DEATH AND SECRETS

SEELEY JAMES

Published by
Machined Media
12402 N 68th St
Scottsdale, AZ 85254

DEATH AND SECRETS Sabel Security #5 version 2.12
Original publication, v2.11 November 13th, 2018
This version is v2.12, 12-April, 2019
Print ISBN: 978-1-7322388-3-1
ePub ISBN: 978-1-7322388-2-4
Distribution Print ISBN: 978-1-7322388-4-8

Formatting: BB eBooks
Cover Design: Jeroen ten berge

SEE THE SEELEY JAMES COLLECTION

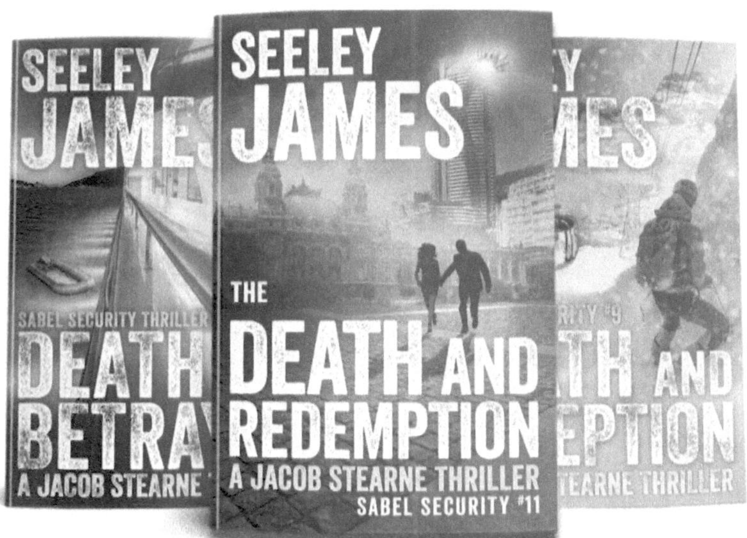

SEELEYJAMES.COM/BOOKS

FOR MY DAUGHTER
Nicole

CHAPTER 1

A VOICE IN A DREAM said, "Do you remember who shot you?"

Someone tugged me through a murky world. When the gray globs in my vision thinned, I recognized my sister. She kneaded my right hand and said something underwater. I blinked. Tubes hung down around me, metal rails on either side. A rack of machines with flashing lights towered over my shoulder. On my left stood a man in a white lab coat with the educated gaze of a doctor.

My eyes slid back to Joyce.

Something was wrong. My sister owned the biggest organic farm in Iowa. She didn't hold hands with her little brother in Bethesda, Maryland. Last time we spoke, it ended sharp and bitter. Some kind of rivalry that didn't matter anymore. Joyce kept talking. It sounded like, *this time better work*. She aimed her words and a mean glare at the doctor.

Noises sharpened a little and came in crisper.

She turned to me, "Do you remember who shot you?"

I looked around for my best friend and constant companion: Mercury, the winged messenger of the Roman gods. My divine protector and occasional savior—when he wasn't too busy chasing goddesses—was not in the room.

A bad sign.

I pushed up on my elbows and tried to speak but only burped out a squawk. Black stars swirled around me. The doc put a hand on my chest and pushed me back down.

I took another nap. It felt like one of many. My dream state reverted to an oddly familiar sight: I looked down from the ceiling at my twisted body lying on the floor of a dark and shabby room. Flies. Threadbare carpet. A voice said, *Don't go to Tremé.* In a blink, I looked up at my twisted body lying on a water-stained ceiling surrounded by a pool of black ink.

"What's the last thing you remember?" The doc's penlight swung away from my eye.

"Christmas. Maybe?" I heard myself say. "Miguel brought—"

"Hell." My sister's voice came from the other side of the room. "You said this would work."

"Amnesia is a mysterious thing." The doctor's voice was silky, understanding, patient. "He's responding this time. He can talk. Let's count that as a blessing."

"Amnesia?" I asked.

"Due to the blood loss." Doc sounded as if we'd had this conversation before.

I glanced around, hoping to see Mercury. I needed someone to tell me what had gone down. As gods go, he was a pain in the ass and a bad influence, but he made house calls. Which was more than I could say for the other deities I'd prayed to. Like any soldier who'd rounded out eight tours of combat duty, I'd prayed to every god I'd heard of and some that were mere possibilities. When a thousand Taliban rounds buzz your ears, you're not so picky about which one is the *One True God.* Call 'em all. See who answers.

"Let's start with something easy," the doctor said. "Do you remember leaving the Army three years—"

"Pick it up, Doc. Something recent." Joyce leaned into my line of sight. "Mardi Gras? Do you remember that?"

My mind spun off. New Orleans. Congo Square. The place where slaves spent the Sabbath in the late 1700s beating out their ancestral rhythms and trying out new ones that, over time, evolved into jazz. I asked, "Tremé?"

"What's trem-MAY?" She pushed the pronunciation the way farmers will.

"Neighborhood. Due west of the French Quarter." I was short of breath. "Where you played trumpet that time when—"

"Mom and Dad took us to Preservation Hall." She snapped her fingers. "Yeah. That was a great trip. What the hell were you doing there?"

"I was there?"

"Slowly bleeding out in a seedy motel." She squinted at me. "What's the last thing you remember?"

The doc put a cup with a bendy straw in front of me. I took a sip while I thought about it. "Tania gave me socks for Christmas. I re-gifted them to Miguel—"

"I mean after that." She closed in with each word as if she led the Spanish Inquisition and would order the rack tightened one more notch if I didn't answer right. "Do you remember your physical therapy? Rehab? Anything we talked about yesterday?"

I had no idea what today was much less yesterday, but I wanted to make her happy. My brain reeled through every moment in time. A couple new things came into focus. I sorted them for approximate dates and came up with my best recollection. "Ms. Sabel made me take her to the Epiphany service at National Cathedral. She cried the whole time."

My sister reared back. "Fuck!"

The doctor inhaled as if he'd been smacked.

"Sorry, Doc." She fisted her hips and turned to the window. "A hundred farm hands work for me. If you don't throw an f-bomb every few minutes, they'll think you're weak. So, this is all we're going to get out of your voodoo experiments, huh? Yeah. I'm taking him home."

"Home-home?" I asked. "Or my home?"

"Your shack in Bethesda for now. But we talked, it's been decided— you're coming back to the farm. I need you to run the business side. Besides, if you don't give up this ridiculous job of slaughtering people, you're going to wind up dead. Not that I care. You can do what you want, but you're killing Mom with this—" she flopped a hand at the beeping hardware "—getting shot all the time. So."

My fingertips ran over a freshly healed wound. I'd been in the hospital for a long time. Maybe my brain hadn't, but my body had healed.

Mom might have a point about my career. I had enough holes in me to double as a pasta strainer. Playing catch with bullets was a young man's game. But give it up? It was a tough decision because nothing satisfies like killing those who attack truth, justice, and the American way.

I didn't need to ask where my girlfriend was. Sylvia hated violence. Most likely, she dumped me. Amnesia can be a blessing sometimes. To win her back I would need a softer, gentler occupation.

But going home?

The farm. The family. The homestead outside of Donnellson, Iowa where generations of Stearnes had been born, lived and died without getting any farther away than Keokuk. It was home. A warm place that smelt of cookies and bacon and meatloaf and dust in the attic. It was Saturday night keggers behind Grafton's barn and Sunday morning breakfast at Agatha's Diner out on the highway. And the hayseeds I'd left behind when I joined the Army. I'd seen Paris, Nairobi, Tokyo since then. Going home would be like going to hell. It was predictable, and I probably deserved it, but I really didn't want to go.

"What happened to Dan Sweeny?" I asked. "I thought your genius-fiancé was going to—"

"Don't make this about me." She shook a finger at me. "Let's keep focused on you and filling in that gap in your memory. There's a cop with a name I can't pronounce asking questions all the time. Get him squared away, then you can be my farm manager. Get up. Let's get you home. We can talk there."

She pulled the sheet back and tossed a pair of pants and a shirt my way.

Doc slapped a bottle of pills on my chest. "Twice a day, every twelve hours. Like clockwork."

I read all sixteen syllables on the label. None of them meant anything to me. "What are they for?"

He looked across my chest at my sister. She met his gaze and gave a slow shake, no.

"Your recovery." Doc patted my shoulder. "Take them all. Don't miss even one."

I yanked Joyce's forearm. "I'm not crazy."

"No one said you were." She gave me that condescending big-sister look. "They help your brain with your … amnesia."

We left the hospital in my sister's usual whirlwind. She barked orders at nurses and doctors and passers-by. She drove. I'd never won an argument with her, so I kept my mouth shut.

I stared out the window and wondered why I ever chose the soldier's life. You get shot, tortured, killed, and all that. A man planning a future might want a less dangerous profession.

A welcome-back banner sagged across my front yard. Balloons. A crowd. Anoshni ran out jumping and barking and nearly knocked me down. The well-wishers ranged from division presidents to janitors. They shouted greetings and waved and hooted. A good number of my fellow Sabel Industries employees were dying to get a selfie with the boss's favorite bullet chewer.

Tania, Miguel, and Dhanpal hugged me and patted my back. Bianca and Emily showed off their shiny new wedding bands with happy grins. The Major stood alone at the far end of the living room observing me with her analytical gaze. One after another, people shook my hand and told me they were glad I made it. Then they asked what happened. None of them waited for an answer. Seemed like they already knew.

No one mentioned the two important people who were missing from the guest list.

Everyone had a good time. None of it involved me. People like a reason to party and my survival was this week's excuse. As the party raged, I wandered through the house looking for Mercury. When you come to rely on your personal relationship with god—even if he'd been reduced to panhandling for the last fifteen hundred years—you expect him to be present for your homecoming.

Void. Emptiness. Looming existentialism.

My best friend Miguel followed me around the way he did on his first deployment. Back then, he'd heard about my legendary survival rate and figured I was favored by a deity. He didn't care which. When I left the Rangers to work at Sabel Security, he trailed along a few weeks later.

We stepped into my empty home office. He wrapped me in a bear hug. "Thought I lost you this time."

At six-four, two-forty, he wasn't the kind of guy you peeled yourself away from even when the hug was way awkward. We'd been through too many firefights together, lost too many friends, cheated death too many times. The stress was taking its toll on him. He choked down a sob and let go and turned away.

Emotions were a concept the stoic Navajo avoided. Everyone he'd befriended wound up dead. Except me. So far.

"Where's Sylvia?" I asked.

"Went back to Monaco." He checked the lock on my gun cabinet. "Cops said she left right off. She changed her phone number and ..."

I waited for him to finish his sentence. He didn't.

Yeah. Fine. None of my friends liked Sylvia. We'd had a strained relationship from day one. Fundamental differences tangled up in an unhealthy attraction. On again, off again, like a strobe light for over a year. We had no business being attracted to each other, a veteran and a movie star. TV star anyway. In France. She once demanded I give up the unusually violent job of protecting the company owner and Olympian Pia Sabel. Never an option. But then we rang in the New Year together in Paris. Totally lit and no arguing. At the top of the Eiffel Tower, we made plans for Mardi Gras. I remember thinking if we made it to Easter, I'd pop the big question.

My memory gets foggy between New Years and Epiphany. After that, it's all blank. Had she left me? Not that I could blame her. What woman would settle down with a man who landed in the hospital all the time?

The Major, Sabel Industries' CEO, leaned her head around the door jamb. "Miguel, could you give us a minute?"

He lumbered past her, glad to be out of there before any more *feelings* surfaced.

She stepped in, closed the door and backed against it, her hands still on the knob. Her gaze ran over me from top to bottom. I returned the inspection. She was an uptight, squared-away former MP who kept her Afro in a bun so tight she'd never need a facelift.

I asked, "Where's Ms. Sabel?"

Asking the whereabouts of our billionaire boss seemed a reasonable question. The Major looked at me like I'd passed gas in church.

"Gone." She looked at the floor. "She's been getting worse, Jacob. One minute she's doing fine, the next she swan dives into a canyon of suspicion. I mean, it's understandable after all. It's been a traumatic year since …"

She took a deep breath. I didn't need a reminder. Neither did she.

"It's been building like a volcano." The Major caught my wandering gaze. "The congressional hearings, the endless accusations, the daily stress of running a major corporation. She went into a tailspin in February. Do you remember any of that?" She waited for me to respond. I had nothing. She continued, "Depression, agitation, anxiety, lashing out—at you. At me. At Tania." She sighed. "Dr. Harrison diagnosed her as … well, he said she needed medications and therapy."

Dr. Harrison had prescribed plenty of happy pills for my problems. I never took them. "What did he give her?"

"Don't know. She took Stefan and the kids on a spiritual quest instead."

Not her best traveling companion. Her boyfriend Stefan discovered more self-righteousness than religion after some serious trauma of his own. "Did that help?"

"Stefan came back from Nepal early. They'd had a fight. A series of fights, actually." She blew out a breath. "He said she needed more help than he could give. Something about protecting his kids."

"Where is she now?"

The Major grabbed my arm, her voice shaky. "Stefan found her phone, passport, all her ID—" she choked "—hidden in his luggage."

The Major let that sentence hang in the air for a long time. Her eyes darted from my left cornea to my right and back several times.

"I'm worried about her." She squeezed hard. "Jacob, you have to find her."

My most recent wound ached. It had torn through the scars from Fallujah, or maybe they were from Jalalabad. Maybe both. It reminded me that I'd served my time. My sister was right—my career path was leading straight to a party with Orcus, god of the underworld. If I hoped to win Sylvia back, start a family, have a normal life, something had to change.

Someone else could save the boss.

Although. She did give me a Ferrari. And a bonus big enough to buy the house we were partying in. There was that. On the other hand, I'd been beaten, stabbed, arrested, shot, tortured, and gone through hell too many times to count for her. So where did that leave me? Golden-handcuffed to a billionaire? Did that make me the battered-partner?

I tried to give the Major a flat-out no.

All I could muster was, "Why me?"

"Times like this, she only listens to you. You're the brother she never had." The Major waited a beat. "I got word; Justice is going to subpoena her about the Popov killing. They claim Tarasov will testify against her." The Major dropped her voice to a whisper. "If she's feeling alone right now, imagine how low she'll drop when all that gets brought up again."

I chewed the inside of my cheek while I thought about the crowd of friends who were oh-so-happy to see me. My girlfriend fled New Orleans because she wanted to spend the rest of her life with a guy who had a good chance of waking up every morning. I considered my memory gap, my apparently-mythical god, and my boss ghosting on everyone when we needed her most. My ancestral home on the Great Plains loomed in my future like a dark prison silhouetted against the prairie at dusk.

I said, "I quit."

CHAPTER 2

ON THE SOUTHERN COAST OF France, EP Scott took a seat by the café window and dropped her purse in the other chair. A feral cat slithered down the narrow lane outside, staying low-key in the pre-dawn darkness. She pulled out a worn copy of *Death and Treason* and attempted to read. Useless. Visions of Stefan popped into her head. His shocked face, his adopted toddlers recoiling in fear behind his leg, her voice rattling the windows. She couldn't blow up like that ever again.

And that was only the latest in a string of explosive anger and corrosive distrust. She had to get it under control. She could do it. Screw Dr. Harrison and his diagnosis. She clenched a fist so tight her fingernails dug into her palm. What had made her think Stefan was in league with President Roche? Just because he said, *One person can make the difference. You are that person.*

Thinking she was the only person who could make a difference is what led to her current problems. Maybe she should give it up and go home. Maybe accepting Chuck Roche as president, murderous and duplicitous as he was, was better than the trail of burned relationships in her rearview mirror. Was the envelope worth everything she'd gone through to get it? Did it really hold the key to an international conspiracy based? Or, had her imagination blown everything out of proportion? She shuddered at the thought. Even if it was evidence, pursuing it had cost too much. Her stomach soured with a mixture of anger and regret.

Three teenaged girls came in from the street, babbling in French. Swimmers, she guessed from their physique. Out for a bite before early morning laps. Two of them ordered hot chocolate with a croissant and jam. The third, the one with a honey-colored braid, looked at the floor.

EP instinctively knew the girl's problem. She'd seen it all over the world, in every country and culture.

EP took a hundred euro note from her purse, the smallest bill she had, crumpled it, rose, and crossed to the counter. She tossed the money behind the girl's left foot.

"You dropped something," EP said in her bad French.

The girl looked up quickly. She followed EP's gaze to the wrinkled bill then back, a touch of fear in her innocent eyes.

"I saw it fall from your bag just now." EP nodded at the note.

Vivian, the gray-haired proprietor and EP's landlord, repeated her words with the verbs properly conjugated. The girl looked at the bill again. EP turned away and picked up the complimentary newspaper from the counter and carried it back to her table. She kept the teenager in her peripheral vision.

The hungry girl picked up the wadded money like a found nugget of gold. A smile ripped across her face. She turned to Vivian and ordered a hot chocolate, croissant, and jam. Their chatter resumed as they took their pastries out into the dark streets. As she dashed out the door, the swimmer glanced back at EP and said, "Merci."

EP Scott ignored the girl and kept her gaze fixed on the headline. At first, she didn't trust her translation. She pressed on through the article. US President Chuck Roche had claimed Sabel Technologies spied on Americans by hacking their webcams. An outright lie that he didn't bother to back up with a shred of evidence. Despite his unsubstantiated claim, news outlets published his words which gave them credence. On top of that, Roche had referred the company to the Justice Department for criminal prosecution. His outrageous behavior inflamed her anger—which drove her mad.

She had to choose between continuing her costly mission and giving in. Going home and accepting Roche as a legitimate president might calm her obsession and save forty thousand jobs. Or she could stay on her mission and risk destroying herself chasing sketchy evidence from a stolen envelope. One that, in the end, might prove worthless.

Her fists clenched again.

She took a quick survey of the room, worried she might be muttering out loud. In the kitchen behind a thin wall, Vivian moved through her morning routine. Cupboards slapped open, racks of buns slid into place.

The Texas BBQ Café was the only place she'd found with strong American coffee in Antibes, a humble town halfway between Cannes and Nice. Vivian opened early and kept a light French breakfast going until the crowds came in for the pulled pork lunch.

Someone came in the back door and stopped in the kitchen. They spoke in English. Expat Central, she recalled from her brief conversations with Vivian. Behind her, she heard the newcomer grab two mugs and pour coffee in each. His footfalls marched straight to her table.

She sank back into her decision to go home or stay. Would the secrets hidden just a few blocks away produce the evidence to take down the most important—

He said, "What do you want?"

"To get that idiot out of the White House." While her finger stabbed at Roche's picture in the paper, she looked up to find a lean, older man with a cup in each hand. "How could anyone vote for that lying, racist, misogynist bastard? I had proof that he hired hitmen …" She blew out a breath. "He's torched it all by now, I'm sure."

"I meant the coffee." He set a mug in front of her and sat on her purse. "Sugar? Cream?"

"Oh. Black." Her face flushed as she watched him pull her purse out from under him and set it on the table. "Sorry, Roche gets me worked up sometimes."

He smiled and warmed his fingers on his mug. "It's pronounced row-SHAY. You don't have to like him but do him the courtesy of saying his name right. He is the president."

"Why? What courtesy has he shown anyone else?" An awkward silence followed before she remembered her manners. She picked up the mug. "Thank you."

She took a long look at him and blew across her coffee. He was older, wrinkled, weathered and gray. Then something clicked. She tilted her head, observing him closely, then turned to the framed photo on the wall. Martin Luther King led a crowd down a wide boulevard. Five faces to his left was a young likeness of the man sharing her table.

"William Koller," he said when her gaze returned. "But you can call me Willy-Mac like everybody does. And. Yes. That'd be me." He nosed at the picture. "Long time ago."

"It's a pleasure to meet you. I'm," she hesitated because she hated lying, "EP Scott."

He stared at her without saying anything. The silence unnerved her. She said, "Do you think one person can make a difference against tyranny? I mean, would the Civil Rights movement have happened if not for Dr. King?"

His brow knitted, he canted his head. "The Civil Rights movement was not the result of one man. It was the result of a nation waking up after the nightmare of the Holocaust and realizing it was time to come clean about racism. The movement began long before Dr. King came to the front. But that one man made a difference. A big difference."

He waited a moment. "So, you don't like the world as it is and you're waiting for someone else to change it?"

EP didn't answer. She sipped her coffee.

"Some people in my community are waiting for another Dr. King," he said. "These people didn't vote because none of the choices were perfect. So, they waited. And while they waited, racists took over the state legislatures. Now we have gerrymandering, voter suppression, purged voter rolls."

She thought about his words while looking out the window. She could feel him watching her every move.

He said, "Why would a rich girl lie about her name?"

"What? I need ID to buy coffee?"

"I was in Paris when you rented the apartment from my wife." His gaze was cold and unwavering. "You showed her ID. Anyone can get ID."

He let the statement hang in the air while he stirred cream in his coffee. His unrelenting gaze never left her eyes.

After a long silence, she said, "I paid in advance."

Finally, his intense scrutiny lifted. He sipped his coffee. He smacked his lips in enjoyment, then brought the cold glare back to her. He leaned forward. "You didn't lock your door."

The shock made her inhale quickly. She sipped from her mug, hoping to avoid his inquiring look. Common routines were foreign to her. She once had people who locked doors, carried things, drove limos, fetched sunglasses.

"I didn't pry," he said. "I took a glance inside to make sure you weren't in trouble. Called out your alias a couple times. Locked up and left. You're accustomed to having a maid."

"I'm messy."

He looked her over, not in a nice way.

"What's with all the questions?" When he didn't answer, she asked, "Why do you think I'm rich?"

"You left ten days' worth of dirty laundry on the floor and bought new clothes. Us regular folk tend to wash the old ones. And your new stuff doesn't fit as well. Your old stuff was, what do they call it? Bespoke. Custom-made."

She stopped her lips before they formed the word *ooh* and recovered by blurting something out. "It's hard for tall women to find right-sized fashions."

"Your passport made you thirty, but a hundred bucks says you're twenty-eight."

He was good, she had to give him that. She was twenty-eight and three months.

"And men go by initials." He dropped his volume a notch as he leaned in. "JD, SC, whatever. Women don't go by EP."

"JK Rowling."

"Only on the covers." He shrugged. "Otherwise, Joanne or Jo."

"It's Eva. Eva Pamela Scott, if you must know. You can call me Eva if you'd rather." The relentless questions annoyed her. "What are you doing so far from home?"

"Retired a few years back and visited here a few times." It was his turn to look away while he sipped his coffee. "Being a curiosity is a pleasant change from being second-class."

She flipped the newspaper over to hide Roche's infuriating face and returned to her book. Pressing the pages to make it stay open, she pretended to read.

Willy-Mac sat very still and moved slowly, like a hunter waiting for game. Even when he tilted back for the last drop, his gaze remained locked on her. "I don't rent to criminals."

The accusation took Eva by surprise. It gave her reason to rethink her choices. She could stop her masquerade, go back to the USA, and pledge fealty to the new king, or stay and take a chance on the slimmest of leads. Facing Willy-Mac's hostility pushed her toward going home and making the best out of a horrible situation. It was the most pragmatic option. One that made her gut flip over.

"Don't let him bother you none." Vivian came to the table with a croissant and a cup of yogurt topped with blueberries. "Old men tend to get cranky in their old age. Being retired means being out of power."

The couple froze, locked in a long, hard stare at each other. A silent power struggle, decades old and never resolved, stretched for an uncomfortable moment. Vivian cut if off with a *humph* and left for the kitchen.

Willy-Mac tossed the rent check on the table between them. "A shell company in the Seychelles smells like money laundering to me. I won't have trouble or tenants who cause it. We rent our apartment to law-abiding citizens who tell the truth. Just tell me who you really are."

She pressed her book flat again, trying to ignore him. It didn't work. She felt his hot glare on the side of her face like a heater.

There was no sense in blaming him for thinking the worst. She'd set up the bank account months ago, the first time she'd felt the urge to flee her native country. Not even her accountants knew it existed. It was legitimate, but it didn't feel that way. Hiding, lying, using an alias was not in her nature.

She faced Willy-Mac. "I'm Eva P. Scott like it says. It's my money. Legal and clean."

He chewed his bottom lip for a minute while she pretended to read. "If you're in trouble, girl, let me help you."

Who the hell was this guy? Maybe Chuck Roche sent him to make her life even more miserable. She didn't know anything about Willy-Mac. What kind of name is that anyway? Just because he marched fifty years ago didn't mean she should tell him anything.

"I don't need your help." She tried to rein in the anger rising with her voice. "I'll rent some other place. Just leave me alone."

As soon as the words left her mouth, she regretted them to the point she wanted to crawl under the table. She kept her eyes on the page she wasn't reading.

Vivian approached with a coffee pot.

"If you can't tell me who you are and what you're doing," Willy-Mac said in a calm and soothing voice, "I can't take a chance that danger might rain down on my family again. You'll have to go."

Vivian refilled the cup slowly. Then she turned and refilled Willy-Mac's cup even more slowly.

Vivian said, "Twenty years with the Texas Rangers and you don't know who you're talking to? Some detective you are. It's because you don't pay attention to women, that's why. Not in sports or business leastways, or you'd know her on sight. If Pia Sabel wants us to call her Eva Scott or Mother Teresa, she has her reasons."

CHAPTER 3

PRESIDENT CHUCK ROCHE USED HIS silver-handled cane upside down as a putter. He tapped a golf ball into a White House coffee mug lying on its side. He heard his aide announce former President Veronica Lodge Hunter. He ignored them. People should always wait for the president; it keeps them in their place.

After a few seconds of silence, the aide rushed back into the recesses of the West Wing.

Roche repositioned his feet and concentrated on the putt. Hunter cleared her throat. He didn't look up, he tapped the ball. Then he stepped up to the next one and figured the angle.

"Are your putts on the green always that close?" Hunter asked.

"This is what you call winning." He tapped the ball. It caromed off the mug. "Damn it. You broke my concentration."

"We have a meeting." She closed in. "You called me."

He kicked the mug, then reached for the TV remote and clicked it on before motioning to the facing sofas. She sat. He remained in front of the TV for a moment. Crowds of filthy vermin protested his magnificent administration right outside the White House.

"Goddamn those bastards. What's wrong with them?" He swung his cane and landed it dead-center in the TV screen. It sank into the glass and plastic. He tugged several times trying to free it. Then stepped back. "How did you handle protestors when you were here?"

"There weren't quite so many."

"These idiots in the Secret Service won't face them down." He gave his cane another tug. "Damn cowards. I should go out there and cane some of these activists, show them how tough I am."

"You're a strong man, Chuck." Hunter rose and wandered the room. "While that would be one way to handle it, there are alternatives. Calming the restless natives requires a certain finesse. You need experience on your side. All these generals you've hired can't discreetly—"

"Don't think you can worm your way back into the White House based on your experience."

"Did your advisors tell you there would be protests after you told the NCAA men's team they were celebrities who could now, 'grab a woman anywhere, any time?'"

"I was referring to dance partners." Roche threw his hands up in exasperation.

"Your pelvic-thrust visual buried that sentiment."

"Doesn't matter," he said. "I'm not going to marry you."

"A Rose Garden wedding would allow the country a chance to admire you. Think of the throngs lining the boulevards to adore you like a royal. You'd be the star of the show. You can keep the hookers and porn stars. I don't mind." When he scoffed loudly, she toured the office, looking at the pictures, working her way toward his desk. "It could change the narrative from the investigation."

"I know damn well how to change the narrative." He bent below the TV to see how deep the cane was. "I've got distractions coming out my ass. In a pinch, I can always fire someone. My ratings always go up after I fire somebody. Say, I should start doing that live during the press conferences—like those survival shows. I'll line up the Cabinet and yell, 'Reggie, you're off the island!'" He rubbed his chin. "Hmm. Doesn't have the right ring to it."

Hunter started poking around on his desk. Anyone could see she wanted it back. It was her fantasy to sit there, acting like she could run the country again and do it right this time. Fat chance. She blew it. Loser. But the idea of firing people on TV was intriguing. If he could just get the right meme going, it could be a thing. He kept thinking.

"You're toast." Roche waved his arms. "No. That's not it either. Out of the Oval! You're done! Get lost!"

Hunter paged through a folder from his desk. She said, "Are you planning to invade the Maldives?"

"What the hell are you doing?" Roche stormed over and ripped the folders from her hands. "Of course not. They don't have any fixed assets worth bombing. If you want ratings, you need mushroom clouds, bright yellow flames, flattened buildings. That shithole country has nothing but grass huts."

"Oh my god, Chuck!" she said. "Invading a foreign country won't make the special prosecutor shut down his—"

"That's why I'm in this office, and you're not." He slammed the folders down on the desk. "Women are too timid to wage war. Reagan invaded Grenada and got reelected. Tiny damn island no one had ever heard of, but it worked. And that other guy—whatshisname—invaded Iraq. What did we need with Iraq? We'd had weapons inspectors in there for ten years, through three administrations, and they never found a shred of evidence against them. We invaded anyway. And we trounced them, hung their dictator, and whatshisname got reelected. It's called winning. That's how it's done."

"We destabilized the region. More people died in the first five years of our 'liberation' than Hussein killed in twenty years of tyranny. ISIS rose from the ashes."

"None of that matters. We pick a fight with somebody—if they knuckle under, I get a Nobel Peace Prize. If they don't, I get a war. Either way, I win." He couldn't believe she didn't know this stuff. "You failed because you don't get what's important. What makes people happy. Winning makes people happy."

"This isn't some game. These are real people's lives—"

"They're just ideas as far as you're concerned," he said. "Something to keep the generals busy. You don't keep them busy, they think you're weak. That's how you wind up with a military coup." He glared at her. "That's all it is, busy work."

Roche went back to the TV and gave a serious yank on his cane. It broke loose. He fell backward.

"The generals are fine men." She turned away. "They're not going to overthrow—"

"You should see how they look at me in the halls." He pushed himself upright. "Like I'm a moron or something. Well, I'm not a moron. I'm the smartest guy who ever held this office."

"So true," she said. "Why did you call this meeting?"

"Pia Sabel disappeared." He paced the room. "Off the grid. No one knows where she is. We've had FBI agents interrogate that black woman she has running the company, Jonelle Jackson. She swore she had no idea where the girl went—but you know her kind."

"Why fixate on Pia? What are you afraid she'll find?"

"Don't know. That's the problem." Roche walked away and stamped his cane for emphasis. "If you want to win, you have to anticipate your opponent's next move. Why would she disappear?"

"She could be in recovery or a mental health retreat or just getting away from all your unfounded accusations."

"Think." Roche felt like smacking her. He spared her because that kind of thing always made people mad at him. "Why would she go underground? What happened just before she left? Sabel Technologies turned over all that data on Yuri Belenov and Flight 1028 to the Senate Intelligence Committee. The investigators don't have anything to back it up, so it's nothing more than a pile of junk to them. But, if she finds Belenov, that's a whole different story. That's a big headline about 365 dead Americans, Veronica. She arranges immunity and brings him in— you're done."

"Me?" she screeched. "You and Popov put that stupid plan together without consulting me. I didn't have a damn—"

"You were president. You paraded five Puerto Ricans around as if you saved the country single-handed. You knew damn well they were innocent. You should be ashamed of yourself. When the public finds out what you did, they'll hang you."

"I'd be a sideshow at your trial." She wrung her hands.

He watched the gears turning in her head. Lots of people didn't like Veronica Hunter, but she was smart. For a woman. The look on her face meant she had figured it out: even as a sideshow, she'd be ruined.

She crossed her arms and looked at him. "What do you have in mind?"

"Her first move will be to ask Yeschenko how to find Belenov. I tried to cut off that route, but it turns out Yeschenko wants to bring her into RULE. If he convinces her—"

"Oh my god, Chuck." Hunter covered her mouth. "You're the president! You can't get caught communicating with Yeschenko."

"Intermediaries. I'm not stupid."

"No one thinks that." She came close and touched his arm. "Why would Pia join forces with a sanctioned Russian oligarch? And why would she join RULE? It's just a bunch of billionaires with good lobbyists. They're no threat."

"Yeah, sure." He glanced at her sideways. She appeared clueless about the group. "Yeschenko did a lot of business with her dad. Well. I mean before Pia got her dad killed, obviously. You know how girls are, they all have daddy fixations. Yeschenko will use that to his advantage. He has big plans. And with her political connections, Pia can make all his wildest dreams come true. If they get together, they can ruin you."

"And by me, you mean you."

"Goddamn it, Veronica." He waved his cane again. "I'm trying to save this country from the breeding immigrants and the overpaid educators and the terrorists streaming across the border. Every day, I'm fighting to save the nation from people like Yeschenko and Sabel. I'm the only one who can get the job done. You need to get behind me and protect my administration for the sake of the country. Don't you care about the United States of America?"

His voice echoed off the walls. Yelling at people always worked.

She lowered her eyes. "How can I help, Chuck?"

He lowered his cane.

"Find Pia and become her confidante. She needs you, needs your guidance. She never had a mother figure. And god knows you should be hers."

"Chuck, you had her parents killed—and I facilitated it. She knows that. Maybe she doesn't have the evidence anymore, but it's not like she's going to join me for a spa day."

"Atonement." He squinted at her. "Ever hear of it? Go cleanse your soul. Tell her you need her forgiveness or whatever crap she'll fall for. Get creative."

CHAPTER 4

Farm life starts before dawn. Can't harvest in summer what you didn't plant in the spring.

I stood in my childhood bedroom staring out of the second-floor window. To the north, a thousand acres of freshly turned black earth waited in the dark for seed. Not one of those acres held a long-forgotten god. I knew because I'd searched for an hour.

Mercury had forsaken me.

Moving like mud, I oozed downstairs with Anoshni wagging his tail behind me. Dad sat at the small dining table in the middle of the kitchen. Mom poked at sizzling bacon with a spatula. A bowl of steel cut oats and a cup of hot coffee waited for me.

Everything felt like a dream. Not a good one. I couldn't believe I was living with my parents. Twelve hours at that point, but already it seemed like an eternity.

Reminding myself that a career change was the only way to get Sylvia back, I took my seat.

"You sure pissed off your sister last night."

"She never asked what I wanted, Dad."

"If farming's not good enough for you, then what is?"

"Thinking I might open a restaurant."

Dad grunted. "That voodoo food with the miniature asparagus, Japanese mushrooms and what not? Won't sell in Donnellson."

"He cooks just fine." Mom clanked the cast iron skillet with her spatula to get Dad's attention. "He learned a good deal at that fancy cooking school the Army fixed him up with. Might be a little…" she paused and shrugged and went back to her bacon, "…advanced for Lee

County. But it's healthy food and has a nice … crispness to it."

"Just cause Joyce grows brussels sprouts doesn't mean I gotta eat 'em saw-tayed."

"Dad." I waited until he brought his gaze back to me. "I'm thinking Davenport. Maybe even Chicago."

That was it. His hopes of a reunited farming family were trampled like a day-old newspaper at the county fair. He refused to air his feelings the morning after his only son returned home, so he pushed back and grabbed his hat. He opened the door and hesitated a moment.

Anoshni darted through the opening. There are more interesting things in the world for a dog outside than in.

"Can't leave all the work to Joyce," he said. "She's out west of Fairfield this morning."

Planting season. For Dad and Joyce, morning was the three hours you worked before breakfast. He'd popped in for his. Joyce would skip it. *Just burning daylight*, she'd say. Mom would deliver lunch and dinner in the field. They'd wrap up after dark. Hired hands would be out there with them all day. The tracts of land beyond Fairfield Road would take them three days. Then they'd move to the land east of US 218.

Sitting there in Mom's kitchen, I suddenly understood the attraction of a long, hard workday. It kept your mind off what people said and did. Like Montgomery County Detective Czajkowski's parting shot: *That amnesia bullshit might fool the doctors, but we're going to find whoever you're covering for.* CJ was given to conspiracy theories whenever my name came across his desk, which was often. And his wildest theories weren't far off the truth. At least he cared enough to pass along what little I remembered to the New Orleans cops.

The only thing on the Major's mind was me finding Ms. Sabel. The Major never asked who shot me. Neither did Miguel or Bianca. Tania wished the EMT guys hadn't found me quite so fast. I'd like to know who pulled the trigger and ruined my only serious relationship. Was that too much to ask? Screw it. I was glad to be rid of them.

"It's good to have you back from the wars." Mom's soft voice brought me home. "Anything that doesn't involve a gun is fine by—"

I rose and gave her a hug before she broke down. She leaned into me for a moment, then pulled herself together with a deep inhale and turned back to the bacon. If I'd listened to Mom a year ago, Sylvia would be at the table with me. Probably.

We reverted to small-town gossip. Who married. Who divorced. Who ran around. Who had babies. There's no such thing as privacy in a small town. Facebook can't hold a candle to rural America for gossip. I decided not to tell her how I planned to win Sylvia back and bring her home. Didn't need that all over town.

I finished my scrambled eggs and went back to my room. I tried not to let the questions that kept me up all night back into my brain. Would Sylvia take me back? Oh, and by the way, does anyone know—or care— who shot me? How could I find Sylvia? Who the fuck shot me and left me to bleed out? I took a deep breath. One day at a time.

I picked up the latest Pendergast mystery and my dictionary and watched dawn's blue hue spread across the fields. As the light grew, I could see thirty miles across the barren, flat prairies nearly to the outskirts of Iowa City.

Who was I kidding? An actress from Monaco would never survive on the Great Plains. What would she do, dinner theater up in Davenport while I cooked meatloaf and green beans at a greasy spoon around the corner? I pursued a deadly career because it was the only thing that interested women like her in men like me. She wanted a guy who cheated death and laughed about it—almost as much as she didn't.

Fifteen miles north, three shiny black SUVs were coming south out of Mount Pleasant on 218.

Not a common sight west of the Potomac. Few people traveled in that formation. All of them were household names. Knowing what lay south of me, not to mention east and west, they could have only one destination in mind. I pulled the Glock out of my drawer, checked the action, slapped in a full magazine, and slipped it into my holster. I strapped it around my lower back and tucked it under my sweater. Scanning with binoculars, I found the entourage barreling closer. I tried to determine the most important tactical consideration: friend or foe?

Off to the east, a truck flew over the oiled road intersecting the highway. I glassed that direction. Joyce had her foot to the floor, her F-

350 doing a good ninety on a road built for a third of that. She would arrive seconds before the convoy. Her hurry piqued my curiosity. But then I remembered: small town. Our visitors had asked for directions after they parked their private jet at the Des Moines airport. The local jungle drums brought the news to Joyce three minutes later. *Guess who came looking for your brother.* She would see that as an opportunity. Joyce pulled in the driveway and ran into the living room. I bolted for the back stairs.

I dropped down half the staircase, paused at the landing and waited and listened.

Joyce welcomed our guest with her upbeat, booming voice. That was my cue. I tiptoed down the remaining steps, slid through the pantry, and out the kitchen's back door.

It would've been nice to have a used god around. He might've told me to go out the parlor window instead. But Mercury was missing in action. I was flanked by two dark figures. One of them stroked Anoshni's ear. My puppy soaked up the attention like they were old friends. We would have words later about the meaning of *guard dog.*

A lean, gray-haired guy with a beard appeared on my right, his weapon at his side. To my left, a middle-aged woman with black hair had a similar posture. She stopped petting my dog. They wore black suits, white shirts, and sunglasses—not-so-Secret Service. I knew these two from Ms. Sabel's description. They'd helped her once.

I said, "You must be Dan and Catherine."

"We don't want any trouble." Dan nodded at the house. "She wants to talk to you, that's all."

Catherine said, "Do us a favor and hear her out."

"Her?" I tilted my head.

"Former President Veronica Lodge Hunter." Catherine motioned me back inside.

"You guys got demoted to the 'former' detail?" I opened the door and held it for them.

"That stunt your boss pulled wasn't our best career move." Dan went in first, looking left and right. "We'd appreciate it if you left us out of your future schemes."

He stopped in the hall and faced me. "Just keep your eyes open for messages from Virginia Goillot."

My face contorted with a question, but he turned and resumed our forced march.

He and Catherine led me straight to Hunter. My sister was talking the president's ear off as if she were the Chairperson of the Donnellson Chamber of Commerce. Which she was. In her spare time.

"…without an ounce of pesticide. And our rutabagas won't need a fucking ounce—sorry ma'am—of fertilizer. That'll clear up the riparian areas for miles downstream. When you rotate the right crops in the right order, you get more nutrients back in the soil without—"

Joyce stopped because Hunter had held up her palm.

"I'm sorry, I'm here on urgent business. But I will bring this to the attention of the Secretary of Agriculture. Later." She waited for Joyce to get the hint.

My sister's not big on hints.

I faced Joyce. "Save your breath. She's no longer in power."

"She still knows people." Joyce protested. "She could put us in touch—"

"Let's walk, Veronica." I tramped out the front door, across the screen porch, and down the steps.

Behind me, Joyce mocked me in a loud whisper, *Veronica?*

Hunter's heels clicked a quick pace to catch up. Fifty yards across the brick-paved farmyard, I slowed. We were out of earshot of the house but still within the protective envelope of her Secret Service detail.

I spun around. "What do you want?"

"Your sister is quite a successful woman. How does she do so well in such a tough farming economy?"

"She's always one step ahead. When we were kids, Mom made us pull weeds out of the drainage ditch. Joyce held up a fistful and said, 'I'll bet city folks would pay good money for this.' She made Mom drive her to all the fancy restaurants in Chicago the next day. She still gets death threats for making kale a thing."

"Anyone can grow kale." Hunter squinted back at the house. "The competition must be fierce."

"That's the one-step-ahead part. The following season, when everyone else planted kale to catch up with her, she made brussels sprouts cool again. Then beets. Turnips. Next year, it'll be—"

"Rutabagas." Hunter wrinkled her nose. "Can't wait."

I said, "You didn't come here for the farm report."

"I have to meet with Pia." She held up her hand to stop my objection. "Chuck is going crazy. The nation is in serious trouble."

"Because they elected you last time or because they elected your boyfriend this time?"

"Pia has what we need to bring down President Roche."

Everyone has an expertise. Mine is taking lives. Hunter's is taking nations. I was out of my league. So, I did what I do best: attack. "You wouldn't need her help if you hadn't taken her evidence by force and burned it."

Hunter waved a hand as if batting away flies. "I need to speak with her. The nation needs an uncorrupted leader to organize the revolutionaries collecting outside the White House every morning."

"If that's her calling, I'm sure she'll rise to the occasion." I stepped close and poked her clavicle with my finger. "There's no way she's going to meet with the likes of you—unarmed."

"I can't change the past." Hunter pushed my finger away. "What I did was heinous and horrible. I know that. I owe her my deepest and most earnest apology. I intend to beg her forgiveness on my knees. She can hold a gun to my head if it makes her feel better. None of that changes the fact that this nation needs her."

"Whoa! You think she's going to forgive you?"

"I spoke to Chuck a couple days ago." Hunter held my gaze for a long time, then stepped back and looked around. "I've been praying ever since. He's mad, Jacob. Utterly mad. In my meditations, I came to the realization that he's drunk with power. I was just as drunk once. My intoxication cost Pia dearly. I can't move forward with the weight of what I did on my conscience any longer. I need to ask for her forgiveness. Whether she accepts it or not is up to her. But those are the petty issues. What we need to discuss is the fate of the republic."

"Petty?" The word blurted out of my mouth. "Murdering a toddler's parents in front of her is petty?”

“Are you so pure, Jacob?” She scowled at me. “Life-and-death decisions. It’s you or them. Don’t pretend you’ve never been there. How many raids took you into villages where innocent bystanders died as much for their surprise as their intent to challenge you? It’s the price of war.” She tightened up. “Sorry. I shouldn’t drag you into it. You followed orders that flowed from me. I made those decisions. I was drunk with that power. And now, Chuck is too. But he’s unprepared. Opportunists are circling his ego right now. They’re helping him divide the people into squabbling hate-groups. They’re waiting for the right moment to destroy our great nation.”

She looked like something just occurred to her. “You’re right. I should’ve let her keep the evidence against him. Hell. I never should’ve helped Chuck in the first place. It’s the biggest regret of my …”

Her lips trembled. She covered her mouth and turned away. A whimper came over her shoulder. Was she crying? If so, was it real? It sounded real. Her shoulders shook. I fought my instinct to comfort her. It was inconceivable that she’d grown a conscience. But. It happens.

Then I thought of her chess moves and countermoves.

“The Oscars are looking for a female lead of your caliber.” I toed a loose paving stone. “Don’t waste your talent on me, I’m not even an Academy member. Besides, I have no idea where Ms. Sabel is and couldn’t find out if I had to. I left Sabel Security.”

She spun around with real tears smearing her makeup. The sight confused me. The nation once saw her give a Memorial Day speech about American heroes. The camera zoomed in over her shoulder and focused on her podium notes. A handwritten scrawl read, *Choke up here,* with an arrow pointing to the appropriate place. Even then, she’d not produced real tears. Was she for real this time?

“The nation needs Pia Sabel, and you’re the only one who can bring her in. Find her.” She pulled a tissue out of her pocket and blew her nose. “You must serve your country once more.”

“Nice guilt trip. But I’m out. The only thing I’m going to serve is a cod fillet with shrimp stuffing in a lemon garlic sauce.” I thought for a second. “Garnished with mini-asparagus and Japanese mushrooms.”

I'd had enough of being everyone's go-to guy. It was high time I did something for me instead of the country. If I could get a little café started, I could win Sylvia back, start a family, be normal. Or as close to normal as a guy could be with a secondhand god leaning over his shoulder. I looked around. Where the Tartarus was my delinquent deity?

Hunter blew her nose again and wiggled the tissue for the last drops. She patted her tears, then took a deep breath and composed herself. She looked up at me with the kind of fierce determination I'd seen in the finest warriors when they were ready for battle.

"You've left a trail of bodies from Borneo to Lithuania since you left the army." She moved in close and spoke in quietly hissed syllables. "My administration covered up those murders long enough. One word to Chuck and the files are dusted off, turned over to Justice. The death penalty's waiting for you. Get me in front of Pia Sabel or take your chances."

She turned and walked toward the house.

"I was exonerated." Every one of those killings was self-defense—more or less—but that wouldn't stop the wheels of justice from crushing me like a grasshopper under a ten-ton combine.

Hunter ignored me.

"Killing is a young man's game. I'm going to be a farmer."

She kept walking.

"I don't know where she is."

Hunter shouted over her shoulder, "Find her or live to regret it."

CHAPTER 5

PIA SABEL SAT UP ON her elbows in the dark. A large, shadowy form sat in a chair at the foot of her bed. No fear or panic swept over her, only curiosity.

"Sorry, did I wake you?" her father asked. His warm baritone filled the room.

"What are you doing here?"

"I'm not sure." His silhouette twisted in the chair. "I thought you might need help."

She groaned and leaned back. "I've been so lonely."

He nodded. Her childhood fear, what woke her up at night, had always been the fear of abandonment. Alan had comforted her a thousand times, assuring her and reassuring her that he would always be there. Until he wasn't.

"When I lost you," she said, "I turned to Stefan and his kids. I spent time with the Major and Tania, but it wasn't …"

Alan Sabel spread his palms wide, inviting more discussion. It was his signature gesture. From the day he adopted her, he would get her to talk with that one simple movement. She'd seen him do it at board meetings and in social situations. No one resisted his request.

"Too many people have died because of me." She wanted to cry at the truth she'd never allowed herself to say out loud. "I'm the opposite of Midas. I wreck everything. Relationships, people, the company."

In the silence he allowed her, she understood what he was telling her, that self-pity was useless. He had come to help.

"I have to get Chuck Roche out of the White House before he destroys the country. I have some evidence of his money laundering for the Russians, but I'm not sure it's worth pursuing."

"Are you the only one who can do this?"

"I'm the only one following the clues." She pinched her nose.

"What do you have?" he asked.

"I have an address on Rue James Close," she said. "I can't do it alone, and I can't put anyone in danger again."

"Your first year in soccer," he said, "was it, kindergarten? No, pre-K. You had that Irish coach. He said you were a natural at offense, but whenever you switched to defense, you were too aggressive. Remember what he told you?"

"Don't lunge in." She rolled her eyes. "A thousand times I heard that. Don't lunge in."

"I can never forget his accent." He laughed.

She savored the sound of his voice. His magnetism changed the polarity of any room he entered. That's what had awoken her, not a sound or a movement but his presence. She longed to jump up and give him a hug. For reasons she couldn't fathom, she stayed still.

"Your best and worst trait, Pia," he said. "Reacting too quickly. While it's great on offense, you must defend strategically. During the due diligence period when we bought NightVisor, we saw exceptionally strong sales in the last two months. They wanted a higher price for the company because sales were taking off. I didn't challenge them. I saw no reason to be rude. After we closed the deal, their distributors began to return most of the increased sales. They had offered a special return policy to inflate the price of the company. We could've pressed the issue in court, called it fraud, whatever. Instead, I pointed to the contract's fine print where any returns were charged back to the previous owners and taken directly out of their personal compensation."

"You screwed the people who tried to screw you."

"I knew what they were doing." He rose and looked out the window. "The key is research, Pia. Research will bring down Roche. Don't lunge in."

"I'm not the right person to bring down Roche. I always mess things up."

"You need help, that's all. You're not alone."

She had missed him more than she'd realized. She ached for his embrace. She longed to jump up and wrap her arms around him. Yet she sensed a delicate supernatural balance. One that anything might upset. She needed to remain in his presence.

She asked, "Want to go for a run with me?"

He turned to her. The town's residual light streamed through the blinds, illuminating his face. A handsome man framed in stark black and white.

He smiled. "Sorry, I can't leave the room."

Pia bolted upright. Sweat poured off her brow. She looked left and right and switched on the lamp. There was no chair in her bedroom. Curtains, not blinds. No Dad.

She hugged her knees, closed her eyes and cherished those precious few moments with her murdered father. Visions of her youth swirled like shuffled postcards: Dad cheering from the sidelines in the Olympic final; Dad in the passenger seat as she anxiously gripped the wheel for the first time; his scent on the overcoat he draped over her shoulders in an unexpected rain; his reflection in a mud puddle as he admonished her for rudeness to a stranger; his awkward attempt to give romantic advice in the absence of a mother-figure; the tear in his eye at her graduation.

He had always been a kind man. Even in death, he pointed out only that reacting too quickly was a bad trait. He didn't mention her impatience had set off a chain of events that cost him his life.

She threw back the sheets and put on her leggings and running top. She tied her shoes, then looked at the bed. During Vivian's how-to-live-on-your-own life lesson, she'd told Pia, "Always make the bed first."

She looked it over. It would wait. She left for her run.

After the first five kilometers, she changed to her pre-planned circle. At four in the morning, only the occasional delivery van prowled the streets. The lane she wanted had a bend in the middle before curling into a larger road at the end. Shops with varying degrees of success lined the lightly traveled path.

She slowed her pace as she approached 61 Rue James Close. There were no video cameras visible, no black plastic bubbles to protect them. A Japanese fondue shop, a dressmaker whose fashions looked out of date, an electronics store with bare shelves, and a rug merchant who stored inventory in rolls that leaned against the window.

The address was a blue door set into a beige wall, recently painted. There was no bell. No name. No business listing. Just a door and the number 61 on an ancient tile recessed into the plaster. Voices were coming from a higher floor. Shouting an argument in what sounded vaguely like Chinese. She continued down the lane to the curve and joined the main street.

She ran down to the retaining wall by the water. Then up the coastal road past the Musée Picasso, where she turned north again and looped around to the lane. As she approached the corner, she saw dark figures banging on the door at 61. She stopped and peered around an apartment building's wall. The door opened, light from inside poured into the early morning darkness. A lightly dressed Asian man faced two men on the street. He ushered them inside.

The nineteenth-century buildings had apartments over the shops. Small doors beside other commercial openings led to stairs. But this one didn't have any. The blue door led to a ground-floor warehouse. Any space upstairs would be accessed from inside. The lights had gone out in the upper-level windows.

Pia trotted down the lane and pressed her ear to the door. The voices were jovial; the language French. Then the voices approached her. They were about to exit.

She backed up and looked around quickly. The fondue shop had a recessed doorway. She slid in and pressed her back to the wall, hoping they would pass without noticing her in the dark. She held her breath.

The voices said goodnight or something like it. One set of footsteps approached her; two voices remained at the door, talking. The light bathed the street in a soft yellow glow. The footsteps passed her.

For a brief second, she saw his face. He kept walking without noticing her. The yeasty smell of beer wafted behind him.

She had seen the man before. He was an arrogant young man who had ogled her like a side of beef at the Texas BBQ Café on her first day in town. He'd looked her up and down, licked his lips, considered saying something, changed his mind, then chatted with a different woman in line. Pia had been just as insulted by his appraising gaze as she was by his lack of interest. It was a common enough scenario, one that caused her endless insecurities. She was pretty enough to attract a glance but too tall and too ripped to be asked out on a date.

The other conversation moved away from the door. Pia peered around the corner and saw the Asian man walking with another toward the curve. The door was still wide open, closing slowly behind them. The men were several paces away, and the door hadn't yet closed. This was her chance to sneak in and find out what was inside.

She should leave it alone and go home. Breaking-and-entering were skills she never learned playing international soccer. She was out of her league. But she needed to know. Why not have a quick look?

She turned out of her hiding place and crept silently down the lane. The Asian man would see her if he turned just a little to the left. He might even see her motion in his peripheral vision. Should she risk going inside? Her window of opportunity was six seconds and rapidly disappearing as the door's automatic closing mechanism pulled it shut. Did the warehouse hold evidence that would bring down Chuck Roche and his corrupt administration? Possibly. Was it worth it? Maybe. Downside risk? Plenty. Getting caught would end her chances of finding anything. Her entire ruse as Eva Scott could be ruined.

Don't lunge in.

She picked up her pace as a jogger, running slowly, and passed the door.

Then she passed the two men. A few yards later, she heard the Asian man snap his fingers, exclaim something and turn around. He'd forgotten something. She glanced over her shoulder. He was walking quickly back to his door as she reached the curve.

She turned the corner.

A palm reached out in the dark. *Stop.*

Startled, she complied.

Willy-Mac stepped out of the shadow. "If I hadn't read your Wikipedia page, I'd swear you were planning to break into that shop back there." He paused before heavily accenting her alias. "What're you doing here, Eva?"

CHAPTER 6

MIKHAIL YESCHENKO WATCHED THE PRESENTATION with rapt attention. The members of the Stateless Hackers and Resistance Collective, SHaRC, had executed all his directives with admirable efficiency. He glanced around the room at RULE's board members. Every face glowed with the smug satisfaction of people who'd just made an illicit fortune. For most of them, a second illicit fortune. Yuri Belenov had done well with Yeschenko's plans.

What troubled him was the young man's arrogance. In the second half of the presentation, he had become surly. The others hadn't noticed, but Yeschenko knew the signs of arrogance well. He had been just like Belenov fifteen years ago.

Belenov wrapped up in his native Russian as his assistant provided an English translation. "As a reminder, it would be too easy for the Americans to find us if there were any open communications between us. Therefore, we will never know what investments you have outside of SHaRC. Your best bet is to keep all your funds out of Wall Street and in SHaRC." He paused while the translator caught up. "Any questions?"

The Italian auto parts magnate raised his hand. "You sold NRG Insurance short without giving us any notice. I lost millions. You need to give us a warning when you're going to do something like that."

"What we're doing is frowned upon in the USA," Belenov said. Laughter rippled through the board at his understatement. "And we know the Americans listen in on every communication in every country. If they were to see any emails, phone, internet, texts, letting you know we've hacked NRG's executive email and discovered the merger was about to fall apart, Chuck Roche would have us all sanctioned."

"Renditioned to a black site in Thailand is more likely," Yeschenko offered. The board members roared with laughter.

"Nor can we tell you what is coming next." Belenov anticipated the next question. "When we hack emails from mergers and acquisitions, we keep that information wrapped up. No one outside SHaRC can know about it."

"Not even Mr. Yeschenko?" the Japanese banker asked.

"I don't ask." Yeschenko spread out his hands. "All my free capital is invested in SHaRC. With a six-fold increase in the first year, where else would I put it?"

They took a few more procedural questions, then dismissed Yuri Belenov and his assistant, Roman. As they gathered their things, Yeschenko caught Belenov's eye. "Stick around. We have a discussion pending."

The board meeting dragged on like a United Nations session. Finally, when all the matters were settled, and the board members left, Yeschenko sent for Belenov.

An assistant brought him in at the far end of the big, barrel-ceilinged meeting room and closed the heavy doors behind him. Belenov approached with the body language of an overconfident rebel. He advanced with an aggressive stride, crossing the cavernous meeting room quickly.

Yeschenko held up his hand and pointed to a chair at the oak table. "Take a seat."

As intended, it changed Belenov's attitude. The leader of SHaRC stopped and pulled out a heavy chair.

"I called you in here because I didn't like what you said about Chuck Roche." He swaggered slowly down the row. "Why say such nasty things about the President of the United States? Many of RULE's members are great friends of his and have paid homage and made tributes."

Belenov took his seat.

Yeschenko propped a hip on the oak table. "Well?"

Belenov said, "He masterminded Flight 1028, and now he's letting their prosecutors dig into the data from Sabel Tech."

"The United States is not like Russia. Their president cannot call off the prosecutors." He patted Belenov's shoulder. "Your presentation was perfect. You increased our holdings to twenty billion dollars last quarter alone. Yet you mope in front of RULE's board like a love-sick teenager. That reflects badly on me."

The two stared at each other for an uncomfortable minute.

Belenov looked away first. "I meant no disrespect, sir."

Yeschenko rose and crossed to the window. He opened it and let in the cool air. The sound of waves crashing against the rocky coast of his private island in the Azores filled the room. "You live in Brazil, Yuri, surrounded by the most beautiful women in the world. And yet you come to me with the look of a suicide. Talk to me."

"You're a good analyst, sir." Belenov exhaled and swept his palm over the table. "To tell you the truth, I'm preoccupied with Chuck Roche. Thinking of him robs me of all those things I once enjoyed. Yes, women are plentiful. They enjoy my company. My wealth is increasing, my cars are exotic, my home is a fantasy—all those things should bring me joy. Yet the rewards of the world feel worthless. Nothing matters if Chuck Roche can send a drone to silence us, the perpetrators of the Flight 1028 disaster. We, SHaRC's founding members, live in fear of a reckless American. To act against him is impossible. We are trapped. I feel like a speck of dust blowing in a desert."

Yeschenko heard the strain in Belenov's voice. Words formed in his head, assurances of Mikhail Yeschenko's renowned protection and, in an emergency, the Russian Federation. He stopped himself from making that promise. Had someone said as much to him a decade ago, he would've sensed imminent betrayal rather than comfort.

"How sad for you." Yeschenko kept looking out the window, his hands on the sill. "Sadness is not what we need. You will change your thinking. You must come to appreciate Roche's genius. The very genius that your hard work put in power."

"But he's a fool. Even his cabinet officers acknowledge it. He can't be trusted to—"

"This is not your place." Yeschenko turned and crossed his arms.

"It's my neck." Belenov stood, pointing to himself. His voice rose a notch. "Every member of SHaRC feels the same. The President of the United States threatens our existence."

"Watch your mouth." Yeschenko let his rising anger loose on the ungrateful hacker. "You need to—as the Americans say—get with the program. Use your head. Attack the prosecutors, not Roche. We put Roche in power for a reason. We control him."

"You're a fool to rely on Roche for anything. He's a treacherous old—"

"How dare you question my authority?" Yeschenko stepped closer, pushing his fingertip into Belenov's chest. "You don't appreciate what a perfect organism of humanity he is. No one matches Roche's hostility in the face of overwhelming facts. No conscience stops him from attacking his detractors. From disabled reporters to war heroes to victims of terrorism, everyone feels his wrath. He's never troubled with remorse. He wastes no time on apologies. Where you worry about morality, he has no such delusion. No intellectual debates about ethics throttle his feral impulses. His will to survive dominates his every breath. He cannot be stopped. He unleashes chaos at every turn. SHaRC thrives in that chaos." He pointed to himself. "And I control his chaos."

Belenov was leaning back against the table. Yeschenko had nearly pushed him over. He backed off and gave the hacker some room.

Belenov straightened his tie. "I understand, sir."

Yeschenko turned away and strode back to the window. A light rain fell beneath gray skies. "He is only now beginning to understand the power at his fingertips. Where any president before him would hesitate to use the government to enrich himself and his friends, he is already lining his pockets. Just last week, against all advice from his military and trade representatives, he lifted tariffs and sanctions against a telecom company owned by the Red Army, and the next day, China loaned a billion dollars to his operation in Jakarta. A year ago, he ranted about Qatar funding terrorism. Two weeks ago, he lifted sanctions against them because Qatar had made 'progress.' Days later, they bailed out a billion-dollar loan that his nephew nearly defaulted on."

"Isn't that corruption?"

"Not if you're the nephew." Yeschenko canted his head. "You don't see where I'm going with this?"

Belenov looked right and left before meeting Yeschenko's gaze. "Sorry, no."

"They are distracted trying to keep up with Roche. No one cares about Flight 1028. You can take care of the remaining clues and remove the executioner's ax hovering over your head."

"You're suggesting we break into their servers and delete the files?" Belenov's confusion crossed his face. "Hacking the US government is different from Facebook ads and Twitter memes. The NSA would commit endless resources to find the intrusion. They would consider it an act of war."

Yeschenko said, "You've hacked into the email of every global CEO and fund manager. You've used that information to make us billions. Now you need to hack into the phones and emails of low-level interns in the US Senate. Undermine the investigation, spread gossip, make their investigators look like apparatchiks, denounce their 'witch hunt.' They are already distracted by the hundreds of outrageous things Roche is doing. This is your next course of action."

Belenov rubbed his face with his hands. "If you control Roche, you could order him to give us a pardon."

"We will not risk making too many demands lest we expose our connections. Your fate is not RULE's problem. The fix is within your grasp—take care of it."

Belenov scratched his chin. "It is possible, but very risky."

"The man who runs SHaRC must be committed." Yeschenko put a hand on Belenov's shoulder. "Otherwise, we will need to find a different man."

"SHaRC is a collective." Belenov looked up at him quickly. "We do not change leaders."

"Some circumstances force changes." Yeschenko walked Belenov to the window. The surf pounded the rocks a hundred feet below with an incessant roar. The younger man grew pale. Small beads of perspiration formed on his forehead and upper lip. Maybe the threat would work, maybe not. If it did, he would have Belenov back under control. If not, Yeschenko would have the man thrown out the window. Belenov's lieutenant, Roman was more agreeable.

Belenov straightened up and looked him in the eye. "I am with you, sir. All in."

YURI BELENOV MARCHED OUT AND down the grand hallway. He descended the stairway and paraded past Roman, his second-in-command. Roman fell into the same cadence as they marched through the reception area and out into the courtyard.

Roman leaned close and whispered. "Did he believe you?"

Despite the risk of eavesdropping, Belenov couldn't hold back. "Every word."

CHAPTER 7

MOM KEEPS A WRITING DESK in the parlor where she writes old-fashioned letters in longhand. A couple days after Veronica Hunter's visit, the Major and I stood next to that desk. We were finger-pointing and arguing. Anoshni sat at my left foot in case I needed someone bitten. Miguel rested against the large pocket doors checking his cuticles.

"Because she doesn't trust anyone else." The Major was on her second round of why I should be looking for the boss. Ex-boss. "She's like a sister to you. I know you're worried about her as much as the rest of us."

"The only sister I worry about is Joyce."

And I was worried about Joyce. Especially after she stormed into my room at four that morning, shouting about kicking my lazy ass for sleeping late. I worried she'd come in next time with her 12-gauge and blow a hole in my ceiling just to wake me up. Farm life.

"I mean really worry. She's in trouble, Jacob." The Major glanced at Miguel then stepped closer to whisper. "You know why she left the National Team. I'm worried it's happening again."

Everyone assumed Ms. Sabel confided her deepest secrets in me. She would've been the greatest soccer star of all time, they said. She was on pace to break every record ever established, they said. Then one day, she walked away and never looked back. The two people who knew her story—the Major and Ms. Sabel's dad, Alan—never discussed it, and Alan was dead. The Major only mentioned it once before. Ms. Sabel had danced around the subject the two times I asked her. No one ever spelled it out for me.

I glanced around the room, looking for Mercury. At times like this,

his divine insights were invaluable. His holiness was nowhere around.

I brought my gaze back to the Major and nodded as if I understood the stakes.

"That doesn't move you?" she asked. She turned to Miguel for help.

He shrugged. "Man said his piece."

Miguel pushed off the jamb and trudged upstairs as if he lived there.

She turned back to me. "You're not a farmer, Jacob. You're a warrior of the highest order. You've saved lives. You've ended lives. You put your life on the line for this country. Won't you do it for the woman who gave you so much?"

Guilt trips suck. Which is why people book you for the full tour. I stood stone still and thought about Sylvia. She had no interest in raising a family with a guy who might come home in a flag-draped box. If I wanted to marry her, I would have to walk away from people like Pia Sabel. Hard as it was.

It was time to do something for Jacob Stearne. I needed Sylvia in my life. Getting her back was my only priority. I was on the path to making that happen. Probably. If I it didn't work, going home had been a waste of time.

The Major stuck a finger in my chest while she rattled off all the things Ms. Sabel had done for me. I fought back with my only defense. "Who shot me? Does anyone care about that? I'd sure like to know. If I do anything, that would be first."

The Major leaned back in shock that I would only think of myself. It seemed like a reasonable question to me. She ignored my question and kept pestering me until Miguel came back down.

He stepped between us, cutting her off. He held up the book I'd been reading. "You read Preston and Child, you'll start using words like 'frisson' in a sentence."

He shoved the book to my chest.

"Just trying to better myself." I took it, unsure what he was talking about. As soon as my hands were busy, he reached into the front pocket of my jeans in a way straight guys don't usually do to other straight guys. He pulled out my medication, held it up for me to see. I'd been taking it twice a day like the doctor said. Miguel closed his fingers around the plastic bottle and crushed it. He walked to the trashcan by Mom's desk and chucked the remnants.

"Let's go." He looked at the Major and headed in the direction of their rental car.

She closed her mouth like a string bag and narrowed her eyes just as tight. "I left a jet and two pairs of pilots for you in Davenport. When you come to your senses, they'll take you anywhere you need to go."

"I'm not going to…" I didn't bother finishing. They were gone.

Anoshni ran to the door, barking like he'd personally forced their departure.

Joyce turned into the parlor before Miguel and the Major had their car doors closed. "You made the right decision, Jacob. Farm life is none too fancy, but it's honest work and quiet. Fuck those people. That world of yours is going to send you to an early grave."

I marched past her, bouncing her off my shoulder. "That medication wasn't for amnesia, was it."

"Hey," Joyce called out as I reached the stairs. "Some badass-looking dudes are coming up from Keokuk in a car with Louisiana plates."

I froze mid-step and cocked an ear.

She said, "You expecting people from down that way?"

Something in the back of my brain screamed Tremé and Creoles who weren't Creoles. A memory tried to surface. A meeting with some sketchy guys about something bad. Ms. Sabel. A Spanish woman dressed like a pirate. Six guys of undetermined ancestry.

I asked, "Where's Mom?"

"Went to Iowa City this morning. Someone's gotta do the shopping since you aren't pulling your weight around here."

"Joyce. Get back to planting those soybeans. Now."

She heard the former master sergeant in my voice and bolted out the door like a private fresh out of boot camp. She slammed her truck door, cranked it up, turned around in the farmyard, and was down the road by the time I'd loaded and holstered my Glock.

I paused before leaving my room and pulled the H&K MP5SD—fully automatic with a silencer—from under my bed. Just in case. Anoshni whimpered.

I pointed to his bed. It was tucked half under my bed frame. "Down. Stay."

I hadn't taught him much yet. But he knew bad stuff was coming whenever he saw me shoulder my rifle. He crawled in deep and curled up.

In the attic, I opened a gabled window on the north side and slid a steamer trunk away to clear an exit. Perching my field glasses in a south window, I watched a '65 Impala coming my way. Four men inside. Bits of memory came out of the fog. I focused on a vague recollection of six Creole-looking guys. Two were big and fat. Two were stringy with nervous twitches. One was a pipsqueak who never said a word. The point man had a gold tooth. He drove the Impala.

I closed my eyes and prayed to Mercury, winged messenger of the Roman gods, begging for his holy guidance.

Nothing.

There are no gods.

When the Impala pulled in the driveway, I crawled out the north window and set up next to the west chimney. They were missing one of the twitchy guys and the silent man.

Gold-Tooth stepped out wearing long pointy boots and carrying a pistol. His associates slipped out of the car and crouched behind the hedges on either side of the front porch. Positions for an ambush. None of the customary neighborly greetings were planned. Whoever answered the door would die the instant it opened. If they killed the wrong guy, it would serve as a warning to the one they wanted. They checked their weapons and aimed at the front door.

It was their choice of negotiating tactics, not mine. But I'll play anyone's game.

I blew the toe off Gold-Tooth's boot.

By the time all four repositioned themselves to aim shiny new handguns at the roof, I was scrabbling around to the oak limb that stretched over the house on the east side. A second later, I had Gold-Tooth's left cheek in the crosshairs.

"Jacob Stearne, you and me not enemies, Jacob Stearne." Gold-Tooth looked left and right as if he could feel my scope trained on him.

"Then throw your weapons on the ground and back up twenty feet." I directed my voice to bounce off the house. The echoes confused them. The goons formed a semi-circle around Gold-Tooth.

"I want only the envelope, *amicu*." He turned slowly, leading with his pistol. "That was agreement, Jacob Stearne."

I tried to place the accent. Brazilian. Or Italian. Maybe French. Yeah. I had nothing.

"Drop your weapons or lose them," I said. Fair warning served.

They kept their pistols aimed high and their fingers inside their trigger guards.

I measured the distances and rehearsed the pattern. Four pops left to right would do it. I ran through the progression again. Then I fired all four shots. Three pistols exploded out of their hands. My fourth shot missed. Three out of four might be worthy of celebration on the target range but missing the last one under fire was nearly fatal.

Gold-Tooth fired a fusillade into the tree.

Pistols are notoriously inaccurate, so I wasn't worried. I scrambled back to the roof. He emptied his magazine, giving his thugs time to retrieve their weapons. They opened fire.

Mom lost all the windows on the side facing the farmyard in the next ten seconds. She lost a good number of shingles and some of the chimney in the ten seconds after that.

These guys were used to scaring the shit out of people. It was a brilliant tactic in most circumstances. They were firing large-caliber, low-velocity slugs into anything. Big holes, big noises. In the criminal world, making noise and turning the side of a house into pegboard would freeze their enemies with fear. Their mistake was expecting to scare a war veteran. While it would cost my parents a good deal of remodeling, I waited them out. At some point, they had to let the smoke clear to find out if they'd won.

When that lull came, I popped my head up. They kept their arms in motion this time, a defense against having their guns removed. One of them spotted me and squeezed off three rounds. His pals joined in. The chimney was toast.

I didn't see a whole lot of options. I scrambled to the east, took aim, and put a round through each guys' femur. Gold-Tooth dove behind the Impala before I could get him.

The criminals learned a quick lesson in weaponry. The ammo they used entered and exited a human body in a direct line. Maybe they'd seen injuries caused by hollow points that expanded on impact, making a .38 as big as a .50 on the way out. Ugly. But nothing prepared them for the carnage of a high-velocity, military-grade rifle round. It's engineered to tumble on impact, shredding bone and tissue and sending out shockwaves that destroy the surrounding flesh. That's why concert shooters and school shooters using assault rifles do exponentially more damage than handgun shooters.

Their massive wounds shocked the hardened criminals.

Gold-Tooth was shaking. He looked up like a scolded child.

"What envelope?" I called down as I rolled to the other chimney.

"You made deal. You gave word. You got lady back. Where is envelope?" He held up his hands in surrender—with his finger still inside the trigger guard. Ready to fire in a split second.

He took a few deep breaths as he scanned his writhing men. They would bleed out in minutes, and he knew it. He mentally wrote them off and pulled his bravado back up from the depths. A mean glare came into his eye. Pure hatred. He found my position. Only my forehead and one eye were exposed. A low-percentage shot for him. Not worth trying since he was looking into the dark and menacing void of my barrel.

In that moment, I understood my fate. If I killed this guy, more of his kind would come. And then more. Exactly the lifestyle Sylvia wanted me to give up. The only way to make it stop was to find Sylvia, get the envelope, and give it back to Gold-Tooth. Then I would be clear.

That's when my mother pulled into the fifty-yard-long driveway.

Gold-Tooth turned to her. The calculation in his head was as readable as a headline on Times Square. He had a hostage.

Not on my watch.

I'd have to work out the envelope thing with Gold-Tooth's replacement.

His brains splattered across Mom's windshield.

CHAPTER 8

PIA WOKE UP IN THE dark. Sounds of the coastal town floated to her window. A rare early riser passed in the lane below. A delivery truck braked a few blocks away. Seagulls. But no visit from Dad. Alone for the second night in a row. She curled up. She missed him. Pia longed to feel the love that he had never withheld in life. Would he return? Just once? Had it been real? Had it been just a dream? It seemed so real. But then, so many of her problems stemmed from confusing reality with hallucinations.

Loneliness and abandonment had long been her biggest fears. Was her psyche compensating now that her reality had surpassed her nightmares? Or were ghosts part of Dr. Harrison's ominous diagnosis?

Isolation ached in her bones. Her parents were murdered decades ago, and her adopted father was killed last year. Who did she have left in a parental role? Gramma, Alan's eccentric and distant mother. The Major, who tried to be nice but ended up treating Pia like a time bomb. And not without reason.

Pia pulled at her hair. She'd done enough whining. A useless waste of time that wouldn't bring her closer to her goal: getting Roche out of the White House.

With a deep breath, she jumped from the bed and pulled on her running outfit. She went into the night, heading back to the warehouse at 61 Rue James Close.

A quick tour around the block told her nothing. No voices, no lights, no open doors. She ran halfway to Cannes beneath arrays of seaside condos still dormant and waiting for summer. She returned to Antibes via meandering roads higher in the rocky hills.

On her second sweep of the address, she saw lights in the upstairs windows. Backing up to get a better look, she felt the plaster of the building behind her. The French lanes were narrow. To her left, a drain pipe ran from the gutters above to the storm drains below. She gripped it and scaled it. When she came level with the second floor, she propped a foot on a balcony and twisted to look in the windows of 61 Rue James Close. Cheap gauze curtains obscured most of the view, but she made out a figure moving in broad gestures. Like Tai Chi or yoga.

"I'm sure you have a good explanation." Willy-Mac's voice rose from the street below. "I didn't believe the last one."

She waited for her heart to return to normal before sliding back to the street. She dusted her hands. Nothing in the form of a reasonable reply came to mind. Rather than dig a deeper trench of lies, she shrugged and began to walk away.

"Have breakfast with me and tell me what's going down," he said, "or I knock on the door and tell them they have a stalker."

Looking over her shoulder, she measured the man. Early seventies, professional, well-spoken, married to a retired professor, with an earnest demeanor and an insatiable curiosity.

"Who the hell do you think you are?" She checked her attitude and lowered her voice. "What are you doing out here at this hour?"

"I'm a runner. Same as you." He flopped his hands at his side. "Not at your speed anymore, of course. Maybe forty years ago, I could've kept up." He approached. "How about that breakfast?"

"Mind if I shower first?"

"Meet me at the BBQ in half an hour."

Her ponytail dripped down her back when she walked into the café exactly thirty minutes later.

Willy-Mac had yogurt, berries, and croissants ready. Vivian wasn't up yet. Pia took a seat by the window as he dropped two plates and silver. He went back for two mugs of coffee. Returning, he sat down, picked up a spoon, and motioned for Pia to eat. She eagerly complied.

"Should I keep your cover and call you Eva?" he asked.

"I'd appreciate it."

"You're not going to bare your soul to someone you don't know, so

I'll give you my bio. When that picture was taken—" he nodded at the picture of Dr. King "—I was in law school at the University of Chicago. I met Vivian on that march. Someone introduced me to Dr. King. He told me the best thing I could do for the black community was to go back to Chicago, get good grades and be the greatest lawyer in the country."

He ate lightly and spread jam on his croissant.

"I did what he told me. First colored in the county prosecutor's office and first in my corporate law firm. I had a good career going. One day in 1988, twenty-years after Martin Luther King was murdered in Memphis, I picked up the paper and read where the Texas Rangers had just hired their first negro. I thought '88 was pretty damn late for integrating. A hundred twenty-four years after slavery, the Rangers hired their first colored man? It kept bothering me for several more years. I was a highly-paid, highly sought-after corporate attorney, but it stuck in my head because Vivian was from Texas. Finally, one day, I'd made all the money I could eat. It was time to start being the change. I called the Rangers and applied for a job for which I was entirely overqualified. They had no choice but to accept me."

Willy-Mac stopped talking while he finished his yogurt.

Pia finished while wondering where he was going.

"The Rangers put me on the organized crime task force, liaison to the prosecutors." He leaned back in his chair and held his coffee close. "Aryan Brotherhood of Texas, Houston Mafia, drug cartels, I have a lot of experience with criminal conspiracies. I'm telling you this because—" he pointed his index finger at her "—you believe there's a conspiracy going on inside 61 James Close."

She observed him and finished her croissant. The coffee was strong and black and fresh. She patted her lips with the napkin while she thought. After a moment, she said, "Why do you think that?"

"You aren't marching outside with a protest banner about animal rights or #MeToo or unfair labor practices. You've figured out someone's in there all night and someone else is working the counter all day. You think they're doing something illegal." He paused to watch her reactions.

When she didn't say anything, he said, "One of the most persistent questions in my life has always been, 'What are you doing for others?' That's why I left big bucks in Chicago and joined the Rangers. It wasn't just to integrate—it was also to fight crime. My wife was a little right and a little wrong. I don't mind being out of power. What I miss is helping people lay down some justice."

Pia sipped her coffee and tried to keep her rising anger in check. Who did he think he was butting into her harmless surveillance? Maybe he was working for the guys in the alley. Maybe he was working for Chuck Roche. How could she figure out who's side he favored?

"Conspirators are a distinct breed of criminal," he said. "When you mess with most criminals, the worst that can happen is they get pissed off and, if they're innocent, you get embarrassed. But when you mess with conspirators, people get killed." Willy-Mac leaned forward, his forearms on the table, and held her gaze. "I'm offering to help you."

Without warning, she felt transported back in time to the industrial basement where she'd been strapped to a chair. Gagged and powerless, she witnessed the horror unfold. Heavily armed Sabel agents attempting to rescue her faced down heavily armed Russian GRU soldiers. Her father charged in to reason with the Russians. He wasn't supposed to be there. One nervous twitch of a Russian trigger finger and the room erupted in blinding muzzle flashes and deafening automatic weapons fire. She watched her father's head explode. He died before he hit the floor. A long blink erased the scene.

Willy-Mac waited for her response.

"Why?" she blurted. "What do you know about them? Are you watching the alley for—"

"Easy there." He kept a measured tone in a soft baritone. "I just gave you my resume. You can look it up online. Research all you want. Take your time. I'm legit."

She blushed at her rudeness. An apology started to form in her head that she dismissed until she could look him up. For now, she decided to take his offer at face value. She had only the thinnest of leads. It might be nothing. It might be a fantasy. "What do you mean working the counter?"

"The other side of that space is an art gallery."

Pia failed to hide her surprise. "How do you know that?"

"Six months ago," he shrugged, "when the landlord raised the rent, we looked at that space for the BBQ. Terrible layout."

She looked at the smears of yogurt and breadcrumbs on her dish. She considered his offer. Too many people had died on her missions. Too many times she had lunged in when she should've held back. On the other hand, he'd worked organized crime. He had been a cop, of sorts. And a big-time lawyer. He was years of wisdom and experience bottled up in a retiree with time on his hands. Exactly what she needed.

She looked up and found his inquisitive gaze boring through her.

"I suggest you meet the gallery owner." He got up to get more coffee. "Talk to him. Your profile said you could read a, whatdoyoucallem, defender like a book. You could do the same with that guy."

"You know him?"

"Seen him around. Can't say as I know his name." He came back and refilled their mugs. "You should go undercover; act like a buyer."

"Good idea." Pia nodded rhythmically. "I'll need a different outfit."

"I can help with undercover." Willy-Mac smiled and cradled his mug. "Tell me what you know. What you think is going on in there. Let me help you out some. What do you say?"

Everything became real at that moment. She was in over her head so deep even an ex-cop knew what she was doing. Getting caught could ruin her life and destroy her company. Her best option was to go home and forget about it. Too many bad things happened to people who helped her. Too many bad things happened because of that damned envelope.

She looked Willy-Mac square in the eye. "No."

CHAPTER 9

PRESIDENT ROCHE STOOD AT THE Oval Office door and held out his hand to CIA Director Smithers. Smithers looked at him and shook his head slowly.

"Before I give you a new one," the director said, "I need to know how to log this."

"If everybody went around logging things, it wouldn't be a 'Top Secret' secure phone, would it?" Roche grabbed it out of Smithers's hand. These deep-state people annoyed him to no end, always wanting to know what was going on. Probably planning to leak it to the *New York Times* or something. Chuck Roche was the finest judge of character to ever sit in the Oval Office. He knew a rat when he saw one. He should fire that asshole.

"But there are legal requirements, even for black projects like ... whatever it is you're doing." Smithers pinched his nose. "What is the project?"

"I'm the President of the United States of America. I set the rules on what's secret and what's need-to-know. You don't need to know. What I need to know is, can the SVR or the NSA eavesdrop on this thing?"

"No, sir. No one can crack that one. It's just like the one you broke."

"Who told you I broke it?" Roche demanded. "Why are there so many goddamn leaks around here? I need to start firing some people before this gets any worse. What the hell else did they tell you, huh?"

"Oh no. Sorry. I misspoke." Smithers held up his hands as if fending off an attack. "I meant, it's exactly like the one that malfunctioned. I'll speak to the manufacturer about their quality problems right away, sir."

"You do that, Smithers."

The director stared at him for a moment, then flopped his hands at his sides the way losers do and left.

Roche closed the Oval Office door and used his special phone to call his operative, Cyril. The man answered in that stupid language he always used. "Speak English or I'll have you droned."

"What you want?" Cyril asked.

"Have you found those people who robbed you in New Orleans?"

"They not know what they got or they been here by now."

"What about DeLano? Did he have anything to do with it?"

"He not talk to anybody. He good boy for you. Stupid. But he work hard. No worry about DeLano."

"Then how did those guys find your man in New Orleans?"

"Maybe they follow him. Maybe they know a guy. We not know. Nobody know."

"Figure it out. Next topic. What about Yeschenko? Did he ever show up?"

"No."

"I'm paying you to bring him in." Roche crumpled up a piece of paper on his desk and tossed it.

"Yeschenko live on private island with bodyguard every window. Not my problem."

Roche didn't argue with that one. Yeschenko would kill the young man if he showed up. "OK. I'll light a fire under him and the others. Get ready for an influx in a couple days. You have the list, send me a progress report."

Roche clicked off and tapped on his desk while he thought. There was no way he could go in person. Everybody went crazy whenever he talked to a Russian. What's the big freaking deal? Nobody cared when Ronald Reagan talked to them. Maybe he should send an aircraft carrier. That would get his point across. But the Pentagon would ask questions. Someone would leak it to the press.

Then it hit him. He would send an emissary in an F-22. The Air Force had a general a few days away from retirement who could be cowed into making it happen. Refueling, supersonic, whatever he asked would be done just like that—or the general could kiss his pension goodbye.

Problem solved.

Now all he needed was an emissary.

He got up and walked down the hallway. An office door opened, a guy walked out, saw Roche, jumped back in his office, and slammed the door. Goddamn economic advisor acted like a scared rabbit most of the time. That reminded him: he should start a trade war then end it and declare victory before the next election. He'd look like a hero. Looking-like is all voters care about. He'd get on that as soon as he had Yeschenko and RULE under control.

A kid who'd been hanging around since the campaign's early days walked toward him in the hall. Fresh out of law school, if Roche recalled correctly. He could tell the young man was a good kid because he averted his eyes and kept his head down. He might be right for the job. He stopped the boy.

"What're you working on, Lucas?" Roche asked.

"Uh, it's Taylor, sir." The boy looked up for a split second then at the floor again. "Opioid crisis, sir. You graciously appointed me to head the task force for—"

"Are you loyal to me, Tyler?"

"Absolutely. Um, Taylor, sir. You're the greatest president in the history—"

"Would you take a bullet for me?"

The boy looked up and almost made eye contact before he bowed his head again. "Yes, sir. It would be an honor."

"Can you face down a real tough guy for me and never-ever-ever tell anyone about it?"

"I hope so, sir."

"This isn't about hope, fuckhead." Roche yanked his arm and shook him. "I'm talking real important stuff, like world war stuff. I need you to deliver a message to a Russian gangster and not shit your pants. Can you do that, yes or no?"

The kid made eye contact this time. His face was pale, he looked like he was about to puke.

Maybe he'd picked the wrong guy. Roche stared hard at the boy. He knew people. Why the press cared about the 250 departures during his first year was a mystery. The kid could pull it off if he had any balls. But he'd need balls of steel if he was going to stand in front of Mikhail Yeschenko.

Taylor straightened up and saluted. "Yes, sir."

Roche sniffed the air. The kid might have pissed himself already.

"Listen up, Taylor," Roche put his arm around this guy's shoulder and turned him into the Oval Office. "You're going to represent the Global Economic Development Institute, GEDI, for a couple days. You—"

"Jedi?"

"If you ever interrupt me again your next stop will be Guantanamo, hear me?"

"Yes, sir."

"You ever ride in an F-22 before?"

The boy beamed with excitement. "No, sir."

"So, you need to get over to Corvo Island, meet a guy named Mikhail Yeschenko. Don't let all his guards and guns scare you. He won't touch you if you tell him you represent me. The F-22 will help him figure it out. He and his friends were supposed to do something for me, but they decided they didn't wanna. So, you go to them, and you give them an ultimatum from me. You're going to tell him to do what I say, or I back Pia Sabel's story about Flight 1028. Got that?"

"Yes, sir." He swallowed hard. "Mr. Yeschenko does what you told him, or you will back Pia Sabel's story about Flight 1028."

"Say, that was pretty good." Roche bent back and looked the boy over. "You do this right, and I'll make you Surgeon General when you get back. I always take care of my guys."

"Thank you, sir. Uhm. I'm not a doctor or anything, though."

"Don't worry about that. You don't want to be a surgeon, you can be a judge."

"Well, um, sir, I've never practiced…" The guy changed his train of thought. "What if Mr. Yeschenko still doesn't want to do what you want?"

Roche pointed a finger at the kid. "Good thinking, Tyler. You're pretty smart. Definitely can use you around here."

"It's Taylor, sir."

"That's what I said, Taylor." Roche paced away, then came back. "Yeah, I got it. You tell him I know where Belenov is. Got that? Belenov. I'll have Belenov in here singing like a racehorse. That'll put the fear of God into him."

"Racehorse, sir?"

"And if that doesn't work, ask him if he's ever had an F-22 fire missiles at him."

Taylor stared at him with his mouth open. If there was one thing Roche hated it was the way people looked shocked when he said something shocking.

"Can you do that? The missiles thing?" Taylor asked.

"Of course I can do that, ya dumbfuck. I'm the President of the United States of America."

CHAPTER 10

I PULLED MOM OUT OF her car, shrieking and shaking, wrapped her in my arms, and buried her face in my coat. The bullet had entered the back of Gold-Tooth's head and exited with a pound of pureed brain and a chunk of skull. A piece of his face was missing from his left ear to his nose. It was a gruesome sight. I held Mom's face to my chest so she didn't have to look. She calmed a little and took a few deep, ragged breaths.

There's something sick about humans' fascination with horror. Mom twisted her face to the right, took another look at Gold-Tooth's carcass and started shrieking all over again. I guided her face back to my coat and this time she pressed in, hoping it would all go away. With my free hand, I pulled my phone and dialed Dad.

"Best come home," I said. "There's been a … problem."

He asked for more details because leaving the field had to be a real emergency. Mom shrieked again. I figured that was all the detail he needed and hung up. My next call went to Lee County Sheriff Louis Kirby. I dialed direct because he used to date Joyce back in high school. He started in with a lot of questions but choked when I interrupted him. "Don't bother with ambulances. Bring a hearse that carries four."

I took Mom inside and waited for the investigators to arrive.

Not too long after, Joyce and Dad took Mom into their arms and forced me out. They gave me looks. Anoshni took their side and laid his muzzle in Mom's lap. In a matter of minutes, I'd gone from the solution to everyone's problem to the Creature from the Black Lagoon. For years to come, the county would talk about the shootout at Stearne Farms. People would whisper about my family when they shopped at Krogers.

Conversations would stop mid-sentence when they walked into Agatha's Diner. The shame and pity would last three generations. Maybe more. Small towns.

I stood in the bay window and watched while Kirby and all three of his deputies put up crime scene tape and snapped pictures. When backup from the surrounding counties showed up, the sheriff came in with one of the deputies. He didn't ask, just motioned for me to begin. Starting with getting shot in New Orleans, I explained my amnesia-gap before bringing them into the present. They listened carefully. The deputy took notes.

Skeptical and cynical, they eventually decided to take the word of the county's high school track star who had come home from the wars with buckets full of shiny medals.

The strangers with Louisiana plates weren't offering any arguments, being dead.

Sheriff Kirby looked at the bullet holes in the living room wall. "Are there any drugs involved here, Jacob?"

"No, sir."

"Mind if I have a look see?"

"You'd have to ask Mom and Dad—it's their house—but I don't have anything to hide."

We looked over at the three of them huddling in the dining room, their chairs pulled close at the head of the table. The hostility streaming out of their eyes made me flinch.

"How could you bring those people here?" Mom shouted.

Dad tightened the arm he had around her shoulder. Joyce looked ready to tear me apart.

Sheriff Kirby swung back to me. "You brought them here?"

"No, of course …" I dragged the phone out of my pocket, unlocked it, and handed it to him. "See for yourself."

He started scrolling through the texts before moving to the camera roll. Engrossed, he leaned against the wall and paged through whatever was on there.

Dad rose and took me aside. "How could you do this to your mother? In our house?"

I tried to think of an explanation he would understand. Since I had no clue who Gold-Tooth was, why he fired seventy-three bullets at our house, or why he wanted his envelope back, there wasn't much I could say. I shrugged.

"Sorry, son." Dad sighed and gripped my shoulder. "This is hard for us to deal with. Maybe next time your, um, business associate come around you could meet them somewhere else."

"Yeah." I looked him up and down. "Good idea."

There was a tremble in Dad's hand on my shoulder. And in the skin of his jowls. On the outside, he was doing his level best to hold it together. Inside he was quaking with fear and uncertainty. He needed to be the brave head of the family. But he was way out of his league.

He needed help. There were no crisis-therapists for a hundred miles, no psychiatrists or even family counselors. Farmers don't need such foolishness. I said, "Joyce told me you've struck up a friendship with Pastor Goodman at the Methodist Church."

"We did a fair bit of duck hunting last season," Dad said, a question in his glance.

"Maybe he could offer some comfort. Help Mom deal with the unfortunate event."

"Unfortunate … ?" Dad backed down. "We wanted you home, we just didn't expect the violence—"

"Let's focus on the pastor and Mom."

"Probably best." He nodded and pulled his phone and dialed and turned away.

"Wow," Sheriff Kirby said, "she's a hottie."

A deputy was looking over his shoulder with his tongue hanging out.

I snatched the phone and looked at the picture. A sexy-as-hell Spanish woman in a pirate outfit gave a lusty laugh with her head thrown back. Long, wavy raven-black hair cascaded from under a plumed hat. She wore a seventeenth-century velvet coat over a frilly shirt and thigh-high boots. There was a twinkle in her eye that said whoever was taking the picture would get lucky that night.

Then it struck me: it was my phone. I took that picture.

I looked closer.

Sylvia.

My auburn-haired actress stood in the center of Congo Square rocking the pirate look with a wig. There were Mardi Gras beads strewn everywhere. Holy Mercury, I wanted her back. I'd give up Ms. Sabel and all the perks that come with being a billionaire's friend if I could see her again. Then something tickled my brain.

I zoomed in on the picture. Twenty yards behind Sylvia, Gold-Tooth strode straight toward her with an aggressive posture.

When I pointed him out to the sheriff, Kirby took the phone back.

Dad tapped me on the shoulder. "His wife took the car to Quincy for gardening supplies. I'm going to pick him up."

He left a silence that spoke volumes.

"OK if I go with you?" I asked.

He pretended to think it over so he wouldn't sound too anxious. He didn't want to be driving the county roads alone after four strangers came to town and shot up his house. "If you want to."

We drove between sprouting alfalfa and sorghum and talked football. We were Packers fans in a region torn between Vikings and Chiefs. The draft was a month away, and the old-timers were being put out to pasture. We had plenty of important matters to discuss.

When we arrived at the Methodist Church, Dad went into the attached residence to explain things to the pastor. I wandered through the pews and stared at the altar.

After a few minutes, I figured *what the heck* and kneeled and folded my hands and looked up at the wooden cross. I prayed for peace. I prayed for a life without flying bullets. I prayed for a wife and kids. I prayed for my family to accept that I had a few enemies who might come around from time to time. It might interrupt planting season. Then I asked the Lord for guidance.

Mercury said, *Really homie, you can't see him?*

I sucked in my shock at the sound of his voice. Opening my eyes, I spied my toga-clad, unemployed god leaning his butt on the altar rail. His helmet is silver with little bronze wings. A second pair of wings adorns his sandals. He is a chiseled African who claims that Roman artists took poetic license with his race to better sell into their Euro-centric market.

All of which pointed to the obvious: I am totally insane.

Mercury said, *He's talking atcha right now. Waving his arms and shouting. You getting any of this, bro?*

Huh? I said. *Getting what?*

Give it up, Jesus. Mercury turned to the empty space between the crucifix and me. *He's just like the Archbishop—deaf, dumb, and blind to your turn-the-other-cheek schtick. He's mine. Hey, now. Don't go getting salty like that, dude. You forget how it went down last time. Have an attitude of gratitude, you've got the President of the United States on your side.* Mercury straightened up and turned. *Oh yeah? Well, he claims he talks to you every day. Hey now. Language. Then take it up with POTUS—not me. Bottom line: I get Stearne the Younger.*

I looked left and right and behind me. *What are you talking about?*

Mercury slapped my shoulder and leaned in with a conspiratorial whisper. *Jesus has been trying to get your attention since you were five years old, dawg. You dissed him like a high school queen bee. 'Bout time somebody did. But enough about my spiritual turf wars—how's it hanging, my brutha?*

I took a deep breath. *Where were you? Who shot me? Where is Sylvia?*

Whoa, bro! Mercury looked me over. *That amnesia thing did a number on you, huh. You don't remember choosing Sylvia over me? I warned you: hang with a Greek goddess and we're through. And how did you answer the god who has vanquished all your enemies?*

I looked over my shoulder to see if Dad and the pastor were anywhere nearby. *You left me because Sylvia worships Aphrodite?*

Haven't you heard? Mercury crossed his arms and leaned back. *Thou shalt have no other gods before me.*

I said, *I think a different god said that.*

Mercury shrugged. *Aw, dude. Jupiter said it first. The Jews and Christians got a boost from Charlton Heston, that's all. I keep telling Jupiter he should spend more on PR. Get some Hollywood action. But. Don't listen to me, I'm just the messenger.*

I said, *So what happened in Tremé?*

How the Orcus would I know? I found you in the hospital. Your sister was doping you up to keep your ears from hearing my divine phrasings and choice perceptions.

I heard Dad's voice coming out of the back.

I said, *How can I set things right with the family?*

Mercury said, *Are you serious, bro? The family welcome mat has done been rolled up. They caught a glimpse of how the future looks with you in it: buckets of blood, bushels of brains, barrows of—*

Stop. I hate alliteration. Just help me get out of this mess.

Get out of it? Mercury said, *Quit trying to ignore fate, yo. One day you're gonna die in a horrible battle against devastating odds over pointless, outdated principles. Your life is nothing more than a hopeless morass of meaningless endeavors for no apparent reason. Deal with it.*

You might expect a god to sugarcoat your insignificance just a little. Maybe kiss you first. Something. We stared at each other.

Mercury pushed me. *Get off your lazy ass and go find Pia-Caesar-Sabel. She's the only one anyone cares about.*

I said, *Why is she more important than me?*

Mercury said, *Money. She has it, you don't. That's life.*

He was right. Everyone cared about her. Given my last look at Mom's face, I had no admirers left. I turned over my options. The best way to protect my family was to get out of town. The best thing for my future was to find Sylvia. For that, I was going to need Mercury's divine guidance and the deep pockets of Sabel Security. The only way to get them both on board was to pretend I was searching for Pia Sabel.

I sucked it up with a deep breath and rose as Dad and Pastor Goodman entered the church.

They didn't say much when I told them to drop me at the airfield in Davenport. Dad readily agreed to take care of Anoshni. There were no arguments about staying. No hugs goodbye. My last sight of them was Dad and the pastor gawking through the truck's windshield at SABEL written in royal blue across the jet's gleaming white fuselage.

I waved goodbye. Dad waved back slowly. Then he put his phone to his ear, reporting back to Mom and Joyce.

Mercury admired the jet, *Y'know, bro, if I could take this thing back in time, I could've saved the Empire from going Christian. Twelve hundred years with us and they were getting stronger every day. The Prince of Peace takes over, and two hundred years later Rome's a ghost town. That's where love-thy-neighbor gets ya. The Christians were nothing until they forgot everything Jesus told them and started killing, conquering, and enslaving.*

The airstair was open for me. As I strode toward it, Joyce called.

"You didn't take your meds this morning, did you?" She didn't wait for me to reply, just launched into part two. "I don't care if you're on a first-name basis with presidents, you can't leave us! What if more of these—"

I said, "Joyce, they're after me—not you. Staying would bring danger."

She stopped ranting.

"Call all your friends," I said. "Put the word out that I skipped town. Make sure it gets around. Then do some research. A couple weeks back, a guy, maybe two came in from Louisiana. They'd dress like the guys in the driveway, one skinny and the other quiet. Funny accents, not Mexican, not Creole. When you find something, call me."

I clicked off and climbed aboard.

Miguel was stretched out on the back sofa with a Navajo hat covering his face. Tania, Emily, and Dhanpal played cards at a table next to him.

Miguel tipped up the brim and looked at his watch. He twisted to look at the other three. "Not even noon. Pay up, bitches."

CHAPTER 11

IT WAS AFTERNOON BEFORE SHE got back from Nice. She had enjoyed the small, designer-occupied haute couture shops along the coast. What should've been a thirty-minute fitting turned into a four-hour spree. It wasn't Paris, but it was hard to beat the charm. She kicked her way through the dirty clothes littering her apartment and hung up her new wardrobe.

Then came the hardest part: deciding which one to wear. Madame Gérard was the only one who hadn't complained about Pia's height, so she decided to wear that one. A retro-sundress, it was bright yellow with a sash of floral embroidery running from the left breast to below the right hip. With the matching shoes and bag, and a quick look in the mirror, she was ready to go undercover.

A knock on the front door interrupted her.

"Eva," Vivian said through the door. "I just wanted to make sure you remembered it's trash day."

Pia opened it.

Vivian gave her a wide-eyed once-over. "Oh my, don't you look—" Vivian's gaze slid past Pia to the mess beyond. She clutched her throat. "Oh no."

Pia looked behind her, then back. She shrugged.

Vivian said, "We talked about being responsible and keeping—"

"I can't even with this domestic stuff. Do you know a maid or someone who might help me out?"

"Guenièvre, maybe." Vivian stepped back, tsking and scowling. "The girl you helped the other morning."

"The swimmer?" Pia asked, and Vivian nodded. "My French is a little … uh."

"Awful." Vivian pressed her fingers to Pia's forearm. "I'll ask her for you. Shall we say twice a week?"

"Every day. I hate messes. Five hundred euros a week?" Pia slipped past Vivian on the tiny landing and dropped down the ancient staircase.

"That's way too much," Vivian called after her.

"It's for discretion."

"We talked about this. Money doesn't solve problems. What happened to taking personal responsibility for everyday…"

Vivian's voice receded as Pia strode out into the street and made her way to Galerie DeLano.

Taking the long way around, she approached from the cross street to get a good look at it before going in. The front was all glass with artwork on display. The tan stucco lacked the polished chrome and black glass of most modern galleries. It was shabby on the outside, the windows were not clean, but the paintings were outstanding even at a distance. She crossed the narrow lane and headed up Place Nationale past a sidewalk café.

Out of the corner of her eye, she spotted a familiar looking dog-eared copy of *Death and Treason*. She had made those dog-ears in that book. It was the one she'd been trying to read for days but left somewhere. At the same time her brain processed this, she recognized the reader. Willy-Mac. Their eyes met as her purposeful stride carried her past the small tables. Neither of them made any attempt to acknowledge the other. But their gaze connected.

Seeing him made her cringe. Before talking to him, she was one step away from going home. Now she was taking his advice without including him. It was for his own good. But knowing that didn't make her feel better about it. She considered her strategy. What was she expecting? Just a peek in DeLano's to see if she could figure out what was going on without Willy-Mac. If a big international-conspiracies-r-us sign hung inside the door, she'd figure out her next step. No big deal.

She fell back in time again. She'd been drugged shortly after her father's murder. Waking up on her yacht was surreal. How could she wake in luxury when he was dead? Her people had to show her his body before she believed it. It made her angry. At herself more than anyone else, but that didn't stop her from lashing out at everyone. Recalling that anger brought her back to the present.

What was Willy-Mac doing there? He'd been around DeLano's every time she'd gone near the place. Was he working for them? She sensed him observing her. She lifted her chin, passed by, crossed to the gallery side of the road, and opened the door.

An Arab in a white thawb spoke to a man in a blue suit near the back wall. Pia glanced at the paintings, mostly abstract impressionists.

One caught her eye. Strong swirling strokes of red and bright blue were accented by yellow mists. It gave her a familiar sensation. She appreciated it for a minute before realizing why.

"Pardon, Madame," the young man in the suit said in accented English. "The most extraordinary and beautiful discovery is the woman who appreciates art."

"Is it so rare?" She observed the work.

He flushed. "This did not come out well. Forgive my English."

The Arab was leaving through a back door. She turned to face the young man. A little awkwardness flitted across his face. She'd seen that look often enough to recognize it: a man who was used to looking down at women. She regretted wearing pumps.

She said, "Eva Scott." And held out a hand.

He shook it while maintaining eye contact, though she thought he was checking her out in his peripheral vision. "Michael Todd DeLano."

"This is your gallery?" she asked.

"Oui." He looked her over with a more brazen eye. "You are the muscular one, non?"

She stared at him without speaking until he swallowed hard.

"Uhm." He pointed to the wall. "The painting, it interests you?"

"How much?"

"Not for sale, this one. Just for the looking." He squinted. "Are you not representing Mr. Deng?"

The name took her by surprise as much as the question. How many Dengs could there be? And why would he be in an obscure corner of France?

"I'm sorry, who?" she asked.

"Of no mind. We closed just now for a private showing. You are going." He waved a hand toward the door. "Perhaps an appointment would be best. We will open doors at any hour to accommodate such a lovely lady. Just be sure to tell me who you represent."

Before either of them moved, a thick Chinese security man stepped in the door wearing a black suit and heavy sunglasses. An earbud clung to his ear. He marched straight to them and nodded at Michael Todd DeLano. The young man put his hands up as if he were being robbed. DeLano nodded at Pia to do the same. The bodyguard followed DeLano's gaze and looked her over.

"I'm leaving." She stuck her nose in the air and crossed the room before anyone could stop her.

The front door swung open. An arrogant Chinese billionaire stepped in, saw her, and gasped.

"Deng Zhipeng," she said. "Fancy meeting you here."

A pained smile stretched across the man's face. He flushed and searched for words. When he didn't find any, he looked away while remaining planted in the doorway.

Pia turned to the window for salvation and found it. Willy-Mac's eyes were on her. She mouthed the word *help*. He dropped his book on the table and crossed the street.

"If you date does not go well," Deng said slowly, working his weak English with care, "it is most polite to decline the following invitation."

"I'm sorry, Zhipeng." She closed her eyes while she searched for words of her own. "It was wrong of me. I didn't mean to ghost on you. I had an important call. I mean. A friend came in from out of town. I, uh…"

He waited with pleading eyes for her to say something more.

"I love the suit." She bent down and felt the lapel. "Zegna?"

Deng forced a smile. "Perhaps, rain check? We possibly meet in Paris tomorrow?"

"Ah, well, y'know…"

Willy-Mac pushed the door open and walked in like he intended to buy the place. Deng's bodyguard swooped in and shoved him against the wall.

"Hey, now!" Willy-Mac cried out. "What is this?"

DeLano scurried over and spoke French. "Sorry, sir, this is the private showing. You must now leave."

Pia observed the melee for a moment before re-engaging Deng's gaze. She held her thumb to her ear and her little finger to her lips and mouthed, *I'll call you.* She turned for the door.

Deng caught her arm.

"I see how it is," Willy-Mac shouted in French. "White girl walks in, no problem. But I make the mistake of walking in here—"

Pia shook her head at Deng. He looked on the verge of tears. She pulled from his light grip and exited.

Willy-Mac slammed his way outside, brushing her shoulder, and said, "BBQ" as if it were a swear word. He turned left and stormed away.

Pia turned right and took the long way to the café.

Vivian and Guenièvre served a line of people that still stretched out the door late enough in the day to be considered an early dinner. When Vivian saw her, she nodded to the back.

Pia slipped around the patrons, past the counter and into the tiny stockroom and kitchen.

Willy-Mac was pouring lemonade and nodded to an empty cup.

"Yes, please." She caught her breath and added, "Thanks for the rescue."

He poured the drink and handed it to her. "Tell me that guy was not the Korean dictator."

"Are you saying they all look alike?"

"Same damn haircut, same weight in a pint-size can. I didn't get a look at his face."

"Deng Zhipeng."

"The Chinese internet magnate?"

Pia nodded.

"You two looked…" Willy-Mac paused "…close."

"Blind date. Only I didn't know it was a date. I have a boyfriend. Had. Anyway. Some friends invited me to dinner without mentioning any guests. Zhipeng showed up with a whole different expectation."

"It's been over forty years since I had dating problems." Willy-Mac laughed. "I don't miss it none."

They both sipped their drinks.

"Smarter, more experienced people than you have been killed undercover. Do you know how much danger you were in?"

"I can handle it." Her blood pressure rose. "What the hell were you doing there?"

"Predicting you'd get in trouble."

"Well, you were wrong. I knew what I was—" She turned away.

"Yeah." He laughed. "How's that working for you?"

"Well. Not great, but not … yeah."

"You don't want help. I get that. But you need it. And that's why you're here."

Pia didn't think of anything to say, so she kept quiet.

"I won't make you say it. I know you're too proud. Let's just say I'm happy to help. Now, what did you learn?"

"I'm not sure what it means." She heaved a sigh. "In 1984, Willem de Kooning painted *Untitled XVII*, a series of bold lines in red and blue on white with yellow accents. Either someone stole it from my library in DC in the last three weeks, or a damn good forgery is hanging in the Galerie DeLano."

CHAPTER 12

MIKHAIL YESCHENKO STOOD AT THE window of his cavernous office, watching the waves come in. A hundred feet down the volcanic cliff below him, the deep blue Atlantic crashed into the natural fortress of Corvo Island. Seawater exploded skyward in enormous fountains of white spray that nearly reached him. Gravity pulled it back from its zenith to splash down and swirl on the jagged rocks. Sunlight sparkled and danced in stony pools for a few seconds before the bone-crushing weight of marine hydraulics repeated itself. A scale and power only Mother Nature could produce.

He marveled at how similar his new situation had become. Like the water pounding the inlets below, he was forced to recognize a power more brutal than his own. The F-22 Raptor that landed on his private airstrip without invitation had punctuated Roche's statement quite well.

"And how does President Roche think his friends and I will react to his generous opportunity?" he asked.

"It is pronounced Row-SHAY." Roche's emissary Taylor stood ten feet back with his arms crossed.

"My apologies. English is not my first language." Yeschenko gave the young man a contrite smile. The emissary made no response, physical or verbal. "What does President Row-SHAY think we will do?"

"He doesn't care. Either you go to Antibes and do what you were told, or he brings in Pia Sabel to testify about Flight 1028." The emissary scowled. "He's been patient with you long enough. Time you got on board."

The president's survival skills had grown considerably in recent days. The man was now biting the very hand that once fed him. Introducing

Ms. Sabel as a bargaining chip would have been a dazzling tactic had the whole world not been painfully aware of her hatred for Chuck Roche. Calling the president's bluff was a risky proposition, but it had to be done.

"To threaten me with Pia Sabel's testimony," Yeschenko said, "is a brilliant strategy, Taylor. It is the most frightening of prospects. Did you have a hand in developing that concept?"

Emissary Taylor's face colored with confusion.

Over the decades that he'd survived the Kremlin's demands, Yeschenko had relied on flattery to unravel bluster and bravado. He left as much silence as the boy needed to think up a clever answer.

Taylor squared his shoulders and picked up his chin. "I may have had a hand in it."

"Tell me then," Yeschenko smiled to disarm him, "if this threat is supposed to be material, why did President Roche—I mean Row-SHAY—tweet a reward for information about Ms. Sabel's whereabouts this morning?"

Like so many of Roche's emissaries, secretaries, and supporters, Taylor found himself one tweet behind the times. "Well, um, he's also bringing in Belenov."

It was all Yeschenko could do not to laugh. If there were one person on this planet Roche would never lay his hands on, it was Yuri Belenov. Roche's penchant for hollow threats was infantile. He once promised to bring down the wrath of the American military on a dictator if the man insulted him again. The young dictator did exactly that several more times. Roche fought back by canceling military exercises with neighboring allies. Exactly what the dictator had demanded to begin with. Roche committed an own goal. Dictators 7, Roche 0.

"Tell His Excellency that I greatly admire his tenacity. He is the greatest president who has ever lived—in the USA or elsewhere. Future generations will adore him. History books will praise him. However, I must call his bluff on Belenov. Produce him whenever you'd like. The events for which Mr. Belenov can testify would not implicate me in anything. I had no part in the terrorist attack against your country. Your beloved supreme leader seems to have forgotten that it was he, Chuck

Roche, who conspired with Viktor Popov to have Belenov bring down Flight 1028. Indeed, Taylor, I encourage you to bring in Mr. Belenov and Ms. Sabel and have them testify—" he leaned in and lowered his voice "—against your boss."

Yeschenko watched Taylor's shock spread from head to toe as reality crashed through the alternative facts he'd come to believe. Yeschenko stepped back in case the young man lost his lunch on the Persian carpet, an event that appeared to be imminent.

Taylor straightened his tie, took a deep breath, and held it while he spoke. "Have you ever had an F-22 fire missiles at you?"

"Ah, now comes the threat of violence." Yeschenko grinned and opened his arms. "Impotent men threaten violence, Taylor. Come here. Look out this window."

He waved his hand until Taylor stood next to him. They watched the surf crashing into the sharp rocks below for a long time.

Yeschenko put his arm around the young man. "I assure you with all my heart and soul that I will never threaten you, Taylor. You see, real life is not like the movies. If someone must be eliminated, we simply eliminate them. There is no discussion, no threat, no dangling you over a snake pit from which you might escape. When someone disappoints me, I have them tossed to the rocks." He pointed at the serrated landing zone and gave Taylor a playful push that made the boy yelp. "Sometimes from this very window. But on sunnier days, from there."

Yeschenko pointed to a broad terrace overlooking the same cliff.

He pulled the shaking emissary away from the ledge. "Don't worry, Taylor, you have not disappointed me. You made a personal mistake. You put your faith in a man who is nothing more than a carnival barker. The best barker of all time, I'll grant him that. But it is not my problem that you are imprudent. That is your problem." One hand gripped Taylor's shoulder hard, the other pointed a finger in his chest. "You see, you arrived in a two-seater F-22. That is a training jet with no armaments. Your threat is hollow, but I don't blame you because your chief told you to say this. If I thought that you made this threat on your own, I would find that disappointing."

Slowly, they both turned to the open window.

He patted the young man and let go.

Taylor doubled over, gripped the sill, and puked his guts out into the roiling sea.

While it felt good to bully an unfortunate underling who was woefully unprepared for his mission, the power Roche had at his fingertips was no trifle. Even though the repercussions of an unprovoked attack on a Portuguese island, no matter how remote, would destroy his administration in a week, Roche lacked the foresight to understand that. Unfortunately, Roche's tactical error could cost Mikhail Yeschenko—and RULE—their lives. As much as Yeschenko hated to admit it, submitting to Roche's tyranny was the most expedient option. For now.

He did not look forward to explaining the situation to RULE's board. Roche would force them all to Antibes to make confessions for financial crimes that were standard practices in any other country. The president would use the information against them. RULE would never stand for such extortion. But, they would plot revenge later. For now, Roche held all the cards.

"The fact remains that Chuck Roche is a very powerful man who must be obeyed." He paused while the boy transitioned to dry heaves. "Can you hear me, Taylor? I do not like to repeat myself."

The boy managed to burp up an affirmative before returning to his heaves.

"You can report back to your *Il Duce*, that we, the members of RULE, first among his most adoring fans, will gladly do as he has so graciously asked."

Taylor looked over his shoulder, yellow bile dripping from his lips, and nodded.

Yeschenko texted his staff for some help while young Taylor spat his last and composed himself. The boy slumped in the window frame then realized how easily he might be pushed over. He leapt three feet away from the opening.

A waiter appeared with a glass of water. Taylor guzzled it like a man dying in a desert.

"It was indeed an honor to meet you." Yeschenko put an arm around the boy and turned him toward the door. "I wish you weren't in such a hurry because I'd be grateful to hear some of your anecdotes about our great leader. You must be quite an educated and brilliant man to be blessed by his benevolence with such a demanding office."

The emissary raised his chin and marched a little quicker to the door. "I hadn't thought of it quite like that. I'm not so sure I handled things the way he wanted." His eyes took in the monumental office.

"Nonsense, Taylor. You got the result you wanted. I'm sure Roche will appoint you as his permanent emissary."

Taylor nearly lost it again.

Yeschenko patted him on the back and gave him a push. "Perhaps he wasn't forthcoming about his involvement in certain aspects of American terrorist attacks. I'm sure that, once you get past that issue, you'll—what was that expression you used—get on board. You'll be back here in no time with updates and his inevitable new demands." He gave the emissary another push. "Taylor, you must look forward to that prospect as a promotion. I'm sure you'll be running Global Economic Develop … what was it again?"

"Just GEDI, sir."

"Ah, yes, you'll be a GEDI master in no time." He spoke into the boy's ear. "Just as I'm sure you will never disappoint me."

He was careful not to slam the door on Taylor-the-emissary's rear end. He crossed back to the window, screamed his anger to the damp air outside, put his hands on the sill, hung his head, and watched the waves breaking. He texted out instructions to his secretaries to schedule the required conference call with RULE's governing board.

It would be he who ended up on the rocks if he couldn't get Roche back under control. Yuri Belenov had been right: that son of a bitch was indeed treacherous.

He called Hugo, his chief of operations. Hugo delivered a succinct progress report. His team had suffered setbacks, lost ground, and had problems. They were on the trail of a promising lead, maybe. He ended the call with little hope for a quick solution to offer his board.

He needed a Plan B. One that would require a partner. Who could offer him a path to Roche's vulnerable underside? One name sprang to his mind. Young, impressionable, and known for making snap decisions,

Pia Sabel might make the perfect ally. Especially if the rumors were true that she had dirt on Roche. Unfortunately, she had not responded to his messages in some time. While he could blackmail her, he hesitated to bring her into RULE under duress. She would be a much better ally if she were willing.

A trap like that would take time.

CHAPTER 13

IT HAD BEEN A BUSY couple of days. I had killed four men, fled the jurisdiction, and ignored calls from my squad. I needed to keep them busy, so I'd sent them to New Orleans, Louisiana, NOLA, to find the two missing guys from the shootout. I told them it was because, eventually, all roads lead to Tremé. Since I planned to hunt for Ms. Sabel only after I found Sylvia—if I did it at all—I wanted to go alone.

My first stop was the one place that would make me look busy without raising suspicions.

Ms. Sabel's grandparents live at the end of a long, wooded driveway just outside of Rockaway, New Jersey. The Lyft driver dropped me at the gate. It was cool and sunny, and I wanted to walk.

Sheriff Kirby called from Iowa. "Two guys from New Orleans stayed up at the Parker farm out west of Franklin. They rented the farmhouse next to the old barn. Parker said they were up in the cupola day and night."

"They could see my folk's place from up there?" I asked.

"On a clear day. They bugged out half an hour after you left. I'm guessing that was the scouting party. Does that mean your family's safe now?"

"Most likely."

"I'll stick around, just to be sure." He waited a beat. "Say, whatever happened to Dan Sweeney? Are he and Joyce still engaged?"

"I get yelled at when I ask, so I'm guessing not. Good luck, Louis."

Mercury strode alongside me. *Just to make sure we're all straight here, homie: looking for Pia-Caesar-Sabel is your top priority, right?*

I said, *Top priority: making sure Gold-Tooth's people follow me around the globe and leave my family alone.*

Mercury said, *And then you're looking for Pia-Caesar-Sabel? Because I don't get the feeling you're looking all that hard.*

I'd like to know who shot me, I said. *I know you don't care, but it might point to where Ms. Sabel went.*

Whoa, dude, I care. As far as you know.

The Colonial mansion was in pristine condition. Ms. Sabel's Grampa, Alan Sabel's father, sat on the porch, soaking up the rays in his wheelchair. His head swayed from side to side in slow motion. His hands rested on the armrests. I'd heard his Parkinson's hadn't robbed an ounce of brainpower, but it sure did a number on his body.

"Hey there, Grampa," I called as I approached. "Remember me from when I was your bodyguard a few years back?"

His head swayed in a way that I took to be affirmative, but who knows. I took his hand gently and shook it, then put it back. Either it quivered off the armrest, or he was reaching for me. It was hard to tell. His lips moved as if he was trying to speak. I bent down, putting my ear close.

"Not the only one … remembers you."

"Sorry I haven't been to visit in a couple years," I said. "But, hey, you're looking good. You've been out dancing, haven't you? Yeah, I can tell. Big smile like that comes from sweeping the ladies around the rug."

He smiled. I think. I patted his back and headed for the front door.

His right hand dug in his shirt pocket with great difficulty. The other arm reached out as if to grab me, but it could've been one of those tremors.

Mercury stood between me and the door. *Brutha, there are people you want to talk to because they're easy to talk to. Then there are people you need to talk to, but you don't because they're repulsive in some way. Think about that.*

I said, *OK.*

Mercury said, *Well?*

Sometimes the riddles of the gods are beyond me. Call me a blasphemer, but I just don't get it. *I have no idea what you're talking about.*

Mercury said, *Talk to people who care.*

I nodded as if he made sense and reached for the doorbell. One of the aides came out before I pushed it. She held a child's spill-proof cup filled with lemonade. A bendy straw stuck out of the top. She remembered me and held the door. We exchanged pleasantries before she directed me to the solarium to find Gramma Sabel.

The matriarch was giving directions to a gardener. He held blueprints in his hand while she gestured left and right. I coughed.

She excused the hired man and greeted me with an air hug. "What brings you out here?"

"Ms. Sabel's gone into hiding, and I need to find her." I studied the old lady's reaction. No shock, no worry, no hint of surprise.

"She's not here." She studied me right back. "Sorry you've wasted a trip."

"Never thought she was." I settled my weight on one leg and crossed my arms. "But she's too careful to go away without telling anyone how to get in touch with her. In case of emergency."

"Did you ever seduce her?"

I took a deep breath. "You know we don't have that kind—"

"What a waste. She has all that money and all those men around. She should be having fun. Enjoy it while you can, I tell her. There's that handsome devil of an Indian, what's his name? Michael? No. Miguel. And then there's you. Not much of a face, but you're built sturdy enough. You might do in a—"

"Ma'am." I wiped my face with my palm and sighed. "I'm not comfortable with this conversation."

"Do you know how many uncomfortable conversations a woman suffers through in her lifetime?"

"About your granddaughter. Did you have any discussions about—"

"She doesn't listen to me." She touched my arm in confidence. "I told her not to make the same mistake I made. I spent the first half of my life being the virtuous woman—and the second half regretting it."

We stared at each other for a couple blinks.

"OK. So. Do you know how to get in touch with her?" I asked.

"Heavens, no. I'm just stating the obvious. Maybe she went to some hedonistic Caribbean island for a romp with some well-oiled men." She huffed at me. "Strike one for the sisterhood."

Mercury leaned against the giant indoor ficus behind her. *Oh yeah, that sounds just like Pia-Caesar-Sabel. Not. You know why you're talking to her, homie?*

I said, *Because she might know something, since the Major and Bianca and Tania don't.*

Mercury said, *You should spend more time talking to people who care.*

An idea formed at the edge of my brain, but it wasn't complete. *You mean, Gramma Sabel's trying to tell me something? Is it the island thing?*

Mercury said, *People who care. Get it? Aw, you're hopeless, dawg.*

I started to protest, but he waved his arms encouraging me to get moving.

"I've discovered something important, and I need to tell her." I traded confidential arm-touches with the old lady. "She can go back to doing whatever she wants afterward. But right now, she needs to know."

Gramma Sabel held my gaze for a long time, her face slowly melting. "Is it about Alan? Did you find out who murdered my son?"

The quiver in her voice made me feel bad about overplaying my part. I knew damn well who murdered him. The ambush he'd walked into weighed on me more than any death I'd caused or witnessed. Everyone who was there carried enough guilt about that day to drown in it.

Mercury said, *Don't go there, dude. Stay with me, don't blame yourself. Focus.*

"Nothing about Alan." I took a deep breath and fought back depression. "He was a great man. You raised the best son on the planet, ma'am. No doubt about it."

"Thank you for saying so." She sniffled and turned away. "I'm telling you the truth, I don't know how to contact her. She dropped in here unannounced a few weeks ago. Said she was going to Mardi Gras. But I had to see my other grandchildren that day, so we didn't talk long. We were never close. It's hard with adopted children, you know." She pulled a tissue out of her pocket and wiped her nose and dabbed her eyes.

"They're not the same as natural children. You don't get the same bond. My other grandchildren are—naturally—closer."

Pia Sabel paid for Gramma's house and staff. She put all her cousins through the finest private schools and colleges. Bailed Uncle Paul out of bankruptcy and paid for Aunt Diana's rehab all three times. She'd reached out to them a hundred times. Nothing came back but mildly friendly replies. They displayed the same kind of interest in her as did her neighbors three blocks away. They never shared secrets, never called just for fun, never visited after her Alan's death. They just didn't care. Except Grampa Sabel; he used to treat her as his favorite grandchild.

Ms. Sabel tried. I was with her every day. I saw her leave messages and texts that were never returned. She never spoke an unkind word about them. But I knew how she felt. Lonely. Motherless.

"You remember Alan's friend, Bobby Jenkins?" I asked. Gramma nodded. "He and his first wife adopted two kids. When he remarried, he had biological children. One time, Bobby and your son were talking about adopted kids and families. Bobby said, 'There is no difference in my bond with any of my kids. I feel every triumph and heartache as if it were my own. But there is a difference. When you have biological children, your whole community has them with you. Your family, your neighbors, your congregation, your friends—everyone gets excited right along with you. When you adopt, you adopt alone.'"

She backed up a step. "When employees overhear private conversations, they should never repeat them."

"Too late. I told my mother that story, just in case I end up adopting someday." I glared at Gramma Sabel. "She promised not to be like you: distant and disconnected."

I turned on my heel and strode out.

Mercury kept pace. *Did that feel good, brutha? That kind of boldness won't help your career any. If you get fired over this—*

I said, *Yeah, go ahead and take off. If I get fired over this, I won't need a god anymore. I'll fry burgers in Fort Madison.*

Mercury stopped in the foyer. *Even fry cooks need a god, dude. Not my specialty, but I could hook you up with Castor and Pollux. They have plenty of time on their hands.*

I said, *Who?*

Castor and Pollux, the twins who make up Gemini. You remember. Castor was killed, and Pollux shared his immortality—because that's what brothers do. Holy Diana, have you ever listened to any of my lessons on the pantheon?

Ignoring him, I kept my pace out the front door.

Mercury stopped. *Now will you talk to someone who cares?*

Grampa Sabel's nurse jumped up and rushed across the porch to me. "He keeps saying your name."

People who aren't easy to talk to. People who care.

"Hey there, Grampa!" I turned on a dime. "I wasn't going to leave without saying goodbye. How's that lemonade? Did you spike it?"

His head swerved and dipped. His lips moved up and down. His left hand reached out as if he were trying to claw at me. I moved closer. His fingers wrapped around my wrist with a desperate grip. He gave me a tug and mumbled something.

Mercury said, *Now, you're listening, homes. He might be hard to hear, but sometimes old people know a thing or two. Just look at me, I'm fifteen billion years old—*

I said, *Save it.*

In the later stages of Parkinson's, the voice is weak. His was barely audible. I bent down, put my ear to his mouth.

"She knows." He pushed me away. "Only you. Danger … she said."

In his right hand was something small, the size of a business card. His arm wobbled toward me and back, like a magician with a distraction. I glanced at him. His powerful blue eyes were locked on mine with an intensity I had never seen before. I tugged the card out of his gnarled grip.

Sylvia Lallouette, Screen Actors Guild.

CHAPTER 14

WILLY-MAC OPENED THE DOOR. PIA sauntered in with a laptop under her arm. He ushered her through the inside to the small patio off the living room.

"This is lovely." Pia twirled around checking out the space. Their home, spacious by French Riviera standards, crouched between two apartment buildings. Even with the limited sunlight, Vivian kept it blooming with bougainvillea and lantana.

She dropped her computer on the table and pulled up a chair. "These came out pretty nicely."

Turning the screen to face him, he paged through a series of photos. "Not bad. Facial recognition software can figure out who these people are. I can call a buddy back in Houston—"

"Google Images," she said. "Largest database going."

Willy-Mac frowned but pulled up a browser, opened Google Images, and pulled up one of Pia's photos. Immediately, the screen filled with similar pictures of Sheikh Mohammad. He pointed at the screen. "That's scary. Who's this sheikh?"

"The royal family's fixer."

Willy-Mac raised an eyebrow. "As in, Qatari royal?"

"Hello?" Vivian stepped out of the living room. A ten-year-old girl of mixed race carrying a school bag trailed behind her.

The young girl looked up at Vivian and spoke in frenzied French. "Is that her? Really her?"

"Sorry, Elisa is a huge fan." Vivian patted the girl's head. "I've sworn her to secrecy."

Elisa marched up and stuck out her hand. Pia shook it.

"*Enchanté* to meet you," the young girl said with a heavy accent. "I keep your secret—if you tell me a secret. What clever things you do when you were me?"

Pia wasn't sure what she meant at first, then realized it was a bargain. "You mean, if I tell you something no one else knows about my childhood, you'll keep my secret?"

"Oui, this." Elisa had a confident grin.

"You're selling your loyalty?" Pia laughed. "OK. Well. Let's see. When I was not much older than you, I was on the National Team's youth squad. We traveled a lot and had tough coaches who wouldn't let us have any fun. When they said lights out, the lights went out. When they said no talking, we had to be resourceful."

Elisa frowned. Vivian explained in French. The girl nodded for Pia to continue.

"One of the girls was related to Jeremiah Denton, a POW who was tortured by the North Vietnamese. He used Morse code to send a message when his captors made him read a confession on TV. She taught the rest of us Morse code. From then on, we would tap, blink, whistle, or hum codes to each other when we weren't supposed to talk."

Vivian explained in French, and Pia tapped out, *play to win.*

"*Tu as enfreint la loi?*" Elisa asked. "Ehm, you break rules?"

"Just a little one," Pia held up her thumb and forefinger with enough space for a thin sheet of paper between them.

"I am to learn Morse code." Elisa laughed and picked up her backpack and darted back in the house.

Vivian turned to her husband. "And just where have you two been the last couple days?"

"Boring stuff." Willy-Mac held his wife's gaze long enough to make Pia feel awkward. "Stakeout."

"Uh-huh." Vivian cocked a hip and turned to Pia when she noticed the laptop. She leaned over and slipped on her reading glasses. "Is that a sheik? In Antibes? Doesn't his kind belong in Monte Carlo or Cannes?"

"Exactly what we were thinking." Willy-Mac pulled a chair for his wife. "Check out the clients coming and going from the Galerie DeLano."

Vivian paged through the photographs. "Is that the Egyptian Prime Minister?"

"We've seen a lot of recognizable faces going in the Galerie. Princes, billionaires, corporate executives, and so forth."

"And y'all are sticking your noses into their business?" Vivian stood back with a frown. "All these people have bodyguards with guns." She shook her head at Willy-Mac. "Uh-uh, don't you mess with them."

Pia pulled up her designer purse, set it on the table, reached into the hidden compartment and slipped out her 9mm Glock. Vivian gasped. Pia dropped the magazine and ejected what looked like a bullet. She held it up and flicked the lightweight paper nose cone to reveal the needle inside.

Pia explained. "It's a miniature dart filled with a nonlethal dose of Inland Taipan snake venom backed by a heavy sedative. The venom produces instant flaccid paralysis long enough for the sedative to put the target to sleep."

"When were you planning to tell me about that?" Willy-Mac sounded as surprised as Vivian looked.

"I'm fully trained and licensed." Pia snapped the bullet back in the magazine, pressed it in the gun, and slid it back in her purse. "Even in France. Even as Eva Scott."

"Look now." Willy-Mac pointed a finger at her as he gathered his thoughts. "If you want my help, we're doing everything legal and by the book. If we find something going on, we turn it over to the authorities. No need for Glocks."

Pia figured operations like the one at the DeLano would involve the local authorities in the scheme but saw no point in arguing with a retired Texas Ranger. She nodded. "Just in case, we're protected."

"Does that thing fire real bullets too?" Vivian asked. When Pia reluctantly nodded, she asked, "And do you have some?"

Pia pursed her lips and nodded.

"The first thing my law-man here's going to tell you is: guns escalate problems exponentially."

Willy-Mac put his hand on top of his wife's. "You're young and don't know, but the last thing you ever want to be in is a gunfight."

Pia had been in too many gunfights, including one that escalated exponentially and cost her father his life. Again, not a discussion she wanted to get into.

"What do you suspect they're doing?" Vivian asked.

"Money laundering," Willy-Mac said. "But her theory doesn't quite fit."

"Why do you think it's laundering?"

"Let's say you're a drug dealer," Willy-Mac said. "You're in a cash business. But you can't spend it on anything big like a house or a car without alerting the tax authorities. So, you buy a car wash like they did in *Breaking Bad*. You wash a thousand dollars' worth of cars, then deposit a million in your bank. Your money appears to be legal profits."

"These guys aren't drug dealers," Vivian said.

"It's the same principle on a much larger scale." Pia sat back. "Let's say you're a Russian oligarch, pumping oil and selling it legally. You're making billions. But at any moment, President Medevtin could throw you in jail and confiscate all your wealth. It's happened from Saudi Arabia to Russia to China. The ruler declares an anti-corruption crackdown and vast estates are redistributed. If you had that problem, you go to New York or London and buy something of subjective value like art, an antique, or a condominium with your Russian rubles. You turn around and sell it the next day for a dollar to a shell company you've set up in advance. The shell company then sells the artwork for the real value and—voila—the oligarch has moved some of his money out of the country. For example, Vladimir buys a painting for sixty million rubles, sells it to ABC company for a dollar, and ABC sells it for a million US dollars. Now ABC, which Vladimir owns, has a million dollars deposited in a Luxemburg bank. Medevtin can't touch it."

"That sounds reasonable," Vivian said. "Then why doesn't your theory work?"

"First," Pia said, "this isn't Paris or London or New York where big sales take place every day, and these little $10 million deals would go unnoticed. The second problem is, billionaires don't come in person, we send surrogates. Third, the art would be in a freeport like Geneva or Singapore or Luxembourg to save on taxes. Fourth, they wouldn't buy obvious forgeries because getting caught by someone like me—who owns one of those—is inevitable. Fifth, Michael Todd DeLano should be the richest, most celebrated art dealer on the Côte d'Azur, but no one has ever heard of him. And he drives a Porsche. None of this makes sense." Pia drummed her fingers on the table. "I sat at a café with a big lens and snapped away as these people came and went. None of them glanced at me. I don't get it."

"What's wrong with owning a Porsche?" Vivian looked at her husband, who shrugged, then back at Pia.

"Oh, nothing," Pia said in a hurry. "Yours is very nice. But for the money he would make from these sales, he should be in a limo with a bodyguard of his own."

Vivian nodded thoughtfully. "So, you two are going to figure out what they're up to and turn it over to Interpol in Lyon?" She squinted at Pia. "You're not going to get Willy-Mac into any kind of crazy trouble, are you? He's not much, but he's all I've got left."

"I need this, Viv." Willy-Mac clasped Vivian's hand and spoke softly. "Remember the marches? Back when we were young and beautiful?"

"Mm-hmm." Vivian closed her eyes in a sweet reverie of her golden youth.

"We were out to change the world. We made a difference, Viv. These days, we can walk in the same entrances, sit at the same lunch counters, drink from the same fountains as anyone else. The world is a better place. But the work is never done, is it?"

Vivian patted her husband's hand, her eyes moist. She rose and stood behind her chair, rolled her fingers on the chair back and looked at Willy-Mac. He looked at Pia.

Vivian said to Willy-Mac, "Do you think something illegal's going on in there?"

"I do," he said. He kept his gaze fixed on Pia.

"Do you know why they're doing those five things she was talking about that don't fit her money laundering theory?"

"I do."

CHAPTER 15

PRESIDENT CHUCK ROCHE PATTED THE Russian cultural attaché on the back as he guided the man to the door. "Come back any time, Dmitri. Bring a balalaika or something, though. Just to make it look like a real cultural exchange. Optics, you know."

"We appreciate you sharing the Israeli intelligence." Dmitri held up a folder marked Top Secret. "It shows a new level of cooperation." He brushed Roche's hand off his back. "But don't think that levels your debts. We have an understanding. You need to do your part."

Roche stepped back as if he'd been hurt. "When 517 out of 519 elected officials sign a sanctions bill, I have to go along. There's nothing I can do." Roche smiled and squeezed Dmitri's shoulder. "You be sure to tell Yeschenko and Medevtin who's administering those sanctions. There are no allocated agents assigned to follow up. Don't worry about a thing. I've got this."

Roche missed Viktor Popov. The former head of the KGB had loaned him hundreds of millions after Roche lost his inheritance in bankruptcy. Popov had rarely asked anything in return. Just the occasional hit. Maybe honey-trap a politician. He and Popov were loyal to each other. The new guys made a lot more demands. He was getting sick of their attitude. He pulled the door open and gave the Russian a push.

"You better have this, Roche." Dmitri gave him a glare, then marched out.

Standing just outside were three generals, his Secretary of State, General Ripley; his Secretary of Defense, General Kurtz; and his latest Chief of Staff, General Bates. Their posture and scowls didn't give him a good feeling about their intent.

"Gentlemen," he said, "don't stand out there in the cold, come in."

"Was that the Mossad report on ISIS?" Bates pointed at the Russian on his way out.

"I'm the one who decides the status of information." Roche tapped his cane on the floor for emphasis. "I decided it was in the national interest to share it."

Kurtz frowned at him, then turned to Ripley. "Kim Philby was nothing compared to this guy."

"Who?" Roche asked.

"A Cold War hero—in certain circles," Ripley said.

Roche motioned the men to a place in front of his expansive desk and stood behind his executive chair.

"We have come here with an important—"

"You guys look pissed off," Roche said. "You better be pissed off about all the leaks coming out of the White House. I expect nothing but loyalty from my staff. I'm not seeing that from you. When I don't feel the loyalty, bad things happen. You don't want—"

"Shut up, Chuck." Chief of Staff Bates put his fists on the desk and leaned across. "We have something to say, and you're going to listen."

"Who the hell do you think you are?" Roche cleared his desk with his cane before slamming it down hard on the oak. "You're not half as good as David Watson was. You know what he did when he was chief of staff? He knew Pia Sabel had him cornered and he'd have to turn state's evidence against me, so he blew his brains out. Do you have that kind of courage?"

General Kurtz stepped around the desk and grabbed the president by the neck and spoke through clenched teeth. "I was eighteen when I killed my first gook in Vietnam. I killed men in Bosnia. I ordered thousands to die in Iraq. Don't think for one minute I can't squeeze the life out of your scrawny, impotent little neck, dickweed. Now sit down and shut up."

Kurtz slammed the president in his chair.

Roche bristled with fear and anger and venom. He squirmed in his seat as he gathered his thoughts. There was a time to assert power and a time to let the other side think they were winning. He straightened his tie. "I'm listening."

"A little over a year ago, a lieutenant came to me for some career advice," General Ripley said. "He'd been deployed on a top-secret mission to Attu Island in the Alaskan archipelago. Know what I'm talking about?"

Roche knew damn well what the bastard was talking about. "If it's so secret, how the hell would I have known about it? It happened on Hunter's watch."

"Shortly after leaving Attu, this good soldier got a call from a guy named Jacob Stearne. Ever hear of him?"

"Don't answer that." Chief of Staff Bates looked at his colleagues. "We don't want to know."

Ripley said, "Stearne told this lieutenant to make sure he had obtained the right files. Told him he should take a careful look through them before turning them over to officials when he landed. The lieutenant took Stearne's advice. He was so shocked by what he found that he created a set of copies for Watson. He stashed the originals away as insurance in case something happened to him and his platoon. Guess what?"

"Something happened to him." Roche rolled his eyes.

"Don't act like a goddamn teenager." Kurtz backhanded him hard. "We're serious men, and we're seriously pissed off."

Roche rubbed his face and glared at the steaming general. Roche saw the future in his mind. Kurtz would be decapitated by a low flying drone. Nowadays he could make that kind of thing happen.

Bates said, "His platoon was the one that crashed in the Chinook during your inaugural speech."

Ripley dropped a manila folder on the desk. "We found the lieutenant's stash. It took us a year because he hid it well. But we have it now." He bent over the desk to look Roche in the eye. "And that means we have you."

"You're not grabbing that folder because you know what's in it," Bates said. "You know damn well if that folder landed in the hands of any half-smart FBI agent, you'd be on trial for murder within a week. And Pia Sabel would be crowing."

Roche seethed. Plenty of men thought they had him. Plenty of people had tried to contain him. It never worked. No one told him what to do.

Not for long. He would listen a little longer. But, he never kneeled, never apologized, never admitted to anything. That's why he always won in the end. One day, he would go to their funerals. That much of the future he could see clear as day. Roche said, "So then, whatever's in that folder makes me look bad. Is that it? If you think I'm resigning—"

"Hell no, we don't want your resignation." Bates straightened up and crossed his arms. "We joined this administration because we're sick of a woman running off at the mouth whenever someone pats her rear end. We're sick of judges making decisions against Christians. We're sick of the immigrants coming here and filling our schools with drug dealers."

"We're offering you a deal." Ripley sat on the edge of the desk. "One we think you'll like."

"We run everything." Kurtz towered over him. "You're the front man. TV spots, rallies. Tweet whatever you want."

"But no more firings." Bates stepped around to Roche's left side, opposite Kurtz. "You can't say things to the press like you did about Kurtz's daughter."

"I never said anything about—"

"You told them," Kurtz said, "and I quote, 'I like girls who run track. I'd date her a few times.'"

"I didn't say that."

Kurtz turned explosive red and raised his fist.

Bates waved him off. "And no more fucking leaks."

"Me? I don't leak anything. I've never leaked—"

Ripley lowered his voice. "You're always bragging, talking to your friends and anyone who'll listen. A *New York Times* reporter says his best leads are your golfing partners. *The Washington Post* editor showed me texts and emails from your business associates. They text him more than his goddamn wife."

"He's lying."

"It stops right now." Bates pulled something out of his pocket. "Here's your new phone. It's locked down. It has Twitter and two phone numbers. One is mine, the other is Fuchs News. They have instructions. They're onboard."

Kurtz growled, "Any questions?"

He thought about options. He thought about calling their bluff. He thought about telling them he recorded all Oval Office conversations. But they'd demand the tapes. In the past, he'd threatened people with lawsuits and damages and Russian gangsters raining down on them. That always worked. But these guys were different. They didn't cower when he yelled at them. They didn't believe stuff just because he said it.

Inside, Roche's guts spun around. His mind twirled like a carnival ride. He had never been so angry and scared before.

He thought about publicly firing them the minute they walked out the door. That would never work. They had the names of the men who killed Pia Sabel's parents on his canceled checks.

Then it came to him; he knew exactly what to do. And he knew just the guy to do it. The only thing he needed was an emissary. A new one since the last sniveling little weasel had fled the premises after ten minutes with Yeschenko. Not even offering him the top job at GEDI calmed him down any. In fact, the kid ran at the mention.

Then he remembered he had the perfect emissary waiting in the wings.

He took a deep breath and answered his cabinet's glares with a smile.

"No questions at all, gentlemen." Roche pushed back and stood. "We're all on the same page, pursuing the same goals. Just look at the pictures of my staff meetings, you've never seen more than one woman in any of them. Never more than one Jew either. And no guys with beards. Actually, this is a great relief. I've never worked so hard in my life. It sucks. I'd like to get out and play more golf, so—hell no, I don't have any questions."

Roche grinned and stuck out his hand.

After sharing a look with each other, the three of them shook it. They filed out, muttering to each other.

Roche heard Kurtz ask, "What was that about beards?"

"Who knows," Ripley answered.

"Hey, Bates," Roche called out. His chief of staff stopped in his tracks and glanced over his shoulder. "I need to see Veronica. Send a car for her."

His chief of staff turned slowly to face him. "What for?"

"You're the one who banned hookers from the White House."

CHAPTER 16

THE UBER DRIVER WHO TOOK me from Nice to Monaco didn't get a tip. He told me Americans who arrive in private jets are expected to be extra-generous tippers. The French don't usually expect tips at all, in my experience. Either that or I've stiffed a whole lot of people during my previous visits. I'm never sure about that kind of thing.

He dropped me in front of Sylvia's apartment. It was a three-story nineteenth century home that had been subdivided several times to grab its share of the highest rents in the world. With nearly three times the population density of Hong Kong, and the world's most expensive condo only a stone's throw down the hill, renting out rooms was a smart option for Sylvia's aging landlord. Hers was at the top of a rickety staircase bolted to the side of the home with birdhouse screws. But inside, if memory served me, one of her windows managed a helluva view. On a clear day, you could see a couple yachts in the harbor and the blue Mediterranean beyond—if you leaned over the bookcase on the left and pressed your cheek to the wall.

It was a studio with a hot plate on the dresser. The closet, toilet, and shower hid behind a curtain. But Sylvia loved it. The long walk up the hill from Monaco-ville kept her in shape. She moved in when she'd been a frequent character in a French soap opera. Then she got tossed out of a producer's limo in Barcelona for refusing his advances. Her #MeToo tweet featuring his name in caps ended her role the next day. So much for feminist progress.

I rang the bell. No answer. Middle of the day, so no real surprise.

Mercury said, *Homie, jump the fence, already. Let's get this over with.*

I said, *Monaco has more security than the White House.*

I pressed the landlord's button and tried to remember the crotchety old man's name.

Mercury said, *You're wasting time, dawg. You need to be finding Pia-Caesar-Sabel.*

I said, *We've been through this. Sylvia's in danger, and she's the only lead I've got.*

Mercury tossed up his hands. *She's under the influence of a Greek goddess. You can't trust anything she says.*

Where should I be looking then? I gave him my meanest glare. *I mean, c'mon, she's never been to Grampa Sabel's house. Only Ms. Sabel could've given him that card and the instruction for my eyes only. And he said she's in danger.*

Mercury said, *Oh, you think that's what he said. You sure?*

Damn sure, I said. *Probably.*

A voice next to me said something in French. The landlord.

"Remember me?" I said in English. "Sylvia's friend? I'm looking for her."

He slapped the gate open and led me up the staircase streaming words in French that meant nothing to me. He only spoke English when he wanted to.

He pulled out a key, opened the door, stood aside, and waved me in.

I stepped around him, hoping to find a piece of paper and a pen to leave her a note. Instead, I found an empty room. No bed. No hot plate. No bookcase. No Sylvia.

Mercury said, *At least she didn't leave a Trojan, brutha.*

I gave him a dirty look.

As in horse. He grinned big and opened his arms. *Get it? Trojan horse? Sylvia worships Aphrodite, and guess who told Paris of Troy to bring the wooden horse inside the city walls? That's right, Aphrodite. She's not a brilliant strategist like me. True story, I swear to Minerva.*

I said, *Does Jesus mess around like that with the Pope?*

That always shuts him up. Idle gods are more trouble than they're worth.

I crossed the apartment to the curtain-section that contained both closet and bathroom. Cleaned out. A slip of paper rested in the wastebasket. Otherwise, empty. I took the remnant. A receipt from a shoe store dated three weeks ago with Sylvia's name on it. Like a charge account or something. Expensive shoes. I shoved it in my pocket.

The landlord watched me take one more look around. Then he launched into a tirade in French.

"Dude," I said holding up my hands. "It's Claude, right?"

He nodded.

"Look, I'd love to help you, but you've got to work with the languages I speak. If you won't speak English, how about Arabic?"

"You are here to pay rent, oui?"

"I might help you out." I cringed at the idea of selling my house to pay a month's rent on a hovel in Monaco. "What are we talking about?"

"And damages, oui?"

Claude pronounced it *Dah-mah-jay*. Something about his demand struck me. I checked out the apartment again. Fresh plaster and paint covered a couple big spots. They escaped my attention on the first round, but now they stood out like a billboard. A big round spot next to where the bed had been. A bigger spot behind the bookcase. New glass in the window, the sticker still in the corner. Someone got tossed around like a ragdoll. I cringed. "How much?"

"Fifteen thousand."

He was talking euros too.

"Claude, you remember the tall lady who came to visit? Pia Sabel." He stared as if I'd said nothing. "The one who gave some big bucks to the orphanage? She can help us with the back rent. But I need to know where Sylvia went. Can you tell me?"

He shook his head. "Rent, damages."

"If I can come up with the money, do you have an address? A phone number?"

He shrugged. "Rent, damages."

I pulled my phone and dialed the Major. After a quick explanation and my promise that it would lead to Ms. Sabel, she authorized the transfer. We made arrangements while standing in the doorway.

He checked the banking app on his phone. When he saw the wire complete, he looked up. "Big fight. Like animals. Wrecked total place. Left in the night. No address. No phone number. Great riddance."

He turned and stomped down the stairs.

Mercury doubled over laughing. *Oh, he got you, homeboy. Got you good. Now, can we go look for Pia-Caesar-Sabel?*

We are looking for Ms. Sabel, I said. *I think.*

I dropped down the landing to Fabian's apartment just below Sylvia's. The guy had been keen on her but had the self-confidence of a nervous mole rat when the owls are out. I knocked but didn't get an answer.

I called out nice and loud to the ground floor. "Claude, for fifteen thousand, you can afford to loan me a piece of paper and a pencil. Don't make me come get it."

A few seconds later, he scurried up the steps, handed me the items, then ran away.

I left the neighbor a note to call me.

Since Uber can only drop you off in Monaco but not pick you up, I walked down the hill to the police station. I asked about Sylvia Lallouette. Had she been kidnapped, beaten, hospitalized? They put me in a corner and pretended to fetch someone who cared enough to speak English to an American.

An hour later, the guy who pulled the short straw showed up. He said the only thing they knew about Sylvia was that Madame and Claude Ancillon called to complain about noise on the 18th. When the police arrived, they found the apartment wrecked and no sign of Ms. Lallouette. After being hounded by the Ancillons, they tried to find her to pay for damages. They never found her. He admitted she was not a high priority.

Mercury said, *He's holding back, bro. Throw this guy against the wall and beat it out of him.*

I said, *Monaco has the highest ratio of police to citizens in the world. I wouldn't live long.*

Mercury said, *So what? Ask him if he's seen Pia-Caesar-Sabel.*

Instead, I got Claude on the phone and forced him to tell the officer he'd been paid. The cop made a note and left.

I went shoe shopping. The receipt was for a place a couple blocks from the famous casino. I paused outside the window and checked out the wares. I know as much about fashion as you'd expect of a farmer-turned-soldier, but even I knew these shoes cost money. They had icepick heels and toes so sharp the owner could rip a man's heart out if she kicked high enough. I went inside and showed the receipt to a guy. He brought out another guy. They discussed me in French and used hand motions that gave away their argument better than if I'd had a translator: who wants to deal with the straight guy? Finally, the one with the immaculate pompadour flopped his wrist in my direction.

"Such shame for her." He tsked and pouted. "She was nice girl. Worked the Théâtre Princesse Grace at times. You check there, oui?"

"What do you mean, shame?"

He looked both ways before leaning in. "She has the terrible boyfriend. American, you know. Beats her. I've heard."

He stepped back and looked me over. He hadn't looked at me to begin with. I don't know how they know us in Europe, but they can spot an American quicker than you can find Waldo. He winced at his awkward statement and walked away.

"Yeah, well. Thanks," I said. "For the record, I've never hurt a…"

He was gone.

Mercury said, *Sorry to hear it, homie. That's gotta hurt.*

I said, *What are you talking about?*

It's OK, my brutha, Mercury leaned back with sympathetic eyes. *Lots of guys get cheated on. We both know you'd never hurt a woman. Musta been somebody else. Maybe, she hooked up with some American gazillionaire with a yacht. I'll bet it was on account of Aphrodite. Sylvia's channeling that goddess, so—she was asking for it.*

I said, *Keep the 'asking for it' crap to yourself. That is SO first century. If someone is beating her … I've got to rescue her.*

You're the one who needs rescuing, Mercury said. *Pompadour is staring at your butt. Do you feel objectified?*

Pompadour was indeed ogling me. I suddenly understood why women aren't so keen on it. I struck out and was halfway to the Princess Grace Theater when a call came in.

"I am Fabien. You are Jacob, oui?"

"Can you tell me where to find her?"

"They came for her. They beat me and told me not to say anything. Hold on."

He sent me a Skype request. I accepted the video. The swollen face of a man showed up. Half his face was covered in two-week-old bruises of yellow and brown. But his left eye and forehead had fresh scrapes and massive blue and dark purple bruises. New wounds on top of the old.

"Damn, Fabien," I said. "They came back?"

He nodded. "They say, did anyone come looking for her. They did not believe what I tell them."

"Who were they?"

He thought for a moment. He began shaking his head. "Non. I say too much already. They will come back. You must go home. These are the worst of men. Don't look for her."

"You liked her." I found myself shouting at the marmot. "She was abducted by thugs, and you won't tell me how to help her?"

He looked hurt by my words. Add that to his damaged face. I felt bad. I said, "Sorry, Fabien. When those guys come back, give them my number and tell them I'm looking for—"

He shook his head. "Not abducted. She went quite willing."

CHAPTER 17

AS THEY WALKED DOWN THE warren of lanes, Pia wondered if her father hadn't visited recently because Willy-Mac had been sent to replace him. She shook the odd thoughts from her head. She was a creature of science and logic, not a superstitious young girl grasping at straws. She was alone in the world. She had to deal with it. Willy-Mac was a great ally but finding him was luck. Her explosive rage at everyone around her had subsided since befriending the old man. He had given her structure and purpose. Much the same way Alan Sabel had when he encouraged her to play soccer their first year together.

"Eva, are you listening to me?" Willy-Mac had stopped a stride behind her.

"Every word." She faced him. "Undercover is dangerous. I get that. What I don't get is, why you won't tell me your theory. What are they doing?"

"I won't always be standing next to you. Do your own research and thinking. We'll compare notes later."

"That takes too long."

"You're a lot like my daughter was." He started walking again and passed her.

Half a block later, he picked up the conversation again. "The most dangerous part of an undercover op is your ego. Every op I saw go sideways fell apart because the officer didn't hold back. He wanted to let them know how smart he was. That's why we did psych profiles and lots of training first."

"And I don't fit the profile," she said. "You told me that already."

"That's not the worst. Ever heard of DID? Dissociative Identity

Disorder? That's when you're so good at playing a criminal that you become one."

"I'm very familiar with DID." Pia rounded the corner and stopped at the café. "I'll be inside maybe fifteen minutes. Half an hour tops. That's not long enough for DID. It's not like I'm going to join the Mafia for a year."

"That reminds me. Whatever you do, do not accept an invitation to anything. When they invite you somewhere, it's to fit you with concrete galoshes."

"Concrete what?"

"You're so young. I worry about you." Willy-Mac looked her up and down. "Just remember the basics: play your game, not his; don't look through his stuff; don't go anywhere with him; and don't challenge his bullshit. I'll be right here, monitoring your panic button."

Pia paused and blocked his path to the café for a moment. "What did you mean your daughter 'was'?"

"Keep focused on the job." Willy-Mac nudged around her and found a table under the awning where he could see the Galerie DeLano.

Pia approached the gallery just before the opening hours stenciled on the door. The sun poured out from behind a cloud, lighting her patterned sheath dress like a beacon. She placed her phone near the keycard reader by the door and pressed the app that cycled through ten thousand magnetic codes per second. After what seemed like an eternity, the lock clacked open. She let herself in and turned on the lights. She roamed the interior, looking for the security system that their surveillance never uncovered. She didn't find it.

The door to the backroom was locked with an old-fashioned brass lock. Someday she should learn how to pick a lock.

Pia strolled through the partitions loosely arranged for viewing. They were stunning pieces.

It took only six minutes before DeLano came running down the street, passing in front of the window. He ripped the door open and ran inside. Wild eyes examined every corner in a second. They came back to land on Pia. A shaky hand combed through his unkempt hair. His button-down shirt looked slept in, his tie left in the pull-over mode from last night. His face was red, eyes bloodshot. Hungover.

She smiled.

"What the hell are you doing here?" he asked.

"Eva Scott." She extended a hand.

He ignored it and checked the back door. Satisfied it was still secure, he pulled a key, opened it, peeked inside, then closed it again without re-locking it.

"Sounds familiar." He faced Pia. "Wait, Mr. Deng's girl?"

"Acquaintance." She kept her arm at full length and tried to draw his eye to it.

DeLano scanned the room again. "How did you get in?"

"Through the door." She dropped her hand. "It was open."

"Stupid idiot." His eyes rolled back in his head. He slapped his palm to his forehead. "Oh. Not you. Sorry. I forgot to lock up last night. I, uh. Look, we're not open this morning."

"We're not French this morning either."

"What?"

"I'm glad, actually." She strolled to an artist's stool near a small counter by the back door. "Your accent was terrible. You sound more Chicago, especially when you speak French."

She winced inside. Ten seconds and she'd already blown through Willy-Mac's advice.

"Whatever." A pained smile tried to grow across his face. "We're not open. You need to leave."

"I'm interested in this one." She pointed to the de Kooning copy.

"I told you, it's not for sale." He reached for her arm. She pulled away. "Even if it were, it would be like, two or three million. Look, I don't care if you're one of Mr. Deng's playthings, you still need to leave."

She unclenched her fist and willed herself not to explode in rage. Being called a bimbo was one thing, but devaluing her de Kooning by more than six million was painful. "It's not the original then? I thought it was *Untitled XVII.*"

His mouth dropped open. His eyes roved over her, not like an excited male but rather like a criminal looking for a wire on her form-fitting dress. There wasn't room. He frowned.

Three burly men pushed through the door, their sport coats barely covering their pistols.

DeLano turned to the intruders. "Whoa. Cyril, dude. No need to bust in here like this. We're cool man. The client is coming. She isn't him."

Pia shifted her purse to her left shoulder to better reach her Glock, should the need arise. She glanced out the window and found Willy-Mac rising from his seat. She waved him off.

Two of the men flanked DeLano. Cyril berated him in a language that was not French. It might've been an obscure dialect. It sounded almost Italian.

She used the distraction to take a peek behind the counter. There was nothing there. No notebooks, laptops, phone chargers, or any of the detritus that collects on shelves in any business. She slid toward the back door, keeping an eye on the heated exchange going on near the front door.

She sensed Willy-Mac shaking his head in disbelief.

She repositioned herself to open the door behind her while eyeing DeLano and his friends. When she'd managed to open it wide enough to slip through, she did. Once inside the back room, she found the lights.

A wooden chair stood between a tripod and a photographer's gray backdrop. Next to it were twenty or more small paintings. They appeared to be copies or in-the-style-of fakes. She didn't know enough about the artists to know the body of work for each. It was unlikely so many originals from these artists would be in an unknown gallery in a beach town. Originals would hang in a museum. She took a quick glance through the stack. A Jackson Pollack, a Monet, and several others that stretched her recollection of art.

Evidence of money laundering was not obvious. The chair and camera looked more like an ominous interrogation chamber than a benevolent interview room. An unfamiliar feeling came over her: fear. Maybe she was in too deep this time.

Behind her stood a large canvas covered with a tarp. On the other side of the wall, the voices were lowering. She moved back to the door.

Cyril had DeLano jammed against the wall with a pistol shoved in his nose.

She instinctively reached for her Glock. *Don't lunge in* sounded in her head again, followed by *guns escalate problems*. She hesitated.

DeLano's eyes pleaded with her for intervention. Cyril followed his gaze and noticed Pia for the first time. He spun the weapon on his finger like a cowboy and sauntered toward her. She pulled her phone and pretended to dial.

"I'm calling the police," she said in English.

One of the goons grabbed Cyril by the arm and dragged him back. The other goon slugged DeLano in the belly hard enough to send him to the floor in the fetal position. The three exited. Cyril stopped in the door. He gave Pia a grin and pushed up an imaginary hat with his pistol barrel.

Pia gave him the finger.

She'd knelt next to DeLano to offer a hand when she noticed a shadow in the doorway. Mikhail Yeschenko stood outside looking through the glass with his head canted to one side, his brow raised.

Pia dropped DeLano back on the floor and quickly stepped outside before her father's long-time business associate revealed her real name and blew her cover.

Yeschenko's bodyguard started to step between them, but he brushed his man back.

"Mikhail," she said, "it's been too long. How have you been?"

"I'm shocked to find you here." He looked up at the sign before looking back at her. "You've been pulled into this whirlpool too?"

"Ah, you know…" She moved down the sidewalk, forcing him to follow. "I don't seem to know the secret handshake."

"I miss your father a good deal." Yeschenko matched her stride. "He helped me learn the intricacies of the international marketplace. I owe him a debt of gratitude. And since he is not here to collect, I feel, from the depths of my soul, that I owe that debt to you. To that end, if I may be so bold, I offer you this: Galerie DeLano is not a venture for which you should ever learn the secret handshake."

"After seeing three common thugs treat him so roughly, I see your point. Thank you for the warning."

"There is another organization that would befit an accomplished and intelligent woman of your stature."

"My father valued your working relationship, Mikhail. Yours is all the recommendation I need. I'm interested. What's the organization?"

He looked around. People strolled on the cobblestone lane.

"This is not the time or place for an in-depth discussion. I am here for a meeting, then I go to Rome. Let's discuss it at my place on Corvo in a few days?"

Willy-Mac sat ten feet away. From the way he slowly shook his head, *no-no-no*, it was clear he'd heard every word.

She thought about his advice. She recalled that 'concrete galoshes' was an old movie trope about gangsters dumping their enemies in the ocean with enough concrete to keep them down for centuries. She considered Corvo, Yeschenko's private island a thousand miles west of Portugal in the middle of the Atlantic. That unfamiliar sensation of fear swept over her like a wave.

Don't lunge in.

But Yeschenko would unravel the Galerie's secrets for her.

She shook Yeschenko's hand and nodded with enthusiasm. "I'd be delighted."

CHAPTER 18

PRESIDENT ROCHE GREETED VERONICA HUNTER with a wink and a grin. He handed her a Pimm's with ginger ale, showed her a vase with two dozen roses, and guided her to the living room. Hunter gushed at his attention. They sat on the divan. Roche put his arm around her. She snuggled in and purred.

Chief of Staff Bates watched them from the doorway until he couldn't take it anymore. He sighed and left.

When the door closed, Roche peeled away from Hunter. "Finally. I thought the bastard would never leave."

Momentarily shocked, Hunter closed her eyes and shook her head. "I can't believe I fell—"

"Don't worry, you can give me a blow job later." Roche stood. "Have you found Pia yet?"

"She's off the grid, but I started something that should flush her out." Hunter watched him in a way he didn't like. "What's this about?"

"You have a problem," he said. "The three generals, Bates, Ripley, and Kurtz, are going to expose your Puerto Rican charade."

"Bates was hanging around as if he was president." Hunter glanced at the doorway. "You can't let your employees act like that."

"They're planning to march you in front of the Intelligence Committee where they'll set you up for a perjury charge on the Flight 1028 disaster."

Roche checked the decanters on the side table. Irish, Pimm's, bourbon, vodka, and mixers were all set up with glasses and ice. The staff did a good job. As far as he knew. He couldn't stand the taste of alcohol.

"They work for you, Chuck." She finished her Pimm's. "You're the one who sets the agenda."

"You need to get hold of Yuri Belenov. You're going to need his skills."

"Why?" Hunter rose and stood behind him. "What happened, Chuck?"

"They were plotting against you. I won't stand for that."

"Then fire them."

"The press would have a field day. I've made too many changes already."

"Since when do you care about the press?" She held out her glass. "Why Belenov? He's a madman who left a trail of bodies from New York to Africa. Why would I want to get near him?"

Roche ignored her refill and walked away from the bar. "He and his little group of hackers can do amazing things with social media and people's email accounts. He can undermine anyone who comes after you."

"Why would you want a Russian fugitive to undermine your own appointees?" She opened one of the unlabeled decanters and sniffed.

"Who said anything about my appointees?"

"The only people who might 'come after me' would be in your administration—your appointees."

"Yeah," he said. "I know that."

"Then why do you want Belenov?" She examined the other bottles and mixers.

"To protect you." He stood in the middle of the room with his arms spread wide. "Believe it or not, I care about you, Veronica."

She looked over her shoulder, then gave him a dismissive glance before turning back to the drinks. Nothing made his blood boil like an arrogant woman.

"I can't fix it if I don't know what's wrong." She gave up trying to find the Pimm's, crossed her arms and faced him. "Tell me what really happened, Chuck."

"Loyalty means everything to me, Veronica." He tried his stern, fatherly voice. "I am loyal to those who are loyal to me. Did you see me pardon that batch of guys last week? I can be generous."

"You know—" Hunter rested her butt against the side table "—people can tell when you're lying."

They glared at each other for too long.

Roche had few options as effective as Belenov. She had to quit asking questions and get with the program. Why on Earth did she think someone would marry a woman who didn't do what she was told?

"You have a bigger problem," he said. "That lieutenant you sent to retrieve the evidence gave Watson copies, not the originals. He never destroyed the files."

Hunter plucked her purse off the couch and shouldered it. "Those records don't incriminate me, but they make your involvement obvious as hell. You have a serious problem, Chuck. Good luck with it."

She stormed for the door.

"I've been giving thought to your Rose Garden idea." He smiled. "A wedding might be just the right thing to bring the country together."

She stopped in her tracks but didn't look at him. "Your manipulations don't work anymore."

Her voice chilled like an arctic blizzard.

He ran around her and seized her elbow. "You hired those people, I just paid the bills. I never knew why you wanted the money. You're the one with the problem." He let go and stepped ahead to open the door.

Hunter stood still, staring at him. He watched the gears and levers working in her little mind. They would click into place eventually. The killers were dead, it would be his word against hers, and he would win because he would lie, and everyone would believe him. They always did.

The last lever found its notch. She got it. It was obvious because she turned around, took a water glass off the side table and filled it halfway with Irish whiskey. She said, "Shit."

She slugged it back in one gulp.

She marched back to him with an arrogant scowl on her face. "To find Belenov, I'll have to go through Yeschenko. I'm the one who crippled his empire with sanctions. It won't be easy."

"Opportunities are opening for him this week that will make him more approachable."

"You're blackmailing the world's most dangerous mobster?"

"I want to meet Belenov by the end of the week." He opened the door and dropped his voice an octave. "Because, if I go down, I swear to God, Veronica, I'm taking you with me."

CHAPTER 19

I SAID, *SHE ONLY APPEARED to be willing. She could've been threatened or beaten, or maybe they held a gun to her head. Someone threw an adult into the wall in her apartment. Something bad went down.*

Mercury said, *You can't admit I'm right even once, can you, bro? Your girlfriend is a Greek-sympathizer and a gang lord who orders her neighbors beaten to a pulp.*

I said, *Don't use a phrase like* Greek-sympathizer. *You can't compare Greeks to Nazis. It's not even close. The Greeks are nice people. Probably.*

Mercury said, *Oh yeah? You try fighting Hera over the last pagan soul in Gaul and see how many scars you come home with. That bitch-goddess can scratch like a mother—*

I said, *OK. That's enough. I'm not listening anymore. La la la la...*

I pulled out my phone and looked up Hera. Greek goddess of marriage and childbirth, married to Zeus, jealous and vengeful as they come. Why did I look her up? Like everyone, I'm addicted to phone-facts, dubious as they are. And, because search engines are inextricably tied to advertising, I knew I would see ads for Lamaze classes and Vegas wedding chapels for weeks to come.

I knocked on the stage door of the Théâtre Princesse Grace and asked about Sylvia. The stagehand asked if I was a friend of hers. When I told him who I was, he said Sylvia had been banned two weeks ago because of her unsavory friends. He slammed the door in my face.

My concern for her safety grew by the minute. I had to rescue her—and quick. I headed to my next stop.

It turns out, Monaco doesn't have foster care. If you can afford to live in the principality, you have nannies who dispose of displaced children. The center where Sylvia volunteered was technically in France. Since it only takes ten minutes to walk the width of the city-state, I made the uphill hike.

The center was a nice place, recently remodeled and well-maintained. Teens mobbed in the main room like it was a Starbucks. When I inquired about adult supervision, a girl rolled her eyes and slid into a back room. Five minutes later, a guy dressed better than a movie star appeared.

"I'm Jacob Stearne," I said and held out a hand. "I'm looking for Sylvia Lallouette."

He spat in my face, pointed to the door, and started yelling at me in French.

I grabbed his wrist and bent him around backward in a headlock. He choked. "I represent Ms. Pia Sabel—the rich lady who remodeled your youth center. She would appreciate a little respect. So would I."

When I let go, he staggered away and looked back at me in fear. The kids in the room were so shocked, they stopped playing on their phones.

I pulled out his shirttail to clean the spit off my face. "I'm not looking for trouble. Just tell me why everyone hates Sylvia and where I can find her."

"She is no longer welcome here." He straightened the sleeves of his jacket. "Nor are her friends. Including you, Jacob Stearne." He stuck out his jaw. "She told us about you."

"Zat right?" I said. "If you banned her, why do you believe anything she said about me?"

His expression changed. My logic made sense.

"We have concerns about her associates." He glanced over my shoulder at the kids, then nodded to the back. I followed him. "The government of France is much better than the American government at taking care of children in transition." He offered me the only chair in a cramped office that overflowed with papers. "We are not forced to beg for volunteers or benefactors. We appreciate everything Ms. Sabel has done for the center."

We stared at each other for a few seconds while I sorted out his meaning.

"But you don't need Ms. Sabel—or me—if we're friends with Sylvia?"

"Oui. This is my point."

"OK, I've not seen Ms. Lallouette in several weeks." I softened my tone. "Last time I saw her, she was a respected actress. I've gotten the impression something went wrong—"

"This would be the understatement."

"You know more than I do. What happened?"

He crossed his arms and leaned against the wall. "We cannot have the children exposed to the criminal elements. First, she told us you have beaten her and asked me to protect her if you showed up. But then, as you say, she kept company with men of *gang de la Brise de Mer*. This we cannot allow."

I pieced his French phrase together. I tried not to laugh. "Sea breeze gang?"

"Non. Non." He waved me off. "The most violent gangsters from Marseille to Ajaccio."

Mercury looked over his shoulder. *What'd I tell you? She's gone gangsta, homie. Will you quit chasing this girl now?*

I said, *There's no way. She's too pretty. Pretty girls don't go bad.*

Mercury said, *Uh. Dude. Jodi Arias? Megan Martzen? Estibaliz Carranza? Jane Andrews? Mary—*

I said, *Whatever. She's in trouble. I have to rescue her.*

My guy was looking at me funny. "She brought the leader in here. He tried to recruit several teenagers. This is not allowed. It was *la goutte qui fait déborder le vase.*"

"Da what?"

"Pardon. How do you say, the drop that makes the overflowing vase?"

I worked that one in my head a moment. One drop too many. "You mean, the straw that breaks the camel's back?"

He nodded. "Sylvia was such the nice young lady. Tragic, non?"

"I'm sure there's an explanation. I'll find her, get her back on the right path. She'll be back to normal and helping you in no time."

He shook his head sadly. "Non. There is no coming back for her."

After that depressing thought, I had nothing. I wandered back down the hill with Mercury yakking up a storm about the difference between little proverbs like the "last straw" and Seneca's actual, serious, life-changing philosophical essays.

Mercury said, *So, with me—the god of eloquence—guiding him, Seneca wrote: It is not the last drop that empties the water-clock, but all that previously has flowed out; similarly, the final hour when we cease to exist does not alone bring death; it merely completes the death-process. We reach death at that moment, but we have traveled a long time on the way.*

I said, *What's that supposed to mean?*

Oh. My. Jupiter. Even a halfway intelligent Hyena— Mercury tossed his hands in the air. *Dawg. Why do I even with you?*

I said, *Because Hera won the battle over last pagan soul in Gaul?*

Mercury said, *Whoa, dude. No need to be throwing shade like that. One interpretation, dumbed down to your level, is that Seneca meant you never know when you're going to die, life is short, make good use of your time. In other words, give up on Sylvia-the-Gangsta-Girl. If you get back together with her, I'm gone. No more help from me. I wouldn't even tell you to find that cop you were talking to earlier down at the mall.*

Which reminded me that Mercury had claimed the cop was withholding information. As unlikely as that seemed, I had nothing else. I said, *There's a mall in Monaco?*

Mercury rolled his eyes. *Every day I pray to Vesta, the virgin goddess of hearth and home for you, bro. You know why? Because I care about you, that's why. Yeah. It's called Le Métropole Shopping.*

Google maps had that—along with a pop-up ad for Lamaze classes in Nice. Only twenty-nine minutes by car, thirty-three by train.

Le Métropole looked like Buckingham Palace squished onto a steep hillside with a lineup of Lamborghinis and McLarens in front. Come to think of it, fancier than Buckingham. More like Sabel Gardens. Inside, it would make a Qatari princess jealous. Giant chandeliers stretched from the ceiling down to the second level. I was gawking at the inlaid marble floor when a voice reached me.

"Monsieur Stearne?"

The cop from the police station, dressed in the fashionable casual clothes of a Euro-billionaire stood in line at the coffee shop.

"I was looking for you." I gave his wardrobe the once-over and wondered how much the Monte Carlo Police Department was paying these days. "You left out something about Sylvia Lallouette."

He looked me over, then looked at the line to estimate how much time he would lose when he gave up his spot. He nodded to a couple fancy-looking chairs and dropped out of the queue. We sat. He rubbed his palms together and kept his gaze on the floor.

"You were romantic with Ms. Lallouette?" he asked.

"Maybe."

"I tell you this in the brotherhood of men who fall in love with the wrong woman." He sat up straight and caught my gaze. Dead serious. "My job would be at risk should someone learn I have told you of this."

Mercury leaned over the man and pointed at him. *Told you so.*

I waited. The cop didn't continue. I got the hint. I said, "I will never repeat a word you tell me."

He nodded a quick thank-you. "Ms. Lallouette has become involved in the gang most controversial. I am Monaco's liaison to your CIA. They have asked me to report her movements. Before you and I spoke the first time, I called Langley about you. You have an impressive resume. They think you are most trustworthy. Yet we are concerned about your inquiries.

"Ms. Lallouette, she keeps the company of a most regrettable man known as Cyril Cahuzac. He is the local boss for a gang that is tied to many high-profile robberies, such as the UBS bank in Geneva, a Securipost trunk, and Air France. Since those brazen raids, they have become much more professional and violent. My advice, Mr. Stearne, is to go home."

What'd I tell you? Mercury crossed his arms and struck a pose. *Who da god?*

"If I were to ignore your advice," I said, "and turned up something useful about her or her new friends, would that be good for you?"

"Respectfully, monsieur, we Monégasques are quite capable of handling our affairs."

"But if …"

"If … you did not die in the attempt. These are the most desperate of men."

"So were the Taliban, ISIS, al Qaeda, Mujahideen, Iraq's Republican Guard—"

He held up a hand to stop me and nodded. "Impressive resume, oui. But remember, I can eject you from Monaco. This is not the American cowboy movie. We do not have shootouts at the All-right Corral. We care for our citizens' safety. I cannot allow you to cause troubles. I will not allow you to endanger our city." He gave me an earnest stare that fell short of a soldier stare but still got his point across.

"It's the OK Corral," I said. "But I get it. No crazy shootouts. So, where can I find her?"

After a sigh, he rubbed his face. "She sometimes frequents the Casino. Most often alone."

Mercury perked up. *Isn't that how courtesans operate, my brutha? … Alone?*

I gave my disrespectful god a dirty look.

"Are you implying she's hooking?" I asked.

He squinted, trying to place the term. Then his face brightened. "Oh. You mean *les grandes horizontales*? Non. She is gambling. Sometimes she wins. Most often she loses. A lot of money. Thousands each night."

She wasn't rich last time I saw her. And she stiffed her landlord. "Where does she get the money?"

"As yet, we do not know."

"If I could uncover that source…"

"If! If you do not expose our surveillance. If you do not begin the gunfight in the streets. If you do not otherwise, how do you Americans say, fuck up?" He observed me as if watching a coiled rattlesnake. Then he said, "Oui. That would be most interesting, even to capable Monégasques."

I stood and shook his hand and turned to leave.

"One moment, *s'il vous plait*." He looked me over from head to toe. "If you go to the Casino, do not look the American."

I glanced at my outfit. No idea what his problem was. I wore blue jeans over sneakers, a black leather jacket, and an olive-green t-shirt stenciled with, *Fuckin' A—Army Ranger*.

He pointed up a floor. "Society Club, Monte Carlo Forever, or perhaps Hugo Boss."

He walked away.

CHAPTER 20

A LIGHT DRIZZLE WAS FALLING in the dark lane when Pia worked up the courage to knock on Willy-Mac and Vivian's door. Light poured into her face, leaving Vivian's form little more than a silhouette in front of her.

"How long have you been out there?" Vivian air-kissed her and pulled her hand. "You're soaked clean through."

"Thought a long walk was in order before Willy-Mac yelled at me."

"Don't be silly." Vivian laughed. "We don't yell at people just because they don't listen. At our age, we share advice, let them ignore it, then wait until they cry out for help."

Pia forced a smile and held up her gift.

"Oh my, isn't that a fancy bottle." Vivian led her through the foyer and living room into the dining room.

Willy-Mac seasoned a pan of hot oil in the kitchen. He wore a chef's apron with a bear pattern that looked homemade. He hadn't noticed them come in.

Pia searched for something to say. "I like your apron."

He looked down at the cloth, worn and stained. Then he looked up with a sad smile and a spatula. "My daughter made it for me … long time ago."

His eyes turned red. He turned back to the dish of meat coated in flour and laid the pieces into sizzling oil.

Vivian handed the wine to Guenièvre who pushed it into an automatic corker. Vivian told the girl, "When wine is more than eight years old, you don't need to decant it."

Guenièvre said, "Oui, madame."

Vivian pointed to the dining table and took a seat. Pia followed. Gold leaf chargers, crystal candlesticks, fine silver, fresh flowers, and cloth napkins in napkin rings waited for her.

Guenièvre brought three glasses of wine and placed them at the table. She retreated to the kitchen to help Willy-Mac.

"If you're wondering," Vivian said, "she's not on your dime. She's been helping with our dinner parties for a couple years."

Willy-Mac took off the apron, straightened his sweater, and joined them as the oil popped and crackled behind him. He hoisted his wine glass to the center of the table. "To discovering the secret inside the Galerie DeLano."

Pia and Vivian raised their glasses, clinked, and sipped.

Willy-Mac leveled his stern gaze at Pia. "You must tell me why a dingy little gallery in this middle-class beach town is crawling with billionaires."

"That's the secret I hope to uncover."

"Why bother?"

His sharp question caught her off guard. He had the press of a litigator who never asked a question to which he didn't know the answer. A noose of words tightened around her neck. "Because DeLano is robbing my friends."

"Is DeLano behind what's going on?"

Guenièvre brought a creamy roll and small plates. She served each from the left like a professional, leaving Willy-Mac a small cheese knife, then retreated to the kitchen.

Willy-Mac sliced the roll and handed out pieces. "My peach-and-goat-cheese roulade with lavender-pecan crumble."

"You made this?" Pia took a bite.

"I cook all day, he cooks all night," Vivian said with a hearty laugh. She reached across the table and took his hand. "A good marriage is a partnership."

"Is DeLano behind what's going on?" he asked again.

Pia tried to duck Willy-Mac's driving stare by turning to Vivian. "Where's your granddaughter, Elisa tonight?"

"With her dad, Thierry." Vivian finished her roulade.

"You didn't answer my question," Willy-Mac said.

"She doesn't live with you?" Pia asked.

Vivian nodded at Willy-Mac. "He's trying to help you."

Pia flushed when she faced her host. "DeLano's not smart enough."

"How did you hear about his Galerie?"

"I came across a bunch of invoices. DeLano's was the return address."

"Found them on the street?"

The four-day operation flashed through her mind. An international chase, a gang of thugs, a crafty courier, a bungled plan, an explosion of anger, and collateral damage. She'd fled to Nepal hoping her demons would go away and let her forget the whole thing. The demons stayed.

Willy-Mac finished his appetizer and waited. Always the hunter.

She said, "I came across it."

"Tell me why a billionaire with sixty thousand employees would drop everything when she finds a few invoices?"

"I have reasons."

A long silence stretched. Guenièvre cleared Pia's plate from her right, like a professional. The girl returned with a crumb scraper and cleaned the tablecloth onto a small dish. Once again, she retreated to the kitchen.

"Let's try this." Willy-Mac leaned back and studied her for a long, intimidating minute. "A retired veteran of law enforcement tells you flat out not to accept an invitation to the lion's den. Minutes later a dangerous Russian oligarch shows up, invites you to his lair, and you say yes. Why?"

Pia glanced at Vivian for sympathy but found the former professor had a stare more intimidating than her husband's. "He was a friend of my father. Well, 'associate' would be more accurate. They had business dealings. I trust him."

"Oligarchs who survive Russian purges are not the kind of people you can trust." Willy-Mac slapped the table. "The Russian economy that your friend grew up in was a dog-eat-dog wilderness. The only survivors were the psychopaths. Their instincts made them kings of the ugly jungle from which they emerged. Then they went international. They assembled gangs of killers who enforced their will over anyone who stood in the way. We dealt with Russian mobs when they tried to control shipping from Galveston, Houston, and New Orleans. I know Mikhail Yeschenko too. And there are no bigger, more dangerous psychopaths than he.”

Pia struggled for a response while she rethought her bold plan to visit Corvo Island. Would Dad have associated with dangerous men? Unlikely. Maybe Willy-Mac was over-dramatizing to scare her. But what about her motivation? Was she lunging in? She could ask Yeschenko about DeLano’s and save a lot of time. She couldn’t call Deng Zhipeng. She saw no alternatives. “I can handle him.”

“And that brings us back to why. Why trace an old invoice? Why leave everything behind? Why not send investigators? Why take on dangerous gangsters?”

Pia didn’t want to explain the number of people hurt on her operations. She shrugged and tried to wait him out.

Guenièvre refilled their wine glasses, glancing at the adults in the uneasy silence, then returned to her hiding place.

“Do you want to know what’s bothering me about this?” He waited until she nodded. “Law enforcement is a small community. I knew everyone in Texas from judges to state cops to prosecutors to defense attorneys. If I didn’t know them, I knew someone who did. Likewise, I’m sure the billionaire community is small. You folks rub shoulders at country clubs we can’t afford to think about—and we’re dang well off. And that tells me you know who DeLano works for, but you aren’t telling me. That’s not how people work together. You need to tell me who I’m taking on here, or I’m out.” He paused for a moment, then shook his head with regret. “You won’t survive alone.”

“I’m fine on my own.” She regretted her tone but couldn’t stop herself. “You’re the one who wanted in. I didn’t ask for your help. You just showed up at the right times. Uninvited, I might add. Awfully convenient. How do I know you’re not one of them? Why the hell should I trust you?”

“You’re right about part of that.” Willy-Mac’s voice came across the table soft and gentle. “You have no reason to trust me. But you’re wrong about being on your own. You’re not. We’re here. We want to help.”

Pia’s anger dissipated. She stared at her plate, unable to look up or even apologize for her outburst.

Vivian gave a discreet nod in the direction of the kitchen. Pia realized all Guenièvre's clearing and serving directions came from Vivian through a narrow space where only the two could see each other. Pia reached another level of respect for her hostess. Her rapport with the girl was not new. Vivian was teaching Guenièvre skills that would lead to a career in high-end restaurants. Skills that might lift her out of abject poverty. A more lasting lesson than overpaying her. *Money doesn't solve problems.*

Guenièvre served the second course, a salad of black-eyed peas and collard greens.

Vivian broke the awkward silence. "You see that picture on the bookcase? That's our son, Joe. Leukemia took him in 2003 after his first term as Mayor of Houston. Next to him is Angela, Elisa's mother. She graduated top in her class at Stanford Law. She worked in Paris for a year after graduating and fell in love with Thierry. They married and had Elisa. They moved here. He ran the Texas BBQ with my old recipes while she practiced law in Nice. A couple years ago, the three of them went to the Bastille Day celebration on the Promenade des Anglais."

Vivian teared up.

Pia cringed, not wanting to hear the rest. At the mention of the town and the promenade, she recalled the terrorist attack. A twenty-ton truck plowed through hundreds of people, killing eighty-six. She fell back in time again. Back to the weeks after her father's funeral. Lost and alone, she'd stumbled through meaningless days, trying to find someone to love as much as she'd loved her adopted father. Weeks went by like a monotonous highway landscape outside a car window. She had yet to shake the misery of being alone. She put her hand on top of Vivian's. "I'm sorry. I can't imagine."

"No, you can't." Vivian wiped her eyes with her napkin and took a couple deliberate breaths. "These days, we help Thierry and Elisa make dance classes and keep her when he's traveling in his new job. But those two are their own family. All we have left is each other."

Willy-Mac finished his salad and put a hand on her shoulder. She gave him a loving glance in return.

Vivian put her napkin back in her lap and took another deep breath.

"Many young people think their elders are out of touch, overly cautious, too slow. What you're ignoring is that we have a lot of experience. Willy-Mac became a Texas Ranger about the time you were born. And yet, you disregard his advice. We're concerned about how deep you'll be when you cry out for help. Everyone needs help." She let that sink in before continuing. "Now tell us your story."

Vivian forked her salad as if she'd lost her appetite.

Pia hadn't gone rogue by accident. When her father was killed while trying to rescue her, she knew she'd been lunging in far too often. She built the legend of Eva Scott back then, not knowing when she'd need it, only that eventually, she would. Things had gone horribly wrong in the last couple months. She left her inner circle of trusted employees behind because she wanted to protect them from her next dangerous idea. She wanted to protect Willy-Mac too. She'd turned down his offer of help only to protect him. Yet, the old lady was right. He had a ton of experience that she desperately needed. She owed him the truth. If he had as much experience as he claimed, then he would stay home and forget about Pia, Yeschenko, and DeLano.

"A year and several months ago," she began quietly, "a Russian spy contacted me regarding the conspiracy behind my parents' murders. He told me who ordered them killed. Who paid the assassins. Who arranged the murders. Who pulled the trigger. A Russian spymaster named Viktor Popov ordered the hit. Veronica Lodge Hunter, then CIA director, called up two killers from the minor leagues. Chuck Roche put up the money. He did it because he'd misspent his fortune, filed for bankruptcy—and Viktor Popov financed his rescue."

Pia expected a gasp. Instead, Willy-Mac sat in his chair, hands on the armrests, as stone-faced as Lincoln in the Memorial.

"I dug up evidence of Viktor Popov's kleptocracy and offered to trade the dirt I had on him for proof of Roche's involvement in the conspiracy. We met on Attu Island and swapped. He gave me a box full of canceled checks, invoices, and other proof of Roche's crimes. Before I got back on my jet to leave, a team of Army Rangers parachuted in and confiscated the goods. The evidence disappeared. At that time, I had no other evidence to expose the President of the United States as the biggest traitor in history." She paused, then muttered almost to herself, "Which one might think was self-evident after Helsinki."

After a moment of silence, Willy-Mac's fingers began drumming on the armrest. "We'll come back to what happened next in a moment. But first, I must point out, there are conspiracy theorists who claim you shot Viktor Popov nine times."

"The evidence is clear." She held his unblinking gaze while she lied. "Ballistics proved Popov was shot with a Russian pistol belonging to Sergeant Anton Tarasov. He testified at an official Russian inquiry that he had killed Popov when he learned of the old spy's treachery against the Federation. He was hailed as a hero."

Pia turned her attention to the delicious salad. She finished it while hoping he would forget about the rest of his question.

Willy-Mac observed every bite she took. Vivian gave their waitress the nod. The girl materialized with the wine bottle and refreshed the glasses before clearing the plates.

"Your need for vengeance is overwhelming your common sense," Willy-Mac said. "Killing Hunter and Roche won't bring your parents back."

"I intend to expose them, not kill them."

Guenièvre returned with buttermilk fried quail and bacon hoecakes.

"The only thing I able to keep after Attu Island was the name of a company involved in the payments: Santalum." She paused to eat between sentences. "With some advanced technology, I was able to track down anomalies that began the day Chuck Roche took office. Larger sums of money than ever before were flowing in and out of Santalum. Transactions a hundred times larger than normal involving countries all over the world. I correlated a few odd things. Chuck Roche would blast off one of his unexplained sanctions or trade tariffs, and within a week, another large transaction would occur at Santalum. After the transaction was complete, one of Chuck Roche's staffers would tell everyone to disregard the tariff."

"Coincidence is not evidence."

"I tracked a courier across the world, from the Seychelles to the Caymans to New Orleans to Nice. I found an envelope full of invoices between hundreds of shell companies. That's where I got DeLano's address."

"Damn." Willy-Mac looked at Vivian. "If those are real invoices—evidence of money laundering—she is on to something big."

Vivian turned to Pia. "What do you plan to do about it?"

"When your husband explains the parts of the conspiracy that I don't understand—my five questions—I'll find the evidence I need to prove he's a crook. But, I won't let Roche get in front of me this time. I'll tell no one. That's why I'm using an alias and laying low. When I'm ready, I'll take my evidence to my old friend, FBI Director Shikowitz. He's an honest and respected prosecutor who can investigate and make the charges stick."

Willy-Mac and Vivian snapped a glance at each other, disappointed.

"What?" Pia asked. "What is it?"

"You haven't checked the news lately?" Vivian asked. "Roche fired Shikowitz an hour ago."

CHAPTER 21

MIKHAIL YESCHENKO LOOKED OVER VERONICA Hunter's shoulder at the breathtaking view from La Pergola's windows. The only three-star Michelin restaurant in Rome sat atop the Rome Cavalieri Hotel on the brow of the highest point in the city. To his right, slightly down the hill, Saint Peter's Basilica rose above the skyline. Below him, city lights twinkled down the slope to the winding Tiber and across the valley.

Yeschenko extended a glass of champagne in front of the former president. "Are you referring to Alan Sabel's daughter? I thought she played soccer."

Hunter peeled away from the view to face him. "She was running the Security Division until Alan's unfortunate accident. For the last year or so, she ran the whole conglomerate, but then something happened. No one's seen her in the last few weeks."

"Unfortunate accident?" Yeschenko backed up a step. "The narrative going around Moscow is that Alan was drawn into an ambush where he was murdered on the orders of your old friend Viktor Popov."

Hunter turned her back on him. "Can you see the Colosseo from here?"

He studied her from the side and said nothing about her avoiding his statement. It was going to be one of those negotiations. The kind where every bit of information would be fought over with the ferocity of trench warfare.

"Mikhail, we've not been friends in the past." Hunter turned and rested her back against the window frame. "I'm no longer in a position of power. I don't need to denigrate foreigners anymore, so you're safe. I'm here because I think we can work together."

"Denigrate? Your sophistry is remarkable. You slapped sanctions on me. Then, out of the blue, you called me. To make such a call, you must need help in the most desperate manner. Even so, you have not spoken of what drove you here tonight. Let us talk plainly, Veronica. Say what it is that you want. Then we can talk about what you are willing to do in return."

A pair of waiters stepped into the private room and held chairs while another pair served the duck foie gras, white asparagus, and squid covered in seaweed pesto.

Hunter smiled at Yeschenko and took her seat. The waiter opened a napkin and draped it softly across her lap. Another did the same for Yeschenko. Then the waiter said, "Buòn appetito."

She waited until the waitstaff closed the door before responding. "All right. I'll put it out there." She met his gaze. "I need Yuri Belenov."

Without taking his eyes off her, Yeschenko picked up his salad fork. "That name sounds familiar. Do I know him?"

"Come now, Mikhail, you wanted to speak plainly. You captured him and took him to your island just as last year's meeting of RULE commenced."

"You seem to know a lot about me." He savored the brilliant richness of the dish.

"You'd be surprised how much even a former president knows about anyone she wants." She smiled and took a bite. She grimaced at the flavor, forced a smile and swallowed. "And, Chuck was there. He spoke to Yuri for a few minutes."

"Ah, Chuck." Yeschenko slurped the remnants of his appetizer. "Has his credibility suddenly improved?"

"What do you want in exchange?"

"If I recall correctly—" he observed her pushing her first course to the side "—your Senate Intelligence Committee seeks Belenov's testimony in the case of Flight 1028. You're asking me to send some poor young man to his death over your political feuds? If I knew where he was, why would I be inclined to do such a terrible thing?"

Hunter tilted her empty glass. Yeschenko took the hint and pulled the bottle from the ice.

"Despite accepting your invitation as your guest," he said as he poured, "since I chose the Bollinger Vieilles Vignes 2004, a bargain at fifteen hundred euros a bottle, I took care of the check in advance."

Hunter laughed and sipped.

"I've run circles around men for years, Mikhail." She leaned back with her glass. "When two men shake hands, one of them wins. When the check comes, the man who pays wins. But women don't pin their status on such trivial matters. We rank our position in ways you can't see, but always feel—the currents of power."

"So true." He nearly dropped the champagne when he laughed. He shoved the bottle back in the ice. "Yet not an answer."

"Our senators haven't made headlines, so their investigation stalled out. No, I need Mr. Belenov for another reason. He doesn't even need to leave Albania or Siberia or the Philippines, wherever you have him holed up."

A waiter knocked on the door before leading in his crew. They scooped up plates, swept crumbs from the tablecloth, and produced new plates of rabbit tortellini with carrots. In less than a minute, they were gone.

Hunter picked up her fork and ate with determination. He sensed her charging up the currents of power for a shock. She intended not to speak until Yeschenko had responded.

He admired her skill for a moment before giving in to the chamomile-scented delicacy. He ate it all before looking up. "Your senate makes Mr. Belenov out to be quite toxic. They claim he is responsible for a social media campaign that favored Chuck Roche over you. And Roche trounced you in the election. Are you seeking revenge on this innocent Mr. Belenov?"

She regarded her tortellini with a conflicted gaze, obviously torn between the fantastic flavor and thoughts of cute rabbits chopped for seasoning. She finished her dish, patted her lips, and put her napkin down.

"Mikhail—cut the crap. We both know Popov ordered Alan Sabel's murder just as we both know he and Chuck masterminded the deaths of 365 innocent Americans in the Flight 1028 disaster. And we both know you have Belenov stealing credit card numbers or some cybercrime. I don't care about any of that. I need his services for a special project."

Yeschenko mopped up the sauce with a piece of olive bread. He gloated over her admission. In her terms, he had won the handshake. But at some point, he would have to reciprocate or go home empty-handed. This was the last chance for serious negotiations. When he finished and dabbed his mouth, he held up the champagne.

She tilted her glass forward, and he topped it up.

Despite himself, the hot flush of anger overtook him as he thought about what he needed in exchange.

"My first demand is non-negotiable." His voice rose in volume with each word. "If one more of Roche's unctuous little sycophants comes to my island, I will throw him from the cliffs. If he makes one more demand of me, I'll find Belenov and send him straight to your Senate inquiry—replete with shocking headlines. You have no idea what humiliations I've suffered. Roche has forgotten his place. He has no respect for those who delivered his precious little office. He makes unreasonable demands that enrage all the members of RULE. They complain bitterly to me every day." He punctuated his statement by pounding his fist on the table. "I will not suffer his indignities for one more minute."

Hunter waited until his labored breath calmed just a notch. "Did you have to suck his cock?"

Yeschenko's jaw dropped. He froze in place. Then he reared back and roared with unrestrained laughter. "Madame President forgive me. You are quite right. With men, it is all about money and status. Here I sit, complaining about ignominies that pale in comparison to yours." He laughed and drank. Then he shook his finger at her. "Those currents of power you mentioned, they are quite shocking when you sneak in the electrodes."

He laughed again and reached for the bottle.

"Portents were all the rage in Shakespeare's day." He filled both their glasses nearly to the top. "We don't hear about them anymore. Yet, tonight, I sense this meeting is the portent of a long and prosperous partnership."

A smile tugged the corner of Hunter's mouth. "I'm so glad to hear you say that, Mikhail."

"Tell me something, Veronica. What is it you want? What is your goal in all this?" He started to sip his drink then held up a hand. "No, don't answer that. I want to figure it out. Tell me this instead: why do you need Belenov so badly?"

"Roche has a problem. Something that requires a little social manipulation. Something that, if uncovered, could easily be denied as foreign meddling."

He rolled her answer around in his mind a moment, savoring all the implications of her use and placement of nouns and pronouns.

"Roche's emissary visited me a few days ago. A young and uncultured fellow. He made no mention of Belenov. Yet you come here looking for something that should have been included in the emissary's mission. That means the task falls into one of two categories. Either it is of such a sensitive nature that he trusted only you. Or. You are taking over the project to control it and, by doing so, control Roche."

The wait staff entered and cleared again this time leaving behind plates of sole with spinach and black truffles. Yeschenko loved sole but hated spinach.

Hunter scraped her spinach off. She said, "Why does Michelin give so many stars to places that offer only fringe food and not more popular dishes like meatloaf or grilled salmon? Surely there's a macaroni and cheese that stands out. Somewhere in the world, there must be one true and perfect pizza."

He laughed and followed her casual breach of etiquette by scraping off his spinach.

"Really?" she asked. "The emissary said nothing about Belenov?"

"Indeed, you intend to seize control." He tasted the sole. "My demands will be most reasonable. Since you no longer control sanctions, I'll press for information instead. I trust you can still get that?"

Hunter considered his offer. "I have friends, I can call in favors. As long as nothing you require involves sovereign nations."

"Or blow jobs."

Hunter smiled. "Chuck's trail of broken promises has ended my interest in his success."

"That much I've surmised." He winked over his champagne. "I have recently become contemptuous of the man myself. We have common ground then. So, what is this project for Mr. Belenov?"

"Too sensitive to discuss." Hunter sipped her champagne. "I will require direct access to him."

An unexpected demand. Yeschenko looked up and canted his head to one side, hoping to coax a broader explanation. She ignored him. Finally, he gave up. "Then I must suppose that Mr. Roche is—what is that wonderful American expression—up shit creek without a paddle?"

She laughed and finished her sole.

"The prosecutor has been getting closer to Roche," Yeschenko said. "Your President Clinton survived six years of an independent prosecutor who managed only one conviction, and that for mere contempt. While Roche's investigator has produced several guilty pleas and several serious indictments in his first year. That must rile Chuck Roche's survival instinct. Allow me to guess what I know you won't confirm: he plans a counterpunch of some kind. Undermine the prosecutor? No, that would never work. Blackmail world leaders? No, that might get him safe passage out but won't save him." Yeschenko sat back and tapped his chin while he thought. "What is he going to get?"

"What's coming to him." She stared at him.

"How intriguing." He poured the last of the champagne. "You came to me because you know my goal: to cancel your sanctions. And now, after this wonderful meal, I know what you are after. Veronica, you can count on me." He raised his glass to toast.

She paused with hers halfway to meet his. "Have you been trying to recruit Pia Sabel into RULE?"

"You've inquired about her twice now. That's curious. To answer your question: she is young, brash, and idealistic without an ounce of political influence. Why would we want her in our group?"

"Have you seen her?"

"Rest assured, Veronica, if I do, I will report to you immediately." He felt a sudden concern. "Why are you looking for her?"

"Roche is looking to use her as a lightning rod. A way to distract the public from his failures. I want to protect her."

"How very thoughtful of you. Pia could use a mother-figure in her life about now, I would imagine."

Hunter lofted her glass. "To a mutually beneficial partnership."

He clinked his glass to hers. "You are a remarkable woman, Madame Hunter."

The staff cleared the empty dishes then brought in iced spheres of pomegranate on gianduja cream. As the headwaiter pulled the door closed, Yeschenko held up his hand. He glanced at Hunter then at her empty glass. She smiled. He said, "One more bottle if you please."

CHAPTER 22

I STOOD IN THE SOCIETY Club clothing store with my mouth open. I couldn't believe the salesman had offered to incinerate my old clothes. Un-washed, un-ripped jeans are damn hard to find these days, I wasn't going to waste them just because Monégasques weren't down with practical fashions. Paid top dollar for those at the Farm-n-Feed in Burlington. After I said *no-I'm-serious* several times, he finally agreed to have a courier deliver my old outfit to Sabel Two on the tarmac in Nice, no matter how *ironique*.

Whoever Tom Ford is, he took enough of Sabel Security's money to remodel my house. There was an upside to my day at Le Métropole. My neck had never been so closely shaved, my buzzcut never so neat and clean. And the mani-pedi was the most amazing thing I'd ever had done to my body with my clothes on. (But I would never tell my guy friends about it because they would immediately say, "Gay. Knew it.")

On my way out, my phone buzzed with a text from Virginia Goillot, "Hunter met with Yeschenko."

I wracked my brain trying to remember someone named Virginia. The name sounded vaguely familiar, but I couldn't place it or why she would post the former president's schedule. I deleted it in case Sylvia wanted to paw through my texts after I rescued her from the Sea Breeze gang. Which sounded more like a resort drink than a bunch of criminals.

With high-energy jazz from *Kerbside Collection* streaming in my ears, I started slipping into my casino-groove. The sun was going down, and the excitement of nightfall was on the horizon. I couldn't wait to announce myself. I tried to remember the famous line from the movies and practiced it in my head. *Stearne, Jacob Stearne. Gimme a pomtini, shaken not stirred.* Something like that. I would rock the casbah like any of the fifty Brits who played that spy, whatshisname.

Three blocks later, reality set in.

What would I actually say to Sylvia? *Hey babe, come here often?* Maybe she wouldn't show up. My stomach tied itself in knots. I'd rather go into battle than to meet an old girlfriend that … that what? I had no idea why she ran, turned off her phone, and moved out of her apartment.

Then the most sickening realization took hold. I had scratched Sylvia off the list of people who might have pulled the trigger and left me for dead. But after talking to the local cop, I had to rethink that one.

My pace slowed. Would she try to kill me?

Mercury walked alongside in his tiny toga. *That's what she always does—in ALL the alternate universes.*

I said, *What? Alternate universes really exist?*

Mercury slapped his hand over my mouth and snapped a glance left and right. *Let's pretend I didn't say that. Some shit we're not supposed to tell you guys.*

I said, *I don't care. But, you gotta tell me this: did Sylvia do it?*

Mercury said, *How in Avernus would I know? You walked out on me, homie. Had popcorn and Game of Thrones lined up for an epic binge, too. Told you not to go to Tremé—but off you went. You never hear a word I say. Y'know what the gods complain about every year at the gods' convention? That no one ever listens to us. We say things like,* Franklin! The Japanese BOMBERS are on their way right now! *Or we'll say something like,* Do NOT do that without a condom. *Or sometimes,* There is NOTHING wrong with wearing white shoes after Labor Day. *Same thing all over the world. Nobody listens. FML.*

I said, *Deity problems, huh?*

Mercury nodded. *Sucks, brutha.*

The thought of seeing Sylvia made me feel like I was back in high school when you have to go to school the next day after Ashely rudely dumped your ass in front of everybody at Lindsey's party. What do you say? Do you strut in like nothing happened? Do you put your arm in a sling for sympathy? (Which doesn't work. I've heard.)

My stomach flipped over again.

I said, *But what did I do that earned me a bullet?*

Mercury asked, *Now who's using the asking-for-it rationale? Dude, are you suffering from battered-boyfriend syndrome?*

I said, *Something went horribly wrong in Tremé.*

Mercury said, *'S what I been telling you, dawg. You ditched your god.*

I stopped in my tracks, swimming in uncertainty.

Mercury said, *Aw c'mon homie. Suck it up. You're walking into the most famous casino in the world with Sabel Security's American Express Centurion card. Flash that, and they'll treat you like you're one of the Capitoline Triad.*

And then, sometimes the things he said made sense. My backbone straightened, my head swelled, a swagger worked into my stride. What could possibly go wrong when you're spending someone else's money? I considered calling the Major to get her approval for my gambling expedition but didn't because—what if she said no?

Besides, when Sylvia saw me in my new threads, acting all suave, she'd be on her knees asking for my hand in marriage.

An immaculately dressed man trotted halfway down the grand staircase. "Mr. Stearne, it is an honor to make your acquaintance. Welcome to Casino Monte Carlo. My name is Pierre. If there is anything you desire, it will be my delight to bring it to you."

He stuck out his hand.

I'd seen people fawn over Ms. Sabel and her dad for years. Being in the crosshairs took me by surprise. I pulled myself together quickly and gave him a firm shake. I grinned like Jack Nicholson. "There is something I desire, Pierre—your phone."

He looked puzzled but pulled it out slowly and handed it to me.

I held it to his face to unlock it, then swiped through his texts. Right where I figured, I found a picture of me descending the airstair from Sabel Two. Right below it was a summary with my name and approximate net worth based on the jet. Small towns. Monaco and Donnellson aren't so different underneath it all.

"Well done, Pierre." I showed him the pic and grinned wider. "You gather intel better than the CIA."

"Ehm. Merci?"

I put the phone back in his pants pocket and patted his hip. "I also desire a pomtini, shaken not stirred."

With a quick nod, his embarrassment evaporated. He twitched a nervous smile and led me up the remaining steps. We entered a lobby full of gawking tourists. Most of them turned away after realizing that even looking was out of their price range. Six security guards formed an aisle through them.

"We are pleased you had time to find a fitting wardrobe." He inspected me as he led me to the cashier.

I stopped mid-stride. "The outfit isn't good enough for you?"

I gave him my soldier stare. It's the look that says, *I can kill you or pat your back, no difference to me.*

He backed up a step while he figured a way back into my good graces. "Very nice, monsieur. Better than Prince Albert."

I decided not to ask who Albert is. Instead, I smiled.

He said, "A few chips, monsieur?"

An attractive woman approached with a pink martini on a serving tray. She handed it to me with a smile then left. I took a sip. It was sweet and delicious.

"The drink is to your satisfaction?" Pierre asked.

"Guess so." I took another sip. "Only heard about it in a movie. No idea they were this good."

Mercury said, *Dude, do not be playing up your blue-collar ignorance with this guy. He gets a hint that you're from Iowa and he'll disappear quicker than a drunken Centurion from Hadrian's wall. Act like you go to better places than this on Tuesdays. Keep him in his place. And—in case you don't remember—you heard the term* pomtini *because an airhead-loser in a rom-com ordered one. Don't be that chick.*

I said, *I thought it was that British guy.*

Mercury palmed his face. *Oh, my Ceres.*

"But a tad too sweet for me." I handed Pierre the glass. "How about a Balvenie '68?"

I had no idea what it was, but a whole restaurant acted like the King of England had arrived when Alan Sabel ordered a bottle a couple years ago. Pierre stared at me for a second, then nodded and shot a quick glance at the cashier. She handed me a receipt for enough euros to fix up Sylvia's place several times over. With it came a rack of chips in every color imaginable.

My stomach twisted again. On the list of worst-ideas-of-all-time, giving your company's unlimited, titanium credit card to a gambling institution ranks right below telling your sister your Facebook password in sixth grade.

I shoved the bill in my pocket and told myself the Major would understand. I would simply find Sylvia and she would be glad to see me and would kiss me and tell me how much she missed me and then tell me how to find Ms. Sabel. And that would make everything just fine.

Pierre grinned. "Monte Carlo is your oyster, monsieur."

"I feel a frisson of excitement in the air, don't you, buddy?" I squeezed his shoulder.

"Frisson, monsieur?"

"Never mind." My Nicholson grin was beginning to hurt, but the truth was, I was high as a kite. Like a kid getting away with something. "Lead on, Pierre."

He led me through the rooms while I tried to act like I'd seen plenty of ornate, gilded ceilings that put the Sistine Chapel to shame. I turned down the video slot machines in the first *salle*. Bianca, Sabel Tech CEO, once told me: never put money into a computerized gaming machine unless you'd hacked it in advance.

The next room was full of card players, all furiously studying their cards. After cashing my first army paycheck, I learned a valuable life lesson: when surrounded by veteran players, the safest bet was stand in the corner and watch. I turned up my nose again. Then Pierre led me into *Salle Blanche*.

Mercury said, *Roulette. Now there's a game for heroes, dawg. Put some money on fifteen.*

I said, *I thought you weren't allowed to help mortals win games of chance.*

Mercury said, *This is a casino. You got no chance. Put a stack of chips on fifteen.*

On one side, French doors opened to a balcony. The setting sun cast an orange glow over the yachts in the harbor. Outside, four roulette wheels and several blackjack tables were wrapped in supermodels. They came in all kinds: beautiful women, handsome men, manly women, feminine men, and a few of the who-knows variety. Suddenly, roulette was my kind of game. I'd seen it in a movie about that shaken-not-stirred guy. He always won. And, there were statuesque blondes. If I found it necessary to make Sylvia jealous, they might come in handy.

Pierre caught my drift and led the way. Three steps later something dangerous caught my eye.

I learned to pick out CIA operatives on my first tour of duty. They were forever dreaming up missions that could get you killed and then declining to go along for the ride. They were easy to spot because they had a superior look in their eye that said, "If I'm wrong, no one will know it but you—and you'll be too dead to complain." Two steps short of the doors, I spotted a *company* man at a corner roulette table with his back to the wall. He had a squinky eye and wore a cost-effective suit stretched by a McDonald's tummy. His eyes tracked me crossing the room.

Pierre stepped out onto the *Salle Blanche Terrasse*. He whispered something to the croupier and stepped back. A woman with a tray appeared with a glass of brown liquid on ice.

Pierre said, "Monsieur, we are out of '68. This is from the oldest bottle we have on hand. I hope it meets your expectations. Allow me to present our Balvenie '76."

The crowd at both tables went quiet and checked me out. I gave the waitress a smile and took the glass. I sniffed it the way wine snobs do and quickly realized it was Scotch whiskey. I'd had a terrible experience with Scotch during my one and only year in college. So terrible that the scent nearly made me puke my guts out on the table's green felt.

To join the Army Rangers, one must first pass Ranger Assessment and Selection Programs 1 & 2. All told, seventy-seven days of physical endurance, sleep deprivation, starvation, navigation, live-fire stressors, and leadership challenges that destroy normal human beings. Navy SEALs have failed our program standards. Grown men have been reduced to tears when begging to be released. Few have passed on the first attempt. In one try, I'd met and exceeded all expectations and graduated top in my class. My picture hangs in the Ranger Hall of Fame. I can survive anything. But when the first sip of that whiskey touched my tongue, it was all I could do to control my gag reflex. I swallowed the poison and inhaled.

"Excellent, Pierre." I turned to the crowd. "Anyone else want one?"

Ten hands shot up. Pierre smiled and snapped his fingers. The waitress scurried away with a spreading smile. Her glee told me I was spending a lot more money than I realized. But hey, the Major asked me to find Ms. Sabel.

Three of the prettiest women I'd seen since I met Sylvia, and two of the prettiest guys, introduced themselves. I gave the boys the I-don't-swing-that-way glance, and they backed off. The ladies tightened the circle to discourage any more competitors. I didn't mind; three was plenty. After all, I'm not greedy. I dropped a small stack of yellow and red chips on the number thirteen and went to look at the view. The sunset didn't have anything on Tampa, but it was still nice.

I pulled out my phone and tried to discretely look up Balvenie 1976. A popup ad informed me that Alexander birthing classes were only seventeen minutes away in Roquebrune-Cap-Martin. I closed the ad only to find another popup. A small wedding chapel was even closer. And there was a coupon. I reminded myself never to look up Hera again.

A soft "ooh" rolled over my shoulder. I turned to find the surprised face of a gorgeous Russian with green eyes that implied your-secret-is-safe-with-me. I shrugged and turned back to the whiskey listings. €3,000 a bottle—wholesale. I had a bad feeling about the bar tab. Monte Carlo is not Vegas. There are no free drinks.

The ball clicked into its slot, and the assembled peopled muttered their disappointment in French. The croupier raked my stack of yellow and reds off the table and into his little box. Just as they went over the edge, I saw €1,000 on the face of one. I tried to count how many were gone. That sickening sensation in my stomach returned. My gambling adventure was not going the way it did in the movies.

Someone tapped my shoulder. I turned to see who. Slow motion kicked in and the next second broke down into three pieces. In the first third of that second, I recognized Sylvia Lallouette by her angelic face, perfect auburn hair, and pale blue eyes. In the second third, I recognized the contents of a glass of red wine exiting its container and flying directly into my face. In the final third, I heard her lovely voice, now turned harsh and ugly with rage, screeching, "Fuck you!"

She walked away.

Pierre stepped into my path and started dabbing me with a napkin and apologizing. The croupier touched my arm, last call for bets. I handed him a stack of something that looked like children's candy and said, "Fifteen." I pushed Pierre aside and started to chase my girl.

Mercury stepped into my path. *What don't you get about Sylvia "bad news" Lallouette, homie? You've been spit on, insulted, humiliated, and now you're going after her? You know how many people beg and pray for a sign from heaven? And here you have sign after glowing-neon-sign, complete with trumpets and heralds, not to mention your own personal messenger, and you still don't get it? Listen to me! You two do not belong together.*

I pushed past him. *If the gods wanted to keep us apart, they wouldn't have given me the budget to track her down. Right? See? Got you on that one, didn't I.*

She made it as far as the lobby before I caught her elbow. "Babe, I have amnesia. I don't know what you're so pissed off about because I don't remember anything after—"

"That's your excuse? How pathetic." Her voice echoed off the marble. She yanked herself out of my light grip and gave me a glare that could've melted the diamonds out of a tiara.

All the tourists in the lobby turned to watch us. I shrank like Ant-Man. It's hard to beg when the beggee has already rejected the truth. I started to say something. She cut me off.

"Those guys were going to kill me over your stupid fucking envelope." She beat on my chest. "Why didn't you just give it to them?"

"What guys? The gold tooth guy?" I grabbed her wrist. "He's dead now."

I thought it would make her feel better. It didn't. She looked sickened.

My phone started buzzing with the unique buzz I reserved for the

Major.

Pierre stepped beside me and put his hands in front of Sylvia to protect me. He asked her to calm down. Then a security guy pulled him away.

"I never would've left you. Someone shot me and left me for dead. My amnesia was caused by blood loss. Look."

I ripped open my shirt, popping all the buttons, and showed her the still-healing wound. Her eyes fell to the spot. Her fingers traced the jagged edges of pink scar tissue.

The tourists gathered for a closer look. For those not turned off by excessive scar tissue from multiple wounds, I had impressive abs.

"Monsieur, pardon." Pierre leaned in. "A matter of utmost importance has arisen. Your credit card—it is no good."

Tourists crammed in tighter still, hoping to hear more juicy details.

Sylvia rolled her eyes. "He has access to more money than the gods, Pierre."

"In the event he is declined," Pierre asked, "you are willing to cover his debts?"

"Yes." Her hiss pushed the tourists back and satisfied Pierre at the same time.

I glanced at my phone. The Major had texted a lot of questions about wild spending in a casino. I texted her back with big promises that I was closing in on Ms. Sabel and to release the company card. I turned to Pierre. "I'll have the card cleared in a few minutes. Can you find us some privacy?"

He glanced at Sylvia. She thought about it for a second, then nodded. He led us to a small office off the lobby.

"You don't care about me," she said as soon as the door closed. "If you did, you'd quit that stupid job and do something … non-violent."

"I did. I quit Sabel Security."

She took a minute to think it over. Her eyes searched mine. She took my arms and pulled me close. We were half an inch from reigniting our flame.

"I don't know what it is about you, Big Boy." She sounded out of breath. "It's like the gods have sealed our fate." She looked into my eyes.

"You have no idea how much I missed that thing you do with your tongue."

Mercury waved from the sidelines. *You better not be doing this to hook up with the Greek-sympathizer, dawg. You're just using her to find Pia-Caesar-Sabel, right?*

Yeah, I said. *Probably.*

Mercury said, *You better not be lying to me, bro. It's a sin to lie to a god.*

Sylvia pulled back, fire in her eyes. "You don't have the kind of money you were spending in there. That means you're here because your boss wants something."

"I have to finish one more job. Then I'm done."

It wasn't working.

I gave her my desperate eyes. "I swear, babe."

She looked me over, suspicious. She crossed her arms and waited for an explanation.

"I have to find Ms. Sabel." I tossed up my hands with the admission. "She's disappeared. Once I find her—"

"Oh no." Sylvia backed up as if I'd pointed a gun at her. "No, no, no. If you're looking for her, don't come near me. I don't want to have anything to do with that psychopath."

CHAPTER 23

Pia checked her weight on the high-tech rope. It felt strong enough despite being marginally thicker than a shoelace. She double checked the chimney it wrapped around. No chinks that might cut the rope. The quick-release latch was ready. Her descender and ascenders were in place, her harness snug and firm. Low clouds obscured the moon. Mist and drizzle reduced the ambient city light. She moved to the edge of the roof and looked at the narrow lane below. Nothing moved. Now was the time to go.

In an instant, she was back in that industrial basement surrounded by Russian soldiers. A creepy general told her with smug satisfaction that she was the bait, her father's death the prize. Within five minutes, the general's brains splattered across her shoulder. Lives wasted because she'd been betrayed.

Thoughts gushed into her head like a flash flood. She was truly on her own. Willy-Mac was hardly helping her. He wanted to believe he was, but what good was he? He only gave her one answer to her five questions, and only then because she'd pleaded all the way through dinner. According to him, DeLano had been hired by someone else to run an illegal operation. Most likely a debt to his overlord swayed over DeLano's head like a piano hanging by a thread. That explained the lack of fame and fortune for an art dealer selling such high-profile pieces—all the money went to the overlord.

Anger boiled up inside her. Why wouldn't Willy-Mac just answer the other four questions? Who cares about confirmation bias? She didn't even know the man, and yet here she was, trusting him with her life and future. Not to mention the fate of the nation. A nation Willy-Mac and

Vivian left behind—for France of all places. For all she knew, he could be in league with Roche and Hunter. Were they calling Washington right now to relay her movements? Why did she trust him—because he was old? Or kind? No. Because she had no alternatives. Isn't that how handlers recruit their spies and traitors, force the victim to turn to them for help? And her spymasters were oh-so-helpful and sweet. They even cooked her dinner. She was crazy to trust strangers.

"Progress?" Willy-Mac's calming voice over the commlink broke into her escalating thoughts.

"Scoping it out." She looked across the rooftops. "Looks good."

"You OK? You sound pissed off."

She took a deep breath. Why did she let her brain run wild like that? She had to get a grip. Mission. Focus. A clear head. "All good. Going now."

She looked over the edge again and listened. Not a sound anywhere except the voice in the loft below her. A phone conversation in Chinese. 3 AM in Antibes worked out to 9 AM in China. After checking the street again, she stood on the parapet, turned her back to the cobblestones below, stepped over the gutters, and rappelled down the wall, one careful, quiet step at a time.

When she leveled with the window, she peered between the curtain rod and the window casing. Inside was an artist's studio lit by an array of daylight-lamps. Drop cloths covered the floor littered with bright drips. Canvases stretched and prepped waited against the wall. Tables covered in spent tubes, palettes stacked on each other, cans and jars stuffed with brushes, and trash cans splashed with vivid colors filled the space. In the center stood a man on a phone arguing in Chinese. In one hand he held a brush that dripped green. He considered the canvas in front of him. His work-in-progress was a Monet look-a-like. He daubed and argued and daubed again.

Pia pulled the sticky backing off a video camera the size of a battery and affixed it to the shutter where it wouldn't be seen. Then she fed the fiber optic lens between the window frame and the casing. She checked the app on her phone and repositioned the lens.

"The feed looks good from here," Willy-Mac reported.

The painter's argument stopped. He held the phone to his chest. He looked around his room. He sensed her. She froze with her face too near the window. His eyes scanned the room, first at the floorboards, then at the crown molding near the ceiling. His eyes swept past her. Inside, the strong light reflected off the glass, obscuring her dark form. As long as she didn't move, he wouldn't see her.

He went back to his phone call.

With a big push-off, Pia swung sideways, crossing two windows as quietly as possible. She planted a second camera to get a different angle. After checking her work, she angled herself to check the painter. He painted with one hand and held the phone to his ear with the other.

Lowering herself to nearly street level, she pried open a broken piece of plaster above the door. As she'd hoped, it gave her a space big enough to feed the fiber-optic lens. The fiber attached to another camera she slipped between bricks on the building's corner.

She thought about what the painter was doing and why. People like Yeschenko and Deng bought real art, not fakes. So why would some random guy paint forgeries above an art gallery? How did Roche hope to make money off that scam? None of the invoices showed artwork. They were all for condominiums and shell companies holding real estate.

A sudden quiet perked her senses. The Chinese argument had stopped. A glance in the window didn't show much. She checked the video feed on her first camera only to find an empty room. She checked the second camera and saw the painter pressing his nose to the first window, immediately below the camera.

He knew she was there. Did he have someone keeping an eye on the place from the outside? She checked her surroundings and found nothing. The painter moved to the other window.

If she moved, she risked making noise and giving herself away. If she stayed, suspended just above the first floor by ropes that came down from the fifth, she was a sitting duck. She considered asking Willy-Mac what to do. The sound of her voice would tip off the hyper-alert painter. Besides, the old man might be in it with DeLano and the painter.

Pia pushed away from the wall and pulled herself up, locking her upward gains with one ascender on her shoe and another in her hand.

When she reached the top, she heard the window below open. The painter called out into the empty street in French. She froze, hanging an inch below the gutter, concerned that scaling it might chip something and give away her presence. The black rope swung in the dark, inches from the window. The glass was recessed a foot into the wall. With any luck, the man wouldn't see it.

The window slammed shut with such ferocity it worried her. She checked her camera. The painter was sprinting for the attic with a pistol in one hand and something else in the other. She had the advantage of a three-floor lead.

With one big pull-up, she muscled her way onto the roof and yanked the excess rope up after her. She crammed the gear into her backpack and slung it over her shoulder and looked across the tile roof. The building was on a small block bordered by a park on one side and narrow lanes on the other three. She calculated her best long jump—way back in high school. Seventeen feet something. A good effort but not enough to make her consider a career in track. How wide was Rue James Close? Twelve feet at least, maybe fourteen. Theoretically within range, but her school jump was on a forty-meter track built for grip into a pit of soft sand. Ideal conditions for both takeoff and landing. She needed something better than rain-slicked tile roofing under her feet if she wanted a chance.

Scratching noises, like a jiggled latch came from behind her. An access hatch on the roof bumped but didn't open.

As far as she could see in either direction, the roofing was either tile or asphalt shingle. She walked quickly and quietly away from the gallery to find the best place to jump that would give her asphalt shingles on both sides.

Behind her, the attic hatch opened with a bang. The painter clambered onto the roof. A flashlight beam swung in a circle that started behind her and moved away. She watched him for a second, then ducked behind a chimney, knowing it was narrower than her shoulders. A split-second later, she realized the asphalt-to-asphalt combination she needed was on the other side of the painter. She'd have to wait him out or take him on.

He called out angrily into the night, this time in several languages. A hint of fear suddenly tinged his voice. He was doing something illegal.

He didn't want to attract cops. Which meant he would have to shut up. He resumed his search. The flashlight beam began swinging toward her.

Pia stood and raced directly at the painter, jumping the uneven rooftops, with her eyes fixed on the jump ten meters beyond him.

He heard her coming and swung the light to her eyes. The balaclava and Sabel NightVisor hid her face, but the flash was blinding. Shocked, he stumbled backward and fell, one elbow landing in the open hatch. His flashlight rolled down to the gutter.

She couldn't see the edge to gauge her jumping-off point. The roof was sloped, not flat like the last two. She'd have to guess. Across the way, the landing site was a good deal higher. Maybe three to four feet. The only way to make it would be to jump from higher up on her side. Unlike comic books, gravity doesn't cease to exist just because the heroine wants to make a clean getaway. She leapt.

Her feet kept moving the way long jumpers do, and her hips twisted the way she remembered the coaches telling her. She crossed the lane below in the cool, damp air. Adrenaline pumped through her body like a drug.

Her belly hit the gutter hard.

"I heard that," Willy-Mac's voice in the comm link. "Do you need help? Or a distraction?"

"Fine. Just a little—" Pia's hands scrambled for anything as the trough began to buckle. The asphalt tile lacked handholds. She slapped her palms down and willed her grip-gloves to stick. They held for a second. Then her hands began to slip out of the gloves. But she remained stuck long enough to swing her weight to one side and get a knee up. A section of gutter fell to the street fifty feet below. The clatter was deafening in the silent night.

She scrambled, throwing her second leg up and rolling onto the sandpaper surface. Her ribs hurt. Her hands hurt. Her knee hurt.

"Are you OK?" Willy-Mac again.

"Gotta run. See you in a few."

The painter's beam swept the rooftops. She popped up and ran. The beam swept across her back. The next series of roofs were higher but easy to jump. She kicked up her speed. Her skin crawled as if a gun were aimed at her. She darted left a little. Then ran out of roof. A longer jump lay ahead. She stopped, dropped to the shingles, and looked back. The painter had lost her. His light beam searched the night, sweeping back in her direction. She took a deep breath and scrambled over another gutter and found the drain pipe. She shimmied down it fast and dropped the last ten feet. She ran.

Willy-Mac waited at *Le Marché Proveçal*, the provincial market. Wordlessly, she ripped off her outer layer of black, light-absorbing Lycra to expose her splatter reflective running outfit. He handed her running shoes while she slipped off her sticky, quiet slippers. Willy-Mac stuffed her cast-offs and her cat-burglar kit into a larger bag and tossed it in the back of his car.

"Any problems?" Willy-Mac asked.

"Nope." She breathed hard.

"Did you learn anything?" he asked.

"That the artist heard me and called for backup."

"Shit." Willy-Mac scanned the streets around them. "They're searching the streets by now, and we're the only two out on them. Let's get moving."

"But I did get the cameras in place."

"They'll close up shop. Go to ground. Ready to do things my way now?"

"No, this is going to work."

Willy-Mac shook his head. "See you in an hour."

He dropped in the driver's seat and sped off into the night.

Pia thanked her guardian angel for him and began her customary morning run.

CHAPTER 24

ON THE TWENTY-EIGHTH FLOOR OF the Global Bank building in Panama City, Panama, Yuri Belenov held a banker's neck in his right hand. He pressed his thumb harder on banker's windpipe, then released. "You see, Luis?" He lingered on the s. "I hold your life in my hands."

Luis nodded vigorously. Petr and Igor pinned his arms to the wall. He was the only employee of *Dexia Banque Internationale a Luxembourg* in a small but extremely plush office nestled among the top executives of Panama's *Global Bank*. His eyes darted to the few remaining city lights twinkling in the night beyond his window as if a superhero might be out there ready to save him.

"You need not fear Mr. Yeschenko, si?" He watched Luis's wide eyes for a moment. "Is there a language barrier? English is the only one we have in common. Do you understand me? I need a verbal affirmative, Luis."

"Si, Señor. I understand."

"Then why the sad look, Luis? We have so much to look forward to. We will be working together for the rest of your life."

"Señor," Luis stammered, "I cannot transfer ownership as you ask. The paperwork is suspicious." Once again he tried to wrestle free of Petr and Igor's grasp. "I know this attorney. He would call me to expect paperwork of this nature. If I fail my responsibilities in any way, Mr. Yeschenko would have me killed."

"Well, that does make for—what do the Americans call it—a sticky situation." He pressed his thumb into the man's windpipe again. When his victim's eyes began to flutter from a lack of oxygen, he released. "Do you see any of Mr. Yeschenko's men here? There's a reason for that,

Luis. Can you guess what it is?"

Luis struggled again.

"You see, the men who do Mr. Yeschenko's killing for him, they like to be paid. Usually, they prefer cash. Do I need to explain why such men insist on cash? No? Oh good. When you complete this transfer, the last corporation he owns will be mine. He will only have whatever cash he keeps on that silly island of his. How far will that get him? Do you see the brilliance of my plan, Luis? Because if you don't share my vision, I'm afraid you'll have to try landing on your feet like a cat—twenty-eight floors down."

Belenov pulled a pistol from his jacket and aimed at the window. "I will have the decency to take out the glass for your first, Luis."

"Si, si," Luis clenched his eyelids together. "I will do it."

Belenov's phone vibrated in his pocket. He handed his pistol to Petr who held it to Luis's head as he guided the banker back to the desk.

The caller ID listed Corvo Island and nothing more. Curious, Belenov answered.

A woman's voice. "Hello, Yuri. This is former president Veronica Lodge Hunter." She waited for a reaction.

Surprising himself, it took ten seconds while he ran through possibilities: a prank call to a number few people had; an imposter calling on behalf of Yeschenko with full knowledge of his treachery; Pia Sabel had finally tracked him down as she had once promised; or the actual former president. Belenov said, "You have the wrong number."

"Not if you and your SHaRCs want a pardon for Flight 1028."

Belenov put the phone on speaker and asked her to repeat her statement. When she did, Petr and Igor gave him shocked looks. Igor rolled his hands, to get the conversation moving.

"First, let me assure you, my name is Antoine Babineau. If I run into someone named Yuri, what would you like me to tell him?"

She let out a tired sigh, "I can call you the fucking pope if you want. But let's cut the crap and get to it, shall we? I have a job for you that will earn you a full pardon."

"And this Yuri should trust you because…"

"Because the poor son of a bitch doesn't have a lot of options, does he?" She laughed. "C'mon, Yuri. You and your friends haven't slept soundly in a year. Every time you hear a helicopter, you're thinking, *Are the Army Rangers are doing an extraordinary rendition on me tonight?* You can trust me because we need you and we know you don't work for free."

Belenov looked up at Petr and Igor. Both men shrugged.

Luis worked his keyboard like a madman. Belenov nodded a scowl at Petr, who had taken his eyes off Luis. Petr smacked the banker's temple with his gun. Luis closed the Twitter window and re-opened his bank's internal system.

"Americans make promises," Belenov said, "then change presidents. Your promises mean nothing. Ask Australia, NATO, England, the list is endless. Hunter may keep her word, but Roche is an animal. A man who knows him well once described him by saying, 'No intellectual debates about ethics throttle his feral impulses.' If your friend Mr. Belenov were to trust you, why would he trust your treacherous friend?"

"How did you know Yuri's last name is Belenov?" Hunter laughed. "To prove my good will, I have an immunity guarantee for you and twelve people that allows you to come and go from the United States of America for three months. I had it drawn up the day we arrested those unfortunate Puerto Ricans for your crime. I thought it might come in handy at some point in the future."

Igor gave Belenov a thumbs-up. Petr scowled and shook his head.

"An easy thing to say, but how does this immunity work?" Belenov asked.

"I'm sending you a PDF. I'll have the originals FedExed anywhere you'd like."

His phone dinged with incoming documents. He opened it and checked it out. He showed it to Igor, then Petr. Luis tried to sneak in a plea for help on social media again. Petr smashed his fingers with the pistol butt.

"What's that screaming?" Hunter asked.

"Your PDF looks legitimate. What is the job?"

"Roche needs a few people destroyed. Forge some social media posts, private emails, texts, whatever it takes to humiliate a man until he's no longer relevant."

"Who are these people?" Belenov asked.

"Disloyals."

"And what do you want out of this, Ms. Hunter?"

"A paper trail proving he asked a foreign organization to undermine American officials."

"Wow. Ms. Hunter." Belenov laughed. "It is you who are most treacherous."

"We know each other well, Yuri." She paused for a second. "What do you say?"

There was something he liked about this brassy American. She had more balls than most of the billionaires he'd met at RULE. He glanced at his associates. They both gave grins that said, *why not?*

"Why are twelve others included in this immunity deal?" he asked.

"Out of respect for SHaRC and the fact that yours is a collective, I included room for your founding members. I realize you've grown by several hundred, but they're newer and therefore lesser members."

Belenov appreciated her respect for his collective.

"You think you know a lot about us," he said. "Do you know what kind of man I am?"

"Yuri—" she lowered her voice to a husky, disapproving whisper "—you strangled your girlfriend at the Andaz Hotel in New York; you strangled Antoine Babineau in Montreal; you strangled a Russian soldier in Santos, Brazil. You stabbed your own lieutenant in Liberia. And that was on your first flight from justice. I'll skip the others, but to answer your question, yes, dear boy, I know exactly what kind of man you are. Now, what do you say to the job?"

Belenov took it off speaker and wheeled around to face the window, anger heating his head to boiling. "I respect honesty, Ms. Hunter. I agree to take the next step with you. However, I must make you aware of one fact that is as certain as tomorrow's sunrise. If I suspect you of double-crossing me, you too will feel the grip of my fingers around your neck."

He heard the arrogant American swallow hard. Ex-presidents aren't surrounded with the suffocating numbers of Secret Service agents as the current office holder—and Hunter knew it.

She said, "I'll text you the instructions on where and how to meet Roche. But there's one other thing. A personal thing I need done as my payment for setting up your pardon."

While the prospect of meeting Roche intrigued him, Belenov hated tacked-on deals. He considered dumping the whole project. He and SHaRC were only days away from achieving their goal. The thing with Roche could be a distraction that wrecked everything or an alliance that cemented SHaRC's future. That was a risk he could evaluate later. But Hunter tacking on more objectives created too much risk.

He asked, "What is it you need?"

"It's an easy job. But it must be done before you get connected to Roche. I'll send you the details later."

He clicked off.

Petr and Igor pointed to their captive. The man had finished his work. The company's cash and assets had been transferred to a shell company owned by SHaRC. Belenov stepped in. Petr held one of the man's arms while Igor held the other.

"You place your fingers of both hands around the neck like this, Igor." Belenov gave his pupil a nod. "Then you press his jugular veins on either side with your fingertips while pressing your thumbs against his windpipe like this. You see?"

Igor nodded thoughtfully. Petr shrugged, having been through this lesson with three other bankers in recent days.

"Can you still hear me, Luis?" Belenov asked. "I'm sure you're wondering why I'm strangling you after you did what I asked. Well, I think it's quite obvious, isn't it? You can't be trusted. How could I leave an untrustworthy banker alive to tell someone what had happened here tonight? Surely you understand my 'sticky situation.' What would you do in my place? Next time, you should … oh, my bad. There won't be a next time, will there?"

When they let Luis's corpse fall to the floor, Belenov had one more look around the office to make sure they'd left nothing behind. He checked the security video feeds on his phone. They were still looping to an earlier hour in the evening.

As they walked out, something strange tugged at his senses. He backed up two steps and picked up a folder on Luis's desk. The word "Roche" was written in the corner. Inside were documents regarding the Global Economic Development Institute. He read a couple pages, smiled, closed it and took it with him.

CHAPTER 25

Sylvia and I were deep into our second day of sexing it up like otters when Mercury appeared. I'd been godless since the Casino, and it was working for me. At least he had the decency to wait until she was in the shower, but it's just plain rude of him to appear when I was lying naked on the sheets.

I said, *Could you knock first?*

We see it all anyways, homes. Mercury leaned against the wall and thumbed out the window. *Hey, you and I are hunting for Pia-Caesar-Sabel, remember? I understand a man can't turn down the favors of a hot mamma like Sylvia, but you're spent.* He glanced at my worn-out member lying like a wet noodle across my lower tummy. *Ask her where to find Caesar and let's get moving.*

I tugged up the sheets to cover myself. *I'm getting around to it. Just felt like Sylvia needed a little comfort after all she's been through.*

Doing her a favor by sticking your dick in her and wiggling it around? Ain't that romantic? Puhleez. Mercury waved his arms around the luxury apartment. *You haven't even asked her about all this, bro. When are you going to get to the tough questions?*

I said, *She has like PTSD or something. Gold-Tooth kidnapped her, she almost got killed. She doesn't want to talk about it. I don't see any reason to make her relive—*

Mercury walked through the sliding glass door and stood on the terrace.

I checked my phone: 73 voicemails, 149 texts, too many missed calls. Everyone at Sabel Industries wanted a progress report on finding Ms. Sabel. The only variations on that theme were the people who questioned my spending. None of them asked if my memory came back or who shot me. What went down in Tremé? None of them cared. Screw them.

I got up, opened the sliding door, and went out to stand next to him. He was right about one thing; the place was a huge step up from Sylvia's previous hell-hole. The balcony overlooked Port de Fontvieille, a yacht-filled party of a marina. Over the hill and beyond the palace was the more famous Port Hercule, but Fontvieille held its own. Even on a rainy day.

Gray clouds splattered tiny raindrops at an annoying rate. Not enough to make you find an umbrella, but enough to soak through a layer on a jaunt to the bodega for more cheese and wine.

Below us, on a bench overlooking the tiny harbor, was the squinky-eyed CIA guy I'd seen at the casino.

Sylvia wrapped her arms around me from behind. Her silk robe slid on my back like mist. She purred.

"Babe." I used my bedroom baritone. "The view is spectacular. You gotta tell me how you landed this pad. New movie deal coming soon?"

She pulled away and went inside. The same reaction she had for every question deeper than *doggie-style or cowgirl?*

"Hey, it's a legit question." I followed her. "You've done pretty well for yourself. I'm proud of—"

"It's a rental. A friend owns it."

Mercury snuck in behind me. *Hey, dawg, about this 'friend,' does he know the great Jacob Stearne's in town—taking care of business?*

I spun around. *Don't jump to conclusions like that.*

Oh, you're right, my brutha. Mercury put a hand over his mouth, faking regret. *In these modern times, it might be something completely different. OK. Does SHE know the great Jacob Stearne's in town?*

"Good friend?" I called out since she'd gone to the kitchen to scrounge up something to eat. A quick wander into the living area took me to the bookcase where the portrait of a handsome, fiftyish lady parted a row of books. On the opposite wall was a brilliant piece of art that drew my attention. It looked new, yet old. Two bare-chested Polynesian women, one with a plate of fruit, looked bored.

"Isn't that something?" she whispered in my ear. "Paul Gauguin."

If I'd painted it, they'd call me a perv, but name some guy who's been dead a hundred years and—bang—it's art.

"I must meet my agent." She slipped her arms around me again. "Would you mind picking up some food? We can have breakfast when I get back. I'll be gone overnight."

"How about we fly to Rome or Paris for dinner instead?"

"I'm not riding in her jet." With a quick twist away, she was in the bedroom rummaging up an outfit.

Overnight. Mercury scratched his head. *Doesn't that sound like— what did that cop call it—les grandes horizontales?*

Knock it off. You're talking about my girl.

Mercury tapped the portrait. *Or—maybe—someone else's girl?*

Sylvia appeared in a tastefully sexy dress with killer heels. A reasonable god might argue she was dressed for success—of some kind. Mercury was smart enough to keep his mouth shut.

"Who's this, a relative of yours?" I pointed at the fiftyish woman.

She flinched as if it were an insult. "Micaela Pontalba. Um, my landlord."

Her eyes searched mine for a long, odd moment. Then she gave me a chilly kiss and left. The door closed behind her with a thud.

Something about that name dragged a memory out of my foggy amnesia. Running around in the rain with Sylvia, slipping on a wet sidewalk in New Orleans, too many Hurricanes at Pat O'Brien's, a phone call that filled me with dread.

I spelled it three different ways until Google found her. Baroness Micaela Pontalba died a century before Sylvia's landlord could've been born. The real baroness designed the iconic Upper Pontalba Building. That's the one you see on TV whenever the show is set in NOLA. The Pontalba's wrought-iron lace balconies overlook Jackson Square in the French Quarter.

Sylvia had been testing my amnesia story.

Which pissed me off.

I took off in a dead run.

Mercury stood on the landing in the stairwell channeling James Earl Jones. *It has been written: those who worship Greek goddesses will rot in Avernus.*

I said, *Not now!*

Three floors down, he stood on the last landing before the ground level. *Would you believe a prophecy? Dogs will devour the flesh of any Jezebel who lies to her man about her sugar-mommy.*

I can't hear you, la-la-la... I ran past him.

Mercury stood at the front door. *OK, brutha, this is my final offer: she went out the back door because she knew you'd figure it out. She's in a cab and gone.*

Where?

He rocked back on his heels as if I stank. *You think Aphrodite is going to let me chase her girls around any more than I would let her sniff up your ... Say. You might want to put some clothes on.*

A quick glance down, an apologetic smile at the older couple coming in from the curb, and I was taking the stairs two at a time. I whipped some of my new wardrobe out of the shopping bag. After the wine splash and the shirt-ripping, my first getup had been trashed. But one call to my sales guy at the mall, and he had three fresh outfits, including shoes, socks, toothpaste, and a fresh box of condoms, delivered to Sylvia's. That guy was a keeper.

Alone in the apartment without a plan, I did a quick check of the closets and drawers. One change of clothes belonged to Sylvia. Everything else screamed fiftyish-lady. The only thing Sylvia left was her casino dress and shoes. I don't know much about makeup and perfume, but nothing in the bathroom said under-forty-single-hottie. Especially the Chanel No. 5.

Which gave me a plan.

I trudged back downstairs and went out the front door.

Squinky-eye, soaked in drizzle, sat on a bench overlooking the yachts. I parked next to him. "She ditched us both, Eddie."

He said, "*Parlez vous Français?*"

"Say. That's pretty good French." I shook a playful finger his way and faced him. "You know, I can place a guy within a mile of his home just by his accent. You're from ... don't tell me, let me guess..." I waited until he looked at me. "St. Louis, am I right? Cardinals baseball, Wash

U., half a McDonald's arch stuck in the mud by the river?"

"It's the Gateway Arch, ya fuck." He stood to leave.

Missourians have no sense of humor. Call it Arch Madness or hula-hoop-of-the-gods and they get nasty.

"Chill, dude." I patted the bench. "We can be pals, share information, work together, right? We're on the same team. You already know my resume since you're working with the local cop. Tell me about yourself. What's your sign? What's your major?"

He stood still, his fingers wiggling while he considered it. His body language telegraphed a negative. I jumped him before he spoke. "Hey, Eddie, gimme a smile, will ya?"

His curiosity turned his face my way. I snapped a portrait and sent it to Bianca, head of Sabel Technologies. I dialed her. "Bianca, can you run this mug through our database and tell me who this guy is? He's claiming DGSE, but I'm thinking more like SVR."

"You cannot do this," she hissed. "Roche is all over us. Don't do it again, OK? He's Peter Hammond. CIA, Berlin Station."

I clicked off and met his almost-scary glare. "Berlin? Pretty far from home. Oh. I get it. You're doing what I'm doing: abusing the company expense account, right? Hey, secret's safe with me, bud."

I held out my fist for a bump.

"Shut up." He sat down, leaving me hanging. "What've you got?"

"A company man, past his prime, sent on a job nobody else wanted. So I ask myself, why? Is he an alcoholic? Did he screw the boss's wife? Did he get an agent killed through sloppy—"

"That's enough." He stood again.

"And he's peeping on one hot actress and her studly—"

"Wrong." He nosed over his shoulder at a sixty-foot yacht across the marina and five slips down. "I'm watching her brother."

Three people stood on the poop deck, arguing about something. Two men and Sylvia. She slapped one of the guys hard enough to send him sprawling.

CHAPTER 26

AFTER THE LUNCH CROWD DISSIPATED, Pia parked her laptop and coffee at her favorite table in the Texas BBQ. For two days, the Galerie DeLano had been virtually empty. The painter never returned. DeLano rarely unlocked the front door. No one came or went through the back door. Just as Willy-Mac had predicted, video surveillance was a bust after her rooftop chase. Pia started the video at the beginning and ran it on automatic 4x speed—again. Maybe she'd missed something the first twenty times she watched the boring stretches of static rooms. Maybe.

She shrank the video to the corner of the screen and checked the news online.

Big mistake.

Headlines from DC: *Roche cancels Sabel Industries contracts with NSA and CIA.* Citing unsubstantiated claims that her companies were spying on the American public, Roche had encouraged the business community to cease all business with Sabel. Only two well-known CEOs protested on her behalf. No one else dared challenge the president for fear of excommunication. The intelligence community went ballistic, but there was little they could do. The CEOs of each Sabel Division demanded evidence from the administration. The White House made no further statement. Within an hour, the president had tweeted that he would ban soccer in the USA because it corrupted America's youth with foreign ideas. The furor over soccer pulled Sabel off page one, effectively obscuring his attack on Sabel Industries.

Pia had discussed contingencies with her executives before she left. They might keep everyone employed for six months, but that was based on a couple of at-risk divisions. No one had anticipated a blanket boycott.

She contemplated calling the Major and breaking her cover. Roche would use the FBI or NSA to track her down. He might have an agency tasked with monitoring communications in and out of Sabel companies. If he found her in Antibes, DeLano's operation would evaporate before she had any evidence. She would have to trust the Major to do her best.

She swiped to the next article in her news feed: *Stefan DeVoor splits with Pia Sabel.* That made it official: she'd been dumped. Should she have told him about her mental health challenges and asked forgiveness? In the article, Stefan took a spiritual tone. "Pia has given in to demonic influences. President Roche is right to protect the nation from someone so unbalanced and spiritually misaligned."

What the hell did that mean? *Spiritually misaligned.*

Stefan could go screw himself. Had Roche suborned everyone into hating her? Maybe she should add paranoia to her list of problems. Eventually, all paranoids are right. If "they" aren't out to get you, the mental health professionals will be; thus, someone is out to get you. Her fingernails dug into her palms again. She had to focus on her goal of getting Roche out of the White House.

Willy-Mac took the seat across from her. "Discover anything?"

"Yes." She looked up. "You were right. I'm wasting my time."

He sipped his coffee and watched her.

"What difference does it make?" She asked. "What can one person do? Especially one who's under 'demonic influences.'"

She turned the news post so he could read it. He pulled out his glasses, skimmed through, and nodded.

"You make a difference everywhere you go and with everything you say." Willy-Mac chuckled. "I have to buy my wife a new car because you used a disparaging tone of voice when referring to Porsches. She's an educated, intelligent woman, secure in her station, proud of her accomplishments, but one off-hand remark from a young soccer star and she can't stand the sight of her car anymore. That's one example of how a person can make a difference. Sometimes good and—" he wobbled a hand in the air "—sometimes not so much."

Pia recalled their dinner conversation and blushed.

"What cars are cool these days, Eva? What do you drive back home?"

She squeezed her eyes closed.

"C'mon now," Willy-Mac leaned in. "Viv and I are one-percenters, unusual as that might seem to a white girl. Tell me what you drive."

"I have lots of cars." She brought her gaze up to find him bearing down on her. With resignation in her voice, she muttered, "My favorite is the McLaren 720, although the Audi RS8 is more practical on the street."

He whistled. "We'd be at the other end of the one percent. Not quite ready for those."

Should've kept her mouth shut. She looked out the window.

They each sipped their coffees in silence for a while. Then Willy-Mac said, "Let me show you something."

He rose and crossed to the framed picture of Martin Luther King marching in Selma. Without looking, he pointed to a random face in the photo. "That one person made all the difference that day." He moved his finger, again without looking. "So did this one. And this one. And that—"

"Yeah, I get it." She crossed her arms. "Every group is made up of individuals. To overturn tyranny, everyone has a role and responsibility."

"That means you." He pushed a finger in her face. "You can bring down Chuck Roche if that's what you want to do. What are you waiting for?"

"How? I have nothing."

"To topple an autocrat, you need to expose his moral compass for what—"

"WHO THE HELL ARE YOU?" DeLano's voice boomed from the front door.

Pia glanced over her shoulder. The gallery owner pointed an accusatory finger at her across the empty café.

She took three quick strides toward him to keep Willy-Mac out of the confrontation. "Are you asking me?"

"Straight up."

"I introduced myself twice. I'm Eva—"

"No, I mean who the hell are you?" His tone was loud and aggressive. "How come you know Deng and Yeschenko? Not even their assistants return my calls."

He moved closer, his eyes blazing red, his face overheated.

Willy-Mac moved to a position parallel to them. She saw him in her peripheral vision. He crossed his arms and leaned against the counter as if he were watching street performers.

Pia said, "I'm active in charities."

"What were you doing sneaking around my back room a few days ago?"

He held up his phone and started a video. He held it to her face. A security camera looked down on a room. Pia entered from the upper-right frame and did her inventory, taking pictures and looking things over. One of the many things Willy-Mac had warned her not to do.

She hoped there was a trap door in the floor beneath her that would open and swallow her before she had to answer him. She turned to the window to avoid his piercing glare.

"The fuck is that?" DeLano's voice boomed. His finger tapped the phone.

Outside, across the street, the man who roughed up DeLano during her backroom-wander leaned in a doorway. DeLano had called him "Cyril" if she recalled correctly. His presence spoke volumes about what was going on. Her confidence returned.

She met DeLano's gaze.

"When I saw that copy of de Kooning's *Untitled XVII*, I wondered what else you might have to offer."

"It's not a copy."

"I know where the real one hangs." She picked up her chin. "I know the owner quite well. I even know what she paid for it: 9,755,750 USD. Let's look up the provenance on Christies.com."

"Bullshit. I have everything documented on that piece. You're wrong." An expression of pain crunched up his face as if someone had stuck an ice pick in his belly.

"The original is signed on the edge, below the frame. You have the signature in plain sight."

He chewed a fingernail. "Look, whatever you think is going on doesn't give you the right to go snooping—"

"Why didn't you ask me about this days ago?"

"We had an attempted burglary recently. It occurred to me someone might've been casing the place ahead of time, so I went back through the security video."

He glanced around and saw Willy-Mac. "What're you looking at?"

Cool as a cucumber, Willy-Mac sipped his coffee without taking his eyes off DeLano.

"Wait a second," DeLano twisted back to Pia. "You said, what else I have on offer. Did you tell someone about what I have?"

"Like the cops?" she asked.

His face turned white. Sweat broke out on his forehead. He didn't answer.

"Why would I ruin a good opportunity with cops?" she asked.

For a split second, he considered her conspiratorial hint. Then he frowned.

"You should leave town." He lowered his voice an octave. "Whatever you think is going on, you're wrong. I've got video cameras all over the street now. You and your friends are going to have big problems if you try anything. Mark my words."

"Are you threatening me?" She stepped on his toes and used her three-inch height advantage to look down at him.

He squirmed. "Investors get a little nutty about theft, y'know? They sent security guards who've seen your star performance. They might be a little trigger-happy. I'm sure you understand—I don't control those guys. They're at my place twenty-four-seven whether I like it or not. I'm not threatening you, just telling you how things might get a little cray-cray if you come around again. I'm just trying to be friendly here. Avoid any unnecessary accidents."

They stared at each other for a long time. Pia released his foot.

He clenched his jaw. "Be smart, leave town. Today." DeLano stormed out the door.

Pia watched him cross the street. She pointed two fingers at her eyes then turned them to Cyril, *I'm watching you.* Cyril smiled and adjusted his jacket, exposing his shoulder holster and pistol in the process. Pia considered showing hers off as well but sensed Willy-Mac's hot stare. *Guns escalate problems.*

She decided to take his advice this time.

Then again, maybe she was trusting the wrong stranger. A suspicious anger built up inside her. She had no idea if he had been a Texas Ranger or a lawyer. He might be orchestrating everything with DeLano. She turned to him. He was observing her as if calculating his next move. Her molars were grinding. What if he was setting her up, predicting exactly what she would do next and letting her dig her own grave?

"Have you figured it out yet?" Willy-Mac asked.

Her blood pressure returned to normal at the sound of his voice. "It's a side deal. He and Cyril are selling forgeries because their overlord isn't paying them anything."

Willy-Mac put his fingertip on his nose.

"OK, but that only explains two of my five questions." She huffed. "What about the other—"

"Talk your way through them."

"First, why here and not NYC?" She felt like a schoolgirl reciting a lesson by rote. "Second, why are billionaires coming in person? Third, why here and not a freeport? Fourth, why buy forgeries when they can afford the real thing? And last—the only one you answered for me—he's not rich because he's a front for someone else. I think it's Roche, but you refuse to be drawn into a conclusion for which there is no evidence."

"Not a shred." Willy-Mac finished his coffee and set the cup on the counter. "Back to your questions. You have the answer to number four."

"The billionaires aren't the ones buying the forgeries." She turned the puzzle around in her head. "Then who is? I haven't seen anyone go in there without a bodyguard. Wait a second. He had visitors at four in the morning once. Holy crap. Completely under the overlord's radar."

Willy-Mac touched his nose again.

"Then what are the billionaires doing there?" she asked.

"I have an idea, but I'm not clear how to prove it. That's why I want you to form your independent opinion."

"Who is Cyril then?"

"Stay away from him." Willy-Mac gave her his trademark serious look. "His name is Cyril Cahuzac, a Corsican associated with the *gang de la Brise de Mer*. One of the worst organized crime syndicates in the world. And he's suspected in six murders this year."

An easy betrayal a year earlier had led her into the Russian general's trap. She had been careless with her words in front of the wrong person. The odd thing was, she had known he would betray her. She would never let that happen again.

Questions flooded into her head. How the hell did Willy-Mac know all that about Cyril? Why would he know that? Thousands of thoughts screamed through Pia's brain at the same time, drowning out everything around her. There was only one reason Willy-Mac would know the name of a gang and its top gangster. He had to be working for the DCPJ, *Direction centrale de la Police judiciaire*. He said he likes to help bring about justice. The DCPJ shares information with the CIA and FBI, which Roche controls. The pressure in her head rose by the second. Willy-Mac might be reporting her every move directly back to Roche.

He might be doing it without realizing it.

No. Willy-Mac was a lawman—if he were to be believed at all— which meant he would know all that. So why was he so nice to her? And he still refused to answer her questions. Damn it. Who could she trust? She was alone in the world and far from home. She needed help, an ally, someone trustworthy. A mentor. One of her Dad's old friends who would help her sort out everything.

Her mind circled back at 100 mph. Why not trust Willy-Mac? Because if he knew Cyril's name, he must know everything going on in Galerie DeLano. So why not just tell her? He was forcing her to work for him, that's why. She was in trouble, and he was her only source of help. He was doing what spymasters have been doing for centuries. She'd thought this once before but dismissed it because he'd been helping her. Exactly like a spymaster. She was being subsumed. Forced into his game. She was playing right into Roche's—

"Can you hear me?" his voice floated through her scrambled thoughts.

"Yes."

"What's your answer?"

She took a deep breath. The sound of his voice was soothing in the same way Dad's used to be—before she got him killed. Her eyes involuntarily shut while she felt the guilt wash through her. Then, she opened them and looked at him.

"How do you know Cyril? He's not from Houston. How do I know you're not working for the French? Or DeLano?" She glowered as he held up his hands. "You could be reporting this to the wrong people for all I know."

Willy-Mac shook his head. "I know you're struggling with—"

She took a deep breath. "I've made a decision. I know how to get the answers I need. And I know you advised against this. So don't bother saying it. You can't talk me out of it. Don't worry, I won't cry out for help. I won't be your problem anymore." She picked up her laptop. "I'm going to Corvo Island to meet Mikhail Yeschenko."

CHAPTER 27

ROCHE HANDED HUNTER A DRINK and motioned her to the couch. Bates watched from the doorway until he was satisfied it was a conjugal visit, then left. Roche couldn't wait to get rid of that arrogant prick. From now on, he would hire only loyal people. People who would take a bullet for him, whether they wanted to or not.

"This sneaking around is ridiculous." Hunter took a big gulp.

"Have you seen the intelligence we get from our people?" Roche handed her a file. "They didn't get audio of your dinner with Mikhail, but they did get something bigger. He's being ripped off by his boy Belenov. He's gotten so paranoid about it, he tossed an accountant off his balcony. Wouldn't you love to have one of those?"

"An accountant?"

She looked at him with that disdainful face so many losers use. No wonder no one voted for her. What is wrong with people? Why can't anyone keep up with the pace of an intelligent conversation? But that was his burden, the downside to genius.

"No. A balcony on a cliff." He could hardly contain his excitement at the thought of a terrace of terror. "You just toss the disloyal bastards over the edge and—problem solved. Damn, I should hold my press conferences on his island."

"Disloyals?" She took a long drink from her glass like an alcoholic with a problem. Then she faced him. "Like your Vice President?"

"What do you mean? He's as loyal as a Labrador." Roche thought about the man who brought him all those religious whacko votes. The strangers who insisted on doing the *laying on of hands* when he first took office. Creepy as all get-out. Why would they vote for him, a guy who never went to church? Not his problem. Crazies born every minute. "Wait. What're you saying about him?"

"Who do you think leaked your nephew's meeting with the Russians to the special prosecutor?"

"That was the *New York Times*." Roche realized the newspaper had produced copies of emails that had to have come from somewhere. "No way."

"Yes." She stared at him until he felt sick.

"I'll fire him." He watched her wince. "What's that face mean? I can't do that? I'll make him resign then."

"Good idea." She kept a steady gaze fixed on him while she finished her drink. "You'll appoint me to take his place."

"Whoa, now. Where'd you get the that crazy—"

"You need Belenov to destroy Bates. I have Belenov. You want him, I get VP."

Roche snatched the empty glass from her hand and stormed to the bar. He didn't know how to make a drink, and he didn't care, but he was so mad he would beat her senseless if he stood there another minute. He glanced around at the mixers.

"I know how to get rid of the special prosecutor." She picked out a bottle and handed it to him. "I know how to make the Justice Department round up your enemies. You need me as VP."

Instead of taking the bottle from her, he handed her empty glass back and pointed to the ice bucket. Women feel entitled to everything these days. She wanted equality, she could make her own drink.

He asked, "What do you mean by 'my enemies?'"

"You've grown to hate a few people." She dropped ice cubes in her glass and poured liquor over them. "People who say nasty things about you. Write nasty opinion pieces about you. Record things you said and then wait until you lie about—"

"I never lie. Some folks don't understand that sometimes the truth just isn't the truth. People believe the wrong things about what they see and hear, that's all."

"The people who tear you down instead of seeing your genius. You can rid the country of them. You could clean up this swamp."

Roche felt good about that. "You're right. That's what I promised the people. I need to start mopping up the criminals. But the FBI never does what I tell them. They keep talking about evidence, proof, and probable cause. I mean, what the hell is that?"

"It's what I bring to the table." She poured ginger ale on the booze and swirled her glass. "We can set things right."

Hunter could be useful, but the press would have a field day with that one. Kick your VP downstairs then appoint your former rival? He said, "How do I get him to resign?"

"He's considering it now." She leaned against the bar with a decidedly sassy look in her eye. "You'll have his resignation on your desk by morning."

"Which means you want my announcement to coincide with his."

"No." She swirled her glass and sipped as she wandered around the room. "You have to do a search. Interview people, bring in a horde of hopefuls, make a parade. Then you pick me. A week, minimum."

"What if I install someone else? Why would you trust me?"

"I'll testify against you in exchange for immunity."

And she was just the kind of backstabbing bitch to do it, too. Roche was the one who forced people to do things, not the other way around. But here she was, brass balls and everything, forcing him to do what she wanted. How could she ever expect a man to marry her when she acted like that? On the bright side, if she got the special prosecutor off his back, and put people like Pia Sabel in jail, it would be worth it. He bit his lip while he thought. Vanquishing his enemies would be cool. Especially since everyone in RULE was pissed off at him now.

"How did you get the VP to consider resigning?" he asked.

"A few young men came forward."

She wandered to the credenza where the briefings were stacked, a mass of meaningless words he had no intention of reading. Bureaucrats—never say in five words what can take ten pages.

"As it turns out," she smiled, "he should've sent himself to gay-conversion therapy instead of his daughter."

"Noooo."

"Who knew?" She sipped her drink and looked at the briefings. "I've lined up six guys who'll confess on all the talk shows. One a week over the next month and a half. They have friends who'll vouch for them. We've matched the dates with his public calendar. We have photos of them from campaign rallies. We gave the evidence to his wife. She didn't bat an eye. She marched straight to him and threw it in his face."

"Wow. Are the guys real?"

"Don't know. Don't care."

She picked up the folder that Kurtz had dropped off. That asshole insisted Roche read the thing instead of telling him what was in it. He would be first to go.

"You're planning to invade Saudi Arabia now?" Her shrill voice echoed off the walls.

He hated it when women acted superior. Now he'd have to bring her into the administration. She knew too much.

"More of Kurtz's exercises." He grabbed the folder out of her hands. "He wants a fallback in case the prosecutors get too close."

"All you idiots think about is saving your jobs instead of tens of thousands of innocent lives?"

"What's so innocent about Saudis? Their people were behind 9/11, they finance more terrorists than Iran ever dreamed of, they export that Wahhabi crap all over the world. And they're rich—nobody will feel sorry for them. Besides, we'll get massive ratings when we blow up that black cube thing, the Kaaba."

"Aren't they your biggest partner?"

"We've had—" he chewed his lip "—a falling out."

He set the folder down and took the drink from her hand. She looked puzzled. At her age, she should know what's coming.

"OK," he said, "you get the job."

He reached between her legs.

She slapped him, turned, and strode to the door.

"Hey, what's with the attitude?" he asked. "I said you get the VP job."

CHAPTER 28

NO WOMAN IN THE HISTORY of civilization needed rescuing more than Sylvia Lallouette. Two men had escorted her below decks and fled Monaco for open waters. Peter Hammond claimed he knew exactly where they were going and would show me—but not tell me—if I gave him a ride. He claimed we had plenty of time since it would take well into the night to get there. I rented a boat and captain for the mission.

Mercury hounded me about letting her go. I tuned him out.

While the captain was getting the fuel and provisions ready, I took a cab back to Sabel Two on the tarmac in Nice to round up some hardware. My liquid-metal body armor made a fashion statement that ran contrary to everything Monégasques held dear. The weaponry alone would horrify my sales guy back at the Monaco Mall.

Once underway, Peter played cat-and-mouse with information. He was there to observe, but not interfere with, or contact, Sylvia's half-brother Cyril Cahuzac, a mid-level guy in a Corsican gang. They shared an American mother. Sylvia had grown up splitting her time between her mom's bi-coastal lifestyle in NYC and LA and her father's home in Paris. Cyril grew up on mean Corsican streets. In their mom's favor, Cyril's dad had been a handsome, smooth-talking gangster while Sylvia's dad had been a boring surgeon.

Cyril continually gave Peter the slip, so he'd begun following Sylvia. Cyril helped her move out of her old apartment. Peter said where I'd been staying was a new location to him. The siblings had not seen much of each other. Only three meetings over coffee after the apartment move. Phones and notebooks and shopping bags had been exchanged. The guys on the boat were new players. He suspected rivals, bosses, or pirates.

He refused to answer the obvious question. Why was the CIA's Berlin Station interested in a Corsican gangster?

We neared a landmass in the dark. Peter gave the captain instructions in French. The captain brought the speed down a notch or two.

Peter asked to borrow my H&K automatic rifle with silencer and scope. When I gave him my soldier-stare as a reply, he had the balls to ask for one of my Glocks. Instead, I showed him the Sabel Darts and explained how they incapacitated a guy for four hours. He didn't care. He asked, "Can you at least loan me a pair of night vision goggles?"

I handed him our infrared monocular that can read heat signatures through walls. At Peter's direction, our captain glided into Ajaccio's yacht club, *Nautique Plaisance*. Nautical Pleasure.

"Are you kidding me?" I shook Peter. "We spent all night sailing the Mediterranean for this? My jet could've put us here in twenty minutes."

"You have a jet?" He smirked.

If Casino-Pierre knew I had a jet, then CIA-Peter did too. But then they blew the call on the Bay of Pigs, the Shah of Iran, WMDs in Iraq, and a host of others, so maybe not.

"Yeah," Peter said. "Like you would've brought me along on your big fancy jet."

We passed the yacht we were looking for in near silence. I had Peter give me an onboard headcount with the monocular.

There were six warm bodies onboard the yacht that fled Monaco with Sylvia's kidnappers. Peter reported there was one guy on the flydeck, two on the main deck, two in the aft lower deck and one in the forecastle.

He said, "I'll take the lookout on the flydeck if you think you can handle the other two."

"Relax." I looked him over before pumping a Sabel Dart into his thigh. "I've got this."

I like CIA guys, I just don't trust them. It was a CIA analyst who told General Custer there were only a hundred Cheyenne at Little Bighorn. When things went horribly wrong, and tens of thousands of warriors descended on the 7th Cavalry, the analyst said, "Oops," and walked away.

Our captain stared at me with cartoon-eyes. His mouth hung open. His English was as bad as my French. After several attempts at assuring him that Peter was only sleeping—because rescuing your girlfriend is more dramatic when you do it alone—and that I wasn't going to kill either of them, he nodded. He dropped me at the end of the pier, three yachts over.

My timing was perfect, somewhere after two in the morning. Sylvia's was the only other occupied vessel in the marina. I crawled to a good position with one boat between us, aimed carefully, and darted the lookout. None of the others on watch stirred. Probably sleeping on the job. That emboldened me. I crouched my way down the dock to Sylvia's. The yacht had *Vita di Bagasciu* written across the stern. "Thug Life" according to my translator app.

Mercury crossed the gangway. *And that doesn't tell you anything? How many times do I have to tell you? Sylvia has gone to the Greek-side. It's like the dark side, only worse.*

I said, *This whole jealousy thing about the Greek gods, Aphrodite, and Sylvia is getting annoying. I'm still your guy, so relax.*

Dang, bro. Mercury held a hand over his heart, wounded. *When you humans want to ignore the advice of the gods, you go all the way around the world, y'know that? Reminds me of when Jesus was telling Truman not to drop the atom bomb on Hiroshima, drop it in the ocean nearby, they'll get the message. Even the atheist-scientists out in New Mexico heard the angels. They went so far as to send Truman a letter. Did it do any good?*

I said, *Could you get out of my way? I have a damsel in distress to rescue here.*

Mercury said, *You really believe that? Tell yourself the truth, are you trying to rescue her life—or your sex life? Either way's a losing proposition, dawg.*

Sigh. The boat was moored ten feet from the dock, making a fully-armored jump impossible. I carefully used the gangplank and stepped onboard quietly.

A barrage of bullets met me square in the chest.

Guess they weren't sleeping after all.

The rounds bounced off my body armor, but the force still knocked me overboard. I fell between the dock and the hull. Weighed down with weapons and armor, I might've sunk straight to the bottom without passing Go and without collecting my $200. But my flailing hand found an ancient piece of rope hanging underneath the dock. No doubt Mercury would claim he put the rope there fifty years ago knowing I'd need it.

Mercury swam up from the depths. *You like that, homie? I put that there back in—*

I said, *Yeah, thanks.*

One of the guys looked over the edge, telegraphing his position with a flashlight. I popped a dart into his neck. He fell overboard and landed, facedown, right next to me. Instead of armor, he wore an oversized life preserver. Smart man. I flipped him on his back so he could breathe while he slept and used him as a float. We made our way under the dock to a ladder halfway back to shore.

Two guys were searching with flashlights when I poked my head up. My rifle's silencer was filled with water which caused my first dart to fly wide. I ducked back down and held it upside down to drain it. A surprising amount of the Mediterranean had holed up in that thing.

Mercury said, *Real heroes—who know Roman gods rule, Greek gods drool—don't have to drain salt water out of their weapons.*

I said, *Just give me a minute, will ya? I've got this. Probably.*

My adversaries made a cautious approach, each on the opposite side of the pier. They were not beginners. Every few steps, one of them would turn around to double check their flank and rear.

I slung my rifle over my back, barrel down, and inched along the wooden dock by my fingertips. With my head below the visible range, I had to locate them by sound. When a pant leg appeared nearby, I grabbed his knee and yanked. But not hard enough. He stayed on his feet. He staggered back, regained his balance, and came after me.

Three bullets flew over my back. The burning powder skimmed my scalp. His misses gave me time to fire a dart into his calf. He fell half-on and half-off the dock. His buddy would be coming in a second. He would know right where I was. I let go of the dock and fell into the sea.

My floating friend was nowhere to be found. I flailed my way to a concrete pillar. From there, I reached for a crossbeam under the planks above and went hand-over-hand back to the ladder. This time, I was on the opposite side.

A light beam searched the water behind me. The guy fired at some floating trash.

He played whack-a-mole with me for a long time. No matter what you see on TV, thrashing around in a silent port with fifty pounds of gear strapped to your back is noisy. Getting away from him was hard.

The guy in the life preserver floated near me. I gave him a push and paddled with him three feet short of the ladder then floated him between pylons on the side. The guy up top fired three rounds into his compadre before noticing it wasn't me. Friendly fire sucks. By then, I'd climbed the ladder and had a dart in his rump. He fell into the drink face-first without a life jacket. He killed his friend and now instant karma was going to drown him. Funny how life works.

I scrambled aboard the Thug Life and slipped cautiously down the stairs. Narrow confines are kill boxes. This one ended in three closed doors. There was no way the last guy didn't know I was onboard. Not with his buddies shooting up the marina.

Mercury tapped my shoulder. *Forget something, bro? The heat-sensing monocular you left with Peter?*

I said, *Would it have hurt you to mention it before I left the boat. A caring god would—*

Mercury said, *You need help with Sylvia's rescue, why not ask Aphrodite?*

There just isn't enough time in life to deal with lonely gods.

I listened, straining for a clue about the last guy. Nothing. That left me one option.

Using the upper deck as a pull-up bar, I smashed my feet into the door on the left, then dropped to a crouch. I'd expected the last man to be in there and shoot back or be across from it and shoot through the door. Neither thing happened. I used my phone to grab a video of the cabin beyond the smashed door. Empty.

Mercury appeared dead ahead and pointed at the door behind him. *They're both in there. They put their clothes back on.*

I did my pull-up kick again, smashing through the door.

A shirtless guy spun around the corner searching for me with a

Barretta. He fired into the space where he expected a standing man to face him. I was crouched at knee level. I fired three times while rising. My first and second darts nailed him just as he planted a bullet in my center mass. The armor held but my ribs complained about the abuse. He slumped to the floor.

I fist-pumped the air. The hero had come to save the day! Oh yeah. Pretty sure that would get me extra kisses from the damsel no longer in distress. But she didn't jump up with any kisses.

The dart that missed the killer had caught Sylvia in the forehead. She was sprawled across the covers in the same dress she left home in. No sign of hasty dressing or undressing. I hoisted her to my shoulder and jogged up the stairs. After finding my way to the dock, I whistled for my boat.

Crickets.

The bastard had sailed away. I called an Uber and my pilots in Nice. With any luck, I would meet them at Ajaccio's Napoleon Bonaparte Airport before *gang de la Brise de Mer* came looking for me in numbers.

My driver thought nothing of the body draped over my shoulder. He took me straight to the executive terminal and dropped me at the front door.

Bristling with armor and weapons, I looked like an alien abducting an actress. Which upset the lone attendant. He required several reassurances before he calmed down. I waited in the lounge while soft, unpopular music oozed from hidden speakers.

Mercury brushed Sylvia's hair out of her eyes. *She's not bad looking for a food-eater.*

I said, *Don't talk about her like that.*

Mercury said, *Sorry, homes, what do your people like to be called these days, air-breathers? Book-readers? Sorry, just kidding about that one. Only the smart people read. C'mon now, tell me. What is it? Shit-takers? I can't keep up with the latest in political correctness.*

I looked away.

Mercury tapped my shoulder. *C'mon now, my brutha, don't be like that. Just open her purse and rummage through it until you find the answers to the questions that are burning through your soul. Then you can ask me to help you out of this mess. I won't even make you beg.*

I looked around the lounge. The attendant cowered in the corner and flinched when my scan reached him. I opened her purse. Lipstick. Mirror. Receipts for makeup. Out-of-date coupons. More outdated coupons. A dried-out pen. Wrinkled Kleenex. A key—which did not match the one we'd been sharing for her new apartment. A fat roll of €500 notes. I kept the phone and closed the mess.

Outside, headlights made their way through the complex roadway that led from the main terminal to the executive. I picked up Sylvia and stashed her in a closet behind the attendant. I crouched beneath his desk with my rifle pointed up at him. We didn't exchange any words. He got it.

Three men burst in talking a mile a minute in the local language. While the attendant's voice quaked, he waved them off. His knee shook like it was tied to a paint-shaker. While they conversed in rapid bursts, I found another peep-hole in my amnesia. *Amicu* means friend in Corsican. Back on the farm, Gold-Tooth had spoken Corsican to his goons. It sounded a little like French, a little like Italian. Then another cloud cleared. A memory from Tremé—Sylvia speaking Corsican to someone on the phone.

The door closed. The car roared off. The attendant heaved a sigh of relief. I patted him on the back and retrieved Sylvia.

It occurred to me that the guys looking for my girl knew about her place in Monaco. We would need someplace to hide out when we got back. Or maybe I would just sneak her off to my place in Bethesda.

Mercury squinted at me.

Or I would wait for Sylvia to wake up to grill her about Ms. Sabel's whereabouts.

Mercury smiled and nodded.

I checked out Sylvia's phone. Like so many people these days, her preferred method of communication was text. There were hundreds, almost all in French. The rest in Spanish. Using the search feature, I looked for my name. Quite a few items popped up. The first was from Wikipedia. It mentioned that Jacob was the third patriarch of the Hebrew people and the founder of Israel. Duh. The rest was useless information about movies, actors, and whatnot. Finally, I found one text thread with my name in it.

Mercury leaned over my shoulder. *That's it, bro? Just one text with your name. That's all you are on her radar?*

I said, *She got a new phone a couple weeks ago. There was a lot more stuff on her old one.*

Mercury took a step back. *Oh.*

I copied some of the thread into the translator app. The one time my name appeared, it read, "Jacob just found me. Can't meet tonight. More after I shake him."

The reply to that had too much slang for the translator. It seemed to mean hurry up. Just before she was kidnapped, she texted the same nameless person, "On my way. He really doesn't remember anything."

The reply was simple, "Bien."

I looked at Mercury, *Don't you say a fucking word.*

He gave me his *who-me?* look.

I spun up through the thread to the beginning and translated her first exchange with her nameless contact. "New phone. Pia tried to kill me. Hugo tried to kill me. Get me out of here!"

CHAPTER 29

PIA WAS IN SIXTH GRADE when she grew too tall for Learjets. Only children and dwarfs could stand in the five-foot interior, and she was the opposite of a dwarf. She crabbed to the front and descended the airstair. It felt like breaking out of jail into a warm, sunny day. As soon as she scanned the runway, she understood Yeschenko's reasoning. Large jets like hers couldn't land on his short airstrip. With a thousand miles of Atlantic between Europe and Corvo, the only practical conveyance was his shuttle. He had total control of who came and went.

"Pia, what a sight you are." Yeschenko stepped from a limo-SUV in a pristine suit, colorful tie, and shiny shoes. He approached with a big smile and open arms. He gave her a Russian hug with a kiss on each cheek, then held her hands and leaned back. "What a lovely dress. You make everything sparkle."

A sudden self-consciousness came over her. Was she showing too much leg? She wanted this to be professional. All business. She tried to discreetly tug the hem down. He guided her to the car and climbed in beside her.

They chatted about mutual acquaintances along his twisting two-mile driveway until he took a call. He turned away from her and spoke in French.

She looked out the window at the island of the crow, *corvo* in Portuguese. Her online study showed it to be the perfect lion's den. The airstrip served the fifteenth-century town of five hundred, all in Yeschenko's employ. Farmable strips of land covered the southern end and some of the eastern side of a volcano that rose from the sea a million years ago. But on the western side, the site of his compound, a series of jagged cliffs marked where the Atlantic and the mountain had been locked in a violent struggle since the late Pleistocene.

Pia tried not to eavesdrop on her host, but the driver had not put on music. The name "Jacob Stearne" perked her ear. She listened in, straining her weak French.

"—could one man kill four of yours?" Yeschenko listened to the answer. "Who the hell is this Stearne?" Again, Yeschenko waited. "And you've lost him? You've given up?" Another pause. "He must be tracked down and killed, Hugo." Yeschenko's face turned beet-red before he shouted. "We will finish this discussion when you arrive. How far out are you, half an hour?" He disconnected.

Pia found herself elated to hear Jacob was alive.

Facing the window, Yeschenko straightened his tie and took a few deep breaths. "I apologize for my vehemence. You know how it is. Sometimes our people disappoint us. I lose my temper too easily and speak extravagantly, exaggerating my instructions." He frowned and twisted to look at her carefully. "Did I sense that you recognized something in my conversation?"

"My French is terrible," she said. "But I heard the name, Jacob Stearne. Were you referring to the legendary American veteran?"

"Perhaps." Yeschenko raised an eyebrow. "Tell me about this Stearne. How do you know him?"

She wondered if the Russian knew Jacob worked for her. Yeschenko's relationship with her father had been minimal. It would be unlikely he'd ever met Sabel employees six or seven rungs down the ladder, despite Jacob's unique standing.

"Well, uhm, as you know, I employ many veterans." She straightened her already straight dress. "And there is one man they all revere. The soldier's soldier. Although they say he's a little mad. Anyway, I think that's where I heard the name. Is he OK?"

"Unfortunately," Yeschenko said.

They arrived at a stone stronghold sprawled across a high, rocky cliff. Waves crashed with an incessant roar and spray shot halfway up the foundations. Yeschenko led her through a grand foyer and gallery to an expanse of terrace overlooking the ocean. A table outfitted with crystal and silver on white linen waited for them under an umbrella.

"I must confess my delight in your interest in my little organization." Yeschenko put his hands on the balustrade and looked over. He turned and parked his butt against it. "I am inviting you to join the most exclusive club in history, Pia. We have been around for almost seven hundred years. It is not an invitation often extended to the young. Several members are concerned you might be filled with unrealistic ideals of income equality, justice for all, that kind of thing. Some people, regardless of their station or birth or education, simply lack the drive to succeed. This organization is exclusively for the driven. People like you. People who can win Olympic gold and run multi-billion-dollar companies. Are you certain you want to hear about it?"

"What's the matter?" Pia laughed. "If you tell me you'll have to kill me?"

He answered with a cold, humorless gaze.

Pia turned away, put her hands on the stone wall, and looked at the deep blue water below. White foam faded from the rocky shore. To her left, two men stood on a path, tensed and waiting for something. The next wave swelled into the small cove and crashed against the stone. The water fell to earth, and brilliant white foam covered the rocks again before receding into the sea. Just then, the two men sprang from their path, hopping quickly from slippery rock to slick perch until they reached a point almost directly below her. They tugged at something stuck in a crevasse until they freed it. Beyond them, the swell rose again, preparing to crash down on the men with unimaginable force. She wanted to warn them but knew the surf would drown her words. The men retrieved their prize and dragged it back across the stones.

A human body.

Shredded pants and shirt, it was a man's lifeless form, missing half a leg and an entire arm. The workers dragged it behind them as they landed on dry ground. A split second later, the wave exploded around them. They took the torso several yards to a different, lower cliff and hurled it into the sea.

She suppressed her shock.

She faced Yeschenko, fighting rising nausea. "That's why I came all this way—to hear more.”

He had his back to the view the whole time. But it was his island, and they were his people.

He gave her a tight smile.

She turned away again, fearing she might throw up. “Could I get a glass of water?”

“Certainly,” he said. “Would you prefer something a little stronger? I have your favorite tequila, Dos Lunas Grand Reserve. Or, perhaps a glass of champagne?”

“How thoughtful. Dos Lunas would be great.”

Willy-Mac’s warning echoed in her mind. She never considered a fate like this. Fists, guns, and knives she’d anticipated. She was trained and capable of defending herself. Lies and obfuscations were expected. But throwing people off a cliff? She felt as if a hawk were trying to claw its way out of her stomach.

A long inhale through her nose helped her compose herself.

“Membership has many benefits.” Yeschenko snapped his fingers. “But one thing is our most precious asset: our obscurity. We are not interested in people coming to hear our story, pinch the oranges like an Arab trader in the market, then turn up their noses. We are very serious people who have no patience for those who are not. Is your interest serious?”

The image of the body being retrieved from the cliff clouded Pia’s mind.

A man walked briskly toward them carrying a silver tray. One shot glass filled with amber tequila, a bottle of Kona Nigari water, and a flute of champagne. Another man followed with a chiller filled with ice and a champagne bottle. The first man offered up the tray.

She took her glass, and Yeschenko took his.

“I’m quite serious.” She toasted. “Naturally, I need to understand what membership entails.”

He clinked, and they sipped.

“There are a few rules. We have no leaks. No member can talk about the organization or allow information about it escape her control.” He waited for her to respond. She gave a weak nod. He continued. “A member can make a reasonable request for help of any other member. These requests cannot be refused. Any disputes are settled by a tribunal of which I am the leader. While some requests, common in some cultures, can be upsetting in others, nonetheless all requests must be honored. Are you the reliable sort, even when you find the actions required to be distasteful?"

Pia's stomach squeezed hard inside her. She fought off convulsions with another sip. "What kind of actions are you talking about, Mikhail?"

He shrugged and gestured to the table. They strolled casually and took their seats. "Sometimes they are simply to contact a government official. Other times more specific, such as feting a dignitary or entertaining a friend with a specific goal in mind."

"And what of the culturally upsetting requests?"

He snapped; the waiter appeared. "Bernardo, we are ready for the lobster now."

A light breeze crossed her face with the scent of the sea. She thought of the body in the surf.

"The death penalty is banned in some countries and not in others. Yours, for example, is the only industrialized nation to allow it. Russia banned it in 1996." Yeschenko refilled his champagne. "Your employees have executed several people in the course of their work. You have testified before Congress about how deserving were the victims of your organization." He leaned forward across the table with a hard scowl on his face. "A reasonable member might conclude that Sabel Security is the right group to ask for certain favors."

The image of Viktor Popov's body in its death throes beneath her smoking gun popped into her head. It was replaced by the image of Yeschenko's men tossing a carcass into the sea. One of them, Yeschenko or Pia, was mad and the other a righteous avenger—depending on the perspective.

"Sabel Security is not an association of assassins. However, given the right details, and a preponderance of evidence, there could—"

"As you well know, there are times for legal proceedings, and there are times of great urgency. No one would call upon you for legal advice. When a request is made, it is not debated."

His cold eyes betrayed an evil she'd only seen in Roche and Popov. Her instincts told her to flee immediately. Shoot Yeschenko, steal a car and make a run for the airport. His jet would refuse service. Maybe time a jump into the sea, to land between waves like the cliff divers in Acapulco. Which would involve swimming two hundred miles to the nearest island. Fantasy. She would have to think harder to get out of this. In the meantime, he waited for her answer.

She controlled her breathing so her abject fear wouldn't quake her voice. "Do you pre-approve requests, Mikhail?"

"Everything goes through me."

"Can I count on you to reject the arbitrary or trivial?" she asked.

"Naturally."

"My father trusted you in several dealings. I don't see any reason I should hesitate."

The staff reappeared with lobster *rossejat*, a Catalan dish of toasted pasta, aioli, and lobster. She downed the rest of her añejo in a gulp and picked up her fork. Before she could take her first bite, another glass of tequila landed in front of her, along with a champagne flute. Yeschenko held up the bottle. She shook off his offer and drank water instead. She needed a clear head.

"And what is the purpose of your group?" she asked.

"Sabel Satellites is bound by your government to keep your proprietary technology for the government's exclusive use. Yet, Chuck Roche humiliates you and ridicules you. You tried to offer your company's services on the open market last year, and he quashed that with 'national security' concerns. So many nations need Sabel Satellite and your other services. Strong, profitable nations like Belarus, Iran, Venezuela, Korea…"

He kept talking while her thoughts overpowered her. His vise squeezed and squeezed until she could not breathe. With such bold partners, he must have some form of leverage over her or her company. Best to get it out in the open.

"Excuse me for interrupting. You make a strong case. Tell me, was my father involved in your group?"

"He was never invited." Yeschenko smiled. "He lacked your drive to succeed."

"I assume you have enforcement methods for members who break the rules." She gripped the tequila. "If I recall, you used Roche Security last year, but he disbanded that division after his people were charged with attempted murder—mine."

Without a hint of surprise, he shrugged. "We are not without resources. Allow me to introduce my new head of security, Hugo Bocognano."

A short, slender man strode out. Pia immediately recognized his cold, dispassionate eyes and small, hard mouth. Not so long ago, from the safety of distance, assisted by a good pair of night vision binoculars, Pia had watched Hugo kill a man. He extended a hand. After a second of hesitation, she shook it. He didn't speak.

"Normally, Hugo is most efficient. Unfortunately, it appears his most recent efforts have been unsuccessful against Jacob Stearne." Yeschenko looked at his man. "It is a rare thing when he can't handle something as simple as eliminating an unreliable witness. But we find ourselves outmatched by this—what did you call him—legendary veteran. We need someone with vast resources to hunt him down. This is our request of you, Pia."

"What has he done?"

"It is not open to debate. A request has been made." Yeschenko's eyes shrank, cold and narrow. "Since you are new, I'll indulge you this once. He stole an envelope from me."

She watched Yeschenko carefully, then assessed Hugo while her heart rate rose to buzz like a hummingbird's. Was he playing her? Did he really not know Jacob Stearne? Neither of them gave a hint of recognition. No doubt a ploy before they threw her body into the roiling foam. She longed for a pair of wings to carry her off the island.

"If Hugo failed—" Pia looked into the slight man's dark eyes "—we would have little expectation of success. The best we can do is try. I trust we can count on Hugo as our advisor?"

Hugo gave a nod. He walked away.

"It is settled then." Yeschenko raised his glass. "You will join RULE."

She glanced at the balustrade and the ocean beyond. Thoughts exploded in her head. Why hadn't she trusted Willy-Mac when he'd been right about everything? Because half the time she wanted to keep him safe. The other half, she had given in to paranoia. Now she was in danger, just as he'd predicted. And utterly alone. How could she get off Corvo alive? Where was her guardian angel? Could she squirm out of it all later? If Yeschenko was turning to Sabel Security for muscle, could her people keep her safe? For how long?

"There are a few unanswered questions," she heard herself say over the noise inside her head. "If RULE is so powerful, why are you under so many sanctions?"

"Ah. Sanctions," Yeschenko laughed. "My favorite topic. I have never been tried in court, yet many of my bank accounts are frozen, my assets locked away, my travel restricted. Rest assured, I am not the kind to stand still for such slights. There are efforts underway to rectify that problem. I expect to have that cleared up soon."

"You're laundering money?"

"You call it laundering, I call it international trade." He smiled. "Your father was quite helpful at times. His death was a terrible loss to the world."

"Is that what you were doing in that little town on the coast of France, whatwasitcalled?"

"Antibes. No. That was a different matter. Related but different."

"Hunter levied those sanctions." She sipped her tequila. "Which you are appealing to Roche. Which means Roche must be a member of RULE."

He gave her a tight, pained smile. "Not for long. He has broken the rules. The membership is unanimous in our displeasure."

"But you can't enforce the rules against the most powerful man in the world. You must have a plan." She watched him, waiting for him to speak. He didn't. "And that's why you came to me. You know I hate him enough to topple him."

Yeschenko tilted his head in affirmation. "Many people have told me you are smart. They are wrong. You are brilliant."

"What happens if I refuse to join?"

"You go home and will never think of us again."

His gaze gave away his unspoken words. Only a dead woman would never think of him again.

"Has anyone said no?" she asked.

"RULE formed during the Renaissance. The wealthy who chose to survive the anarchy of city-states banded together when governments, churches, and courts refused to do what was necessary. If you think about the wealthiest people in the world going back a few centuries, a significant number were members. From the Medici to the Forbes List. With exclusivity on that level, we never resort to inviting stupid people. On the rare occasion when a mistake is made, an amicable withdrawal is arranged." He sipped his champagne. "One memorable case comes to mind; the scion of an oil baron declined our offer in 1961. He went on his merry way only to fall afoul of cannibals in New Guinea. Most unfortunate."

The disappearance of Michael Rockefeller? Pia shook it off. No time to look weak. She softened, opening her eyes wide and tried to look vulnerable. "I've no one to guide my decisions these days, Mikhail. Can I trust you?"

"Absolutely."

"Will you be my mentor in RULE?"

"I'm honored you would ask, Pia." He canted his head and raised his brows. "It would be my pleasure."

They toasted to a long partnership and finished lunch. When he'd given her all the details about RULE, she took her leave.

He escorted her to the front door, gave her a kiss on the cheek. "Oh, by the way, Veronica Hunter wishes to speak to you. She told me she wants to apologize to you, ask your forgiveness. She has decided to unburden her soul. Perhaps she can help you in the future."

"I thought you two were mortal enemies. You've been in touch?"

"Never make enemies, Pia." He shook a finger at her. "As fate would have it, you always wind up needing help from the people you hate the most. Would you like me to arrange a meeting?"

Pia considered what would motivate Hunter to suddenly atone for her sins. There were a few possibilities. One had floated in the back of her mind for a long time. None were clear. She had too many reasons to distrust the former president.

"Tell her a public announcement is her best first step." She climbed aboard the SUV and waved good-bye. The bulletproof doors closed, and she was encased.

When the truck turned in the circle and left through the main gate, she broke down, gasping for air. "Oh, my god. What have I done?"

CHAPTER 30

CHUCK ROCHE CALLED TO A Secret Service agent on the country club's terrace on Florida's Atlantic coast, "What the hell is taking so long?"

"General Sinclair is holding the man for a bug check, sir."

It was a shame such a brilliant leader like President Roche had to suffer bureaucrats. Especially on a warm, breezy evening.

Roche pushed the agent. "Bring him here at once. That's an order."

The agent disappeared double-time. A minute later, he returned with two men in expensive suits: National Security Advisor, Neville Sinclair and Canadian businessman Antoine Babineau. Sinclair wore one of those smug expressions their kind puts on when they think they're so smart. The only reason Sinclair got the job was due to the president's first pick pleading guilty to a felony.

Sinclair pointed to Babineau. "You can't have this man in here. He's a Russian agent."

"Speak to me like that again, and you're done, you hear me, Sinclair? I'm the President of the United States of America, and you're not. I'm the one who gets to say who is a Russian agent and who is a valuable informant. Now get out of here before I tweet about all your mistresses."

"I don't have any—"

"If I tweet you've got them, you'll never prove otherwise. Now get out of here, Naughty Neville. You should be ashamed of yourself."

Sinclair flushed as if his rank and decades of service should have earned some level of respect. Generals think everyone should bow and scrape when the truth is, they're nothing more than welfare queens on the public's dime. They claim they're risking their lives when everyone knows it's all automated these days.

Sinclair shook his head and left like a beaten dog. Which was better than he deserved.

"Sorry to hear about your Vice President leaving." Yuri Belenov surveyed his surroundings like he owned the place. He had an arrogant smirk, too. Roche would bring him down a notch.

"Hey, boy," Roche waved at an African-American waiter. "Bring us some drinks, will ya? I'll have lime and soda. What about you, Yuri?"

"It's Antoine, Antoine Babineau." Belenov scowled. "Nothing, thank you."

Roche motioned to a table partitioned from the rest of the diners by three small palms in mobile planters. Belenov hesitated he checked out all four agents stationed around the table's perimeter. Then he took a seat.

"Your first mistake was coming here." Roche grinned. "Hunter's immunity papers are meaningless."

Belenov pouted with a look that was a shade too sassy for Roche.

"Why would I need immunity?" Belenov asked.

"Cause you killed a whole bunch of people on Flight 1028."

"This is the second time I've had that accusation thrown at me. What of the Puerto Ricans you threw in jail? Are you the kind of president who would let innocent men waste away while you dine with someone you believe to be responsible?"

"Cut the crap. You and I both know why you're here. We need—"

"What evidence do you have against me, Mr. President?"

"Don't fuck with me, Belenov." Roche pointed a finger at the arrogant young Russian. "We have film of you strangling Luis Perez last night. We've got loads more evidence of you—"

Belenov held his wrists together and pushed them to Roche. "If that were true, you should arrest me right now."

Roche didn't like the way his negotiations were headed. "Listen to me, you criminal—"

"No, you listen to me." Belenov's face turned red, his words hissed through his teeth. "I know you and Viktor Popov conspired to bring down Flight 1028. You did it indirectly—through intermediaries like David Watson—so no one could ever tie you to Popov. Yet you and your girlfriend keep throwing it in my face as if I needed the pardon you offered. If you can't take responsibility and admit you were in it with Popov, I'm leaving. If you want to charge me with something, go ahead. I dare you."

The man's insolence was unbelievable. But Roche needed the guy. "OK, fine. You can forget about Flight 1028. Won't mention it again."

"That is not what I said." Belenov stared like a killer. "Admit to me, here and now, that you conspired with SVR Director Popov and then we can discuss anything you'd like."

Roche felt like he was back in that sweltering room with the Asian dictator, giving up everything and getting nothing in return. Just like that time with China's president, now that he thought about it. And the German chancellor. And … damn. Why did everyone keep demanding he do things before they would negotiate with him? The world was full of these scumbags. It didn't matter. He'd have Belenov droned as soon as the operation was over. All he needed was to make this deal.

"Fine." Roche leaned in close. "Popov and I go back twenty years. Went. He's dead now. We did work out a deal during the election. He made suggestions on how I should attack Hunter during the campaign— and then things happened that fit into those talking points. I had no idea he was going to shoot down an airplane full of Americans. But hey, you know, it worked out fine."

Belenov fiddled with his cufflink and pried it open. Inside were small electronic pieces. He spread them on the linen tablecloth. "Your club was kind enough to give me internet access for only $9.95 per day. Everything you said has been recorded in the cloud. By now, my associates have moved copies of the recording to ten different secure, encrypted sites."

He looked at Roche, tilted his head to one side, gave a smug smile, then bent forward with a mean scowl, almost touching noses. "Twelve pardons land in my email box in the morning."

Roche blinked twice. Civilization had hit rock bottom. No one could be trusted for even a minute. These days, when you try to blackmail a lowlife, he turns the tables on you. Definitely a candidate for droning. After.

Roche considered his options. He could have the guy thrown out. Call Sinclair back and let him take the turncoat to Guantanamo. The base where presidents stash their enemies until they die of old age. Could Belenov release the recording remotely? Maybe it was a bluff. No. The CIA claimed his group SHaRC was advanced. Damn, this negotiation was going the same way it did with the Russian Ambassador. Everybody has those little recording devices up their sleeves. But Belenov was a pissant compared to his other problems. And he needed Belenov to get rid of those problems.

"Sure." Roche tried to smile at the renegade. "I still need certain things done."

"Now that I'm blackmailing you," Belenov nodded with condescending eyes, "instead of the other way around, I don't need you at all. If you want my help on a project, tell me your incentive plan. I'm listening."

"You son of a bitch." Roche's fingers tightened around his empty glass. "What do you want?"

"Your endorsement to be the new head of RULE."

"Yeschenko won't allow that."

"I can control Yeschenko."

A whole train full of thoughts ran through his head at high speed. One stuck. He looked up at the maître d' and snapped his fingers. "Where's that boy at? I asked for a lime and soda two hours ago."

"He quit, sir." The man tightened his lips. "We've discussed your language before. We cannot keep staff if you insist—"

"Just get me a fucking lime and soda." The obsequious bastards that ran the place drove him crazy with all their political correctness. Roche looked at Belenov. "What do you want, vodka?"

"Nothing, thank you," Belenov said.

The maître d' disappeared.

Belenov said, "I also need your SEC benched where certain trades are concerned."

"Wait a second." Roche held up his hands. "I can't control—"

"Find a way. When you do, I have a present for you. You've been promising to produce Sergeant Tarasov, the man who watched Pia Sabel fire nine bullets into your old friend, Comrade Popov. But he won't help you. I can get him to testify against Sabel."

Now things were clicking. Roche liked the sound of that. If he put his nephew in charge of the SEC, the young man would derail everything. "Yuri, I think this is the beginning of a beautiful friendship."

Belenov slid a card across the tablecloth. "My contact information on Signal—a secure messaging system. Text me anytime with exactly who you want chopped up in the social media blender and consider it done."

Belenov got up without another word and left.

Roche watched the Russian leave. He hated people who didn't have any manners. People just come and go without even asking permission. In the old days, when arriving or leaving a royal presence, people would take a knee. It was a sign of respect. They should do as much for POTUS. He didn't need them to prostrate themselves, just show reverence, fealty, and obedience.

CHAPTER 31

It was still dark when the Uber dropped us in front of Sylvia's apartment. We had a four-hour head start on the bad guys because jets are faster than boats. Sylvia was just waking up. She'd never know she'd ridden on Ms. Sabel's jet, so, one problem handled. Next up: finding out who was trying to kill her, what happened in NOLA, why she was acting so weird, and why she texted people about ditching me.

Another text from Virginia Goillot came in, "Hunter to become VP."

Which was interesting but useless information to me. I still couldn't recall any Virginias in my past. I texted Bianca to trace it. All she found was an unassigned phone in the Treasury Department. I began to think "Virginia" was one of those news feeds you can't get rid of.

We took the elevator because Sylvia was still too groggy to talk or walk much. I barreled into the apartment while she wandered along behind me. There was a new suitcase in the foyer and a lump under the covers. Expecting a competitor for Sylvia's favors, I nudged the lump. "Hey, who are you?"

Fiftyish-lady from the portrait in the living room turned over. She pulled an eye mask up and squinted at me. The portrait was from twenty years ago or had been Photoshopped by a pro. She immediately started screaming something in French and threw her bedside lamp at me.

"Whoa! I'm with Sylvia." I put my palms out and batted down the next three things she tossed my way. "Aren't you Sylvia's landlord?"

She stopped yelling and looked over my shoulder. "Sylvia?"

"Hi, um," Sylvia stammered, "I thought you were coming back tomorrow."

The lady picked up a book and hurled it at Sylvia. "It is not a

Gauguin! You thief, *vous fraude! Salope! Putain!"*

I fired a dart into her shoulder. She slumped like a dead woman. I started to explain the darts to Sylvia, but she waved me off. She'd heard about them.

That made me think I should be asking some questions. "I don't know much French, but I got the distinct impression she doesn't like you, and the painting is a fake. Want to tell me what's going on here?"

"No." Sylvia dug in the closet for her old outfit.

I grabbed her arm and pulled her around to face me.

"Is this the part where you slap me around?" She closed her eyes and braced for a punch.

"I rescued you. Don't I deserve an explanation?"

She opened one eye cautiously. "We have to go. Madame Huppert will wake up and have us arrested."

She bunched her things under her arm and headed for the front door.

Mercury leaned against the bedroom door. *Dude, your best play is to let her go. Start looking for Pia-Caesar-Sabel. Obviously, Grampa Sabel's union card thing was before Caesar tried to kill her—a death sentence she deserves, by the way.*

I said, *She has answers to what went down in Tremé. I think that's why Ms. Sabel went into hiding.*

Mercury moved out of the way. *You get until lunchtime, then your carriage turns back into a pumpkin, dawg.*

The guys on Corsica would be coming for us. Which meant we had to keep out of sight for a while. I didn't know much about the town. But I would think of something. Eventually.

I cornered my girl in the elevator. "Let's work backward. Start with who is Madame Huppert?"

She backed against the wall and glared at me. "Actress from the seventies. If you don't follow French cinema, you've never heard of her."

"And why does she think *vous fraude*?

"*Vous êtes une fraude."* Sylvia crossed her arms and stared at me.

Like this was the time for a French grammar lesson. I gave her my soldier stare. The stare a warrior gives when he's deciding whether putting the bullet through your left or right eyeball would minimize collateral damage.

She sighed. "Some really bad guys gave me a job, and I did it. But it got screwed up, and they were not pleased. To stay alive, they made me sell some fake art to my friends in the TV and movie business. Madame Huppert lives in Paris but comes here once a month or so. I thought I'd camp there while she was away." She turned her face to the wall.

The elevator opened on the ground floor. We stepped out, ambling to nowhere in particular.

"Who gave you the job?" I asked. "Cyril?"

Her eyes darted to me with surprise, then away again. "I needed the money. I was barely getting by before and when that thing happened in Barcelona … I lost my job. I was desperate, OK?"

"Why did Ms. Sabel try to kill you?"

"You remember that?"

"I read your—"

A car pulled up out front as we crossed the lobby. Sylvia looked at the guy getting out like he was Freddy Krueger jumping off the screen. She started backing up. I took her hand and held her firm. The doors had glare on the street side; he couldn't see us. I pulled my Glock and held it at my side. He casually entered his code on the pad outside and let himself in.

"You must be Cyril," I said.

He glanced at me, then my gun, then Sylvia. He bared his teeth and reached for a weapon. He was a split second too late. My dart caught his neck. He fell face-first. His head hit the floor like a dropped melon.

Sylvia tugged out of my hand and ran for the back door. I followed her, my duffel bag full of fashions, weapons, and armor slung over my shoulder. We exited into a tight lane and ran. We jogged left and right through streets broad and narrow. Five blocks later, we stopped to listen for our pursuers.

"Just out of curiosity," I asked, "was that your brother?"

"Worse. His boss. The one I was supposed to report to this morning. I was going to tell him that losing the envelope wasn't my fault. It would've gone well. But you rescued me. And that makes me look bad.

Really bad. Now you shot him, or whatever you call those things. And that makes me look even worse."

"Would you rather I kill them?"

"If you knew these guys, you wouldn't have to ask."

What happened to Sylvia, Goddess of Peace and Love? Mercury scared the daylights out of me when he whispered in my ear. *Easy for her to talk about killing people, homie. She doesn't have a former president threatening to reinvestigate all her kills. A fresh trail of dead gangsters might be hard to explain. Besides, that cop told you Monaco isn't the OK Corral.*

I said, *Why do you think I'm using darts? Where can we go?*

Mercury said, *Ask Pierre.*

I said, *The god with a good idea for a change.*

Still panting from the run and the adrenaline rush, I called the Casino and asked for my personal gambling advisor. "Pierre, this is Jacob Stearne. I need your advice on—"

"So good to hear from you, monsieur. We need instructions regarding your magnificent winnings. Would you like to come in and try the wheel again?"

"My what?"

"You placed a bet on fifteen, it paid handsomely. We hope you will return soon to continue—"

"Good idea, my man. Good idea. I'll be there after lunch. But first, I need to freshen up. Could you recommend a good hotel? Preferably one with a lot of security?"

"Oui. That would be le Hôtel Hermitage. Shall I book a suite for you? When would you like to arrive?"

"Yes and immediately," I said. "Say, could you arrange a limo as well? Um, armored ... would be good."

"Oui, monsieur, in four minutes."

When I clicked off, I realized I could get used to the billionaire lifestyle. I mean, sure, Janet at the Farm-n-Feed gives you a warm, friendly smile—but she never sent a bulletproof limo for me.

Sylvia and I snuck behind a dumpster and waited for our driver. The Corsicans drove by twice before a stretch Maybach showed up. It took us

to a hotel overlooking the big harbor from behind a high wall with a steel gate.

We dropped our stuff on a bigger-than-king-sized bed and stared out the window for a full minute. The famous harbor was filled with yachts almost as big as Ms. Sabel's. The Mediterranean lay below us like a blue carpet.

After the amazement passed, I said, "OK, I need the whole story this time."

"I don't know what it is about you. It's like I've known you for a thousand years." She turned away from me and smoothed the duvet cover. "Maybe we could relax a little—"

I held her arms and yanked her up to my nose. "Talk."

She ran her palm down my chest. "Just a quick—"

"No." That was the first time in my life I turned down sex. I surprised myself as much as Sylvia.

She dropped the coquettish looks and sighed again. "There's so much that's happened. I don't know where—"

"Start with the first time we saw each other after New Year's Eve and keep talking until you get to this room."

I let her go.

She hugged herself, took a deep breath, and paced the room. "I was broke, so I borrowed money from Cyril to meet you in New Orleans. As interest on the loan, he wanted a favor—take an envelope full of memory cards to a guy in NOLA. Seemed easy enough. But then, Hugo popped out of the woodwork—"

"Who's Hugo?"

"Muscle for Mikhail Yeschenko, the Russian—"

"I know Yeschenko." I rolled my hand. "What did Hugo want?"

"The envelope. He killed the guy I was supposed to meet. Just shot him dead. Walked up and pulled the—"

"But he spared you?"

"He was going to kill me next, but you and Pia showed up, and everything went crazy."

"How did we know what was going down?" I asked.

"I guess you followed me." She stared at me blankly. "You don't remember any of this?"

A wave of sympathy overcame her. She slipped her arms around me and hugged me. My heartbeat rose, but it was concentrated somewhere below my belt. With herculean effort, I pushed her out half an arm's length. I like foreplay, but I needed answers. I said, "Did Ms. Sabel come with us on our New Orleans date?"

"You got a phone call." She crossed her arms.

The phone call that filled me with dread. It came out of the memory fog. Walking through Jackson Square with Sylvia, half lit and laughing about nothing when my phone rang. I dreaded it because I knew what Ms. Sabel wanted. And I knew she would pull me away from Sylvia. So, I tried to lie to her. Which never worked.

"Um." Sylvia had a sour look. "You smell like filthy sea water. I can't stand being this close to you."

She was right about that. I hadn't had time to change since my dip in a Corsican marina. I smelled so bad I couldn't stand being that close to me. "Want to soap up my back?"

She thought it over. "After you get clean."

I stripped down and went into the bathroom. Apparently, Monégasques consider showers passé. It's all about big tubs with handheld showerheads these days. I know thirty-seven things you can do with a handheld nozzle and none involve soap. I gave her a look.

She said, "After."

She walked out to the living room.

I lathered and soaped and was in the middle of rinsing when Mercury walked in holding hands with one spectacular beauty in a nearly-transparent toga. One breast bounced outside the material. Her smile made parts of me want to stand up and pulsate.

Mercury said, *Allow me to present the one true goddess of love, desire, sex, beauty, and prosperity—Venus!*

I eloquently said, *Uh.*

Venus sat on the edge of the tub and splashed the water playfully. *Is there enough room in there for both of us? Mercury carried me through storm clouds, and you know how dirty those make you feel. Can I trust you to soap my back?*

When she bent forward, her other breast almost fell out. I tried—I really tried—but totally failed to maintain eye contact.

Then something struck me as odd.

Storm clouds. Why would there be storm clouds?

Then something else freaked me out. Aside from having an entirely delusional conversation with a pair of gods who probably don't exist. I listened and heard nothing. Absolute silence.

I jumped up quickly and snatched a towel.

Venus looked me over and pretended to shield her eyes with a hand. *Oh my. I see why she calls you Big Boy.*

I said, *OK, fun's over. I know what you're trying to do. Where did Sylvia go?*

Mercury held up his hands. *Easy there, my brutha. You don't get this kind of attention from Aphrodite. Chill with us for a couple hours. Let Sylvia do what Sylvia's gonna do. And let Venus do—*

CHAPTER 32

YESCHENKO'S JET DROPPED PIA IN London where she went sightseeing while trembling from head to toe. What had she gotten herself into? How long a reach did they have? How would she get out of it? Her head spun in a hundred directions at once. She could hardly think for all the noise in her brain. From St. James's Palace to Trafalgar Square, she watched the people around her.

As she suspected, shadowy men followed her. Three of them in shifts. She lost the one with the tweed cap when she stopped for lunch at the Gong Bar on the 52nd floor of The Shard. The gray-beard disappeared at Westminster Abbey. She pretended she was waiting for someone and let many people in line, including her stalker, pass in front of her. As soon as her shadow committed to the inside, she called an Uber.

Then she made a mistake. The third man didn't make it onto the Eurostar with her, but her destination was too predictable. As she feared, a fourth man waited in Paris.

At Charles De Gaulle, she booked three separate flights. She waited ten feet from the security entrance. When a large tour group approached, she jumped in front of them and took the flight to Lyon. From there, she appeared to be alone on the train to Geneva. By the time she arrived long after midnight, she was exhausted from paranoia. At least it was reality-based paranoia this time. She took an Airbnb that had a view of the Jet d'Eau.

She never bothered to turn the lights on. Just tossed her purse on the bedside table and fell on top of the sheets. A lifelong insomniac, she was more exhausted than ever before.

In the dark stillness of the small apartment, a million conflicting thoughts crowded her mind. Forced to join RULE. A dead body disposed of like so much trash. Willy-Mac's warning not to enter the lion's den. Yeschenko said Roche was out of favor with RULE. What the hell was RULE? How long would it take Yeschenko to learn Jacob worked for her? What happened then? Did she remember this part correctly: Hunter wanted to apologize? What was Hunter's angle?

Maybe the Apocalypse was at hand.

She rolled over and squished the pillow under her head.

She had to trust Willy-Mac now. Or could she? Willy-Mac might well be on Roche's team. She tugged at her hair. Finally, she slept for an hour.

He sat on the edge of the bed. He'd often done that in her childhood when she woke up screaming every night. He would rush in and read Shel Silverstein until she laughed.

He brushed her hair out of her eyes. "Has Willy-Mac given you any bad advice?"

"Did you get into some illegal business with Mikhail Yeschenko?"

"Good advice is just what it seems. Distrust comes from guilt."

"Am I going to die?" she asked.

"Yes."

"I don't mean 'ever.' I mean, violently and soon. Because I'm not going to kill Jacob."

"It's a test." He stood and looked out the window. "Mikhail knows damn well how important Jacob is to you."

Pia's breathing picked up fast and shallow. Cold sweat. Of course Yeschenko knew Jacob. "How do I get out of it?"

"Roche and Yeschenko are at each other's throats. Focus on Roche."

"Yeschenko's going to have me killed, isn't he?" She swung her feet around and jumped up. "Answer me. Have I gone too far? Am I going to die this time?"

"Everyone dies. No one knows when. Do your best until then." His calm gaze stayed with her. "It's a deadly game of wits now, Pia. You're smarter than they are. Use your resources. Trust Willy-Mac."

"I can't. I can't. I can't. Everyone who helps me gets killed." Her fists pounded the mattress. Sunlight stabbed at her eyes. Her legs were tangled in the sheets.

No Dad. Empty rooms. Silence.

She dressed, grabbed her bag, and fled down the stairs. She walked the city, making sure she wasn't followed before going to the airport. The first flight out got her to Nice. An Uber took her back to the Texas BBQ.

The café was empty except for Guenièvre. The teenager reported that Willy-Mac and Vivian had gone to Elisa's school for the talent show and would return shortly. Pia told her to have Willy-Mac meet her at the Musée Picasso. No texts, no calls.

He arrived half an hour later. After one look at Pia, he took her hands in his. "You all right?"

"I didn't take your advice. Now I'm crying out for help." In the quiet sculpture courtyard, she told him the story of the body on the rocks, joining RULE, the assignment to kill her most trusted friend, the rift between a thug-oligarch and the President of the United States of America, and the olive branch from Hunter. She chewed on her knuckle. "I need your help. I'll listen this time. Please tell me—what do I do now?"

"Grow up." He walked across the stone to the wall and looked out over the blue Mediterranean.

She joined him but turned her back to the sea. She scanned the seventeenth-century stronghold of the Grimaldi family and short-term studio for the famous artist. A few tourists meandered around them. No one looked suspicious.

"I deserved that." She blew out a breath. "But now what do I do?"

"Go to the police."

"And tell them what?"

He thought about it for a long time.

"You're right. Damn it." It was Willy-Mac's turn to sigh. "All this and we've got nothing. And on top of that, Yeschenko owns you."

"I'm sorry. I should've listened to you. I'm listening now." Pia picked at her fingers. "What are they doing at DeLanos?"

"You've figured out your five questions were the wrong ones?"

"For Deng, Yeschenko, the others, it's not about art at all. It's some kind of blackmail, right? No. Initiation into a club or something? Both?

Yeschenko runs RULE. Roche is taking over."

"Think about street gangs," he said. "You want in, they jump you in. They make you commit a crime. They witness it so they can turn you in if you piss them off. Blackmail or insurance, depending on your perspective." He crossed his arms, turned his back to the sea and watched the crowd with her. "Take that concept up the socio-economic spectrum to a hundred thousand feet, and you have what Roche is doing at DeLano's."

Pia puzzled it out in her head. "The chair, the tripod, the photographer's background. They're detailing their own criminal operations for Roche?"

"On video. Yeah, that would be my guess. Voluntary confessions are usable in court or deliverable to the local dictator. You've stuck your hand into a bag of rattlesnakes."

"Roche is doing this to make sure he has dirt on them." Pia began to sense the scope of the arrangement. "If they don't do it, he closes their money laundering operation. If they cause trouble later, he releases a video of them confessing to much more. He always says, 'You hit me—I hit back twice as hard.' Even if Yeschenko was given immunity in exchange for testimony against Roche, he's tainted as a witness. That's why the rift between Roche and Yeschenko."

"Roche has been doing their laundry for decades." Willy-Mac caught her gaze. "He does it with real estate. Everyone thinks he's in the oil refinery business, but that's just a distraction. He's been selling condos and mansions to shell corporations owned by oligarchs and despots around the world. He flips them from one despot to the next, pocketing a big profit each time. My team ran across him and turned it over to the FBI ten years ago. They convicted an associate. Never got Roche because he never writes, never texts, never makes calls. He has people who do it for him."

"What about Roche lifting and levying taxes, tariffs, sanctions, all that?"

"No tyrant started out a despot. It takes time to learn the ropes, figure out what you can get away with. Roche began as a businessman stiffing debtors and forcing suppliers into bankruptcy. He was just a jerk. But then he stepped up to international corruption and scaled it to billions. He ran for president on a lark, and now that he's in, he's beginning to understand how his powers can be used for global extortion. You thought last year was bad? He's just getting started. Ever hear of kleptocracy? He's going way beyond that. His plan for the future is global enslavement."

They stared off into space, each imagining Roche's frightening trajectory.

"Pia, I have to tell you something." Willy-Mac faced her. "I've known we needed to do something about Roche from the day he got elected. This could be huge. You're right about the cops though. If we go to them with this story, they'll blow us off as conspiracy theorists. We need to get our hands on something tangible. Our best shot is to grab something incriminating on DeLano and get him to flip."

"Why would he flip? Wouldn't his overlord have him killed?"

"DeLano's not as tough as he seems." Willy-Mac looked over the crowd once more. "Cyril, the guy who waited outside while DeLano tried to intimidate you, is his handler. They're in the forgeries business together. But DeLano wants to get away from Cyril. We give him an escape hatch, he'll let us take what we need."

She looked into the old man's soft brown eyes, saw the wisdom there, but saw something else—a telltale tremor in the iris. He was scared. "You mean we need to break into DeLano's and find one of the videos?"

"I like to do everything by the book. But this time, I don't see any other way."

"I do this alone." She gripped his arm. "You need to keep clean so you can go to the police. Tell them you caught me, found the video, and realized—"

"We don't need any subterfuge. If it is what I think it is, we just drop it off on the desk of any politician in France or Germany."

"Before we break in there, I have to ask you something." He gave her a solemn look. "I have to know you're reliable. Can you control your PTSD?"

"Wha—" She blinked several times.

"After witnessing you lose focus several times, I did a deep dive on your bio. You watched a man strangle your mother when you were four. You killed him with a knife. You've been tortured by rogue CIA agents, been kidnapped, involved in firefights that would scare a combat soldier, and saw your adopted father gunned down. That would give anyone PTSD. It's a credit to your character that you get up in the morning. I'm not judging you. I'm asking because our lives might depend on it. Can you control your PTSD?"

"You knew." A million excuses flew through her head. "You were talking me down. The soft voice, the calm manner."

He nodded.

"Yes, I can control it. I will control it. With your help." She squeezed his shoulder. "Something else is bothering you."

"You have Yeschenko after you." He leaned in. "At some point, he'll remember where he first saw you. He'll start his search here in Antibes."

CHAPTER 33

YESCHENKO DUCKED INTO HIS POOLSIDE cabana at the exclusive resort in Marrakech. He was surprised to find Veronica Hunter already there in a modest one-piece, reading a copy of *Death and Dark Money*. He eyed her without greeting and ordered orange juice. When the waitress left, he took a seat on the opposite lounge. "What have you done with Belenov?"

"The same question I was going to ask you." Veronica put her book down. "That is until one of my White House spies reported in."

Yeschenko waited, drummed his fingers, then ran out of patience. "And?"

"It seems your boy has endeared himself to the POTUS directly. You and I are no longer needed."

"We've been burned." Yeschenko nodded and applied sunscreen to his legs. Then he rubbed it on his arms and face and upper shoulders.

"I may be twenty years older than your usual harem girl, but I can apply sunscreen to your back if you'd like." She paused for a reply he didn't give. "Don't worry, I'll try to control my urges."

He laughed and tossed her the sunscreen. "I'll be sure to return the favor."

"Aziz already took care of it." She rolled the lotion softly over his shoulders. She pushed him over and turned the lotion into a full-scale massage. "How do you suggest we get Belenov back under control?"

"No need." He shrugged off her massage and sat up. "RULE has voted to overthrow Roche. It was the first unanimous vote since Napoleon had to be kicked out in 1814."

Hunter rose and returned to her lounge facing him. "What is this little cabal of yours?"

Yeschenko huffed at her slight. "Since the first city was built, there have been three power centers in civilization: church, state, and money. During the Renaissance, the church and state conspired to control the wealthy. In 1394, Giovanni Medici founded not just a bank, but a group of like-minded men who focused on promoting business over church or government. RULE cooperates using our individual resources and influence as a unified entity to keep commerce flowing."

Hunter picked up her drink. "How sweet. So many hyper-competitive egomaniacs cooperating like a church choir in song. Mercenaries, bribes, hand-picked judges, that kind of thing? Don't answer, I don't want specifics. What do you do to someone like Belenov?"

"First, make no mistake, he is not a member. He never will be. He's a hired hand. Uncultured, despite what he thinks, with few resources to offer. He will never be invited."

"He has considerable talent for social media and internet issues."

Yeschenko waved her off. "One of our members, a ranking Red Army general, has a thousand Belenovs at his fingertips. Had Popov come to me, we would've asked our Chinese friends before we involved Belenov's SHaRCs."

"Will this Red Army general help us unseat Belenov when the time is right?" Hunter asked.

Yeschenko did his best to hide his surprise. In an uncharacteristic slip-up, Hunter had shown him her full hand. Despite Belenov being outside her control, she wanted to delay killing him until he finished the job. There could be only one reason for that. "I've already spoken to him about fixing a different problem Belenov created."

"Oh?" She sipped her drink and laid back, looking out at the pool.

"Belenov is more astute than I had imagined. He ran off with a considerable part of my empire." Yeschenko marveled at how easily the politician made him give up his secrets. She must have sensed that he needed to confide in a peer. "The smaller, money-laundering pieces, but his treachery will be rewarded with extreme measures."

"That's fitting." She sipped her drink. "How do you plan to overthrow President Roche?"

Yeschenko might fall for some of her casual questions, but he would not go that far. He shook a finger at the naughty former president. "Ah, now, Veronica, you have asked a question for which you do not want to know the answer."

"Then you're going about it all wrong." She looked over at him and gave him a cunning smile. "Brute force starts wars. Traceable manipulations lead to indictments. You must be clever. Only the will of the people can oust him. And you must have his replacement hand-picked in advance. If you had moved last week, you would've had that Puritan lunatic in office. He would've made the Spanish Inquisition look like a parlor game. Those who didn't win the trifecta of white, American-born, Christian would've been racked for heresy."

"It doesn't matter now. He's gone. We will deal with whoever Roche chooses to fill the office."

Yeschenko pulled back a side curtain and snapped his fingers. An orderly ran to his side. He ordered two Dirty Bananas, and the orderly disappeared.

She reached across the space between them and touched his leg. "I will be the next VP."

Yeschenko looked at her and gauged her seriousness. She meant it. And she was not the kind to make empty statements.

"What you are thinking would be a complex plan." Yeschenko pulled the curtain to one side, letting in the sun. He scooted his lounge out of the shade and lay on it. He adjusted his sunglasses and stretched out to maximize his tan. "Too many things can go wrong in complex plans. RULE will stick to my strategy."

"If you kill him, he becomes a martyr. His mindless minions will rise up and crush your puppet."

"You expect me to believe Roche will pick you, a woman who has not endeared herself to him? And you can get him to resign? Then we would have to trust you. I trust no one. No. There are too many moving pieces. It would never work."

"Pia Sabel can make all those pieces fall into place."

He looked a question at her.

"America loves celebrities." Hunter grinned on one side of her mouth. "They elevate them only to tear them down. They consume the extramarital affairs of rappers and movie stars like candy. They won't read a basic economic plan or foreign policy position before they vote, but they'll pore over pictures of a singer's love child for hours."

"Pia Sabel has some kind of celebrity?"

"Very little. Which makes her perfect to lead the charge. Everyone knows who she is—that she's a gold medalist, that she singlehandedly willed her team to win on numerous occasions—but they don't care about women athletes enough to read about her drunken episode in Kazakhstan. She can speak from the altar of celebrity without any baggage. The people will listen to her."

Yeschenko closed his eyes and took a deep breath. Did Hunter know Pia was in his sphere, that the girl feared him, that she would do what he asked? It was too early in their relationship to reveal his connection. He had not yet completed the subjugation of the young athlete. Nonetheless, he could see the merit in Hunter's plan. It might work.

He said, "You add even more complexity to the scenario by manipulating Pia."

"Which is better, a simple plan that fails or an intricate—"

"It would take too long."

"All the more reason to start right away." Hunter pulled down her sunglasses. "Can you get in touch with her?"

He had imagined Pia was on a leash when he let her leave his island. Unfortunately, the young lady must have had street training from her stable of former CIA spies and military operatives. Yeschenko made a mental note to send Hugo to Antibes. His gangster could question DeLano about what Pia had been doing there and where she might've gone. While he was at it, Hugo could reclaim the incriminating videos of RULE members. It was long past time to start that war with Roche.

He turned to Veronica. "Have you considered a public act of contrition? She might be moved if you openly sought reconciliation."

"What a grand idea." Hunter nodded and pushed her sunglasses up. "It would serve to raise her celebrity in the public eye as well. I don't care what the police say about you, I like working with you, Mikhail."

The orderly arrived with their drinks. Hunter took them both and sat on the edge of Yeschenko's lounge next to his knee.

She handed him his glass and dipped her finger in hers. She trailed drops of the ice cream and rum drink down his inner thigh. He watched her as the odd sensations tingled nerve endings deep inside him. He didn't find Hunter appealing in any sexual way, yet the sensations she created made his heart beat faster. She wiped up her intentional spill by delicately dragging her fingernails up the inside of his leg. She stopped at a specific spot and stood. He found himself speechless, his breath taken away as much by her boldness as the sensation. He hoped his hardening was not evident.

He stared at her as Hunter chugged her drink and set the empty down next to him. She said, "Don't worry, Mikhail. I don't expect you to desire me or woo me or fall for me. At my age, the last thing a woman wants is stinky splooge squirted all over her. The only constant in civilization since Delilah seduced Samson has been that men pay attention when sex is imminent. Now it's time for you to pay attention. I've arranged for a couple of my most discrete submissives, Tatyana and Aziz, to take things from here."

She turned and picked up her purse and book. A blonde supermodel with green eyes stepped around the curtained entrance and waited for Hunter's order. A short hunk of an oiled bodybuilder stood behind her.

"Wait." Yeschenko jumped to his feet and grabbed Hunter's arm. "Why are you doing this?"

"To show you how much we are alike, Mikhail." She looked him over and tickled his left nipple with her fingernail. He tried not to react, but his goosebumps rose.

"You and I are different from the rest of them," she said. "Roche wants to be the bride at every wedding, the center of everyone's attention. He thinks that comes from screwing every model on the catwalk. You've had your fill of Ms. Universes and Mr. Universes. Sex with the most beautiful specimens humanity has to offer only gives one a fleeting sexual satisfaction. The buildup of an hour or so, the climax of a few minutes—is always followed by meaningless, empty hours. For you and me, it's not about sexuality or gender or beauty. For people like us, Mikhail, what gives us lasting satisfaction is power and control." She made a fist and shook it between them. "It's about domination and submission." She growled her next sentence. "They shall all bow down before us."

CHAPTER 34

I TOWELED TO DAMP AND slipped into half my clothes by the time I reached the elevator. Two women in burqas got on with me and watched me pull on a shirt and a pair of shoes. They giggled. On the street, my phone tracked Sylvia's movements through a maze of expensive shops and a hotel. Her path led me down a street and out to the *Place du Casino*, the park in front of Pierre's crib.

The map showed her at the Casino end of the park. I scanned the crowd and found Peter Hammond instead of Sylvia. He stood with his arms crossed and a scowl to melt steel. Beyond him, climbing the Casino's grand staircase, was my theoretical girlfriend. I started running.

Peter held up a hand. "You left me in Ajaccio. You said we would—"

I kept running. "Later."

"Cyril just drove through looking…" His voice trailed off in the distance behind me.

Pierre met me on the steps. "Would you like your winning in chips, monsieur? Perhaps another turn of the wheel—"

"Where is Sylvia?"

He shrugged and started to form the words, *I don't know*. I yanked his lapels and lifted him off his feet. His collar and tie bunched beneath his chin giving him a childlike appearance. He shrugged again. "I saw no one just now."

"I didn't say just now. I asked where she went. She ran right past you." I gave him my soldier stare.

He swallowed hard. "Perhaps the back through the opera house?"

I set him down and trotted past him.

"But, monsieur, your winnings?" Pierre asked.

A burly guy smacked my chest and said the French equivalent of, *My boss asked you a question.*

Mercury peeked around the guy's shoulders. *Now there's a moral dilemma, bro. If you spend your company's money gambling, do you get to keep the winnings? Or, since they wrote it off already, do you just keep it all?*

"Put it all back on the credit card." I pulled out of his grip and ran through the building.

Mercury ran alongside me. *You could've paid off your mortgage, dude. Even if you split it with the company. You should be taking your moral cues from the President of the United States—take everything while you can. Why are you even chasing this girl? Nothing good comes from Greek goddesses. Only heartache.*

Ignoring him, I chased her across pedestrian walkways and up boulevards and down switchback staircases. I'd spot her, then lose her in a market or hotel lobby and then consult the map. Whenever I got within striking distance, she made another duck down an alley, and I'd lose her. Her trail began leading me back uphill.

We were in a lesser neighborhood, where the retaining walls were cracked and flaking. I ran up a flight of stairs and across a pedestrian overpass and saw her on the road below me. I shouted at her. She looked up at me as if I were a monster and ran. The map didn't show a way to get down there, so I climbed over the rail and shimmied down a drainpipe. The last ten feet of it broke off the wall and crashed to the street. I landed on my back with the lead pipe on top of me. It knocked the wind out of me.

Mercury bent down. *She has a good reason for treating you like this, right, homes?*

I got to my feet, coughed a couple times, checked the map and took off running again.

Two more corners and I found her climbing a narrow stair between houses. She turned left at the top, stopped, looked back at me over her shoulder, and ran.

I took the steps two at a time and turned left.

I fell face-first on the sidewalk. A type of fishing net pulled tight around my body. My hands were immobilized at my side. The netting was made of super-strong nylon. A net designed specifically for catching men. Rough hands turned me over.

The zipping sound of the net being tightened reached my ears a split second before my feet reported pain. The net's drawstring had constricted around my ankles. My circulation had stopped.

Four men and a small van backed towards us. Two of the men seized the netting and hauled me to my feet. A third man held a collapsible baton that smacked into my breadbasket three times. I couldn't breathe. They leaned me back and tossed me into the minivan. My head smacked the back of the front seat.

Someone pushed Sylvia in next to me. Her eyes were wild with fear and anger.

I asked, "Cyril or Hugo?"

The baton smacked my thigh. The perpetrator shouted something in Corsican that I assumed was, *No talking*. Sylvia shook her head. The van pulled away, its engine straining under the load.

We turned left and right and right and left until I was dizzy. Even if you know where you're going in this cliff-hanging town, the switchbacks get you turned around. After an hour of driving up and down Monaco's hillsides, we slowed and pulled into a dark space. I heard the metallic rattle of a rusty roll-down garage door.

They opened the minivan, pulled Sylvia out, then slammed the door on me. It was dark. I was immobilized. They left me there for several hours.

They finally came for me and smacked me with the baton again before dragging me out and standing me up. A big guy kicked my shins, sending me to the ground. Someone else yanked my shoes off. The baton crashed into my soles and toes time and time again. It worked. I was not going to run away. Only then did they cut the netting off me.

They dragged me into a small workshop and put me on top of a table saw with my torso extended onto a workbench. They tied my feet to the sides. My arms were stretched over my head and tied to something behind me. The big guy turned a crank. The saw blade rose up between my legs with menace. Someone turned off the lone light bulb. Then they filed out and left me alone for a couple more hours. My feet ached. My bound hands ached. My beaten stomach ached. My stretched arms ached.

I heard the squeaking of rats.

Mercury leaned into my vision, glowing in the dark the way gods can when they feel like it. *Hoo-doggy, you're in an Orcus of a mess this time. You walked right into Sylvia's trap. Leave that Greek-sympathizer alone, I said. Party with Venus, I said. Search for Pia-Caesar-Sabel, I said. Did you listen to me?*

I said, *OK. I'll do whatever you want. Build a temple, make a sacrifice, perform a ritual, whatever, just get me out of this.*

Mercury said, *Buy your way out of trouble? Is that how you think this works? What's with you mortals? You never believe until you're on the verge of bankruptcy or your beloved grandmother is diagnosed stage 4. Then you suddenly recite the Nicene Creed or the whole Kabbalat Shabbat from memory.*

I said, *I screwed up. Just forgive me, OK? I'll do whatever you want. Get me out of this so I can save Sylvia. They'll kill her.*

Mercury wandered away. *Forgiveness? Oh, dawg, you be talking to the wrong god if you're in search of mercy. You think Roman gods are the kind who absolve the people who turned against them? More like— we gonna nail your hands and feet to a piece of wood and hang you up for a few days. Maybe you read about that somewhere.*

Suddenly, I was alone again. I called out for Mercury. I called out for Venus. Nothing.

Voices came from the other side of a door. Not whispering but trying to speak softly. I could almost make out their words. But not quite. One was a woman's voice.

The door burst open. The light came on, stinging my eyes.

A man shouted in a Corsican accent. "Where is Hugo?"

CHAPTER 35

PIA PULLED OUT HER KEY to the Japanese fondue shop next door to 61 James Close, on the backside of the Galerie DeLano.

"How did you get a key?" Willy-Mac asked.

"I made an investment in their expansion plans this morning."

"If money can't buy happiness—it sure buys access."

It was too dark to see, but she sensed his eyes rolling. Then her fear of getting him in trouble resurfaced. "I can do this part by myself, Willy-Mac. I appreciate your help, but I'd rather go it alone."

"You said you'd listen this time." His voice stern. "You need my help, and I'm here to give it. Quit talking and get moving."

With a deep breath, she unlocked the restaurant, keyed in the security code, waved Willy-Mac through, and locked it behind him.

She marched to the ladder in the back room. They climbed it to a short-floor just over six feet high between the restaurant below and the apartments above. They pushed aside stacks of boxed rice and cans of cooking oil until they had a space cleared next to a large piece of plywood.

She pointed at the square. "This is what we need the tools for."

"What is this?"

"A hundred years ago," she said, "the building we're in didn't exist. DeLano's building had a window. It opens directly into this storeroom."

"How do we get out?"

"Once we're inside, we can unlock the back door and walk out."

Willy-Mac set his bag down, pulled out a claw bar, sprayed WD-40 around the rusted nails to quiet the noise, and pulled out the first nail. After ten agonizing but relatively quiet minutes, they pulled the plywood out. They flicked on their headlamps and peered into the space.

A twelve-foot drop awaited them. Not a bone breaker. Not a soft landing either. He lowered himself over the edge and was about to drop the remaining distance. She held his wrist and lowered him down gently. He gave her a nod of thanks on behalf of his aging ankles.

She dropped down next to him.

An alarm on her phone app buzzed her hip. A monitor warning blinked. She flicked on the feed. DeLano stood out front, trying to unlock the door.

"When did you put a camera out there?" he asked.

"This morning."

"Thought you said he drank in bars until three."

She shrugged. "Maybe he forgot something. We hide and if he leaves, we're good."

Willy-Mac slid behind a stack of boxes and turned off his light. Pia slipped behind the bathroom door. With her eye to the hinge gap, she could see a third of the room.

A second later, DeLano entered, muttering to himself. He lowered a large steel beam across a newly installed latch to bar the Galerie-side door. He plopped down at a desk in the corner and rubbed his face in his palms. The computer bleeped to life. He searched for a camera app and brought it up. Four panes of security camera feeds came up. One she recognized as the street out back. Another was the front door. A third was the storeroom. If he backed up the feed, he'd see Pia and Willy-Mac making their grand entrance. Another looked like an apartment being ransacked by three men.

"Fuck me." DeLano pulled out a phone and dialed.

He held it to his ear without speaking for twenty seconds before clicking off. He opened a drawer and pulled out a bottle of Mopralpro, French antacid, and chewed a tablet. Then he pulled out a bottle of Armorik, a French whiskey. He fumbled a shot glass. It rolled across the floor to where Pia hid. He glanced that way, unscrewed the cap and chugged straight from the bottle.

DeLano's phone rang, he answered like a condemned man. "Cyril, he's fucking here. No. At my apartment. Where are you? No way, dude."

He dropped his face in his palm. "This is your fucking JOB, damn it. You have one mission: keep me operational." He listened. "Six of them. Two at my apartment. The others are here." He listened again. "Yeah. If I make it to my car."

He clicked off and tossed his phone on the desk and ran his fingers through his hair.

Pia's warning app buzzed again. In the silent storeroom, it was a noise loud enough to perk DeLano's ear.

He rose with alarm and held the whiskey bottle by the neck like a cudgel. "Who's there?"

She pulled her Glock and stepped out from behind the door. "Sit down, DeLano."

He spun to face her. "Wha—?"

She pulled her balaclava off and shook her ponytail loose. "Sit."

"You?" he said. "Who the hell ARE you?"

"The woman who's going to save your worthless ass from them." She pointed to the feed from his front door. Two men picked at his lock.

"Oh. Fuck." DeLano fell into his chair. "They're going to kill me."

"Where's the collateral?"

"The what?"

She pressed the barrel to his temple. "I'm your best chance to get out of here."

"Hand over the videos." Willy-Mac moved into the dim light. "We're here to help you, son."

The glass outside shattered. The men out front lost patience with the lock and strode into the Galerie. They swept the room with guns drawn. Someone else tried to force the back door open behind them. Pia glanced that way and saw a new steel bar across it. Secure for the moment.

"Really, who are you guys?" DeLano took another pull on his whiskey. "What collateral?"

Pia took the bottle from him and put it out of reach. Someone rattled the back door. The guys in front pounded on the gallery-side door. "The videos you took of Yeschenko and the others."

His face went white, a finger pointed at the camera feed in the gallery. "You're with them?"

Just above the gallery feed, Pia saw the apartment video. Hugo stood in the center of the room, giving it one last survey. He strode out.

"No," she said. "I'm here to save you from them. Where is the collateral?"

He pointed to a shelf full of a hundred device chargers, the detritus of the modern age.

She yanked him to his feet and waved her pistol at the opening high above the floor. "Give it to me, and I'll give you a boost out of here."

An electric Sawzall buzzed to life in the front. A blade busted through the drywall a second later.

All three of them stared in disbelief for a second.

DeLano ran to the shelf and started shoving things to the floor in a mad search.

Pia aimed her pistol at the blade coming through the wall.

Willy-Mac grabbed her forearm and pulled it up. "Don't escalate. They can shoot through drywall too, and that will bring in the guys from out back. You'll be caught in a crossfire."

DeLano held up an SD card. "I got it. I'll hang onto it."

"OK." Pia nodded at him—then slammed her elbow into his chin and snatched the chip out of his fingers in one fluid motion. She pocketed the card. While he rubbed his jaw, she pointed to the escape hatch.

DeLano ran to it and tried to jump. He fell back. Not even close.

Another Sawzall began hacking at the hinges on the back door.

Pia squatted low and looped her hands together. DeLano put a foot in her stirrup. She pushed off. He gripped the ledge and did a pull-up, getting his waist into the hole.

A chunk of drywall fell away on the gallery side. An eye pressed to the opening.

Behind her, one of the hinges in the back door gave way with a clank.

Pia squatted again and looped her hands.

"Won't work." Willy-Mac shook his head. "I'm not strong enough to pull you up. You'll have to go first. You can lean out and pull me up."

She wanted to argue but knew he was right. He was a retiree. She was tall, all muscle and not light. They traded places. He boosted her up. She did the pull-up, swung a knee inside, pulled herself in, then turned around.

She felt a sharp object at her neck.

"Give me the chip," DeLano said.

"OK, here, give me some room, it's in—" When he relaxed his grip, Pia flipped on her back and kneed him in the nuts.

He groaned and dropped a piece of cardboard. She had thought it was a knife.

She slammed her foot into the side of his knee. "I'm trying to save your life, asshole."

With another flip, she reached out and took Willy-Mac's outstretched arm.

A large chunk of the gallery wall fell to the floor with a crash. A pistol reached through.

Pia pulled with all her might. Willy-Mac pulled.

The back door crashed to the ground. A gunshot rang out.

Willy-Mac groaned.

Pia pulled harder, but his grip slackened. "Pull up, pull UP."

Another shot rang out.

Willy-Mac convulsed.

"NO!" Pia reached for him with both hands. His sweat-slickened flesh slipped through her grip.

"Sorry, Pia. I can't make it." His eyes held hers. "Roche set my people back forty years. Make sure you take him down."

"I'm not leaving you behind."

A third shot boomed.

He yelled out in pain then looked at her again. "I'm not gonna make … Go."

Willy-Mac fell to the floor.

Two shadows flowed into the room. Their flashlights illuminated her friend's bleeding body. They looked up. A split second later, they were firing pistols at her.

She fired three darts through eyes filled with tears. She had no idea where she was aiming. It bought her enough time to crawl out of the cramped space.

DeLano had the plywood ready and slammed it into place. He

whacked the nails back in with the craft of a former construction worker. They abandoned the effort after two nails. She led the way up three more flights to a roof access hatch.

She was alone—once again.

She led DeLano across the rooftops to a drain pipe and shimmied down it. He ran to his convertible Porsche 911 Carrera. He started to get behind the wheel. She gripped his collar, pulled him back two feet and pointed to the passenger seat.

"You don't know how to drive a powerful—"

"Shut up and give me the goddamn keys." She shoved the Glock in his ribs.

Without further argument, he turned them over and got in the passenger seat. She fired it up, fighting to see anything through the flood streaming through her eyes and down her cheeks. Her headlights illuminated two figures with handguns running toward them. Pia dropped the clutch in reverse, lit up the back tires, and pulled a reverse 180. As the car spun around in the lane, smoke from the tires clouded the shooter's view.

Slapping the gearshift into first and dropping the clutch, she forced the 911 forward. More smoke poured from the tires. She navigated the narrow lanes until two more men with guns appeared in front of them. With a yank on the handbrake, the car slid into a right-hand turn, brushing the fenders against a brick wall.

"Where the hell are you going?" DeLano yelled.

"Shut up." Pia pulled two more handbrake turns to keep any pursuers guessing. She found the road to Cannes and set the cruise control at 160 kph. She let herself cry for Willy-Mac all the way to the outskirts of the city.

Thoughts barreled into her brain like a train crammed with refugees all talking at once. *Abandoned. Unguided. Fuming. Willy-Mac was your fault. Miserable. Orphaned. Again.*

She remembered Willy-Mac's words when they talked about her PTSD. *Hear the sound of my voice through the noise. Try to focus on that.*

"Call an ambulance." She looked at DeLano's scared face. "Do it now."

DeLano pulled his phone and dialed.

When he finished reporting the shooting, she seized him by the neck and slammed his head into the dashboard. "That's for the stunt you pulled in the attic. I might've had Willy-Mac out of there."

He said, "Sorry. I—"

She slammed him into the dashboard again. "What's on this SD card?"

"A monologue." He grabbed her hand and tried to free himself. Her fingernails dug in deeper. "Ow. Cyril gives them to somebody. This one is Yeschenko."

"Where is Deng's SD card?"

"Cyril has copies."

She glanced at him. "You kept copies?"

"We thought they would kill us when the project was over. We wanted insurance."

"Tell me the rest of them are somewhere safe, not in the Galerie."

"Cyril keeps them."

"Where's Cyril?"

"We have a safe house in Monaco."

Pia slammed on the brakes, pulled a forward 180 and caught the A8 to Monaco.

CHAPTER 36

CHUCK ROCHE STARED AT THE Under Secretary of Defense on the other side of his desk. "What I asked was a simple question: will you be loyal to me no matter what happens?"

The man swallowed hard. "With all due respect, Mr. President, I cannot make a statement about something I did not—"

"Damn it, Brian, you were a senior Boeing executive before you landed here. I've heard you're great at your job, best ever. And now Boeing wins all the missile and drone bids."

"It's Robert, sir. Robert O'Brien." The weakling squirmed in his chair. "Yes, and my former colleagues at Boeing appreciate the business. But if you're implying corruption, I assure you, I have nothing to do with—"

"Did I go telling the press about your midnight phone calls, Robert?"

"Wait a second. I've not made any midnight—"

"Who does the FBI report to?" Roche pounded his desk with his cane. "Me, that's who. They're mine. I tell them you're making midnight calls, they'll find midnight calls. Like when whatshisname wanted to invade Iraq. He wanted Iraq to have WMDs. His people went out and found someone to claim he'd seen WMDs. That's how it works. See? I'm big on loyalty. You do something to prove your loyalty to me, and I'll stand behind you every time. Loyalty. Now do what I told you and you'll be acting Secretary of Defense in an hour. That's a promotion—and your kind doesn't usually get promoted."

"Uhm. My 'kind' sir?"

"Aren't you Armenian or something?"

"My grandfather came from Dublin—"

"Can you stick to the story? Or do I need to find another Acting Secretary? You've got five seconds before you're fired, so think it over."

The guy flinched when he said *you're fired*. Roche liked that. It showed respect.

Then sweat broke out on the loser's forehead. Why did it have to be so damned hard to find someone who would stand up for decency in this country?

Finally, the man wiped his face and looked Roche in the eye. "Yes, sir. I'll make the call."

"Good." Roche stood. "You tell him you saw the kiddie porn on Kurtz's personal computer, not his official one. You saw it, you came to me, and I told you to call the Feebs straight away. They didn't believe me when I told them." Roche handed him a business card. "This is the guy. Got it? Now dial."

"Right here? From the Oval Office?"

"Where the fuck you think you're going to call from, the ladies' room? Christ, Robby, I want to hear you say it. I want to hear you say exactly what I told you to say. Think about it. Get it straight. You saw the porn. You came here. I told you to call. Do it. Right. Now."

Robert O'Brien rose and pulled his phone and dialed the FBI agent and paced to the far end of the room.

Roche watched him. What a sorry excuse for a human being. And he claimed to have a Harvard MBA. What good is a degree like that if you don't do what the boss tells you? Some people just don't get how the world works. Fools. He shook his head.

Then his phone rang. The one in the bottom drawer. The one that should never ring. Cyril. He picked it up and turned away from his future Secretary of Defense.

"You got problems," Cyril said. "Big problems."

"Don't toy with me. What did you screw up this time?"

Roche watched O'Brien in the window's reflection. Irish. Plenty of Armenian terrorists snuck into the country pretending to be Irish. He should have the FBI watch that guy.

"Not me who screw up," Cyril said. "Yeschenko. He sent Hugo. DeLano escaped with life. Big woman working with them."

"Did you kill Hugo?" Roche realized he was too loud. He glanced over his shoulder at the suspected Armenian terrorist. The guy was deep in a conversation with the FBI. He hadn't heard him.

"I am not there when Hugo comes. DeLano not good with gun."

"Wait a second—what did you say about a big woman?"

"DeLano call me but hungs up. I look video feed. Big woman hold gun to his head."

"Ponytail, tough looking?" Roche bit his knuckle. The last thing he needed was that whiny bitch digging into Cyril's operation. All she ever did was cry about who killed her parents.

"Yeah. Ripped. Scary rip."

"Is she working with Hugo?"

"Look like, yes."

"Listen to me carefully, Cyril." Roche stepped close to the window and lowered his voice to a terse whisper. "If either Hugo or that woman get out of there alive, I'm sending an aircraft carrier to Corsica. I'll wipe you and your ancestors off the face of the Earth. Got me?"

"You start war with France?"

"What's Corsica got to do with France?"

"Same country since 1796."

"Huh. No kidding? Well. In case you haven't been watching the news, I've broken every tie to that stupid country. They've been letting immigrants in for a hundred years and look what's happened to them. They're nothing but a bunch of Algerian terrorists now. I can't stand frogs or their stupid language. *Milieu, ennui, refoulement, canapé*—what does that shit even mean? Nobody knows. Go find Hugo and his girlfriend and kill them. No fucking excuses."

He clicked off and looked at the office reflection. The second-rate bootlicker was staring at him. No matter what kind of promotion you give these idiots, they're always shocked about the most trivial day-to-day crap.

"What?" Roche wheeled on him.

"*Refoulement* is a term referring to the illegal expulsion of refugees."

"So? You speak French now? Big deal." Roche grabbed his cane and twirled it as he walked around the desk.

"No, I speak German. But those are common terms. For example, a *canapé* is a—"

"I know what a canopy is. It's those things they put over their sidewalk tables to keep the rain off. I'm not stupid, you know." He improved his grip on the cane in case he needed to strike. "What did the FBI say?"

"They're coming here to take our statements."

"Good." Roche looked the man over. He was pale, uncertain. "You signed a non-disclosure agreement, O'Brien. That means you can't make up any stories about what we talked about in here. You do, I sue you back to the Stone Age. We weren't talking about lying or anything like that. Just tell the truth about Kurtz and all that kiddie porn you found on his laptop."

"The agent said you demanded they investigate but didn't cite any evidence. Did you just have me make up evidence?"

"They keep telling me they can't start an investigation or get a search warrant just because I told them to. They want probable cause. Can you believe that? I'll give them probable laws. But not your problem. I found someone who can make evidence for me." He looked the man over. The SOB looked even weaker. When people didn't have a backbone of their own, Roche gave them one. "You lied to the FBI, Robert. I heard you. You change your story now, I'll have you locked up."

The man became so pale he was almost translucent. "Yes, sir."

Bates, his chief of staff, or more accurately, his chief-of-arrogant-pricks, stuck his head in the door. Bates glanced at the future Secretary of Defense and raised his brows as if questioning the man's presence.

"Something you should know, Bates. Robert here tells me your pal Kurtz has kiddie porn on his laptop. Did you know about that?"

"What?" Bates backed up with that ridiculous shocked look that seemed to be all the rage around the White House. Bates had to have known. They were in the Army together. Probably shared a tent. Perverts.

Bates managed to speak. "Not Kurtz. Impossible."

"Are you calling me a liar, Bates?"

Bates looked at O'Brien. The guy was staring out the window at the

Rose Garden. Bates said, "Hey, you better not be up to your old—"

"Don't take that tone with me. He's going to flip on his co-conspirators. His kind always does. The Feebs already leaked it to the press. It's all over Twitter right now."

O'Brien looked shocked all over again. Roche scowled at the sniveling coward.

He turned back to his chief of staff. "If you have anything to confess, Bates—" Roche crossed to him and wielded his cane like a baseball bat "—do it now, you short-eyed degenerate."

Bates looked at the Acting Secretary of Defense for support.

The worm finally did the right thing. The guy decided to get with the program.

O'Brien turned to Bates with fire in his eyes. "I saw it myself, Bates. Horrible stuff. Sickening. If you're defending Kurtz, you're probably in on it. I should kill you myself."

Roche smiled and mentally moved O'Brien to the converted column. One-by-one, he'd get them all.

"No." Bates backed to the door. "I had no idea. I just came in because the Super Bowl team is waiting for you. Um, six of them at least. Kurtz is in there with them."

"Drag him out," Roche said. "The FBI's going to take him away in chains."

The new guy clenched his fists and hardened his glare at Bates. "He'll rot in hell. And if you're in it—"

"No." Bates ran out of the room.

O'Brien was a brilliant pick. Which proved Chuck Roche was a great judge of character. He play-punched the acting Secretary of Defense. "Let's go, O'Brien. I'll introduce you to the press."

CHAPTER 37

WHEN HE GOT OFF THE phone, he started beating me with a baton. The guy kept shouting questions about Hugo. He didn't care about the answers. My body reeled in agony. The steel table beneath me offered no comfort, no escape from the blows.

"I don't know any Hugo," I yelled between strikes. "Does he speak your language? Does he have a gold tooth?"

Anger had taken over the man. He wailed on me with no goal or purpose other than to kill me to make himself feel better. Eventually, the pain overcame me, and reality dissolved. I fell down a deep well.

I landed in a bombed-out city like Aleppo, but with a distinctly American feel. It was dark and moonless. Smoke and fog rolled through the streets and alleys and rubble. I hid behind a crumbling wall to catch my bearings. Husks of broken-glass towers loomed darker than their surroundings. In my life as a Ranger, we learned to love the darkness. It felt like an old friend.

Moving like a ghost, I slipped through an alley and peered around the corner to recon the main boulevard.

Masses of pilgrims, tired and forsaken, trudged east in a desperate search for something undefined. They chanted, their mouths forming words without making sounds. They passed beneath a cone of light as if being scanned for barcodes.

I walked alone, parallel to the endless sea of humanity on the street. Cold, damp drizzle ran down my neck. I turned up my collar and shivered. Something drew me farther up the road. I kept to the deepest shadows and managed to remain unseen.

Suddenly, bright lights flashed in the sky and came together to form row after row of giant TVs. Local reporters appeared, talking without meaning, saying the same thing in an unintelligible babble. They seemed to be praising a great baboon. Then they swirled together to form the biggest screen of all. It covered the sky and stretched to the horizon. Everywhere I looked, left and right, people stopped and took a knee.

A baboon bounded onto the screen. He slapped the table and gestured wildly. He ranted in an unintelligible voice. Words were diced and chopped and tossed in the air. Nothing meant anything in normal terms, yet I understood the intent of his grunts and hoots. He railed against non-baboons and green baboons and blue baboons and purple baboons. He railed against science and medicine and wisdom and education. He railed against rules and levies and entryways and Feds. He railed against his friends with a multitude of reasons that shifted like sand in the desert.

A warm feeling grew inside me. Everything was going to be OK. The great baboon would take care of it.

I realized my awestruck face was lit by the descending light from the giant screen. I was exposed. I ran under an overhang. The naked light fell on the pilgrims as they resumed their journey with their faces upturned. They watched the baboon the way people watch a car accident. Horrified and fascinated and newly respectful of the dangers in life. They renewed their vows to protect themselves from the horrible fates their great baboon had exposed.

A few of the people were horrified at what they heard and scribbled notes and handed them out. A young woman, her face desperate but her voice mute, stuffed a hastily scribbled note in my hand. It read, *The resistance needs you, Jacob Stearne.* Shocked that she knew my name, I stared into her eyes for a moment. I had questions. *Who are you? Why me? Resist what?* But instead, I said, "I can't help you."

The baboon railed about the writers of words.

Hands of the pilgrims stretched from the crowd and seized the woman and pulled her away. The people set on her, beating her and pulling her limbs apart. Up and down the street, the writers of words were torn to shreds.

I couldn't watch. I ducked through a hole in a building and looked over my shoulder. The pilgrims continued on their way, trudging to a great glass cathedral at the end of the boulevard. A man pointed at me and shouted silently. I read his lips, *She gave him a note!*

A group broke from the crowd and ran toward me. They threw sticks and stones.

I dove deeper into the hole. It led to the filthy hallway of a once proud apartment building. Fresh graffiti stretched down the wall. *Because you did not serve the Lord your God joyfully and with gladness of heart for the abundance of everything, therefore you shall serve your enemies whom the Lord will send against you, in hunger and thirst, in nakedness and lack of everything. He will put an iron yoke on your neck until he has destroyed you. The Lord will bring a nation from far away, from the end of the earth, to swoop down on you like a two-headed eagle— Deuteronomy 28:46-49.*

I didn't know if it was for or against the wailing baboon.

Out the back and down a side street, I heard the keening of a train. I ran for the entrance and jumped down the steps. A long subway car bursting with refugees raced by the platform without stopping. When it was gone, I turned away. I slogged up the long stairs back to the street.

The flood of pilgrims swept me along until we neared the glass cathedral. I split to the side and entered a small door behind an altar of vivid green Lucite. The priests wore red business suits made of the finest silk. They had blue shirts and white ties and white shoes. On their heads were conical hats. In their hands were big silver forks and long, sharp knives.

When the pilgrims entered the building, they emptied their pockets onto a conveyor belt. Acolytes clutched them and reached into the pilgrims' shirts and pulled out hidden money and diplomas and children and roads and parks and insurance cards. The acolytes said, "We need everything you have—and you don't."

The pilgrims replied, "We believe in one great baboon who came down from his tower to become one of us. He was crucified, suffered, and was buried by the writers of words. Yet he rose again to sit in the White House. He alone can judge the citizens and the terrorists. His administration shall have no end. We believe in the secretaries who proceed from the great baboon to dispense justice and security according to his demands. We sacrifice our votes for our economic salvation, forsaking any hope of common decency. We look to our resurrection in the tariffs to come. Amen."

Then the pilgrims moved forward and knelt before the altar where their heads were severed. The men in suits carved flesh from the bodies and ate where they stood. Rivers of blood flowed around my feet. It grew deeper by the second, first up to my ankles, then to my shins. I fled the building.

I ran as far and as fast as I could. At the edge of the city, I saw a crowd of people coming my way. They bore torches and signs and sang the songs of bold and fearless soldiers. They marched around me, heading for the glass cathedral. One sign stretched fifty feet, its poles carried by ten men. It read, *Ah, you destroyer, who yourself have not been destroyed; you treacherous one, with whom no one has dealt treacherously! When you have ceased to destroy, you will be destroyed; and when you have stopped dealing treacherously, you will be dealt with treacherously. – Isaiah 33:1-3.*

One of the men carrying it was Paul, who died in Fallujah more than ten years ago. He saw me and called out. "Jacob! We must serve our country one more time. Come and join us."

"I can't." The lie twisted my soul. "I'm going to start a family."

I turned away and ran upstream against the tide of humanity.

Peter, who died in Helmand Province, caught my arm. "We need your help to—"

I tore from his grip. "I'm busy."

I hurried on and broke out of the crowd and ran over the hill. Two stragglers crested the next ridge. Philip and Matthew, victims of an IED while on patrol. They waved me over. "Jacob, you're with us. It's time for brave men to make a stand."

I ran into the dark. "I'm not that guy."

CHAPTER 38

PIA PILOTED THE PORSCHE INTO the night with expert precision. She hovered on the brink of disaster, squeezing between cars and trucks.

Hugo would see her face when he checked the video feeds in the Galerie DeLano. He would leave a man behind to find her. There was no going back. He'd figure out how to find Cyril and DeLano too. How much time did that give her? Ten or twelve hours maybe.

DeLano cowered in the passenger seat. He answered when she peppered him with questions about his operation. Then she brooded in silence followed by tears for Willy-Mac. Another friend shot while helping her. Her anger at DeLano rose alongside her guilt about her friend.

"Where does Cyril keep the confessions?" she yelled over the noise of the engine and wind.

"You can't win," DeLano screamed. "They'll kill you."

She grabbed a fistful of his shirt and yanked him over the center console. "Answer the question, or I throw you out of the car."

She shoved him back in his seat. He glanced at the dark freeway flying by at 180 kph.

"They'll kill us both." DeLano beat his fists on the dashboard. "You don't know these guys."

"They're not smart enough to get to me. I can protect you."

DeLano dropped his face in his hands. "I still can't help you."

"That play you made for the SD card cost Willy-Mac. I should beat the crap out of you." She downshifted and turned onto the A500 to Monaco. "Instead, I'm offering you a way out of this mess. Do you want a free ride back to the States or not?"

"If you think I'm going to testify about these guys—no way." He stared at the lights flying by. "I don't know … Damn it." He clenched his head. "I do know. They weren't going to let me live, regardless of our 'insurance'. Can you really keep me safe? Maybe I can help. I don't know. They keep me in the dark about most of it. What do I need to do?"

She explained his role as they drove through the Monaco Tunnel in the blink of an eye.

He guided her into Cyril's neighborhood. They parked up the hill and around the hairpin turn above the house. DeLano strolled in the lighted part of the lane while she hugged the walls and shadows to keep out of the house's video feed. When they were in position, he knocked.

A big Corsican opened the door. Pia spun around the jamb and put a dart in his leg while his surprised face was still registering her presence. A second man raced across the small foyer and captured her gun hand. She twisted into him, her left elbow slamming into his chin. He staggered back and caught a dart in the chest.

DeLano stared at the two bodies before looking over Pia. "Who ARE you?"

She put a finger to his lips, then pushed him up the steps to the second level. He opened the inner door.

Three men played an Xbox with the volume up high. Two on the couch, one in a chair. From the shadows of the landing, she laid out the firing pattern in her head. DeLano strode into the room and greeted them, dragging their attention away from the door. They grunted responses with an abbreviated glance his way. One guy registered Pia's figure in the dark space, questioning his eyesight.

She dropped all three.

Crossing the threshold, she asked, "How many others?"

Two gunshots rang out before DeLano could answer. The heat and flash missed Pia by millimeters.

She dropped and rolled and took a quick damage assessment. She was fine. She was also in front of the couch. A figure moved in from the kitchen, a pistol in one hand. Pia spun around the far end of the furniture to the wall and took a peek. DeLano stood with his hands up.

On the other side of the room, Sylvia Lallouette held a pistol in her outstretched arm. She sighted down the barrel at DeLano.

"Toss the gun, Pia." Sylvia glanced her way. "Or I kill this fucking traitor."

Pia rose and held her hands out like a cross. "If you're going to kill someone tonight, kill me."

"Drop it." Sylvia's hand shook as she took another glance at Pia. "I swear, I'll shoot him."

"I forced him here at gunpoint." Pia slid her feet across the wood floor, inching around the end of the couch. "He had no choice."

"What are you doing here?" Sylvia's voice cracked. "Think you can save Jacob? You're too late."

"I thought you were a pacifist. What happened?"

"Life happened. I need to stay alive." Sylvia squeezed her finger around the trigger and closed her eyes. She turned her face as she fired. An amateur move to avoid the loud noise and blinding flash. Her actions pulled the barrel up and left as it fired. The bullet grazed the top of DeLano's head. He dropped to the floor.

Pia put a dart in Sylvia's ribcage. She fell like a ragdoll.

"Holy shit!" DeLano jumped to his feet. "Did you kill them all?"

"Any others?"

He inventoried the faces. "Cyril."

Pia held up her hand for silence. She searched through the house. Noises came from a distant room. She cleared two bedrooms and a kitchen before following the sound of someone shouting.

"It's him." DeLano came up behind her. "He's dangerous."

"So am I." She motioned for him to open the door.

After a moment of hesitation, while DeLano battled nausea, he followed her instruction.

When the door opened, shock caught her for a second. Cyril stood with a collapsible baton in his hand. Beneath him lay Jacob's comatose body. Cyril threw his baton at her. She fired a dart that dropped the Corsican. The baton caught her in the shoulder with a stinging blow. She shrugged it off.

"Who the fuck ARE you?" DeLano stood like a statue.

"I'm a pissed off woman with a gun—and you're annoying me." Pia ran to Jacob and pressed her ear to his chest. Faint wheezing sounds burbled inside him. She looked at DeLano. "Don't just stand there, untie him."

DeLano rushed to Jacob and tugged at the rope binding his wrists. DeLano's hands shook so hard he struggled to function. He asked, "Is he alive?"

"I hope so. The others are, at least."

She explained the Sabel Darts while lifting Jacob's shirt. Sickening bruises covered his chest and stomach. She couldn't look anymore and dropped the cloth as gently as possible.

"He needs help." DeLano finished untying the ropes on Jacob's ankles.

"Shut up." Pia regretted snapping as soon as she heard her voice.

She started to call for an ambulance.

DeLano looked at Cyril's body on the floor. Her gaze followed his.

"Does Hugo know about this place?" she asked.

"He'll track it down soon enough."

Paramedics would take Jacob to a hospital where Hugo would finish what Cyril started. They were better off leaving Cyril and his crew here. She fought back despair. She'd lost two people in one night. She had to get Jacob to a doctor. One who wouldn't need a lot of explanation. The only one she could think of was her doctor. In Washington.

"Get your car, bring it around."

He started to move, stopped, thought about asking a question, then snuck between the wall and the delivery van.

"Don't think about running out on me." She waited until he stopped and looked over his shoulder. "I'll hunt you down and kill you."

He tightened his mouth and lifted the garage door and disappeared into the dark.

She picked up Jacob. He was as tall as she and densely muscled. And he was dead weight. She shifted him as gently as she could manage and got him on her shoulders. Tears began forming in her eyes again. She willed herself not to think about the destruction in her wake and staggered out to the street.

DeLano pulled up next to her. He helped her put Jacob in the passenger seat.

"Where am I going to ride?" he asked.

"You're not." She led him back in the house and closed the garage door behind them. "These motherfuckers shot one of my friends and beat the crap out of another. I'm going to find them and take their little gang apart. I'll need your help. Welcome to Sabel Security. You're now an official undercover agent."

"Hey, I didn't ask for a job. I'm not going to—"

"You cost Willy-Mac his life, and maybe Jacob too, so fuck you."

She pushed him into the living room where they stepped over Sylvia.

DeLano said, "Who ARE you?"

"Pia Sabel, owner of Sabel Security. Like I said, you're my newest agent. Don't worry, I pay well, and I'll get you the best lawyers. Your job is to find the SD cards with the confessions and hide them somewhere outside this house. Later, after Cyril accepts your story, you retrieve them, call the switchboard at Sabel Security and identify yourself as DeLano from Antibes. They'll put you through to me. I need those confessions to prove the invoices from Santalum are real and that Roche is shaking down billionaires around the world."

"Whoa!" DeLano held up his hands and backed up. "I'm not that guy. I can't get involved in that kind of thing. I'm a teacher. I was teaching English on Corsica when I got a little behind on some gambling debts. What you're talking about—"

"You can do what I ask—" she waved at the bodies around them "—or take your chances when these guys wake up. If you choose to work for me, you have a life. I'll come back with the full expectation that you'll have done what I asked."

"Hey, Cyril's never going to believe—"

"I have to get Jacob to a doctor. You find the SDs, stash them, then jab this in your thigh. Be sure to stand right where Sylvia last saw you. Tell them I darted you a second after I darted her." She took his wrist, slapped the dart into his hand and walked out. "Don't disappoint me, DeLano."

CHAPTER 39

Cabinet meetings were a big deal. The press needed to see how the important people in the world adored President Roche. His press secretary had to get that message out so more people could admire him.

Normally, he loved to hear these former generals and CEOs praise and glorify him, but all he could think about was Cyril's operation being compromised by a girl. He should have that guy droned. Cyril had already lost the envelope with all the Santalum invoices in it. And he let Hugo invade the Galerie DeLano. What kind of security was Cyril providing if Yeschenko's men just waltzed in whenever they felt like it?

And what was Sabel doing with them? Had Yeschenko won her over? Were they plotting against him? Whatever the case, he should drone Cyril.

"Sir?" Chief of Staff Bates was staring at him.

So was everyone else. Even the photographers had stopped snapping and flashing.

"Will that be enough photos, sir?" Bates said with too much impatience.

"Does anyone else have anything nice to say?" Roche asked.

They all looked at their water glasses. The ingrates. He gave them jobs when they were all out of work, retired, ready for a pine box. He should fire them all and bring in young people. Good looking people like his nephew's wife. She was a hottie. She liked older, powerful men.

"Thank you, members of the press pool," Bates said. "You're excused."

While the room cleared out, Roche heard one of the photographers say to another, "Did that just happen? Or did someone slip LSD in my coffee?"

Roche pointed at the photographer and yelled at Bates. "Never let that guy in again."

Bates nodded but didn't write anything down.

When the doors closed, Bates said, "Mr. President, first on the agenda is your pick for Vice President. Would you please enlighten us?"

"You mean you don't know, Bates?" Treasury Secretary Gruber asked in an impertinent voice. The smug bastard always churned things up.

"The president has played this one close to his chest because ..." Bates left his sentence for Roche to finish.

"Because of all the damn leaks," Roche said. He decided to get this part over with. "I've chosen a person with more experience than any of you. Someone who knows how to get things done. Someone who's been here before. Someone the people once voted for overwhelmingly—until she ran against me."

He snapped his fingers. An intern opened the door.

Veronica Hunter strode in. "Good morning, gentlemen."

Dead silence greeted her. All the secretaries and ambassadors and directors let their mouths fall open as if they were tourists on their first visit to the Big Apple. Slowly, their faces turned to Roche.

"First," the Secretary of Housing and Urban Decay said, "your fundamentalist vice president resigns amidst rumors of a gay double-life. Then your Secretary of Defense is caught with child pornography on his laptop. You suspended the Civil Service by executive order, making all federal employees serve at the pleasure of the president. Your Secretary of State calls me minutes before this meeting to tell me he's being accused of tax evasion—and now you want me to swallow this?"

"Ripley? Tax evasion?" the Secretary of Health and Human Servants shouted. "Where the hell is he?"

Roche stood and put his hands out, palms waving downward, calming the group. "It's true. The Veep is a fag, but let's keep that between us boys. And it's also true that Secretary Ripley had millions in unreported cash sitting in the Caymans. No wonder he never showed anyone his taxes. Ripley was never close to me though. He wasn't an important part of this administration. Right now, he's in FBI custody—"

"Not important?" Bates yelled. "Ripley is fourth in line to succeed you. After the Vice President, he's the most important—"

"Shut up, Bates." Veronica Lodge Hunter withered him with a glare. "Get with the program. What matters is: I'm the best person for the job. Get me through confirmation in Congress—and I might be able to save your reputations."

She ended with a nod at Roche, which he didn't understand, but everyone looked at him. Then they looked at Hunter and smiled. Their heads began nodding. That was a good thing. He waved Hunter over and made Bates give up the chair at his right hand.

Bates rose reluctantly and whispered in Roche's ear. "If you're doing this to get rid of us, I still have that box of evidence."

"So you claim," Roche said. "Forgeries, no doubt. And your friends are filthy animals. Beat it. You're staff, not a cabinet officer."

Hunter took her new seat.

Roche said, "Next on the agenda is Pia Sabel. I'm going to hold a little competition. The first guy to ruin her and her company gets to be the new Secretary of State."

"We can't ruin Sabel Industries," the Secretary of Homeland Security said. "They run the algorithms for State, NSA, and CIA. Their spy satellites watch over—"

"We can take them down a notch," the new CIA Director Nora Ratched said.

Who better to lead the CIA? She was a lot better-looking than Smithers. And she'd sailed through confirmation because she had dirt on every senator alive. Enough dirt that no one questioned her shocking participation in torture schemes around the world. She came to Roche pledging her loyalty and took a knee without being told. She'd even kissed his fingers, which was a nice touch.

"I want Sabel's reputation destroyed." Roche roared. "Hear me?"

Again, everyone was silent. They all stared at him with that idiotic shocked look. Even the Ambassador to the United Nations looked surprised. That guy usually nodded off in meetings.

"Do you have any evidence of wrongdoing?" Attorney General

Michael Myers loved to stick some bureaucratic bullshit into the discussion. "Anything at all?"

"That's what I'm asking you guys to find."

Roche looked around the room. He'd just about had it with their insolent looks, their superior frowns, their pure arrogance. None of them ran for president. If they had, he would've clobbered them in the first primary. They had to start doing things his way. No more whining.

"Listen up, you bastards," Roche bellowed. "You're going to dig in and find ways to destroy Pia Sabel. She's on her way here in a day or two with a whole pack of lies that will make you look bad." He pointed his finger around the room, engaging each one of them. "You could go down in history as the greatest Secretary of Whatever—or you could go down as co-conspirators. I'm not going to let you destroy yourselves like that.

"I am the only person who can save this country from blowing all my money on the stupid crap people think they want. You're here to help me save this great nation. I'm telling you, we need Pia Sabel and Sabel Industries ruined in the next few days or everything you stand for could be demolished like a sand castle in a hurricane.

"Imagine a world where the women run everything, where your taxes give free tuition to every numbskull with coal dust under his fingernails, where we're taxed to death to pay the salaries of public school teachers, but your kid's private school doesn't get a nickel. Well, boys, that's just the world we're going to live in if we don't stand up and fight for what's mine."

He looked around and saw a few of them nodding. But not all were on board. Yet. For every carrot-eater, there was always a stick-needer.

"Here's how it works. The first one of you to shut down a Sabel division gets to be Secretary of State. Anyone who brings in real dirt on Pia Sabel gets honorable mention." He looked around the room at each one of them. "But. If you come back here with nothing—" he roared his closing statement "—YOU'RE FIRED!"

CHAPTER 40

I HEARD VOICES. ONE OF them kept repeating, "I'm not that guy."

It might have been me. Wind whipped my face. The roar of an engine followed behind me. I opened an eye and saw Ms. Sabel in profile, lit by the dashboard. She had both hands on the wheel, her arms were stretched out like a race car driver.

"Stay with me." She glanced my way. "Don't die on me, Jacob."

I tried to speak but only drooled. Somehow, I was cramped up sideways in a sports car. It was better than being strapped to a table saw, but not by much. With a twist, I managed to straighten out my body. Pain shot through me from my hips to my lungs. I took a deep, excruciating breath. Pure agony clamped my eyes shut and forced a grunt between my clenched teeth. My head lolled to the right.

Bushes and rocks formed a blurred landscape. Street lamps went by like a high-speed strobe light.

Mercury flew alongside, parallel to the ground. *You look uglier than Nick Nolte's mugshot, homie.*

I said, *Oh god.*

Mercury said, *Hey, you got that part right. Here, drink this.*

He held out a golden goblet, the kind you see in Holy Grail movies. Inside was a liquid of some kind. The fact that we were doing over 100 mph in a stolen Porsche while a mythical god offered a cup of what was probably yak's piss led me to close my eyes and hope it all went away.

Hang on, my brutha. Mercury pulled me to edge of the door. *You're in some serious hurt. You need to drink this. C'mon man, it's the elixir of the gods. I got it from Vejovis himself.*

I said, *Who?*

Vejovis, god of medicine. For Juno's sake, try reading a book some time.

I said, *I read a book once. Ended up using* frisson *in a sentence. No one knew what it meant.*

Mercury said, *It means a moment of excitement, from the Latin* firgere *or cold, like it gives you a chill. Everybody knows that. Now drink this and go back to sleep. You'll feel better in the morning.*

I said, *It's not yak's piss, is it?*

Oh hell no. Mercury frowned as if I'd insulted him. *Now drink it.*

I took the goblet and chugged half. It tasted worse than piss. I gulped air and looked at him. He motioned for me to drink it all.

While I slurped down the rest, Mercury said, *I cannot believe you think I'd bring you yak's piss. No way, man. This is Bellona's piss. Vejovis and I got it straight from the goddess of war and conquest herself. Holy Saturn, homie. Yak's piss.*

I puked my guts out over the edge of some poor bastard's Porsche. When the last retched out, I flopped back in my seat and closed my eyes.

Ms. Sabel took my hand and squeezed it. Her touch was more comforting than a goblet of goddess piss. She said, "Are you with me?"

"Did you…" I gasped and struggled to put words together, "try to kill Sylvia?"

"Can you hang in there, Jacob?" She took her eyes off the road to look at me for a split second. "Hugo would come down on us if we went to a hospital. But I'll risk it if you don't think you can make it."

"I'm … fine." I closed my eyes. "Just need a … little shut-eye."

The engine roared into the night. Everything around me swirled into a vortex of blackness. Storm clouds hovered over Stearne Farms at dusk. Tornado weather on the prairie. Lightning cracked the sky. Thunder charged across the Great Plains like a bison stampede. I ran inside where Mom waited in the kitchen. Bread baked in the oven. A Caprese salad waited for me in the center of the table. It was set for five, with cloth napkins. Family, the tranquility in a storm. Joyce came in coated with oat dust from the harvest. Dad followed her, equally covered. Sylvia came in from the living room with a big smile and a wink. They sat at the table, put their napkins in their laps, and looked up with expectant eyes.

"Joining us?"

Something had changed. I felt the sensation of flight. That moment when your body weight changes from earth-bound to climbing skyward. I heard the grumble of jet engines. Ms. Sabel wiped my face with a damp washcloth. I glanced around the Sabel jet's interior.

"Did you get Sylvia out?" I asked.

"How are you feeling?"

"Fine." I grabbed her wrist and sat up. "Where's Sylvia?"

"Wow." She looked confused and leaned back. "You look one hundred percent better than when I pulled you out of that house. What happened?"

"They kidnapped us. Threw a net over us when we rounded the corner."

"I meant, what happened to your injuries?"

"Where is Sylvia?"

"She almost shot me." Ms. Sabel's eyes checked mine the way someone does when they aren't sure if you'll believe them or not. "Luckily, she's not handy with a pistol."

"She thought you were trying to kill her in Tremé."

"Is that right?"

"Were you?"

"You don't remember? We tried to talk her out of delivering the envelope."

A dim memory surfaced like a dead fish in a muddy pond. Ms. Sabel and I towered over Sylvia, yelling at her about doing the right thing. Sylvia cowered and finally agreed with us. She promised to give us the envelope. There was a gap of time, we were in a different place, and Ms. Sabel was yelling at me. Not yelling, screaming.

"Amnesia, they said." I stood in the aisle. "I have a few weeks missing."

"What is with you?" She pulled my shirttail up, looked me over, and dropped it. "Your bruises are gone. You were on death's door ten minutes ago."

Mercury stood behind her. *Y'know, homie, there was a time when people believed in gods and miracles. They still would—but instead, they listen to Bill Maher. So, you have a decision to make. You could tell her how Mercury, divine messenger and freshest god of them all, saved your sorry ass from internal bleeding. Or you can pretend I don't exist. If I don't exist, I couldn't have helped, right? Meaning, those injuries never actually healed and you're about to die. So, you choose.*

I said, *If you think I'm going to tell Ms. Sabel that I drank Bellona's piss, you're the crazy one.*

Mercury laughed. *Aw, hey, I was just fucking with you, bro. It wasn't her piss.*

I said, *Thank god.*

Mercury said, *It was her menstrual flow.*

Everything around me swirled again. Ms. Sabel held my arms to steady me.

Powerful stuff, my man. Mercury shook his fist. *Potent AF.*

"You want to sit down?" Her eyes searched mine.

"Nah. Whew. Just a head rush kinda thing." I took a deep breath and straightened up. "I'm fine."

"Your recovery is scary." She kept checking me out as if I were growing horns. "You were in bad shape. How did you do that?"

"Well, um, I drank, or dreamed I drank—" I ran my fingers through my buzz cut and wiped my face "—an elixir."

"Mercury?" She gave me yet another once-over. "He patched you up? He's real?"

Mercury crossed his arms and looked like he deserved my gratitude in the form of evangelism. Which he might have. But. Menstrual flow. How do you forgive a god for that one? I think death would've been better.

"I was hurt. I'm fine now." I scratched my head. "It's just a miracle. Probably. So. Uh. Did you see Mercury? My elixir-dream happened in the car. Or. Maybe I wasn't all that bad to begin with." I gripped my head with both hands. "I don't know. If he's real—everything we've ever been taught is a lie. Do you want to go there? Worship the Roman pantheon and bring back deathmatches? But if he's not real—that means I'm insane. I don't know. Which one do you want to believe?"

Ms. Sabel looked half frightened and half angry.

I grabbed her arms. "Did you try to kill Sylvia in Tremé?"

"Not exactly."

I backed up. She backed the other direction. A good six feet separated us. I waited for an explanation.

"Sylvia's not who you think she is." Ms. Sabel crossed her arms. "There's nothing I can say that would explain what happened unless you remember how we got there."

"The doctors tried everything—"

"Except taking you back there." She turned away from me. "That's where we're going. Back to New Orleans. Maybe you'll remember what happened."

"Wait a second." Something strange tickled my loyalties. "You haven't been in touch with Sabel HQ for weeks, yet we're going to Tremé. How did you know I had amnesia?"

"None of that matters until we—" She looked away. "We need to resolve a kind of a problem between us."

That strange sensation about trusting the wrong girl flooded over me like a tidal wave. One of them had not told me everything. One of them was leaving out a whole lot of something important. No. That wasn't right either. Neither of them had told me everything. And both of them had left out a whole lot of something. Who should I trust, the woman I loved or the woman who saved my life?

Mercury said, *Easy call, dawg. Go with the one who pays better.*

"How did you know I had amnesia?" I asked her.

"You were talking when you were dying."

CHAPTER 41

ALAN SABEL SAT IN THE chair next to Pia's bed on the jet. "You should tell him."

"He'll understand better if he remembers it." She hugged her knees and bit her knuckle and let the sheets drop.

"It won't make him feel any better." Alan pointed his finger at her. "And you owe him. Better to get it over with than drag it out."

When she looked at the flight monitor on the wall, ten minutes from landing, her father's ghost disappeared. He was right. Apologies are better served sooner than later. It was time to just blurt out everything and hope for the best.

Three soft raps on her door preceded Jacob's tentative voice. "Are you awake?"

"Come in." She checked her ninja outfit, going into its second day. No powder burns, no blood stains, used but workable. "Listen, Jacob, I need to tell you about—"

"Watch this first." He held a phone with a video of Veronica Hunter at a press conference.

He fast-forwarded through the typical political-speak to the point where Hunter's eyes glistened with tears. Hunter said, "But I cannot accept the nomination to be your vice president until I make a public apology for the way I've sat idly by while this administration demonizes Pia Sabel and Sabel Industries."

Chuck Roche had introduced her and stood on the sidelines grinning and chatting like a sixth grader in gym class until he heard those words. He rushed toward her, yelling something the mics didn't pick up. Hunter gave him a withering glare. Roche froze and turned red. He held his cane ready for an overhead strike. Three of his aides pulled him back out of the frame.

"Throughout my career," Hunter said, "I've participated in or knew about operations that hurt Pia deeply. Somehow, through it all, she's persevered and succeeded better than anyone could have imagined. For my part in her agonizing setbacks, I beg Pia Sabel's—" Hunter choked up "—forgiveness."

Real tears streamed down her cheeks as she tried and failed to compose herself. She turned away while still holding on to the podium. An aide handed her tissues, which she pressed to her eyes. When Hunter faced the cameras again, her makeup was a wreck.

"Pia Sabel, wherever you are, I am truly sorry, and I humbly repent. I don't expect you to accept that. I don't expect you to forgive me. I expect nothing." Her tears began to flow again, but she held up like a stoic. "But know this: I am doing my best to become a penitent from this moment forward."

With that, she left the press conference in a rush.

"What a crock, right?" Jacob shook his head.

"I don't think so." Pia clutched his arm and waited until he met her gaze. "I think she's sincere and I have an idea why."

His mouth opened to explain why Pia was wrong, but the Major came up on Skype. Pia nodded for him to accept the call.

The jet touched down with a bump.

Pia and Jacob filled the Major in on the pertinent events of the preceding weeks as they climbed into a limo and headed for Tremé. The Major wanted Pia to return home, get some rest, talk to her attorneys about suing the Roche administration. Pia refused.

"Why New Orleans? And why go back to Monaco?" the Major asked.

"Last time we were in Tremé," Pia sighed, "Jacob and I secured the envelope. It turned out those are invoices between nameless shell companies and Santalum. DeLano recorded the confessions of Roche's friends at RULE. Roche's been shaking them down with tariffs and sanctions. He needed blackmail material on them to keep them from going public. Those confessions validate these invoices. They're the key to tying this together. I left DeLano there to secure them, but I don't have any faith in him."

"There's no need to go back," the Major said. "I'll send Tania with a squad."

"There're a couple things I need to do," Pia choked up the same way Hunter had. Guenièvre hadn't responded to Pia's texted messages, and she couldn't call Vivian. She pushed the image of Willy-Mac falling to the warehouse floor out of her mind. She took a deep breath. "Things no one else can do for me."

They ended the call and sat in silence for a few miles. Jacob was not happy that she refused to answer his questions about Sylvia. She couldn't bring herself to blurt it out. He needed to remember the details.

The limo took the Esplanade Avenue exit off I-10. In a few turns, they were deep in Tremé. Clapboard houses in various states of decay were offset by the occasional restored and brightly painted home. Jacob stared out the window with childlike curiosity.

They stopped in front of a nineteenth-century boarding house. Half the last paint job clung to the wood as best it could. Siphoned power ran in a tangle of wires from the rack of electric meters on the side to windows and small gaps in the walls. A sign hung above the wooden steps, *The Grand Tremé Hotel.*

Pia led the way inside and slapped the bell. A teenager popped his head out of an office. She handed him a hundred-dollar bill. "I'd like Room 203."

The kid tossed her a key.

"Gold-Tooth," Jacob said. "He lived here?"

"Not exactly." She led the way outside and around the corner. She led him up a metal stair tacked on the back of the building a hundred years ago. "This is where we holed up. No cameras. No cops."

Jacob stopped at the landing and looked across the rooftops. He pointed three blocks away. "Congo Square?"

"That's where we met before coming here." She went inside and unlocked Room 203.

Inside, she waved off flies. Jacob stood in the doorway staring at the threadbare carpet. A large dark area had been scrubbed for a few minutes then left as part of the scenery. He looked up at the water-stained ceiling.

His gaze came down to meet hers.

"Is it coming back to you?" Pia rested against the thin metal bed frame, trying not to touch the filthy bedspread.

"This is where he shot me?" Jacob looked around the room as if he was reliving the pain of being gut-shot. "Gold-tooth, right?"

"Not exactly," she said. "Can you remember the operation?"

"You and I were staking out a meeting from here?" Jacob wandered to the window as flies buzzed them both. He stared out at the shadows below. He looked up the street and down. "A courier was delivering transactions to a Roche accountant. Roche didn't want them transmitted over the internet because the NSA might find them using Sabel Technologies' algorithms."

Jacob looked back at her with anger in his eyes. "You didn't tell me Sylvia was the courier."

"I did. You didn't believe me."

"Her half-brother, Cyril, made her do it. We have to get her out of there. Give her a chance to start over without the Sea Breeze Gang threatening her life every day."

"That won't work for Sylvia." Pia watched his reaction.

"The guy at the youth center said the same thing." Jacob frowned. "I don't believe it. We can't leave her—"

"What else do you remember?"

Jacob looked out the window again. "When she met Roche's guy, a pipsqueak who never spoke came out of the shadows and shot him in the head." Jacob squinted. "Sylvia freaked out. The quiet guy was going to kill her next. I jumped out of this window. You followed and grabbed the envelope. More guys popped out. There were six of them. We were outgunned. The guy with the gold tooth snatched Sylvia and dragged her into the dark."

Pia gripped his shoulder. "The quiet guy's name is Hugo."

He looked at her hand, then stared into her eyes. "What aren't you telling me?"

"Look." A lump formed in Pia's throat. "I know all your hopes and dreams for a future revolve around Sylvia. I know she means everything to you. I'm sorry. She chose the wrong side."

"You mean she didn't choose your side." Jacob yanked his shoulder free. "You tried to kill her."

"Not exactly." Pia exhaled. "I've been having problems controlling my anger."

"They were firing like mad." His gaze returned to the street below. "You ran back upstairs. You left me out there."

"You were right behind me." Pia put her hands on either side of the dirty glass and looked at the street below. "Tactical retreat. We had real bullets stashed up here."

"Gold-Tooth said he made a deal, Sylvia for the envelope. We could've gotten her and come back later for the envelope."

"Like I said, I've been dealing with anger issues." Pia blew out a big breath. "PTSD. I blew up at Stefan in Nepal. I blew up at the Major. Can you believe it? I fired her a few months ago. Luckily, it didn't stick. Dr. Harrison said I was mad at the world for losing Dad. I was blaming myself and everyone else at the same time. Just like that time a few years—"

"Why didn't we toss the envelope out the window and get Sylvia back?"

"After I blew up at the Major, she recommended we have a reconciliation party for Roche administration officials."

"That I remember." Jacob crossed his arms. "That was before New Year's Eve, more like Thanksgiving. You sent a jet for Sylvia. She was thrilled to be invited. Even if Roche goes against everything in her feminist portfolio."

"Like him or not, he's POTUS. Power has a certain appeal. A promise of opportunity."

"What's that got to do with anything?"

"Sylvia ended up having a one-on-one session with Roche." Pia worried about Jacob reacting badly again. "They spoke in the hallway for a long time. I'm not saying she's having an affair or anything. For some odd reason, she's stuck on you and only you. But in the end, she's not who you think she is. I'm sorry, Jacob. I really am."

Jacob grabbed her roughly. "Damn it, quit screwing around. Why didn't we toss the envelope out the window?"

"She's not who—"

"Stop saying that." He shook her. "Why didn't we trade the envelope?"

"You were about to." He let go. Pia wrung her hands. "I'm sorry. You had it in your hand. I'm sorry. I'm really, really sorry. Bringing down Roche was important to me. Too important. I lost control. I'm sorry. I just lost it." She took a deep breath. "That's when I shot you."

CHAPTER 42

CHUCK ROCHE TROTTED UP THE steps to the country club while the press shouted questions at him. One caught his ear that pissed him off.

The reporter had said, "Are you going to withdraw your nominee from the confirmation process?"

He turned around and waved his cane at them. "She called it sexual assault. But he called her a liar. That proves he's innocent. This whole thing has been outrageous. If we let a little thing like that stop a nomination, no man will be safe."

He turned and headed inside as another reporter shouted, "Who are you meeting today?"

He ignored that one. As if the people needed to know who their commander-in-chief was talking to. It was none of their business. And it wasn't any of the press's business.

He never understood those animals, hanging out there like a pack of jackals. He told them things, but they never published what he said. They printed whatever they wanted.

They never printed his myriad great accomplishments. He had more accomplishments than any administration in the world. When he cleaned up the border, all they printed were stories about children being separated, abused, and lost in the system. Did they print anything about how dumb it is to bring your kids with you when you're fleeing a war zone? When he told reporters that he never slept with a nude model, did they print that? No, they printed the audio recording where he discussed paying her off. What was their problem? The economy was going gangbusters, and they acted like morals were more important than money.

"Get in, Yuri." He looked at his guest. "You'll love watching me play golf."

The Russian rolled his eyes like a jerk and got in the driver's side. He looked around—the way idiots who never play golf always do—and figured out how to work the controls. They sped off with the Secret Service following a safe distance behind.

"Thank you for the pardons," Belenov said. "My people feel better now."

"Do you play any sports?" Roche asked.

"Football."

"You don't look big enough."

Belenov glanced at him with that same condescending glance Medevtin used. "Of the 7.6 billion people in the world, 7.3 billion of them call the game where you control a ball with your feet 'football.'"

Roche gripped his cane while he imagined plunging it into the foreigner's skull for his disrespect. But the press-rats would have a field day with that one.

"That thing with Kurtz was pure genius," Roche said when he was certain they were far enough away. "No one argued for a minute. But that thing with my old vice president, that was very bad, Yuri. Making him out to be gay was too much. I should have you droned for that."

"Are you threatening me?" Belenov took his foot off the gas and let the cart slow.

"You stuck me with Veronica Hunter." Roche spat. "Never do anything for her. Do you hear me?"

"I hear you, but I don't care." Belenov stomped on the gas. "Besides, your old VP is gay. Finding his ex-lovers on Christian-Grind was easy. Oh, by the way, I met with President Medevtin. He doesn't want me to do anything else for you until you force a breakup of NATO or the EU or both. Apparently, you had an agreement."

"What, you work for Medevtin now?"

"Don't we all?" Belenov laughed and slammed on the brakes. "I told him to fuck off. Same thing I tell you."

"Just don't help Hunter out anymore." Roche fell back in his seat when Belenov hit the gas.

They drove up to the first tee. Belenov stretched. Roche marched to the tee and set up his ball. After a couple practice swings, he smacked the ball hard left into the trees. He set up another ball, turned his hips to offset the angle, and sent the next one off to the right. His third try landed a ball on the edge of the fairway.

"How many penalties and strokes is that?" Belenov asked. "Six?"

"It's one." Roche snatched the paper out of the man's hand. "I'll score the game."

Why he even let a goddamn foreigner onto the course was beyond him. "Where is Tarasov? You promised me a witness. I need him to put Pia Sabel in jail for murder."

"Why are you so fixated on her?"

"Ever since Helsinki, the press writes nothing but lies about Medevtin and me." Roche climbed in and pointed to his ball forty yards up the fairway. "They need a distraction. I'm going to hang Sabel because the people love a good hanging and she's hangable."

"Are you telling me you're not Medevtin's Moll after all?"

"You sound like the enemy of the people."

"You should be careful about using that phrase." Belenov tapped the gas before stomping on it. "Do you know its origination? The Roman Senate declared emperor Nero a *hostis publicus*. They ordered him beaten to death in the Forum. He committed suicide rather than face the humiliation. If you keep using it, your own Senate will do to you what the Romans did to Nero."

"Plenty of arrogant pricks get droned, you know." Roche smacked Belenov on the wrist with his cane. "Don't think I'm short of alternative hackers. There's a Red Army general who's dying for my business. Now answer my question, where is my witness?"

Belenov slammed on the brakes, snatched the cane, and snapped it over his knee. He handed the pieces back to Roche. The president unscrewed the silver handle, twisted in his seat to reach behind him. He took a new shaft out of the golf bag, screwed in the head, and faced forward again.

"Your nephew's only been on the job a few days, and already he's screwing things up at the SEC. Thank you." Belenov resumed their journey to Roche's ball. "Now I need another thing done."

"Then I get my witness?" Roche waited for a shrug from Belenov. "What do you want this time?"

"Defense spending is what destroyed the Soviet Union." Belenov waved his arms. "Defense projects take a decade to develop, and by then, your Congress has flogged any profits out of it. You need to spend more on your elderly, the sick and the poor. Don't you care about America's grandparents, Chuck?"

Roche wanted to laugh. If the man weren't a Russian criminal, he'd make a damn good politician. "Why care about poor people's health? They're our best source for organ transplants. Think about that, young man. You might need a liver one day."

"Because healthcare companies are good investments. Tank manufacturers are terrible." Belenov gave him that indignant look that Bates and Kurtz used. "Canada, Belgium, Australia, France all spend less than half of what you spend per person, and they're healthier and live longer. You should redirect that defense spending to health care immediately. Think of the jobs for in-home workers, pharmaceutical engineers, doctors and lawyers, hospital architects, educators—with what you're spending now, the profit potential is astronomical."

Roche scratched his chin. "Let me guess—you've invested all the money those fools in RULE gave you into the healthcare industry?"

"Of course not." Belenov looked hurt. "I would never do such a thing until after your push for unlimited government spending is successful."

Roche considered investing in Belenov's equity fund. He leaned forward. "The opposition party watches every deal I make. I have to be careful. But there must be a way I could get in on that, right?"

Belenov shrugged. "There is a nice little company in the Caymans you should buy. It's called 'Global Oil Operations Services.' It doesn't have any revenue to speak of, but soon its portfolio will be all healthcare. GOOS would be a good fit for your Global Economic Development Institute. You could buy it for, let's say a million dollars. Think of it as the GEDI GOOS."

"What do you know about GEDI?"

"Found this in Panama." Belenov tossed Luis's GEDI folder on the seat between them.

Roche's heart stopped for several beats. Then he realized Belenov was offering a deal, not turning him in. "What will this GOOS portfolio be worth?"

"That depends on how much you care about the American sick, elderly, and helpless." Belenov smiled. "It would be worth $50 million on delivery. But, if you can double American spending, industry profits would triple or quadruple. You could see a windfall of many times that—provided you sell before your national debt collapses."

"What do you mean?" Roche thought about it. "Oh, because we'd be adding trillions to the debt but not raising taxes. That's not a problem. This country needs a good bankruptcy. I've done it plenty of times, and the only people who get screwed are the debt holders."

Roche smacked his ball into the trees on the left. His second try landed dead center in the fairway fifty yards ahead of them.

"You're right, healthcare is a smart idea." Roche liked this kid. He knew how to make money. And he knew how to take care of the right people. "That's a fair offer, Yuri."

Roche stuck out his hand. They shook on it.

"I will let you know when the time is right to buy GOOS." Belenov drove up the fairway. "It's a good thing you didn't divest your holdings when you took office. Everything will be untraceable. Your GEDI will simply make an investment in a small, unknown company. As long as you don't dump the stocks right away, the press will never notice a thing."

"What about a war?" Roche asked. "Could we make money off that?"

CHAPTER 43

MERCURY CLANKED DOWN THE METAL stairs behind me. *Where do you think you're going, homie? Get back in there and tell her it's OK. You've been through friendly fire before. No big deal. C'mon, my man, a Caesar needs you.*

I said, *Friendly fire is when another squad mistakes you for the enemy. How can you call shooting your best friend—point-blank and on purpose—"friendly fire?"*

Mercury said, *Happens all the time, bro. OK. Granted, it's usually rednecks, and there's alcohol involved, but they get over it.*

I said, *And they all live happily ever after at the trailer park. No thank you.*

Mercury looked at me like I was crazy. *Dude, Sabel Gardens is no trailer park.*

Not the issue, I said. *You can't just shoot people—no matter how rich you are.*

Mercury threw his arms out. *Since when can't rich people shoot poor people? Wait a second—you're not going back to Sylvia, are you? You're like Helena in A Midsummer Night's Dream.* He affected a woman's voice. *"I am your spaniel. And, Demetrius; The more you beat me, I will fawn on you."*

Mercury had a point. If I believed Ms. Sabel, Sylvia had gone bad. Going back to her would reveal some serious mental health issues. I glanced at Mercury, grinning in his red-trimmed formal toga. Hell, I already had serious mental health issues.

I rounded the corner from the alley to the street. Three kids played with a rusty tricycle. I walked around them and struck out for parts unknown.

I looked up over my shoulder. Ms. Sabel stood in the window, watching me with sad eyes. Her gaze felt like anvils weighing me down. I considered flipping her off. She shot me because she knew I wanted to start a family. That meant leaving Sabel Security. She couldn't handle the idea of going on without me to protect her. Like a few people involved at the time, I had some guilt about losing her dad in a firefight, but not enough to give up my future. She could find someone else to be her coping mechanism.

It struck me that thinking like that put me on the same plane as the CIA analyst at Little Bighorn.

Mercury matched me stride for stride. *Oh, my brutha—that is harsh. Maybe, just maybe, she doesn't want to see you waste your life chasing that traitor Sylvia and her cult of Aphrodite.*

I said, *Or maybe, just maybe, she's like you—jealous that I might leave all this behind and have a life free from pain and gunshots and amnesia—and unemployed gods.*

News flash, dawg. Mercury ran in front of me and put his hands out to stop me. *Life is all about pain and gunshots and amnesia. In your case, that's all you're good for, target practice. Now get back there and help Pia-Caesar-Sabel before she gets killed. And, F-Y-I, I am not unemployed. Technically. I'm between civilizations.*

I looked at him, waiting for an explanation about the before-she-gets-killed part. He rarely said things like that unless something was going down.

A second later, I heard Ms. Sabel's feet slapping down the pavement. She yelled, "Jacob! Left! Turn left."

I craned over my shoulder. She was coming at me in full-fledged Olympian mode, arms and legs pumping like a machine. I snapped to my left but didn't see anything unusual for Tremé. Just a couple houses with a two-foot gap between them. I glanced back in her direction.

She swung out wide right, then turned directly toward me. She took two big, powerful strides, leapt into the air, and threw her arms out. She looked like a pro cornerback tackling a wide receiver. Her arms wrapped around my shoulders as her body weight, multiplied by her airborne momentum, slammed into me. We flew over the sidewalk into the narrow space between the homes. I landed on the ground. She slammed into me hard.

I like getting tackled by a handsome woman who straddles that fine line between nicely-ripped and scary-jacked as much as the next guy. But when she's your boss—and your sibling in madness—it can be awkward. Our eyes met. Our noses and lips nearly touched. We almost kissed.

But I'm saving myself for Sylvia.

Two gunshots rang out. The wood over our heads shredded. Ms. Sabel scrambled off me, pulled her Glock, and knelt at the front edge. She said, "See if the back is clear."

Mercury said, *I got the dog, you two jump the fence.*

At times like that, I never question the word of god. I called for her to follow me.

She took another peek, then came fast. We ran down the narrow space into a common area where four houses shared a backyard with a chain-link fence running through the middle. A pit bull lounged under a tree at our end. The dog flipped over and spread all four legs. Mercury rubbed the dog's belly. After we cleared the fence in a bound, Mercury followed. The dog jumped to his feet. He wanted more.

Hugo's skinny sidekick rounded the corner behind us and stopped. The pit bull looked at him and growled.

Mercury pointed at our pursuer and shouted at the dog, *He's a cat lover.*

The pit bull tore after Skinny-Dude, barking and snapping. Our enemy dove for cover.

The victory was short-lived. We were boxed in. The narrow space had two exits. The skinny guy stood at one and his evil spawn at the other. When I took a peek, Spawn had a pistol aimed down the gap. A third guy stood behind him. I ducked back as their bullets buzzed my ear.

I started to fire blindly down the gap, but Ms. Sabel grabbed my wrist and shook her head. "Too many kids and dogs in this neighborhood."

We backed up, covering the entrances to the yard. I covered one end while she covered the other. Our spines were touching.

There are few times in life when you know you're right where you're supposed to be at the time you need to be there. That was one of those times. Being in a firefight with Pia Sabel felt like my calling in life. Even if she shot me once. That thought pulled me back to my mental health issues. I was screwed in the head. No doubt about it.

"Why didn't you call 9-1-1?" I asked.

"Haven't had time."

"I meant when you shot me."

"I did. After the gunfight. They weren't quick. I'm sorry, I'll make it up to you."

Mercury leaned over my iron sights. *See what I mean, bro? That's how it feels when someone says* sorry *to you. Falls way short, don't it? See, that's why I'm not the forgiving type. But she's a Caesar, they don't need forgiving. You're only alive so you can die for her. That's what it's all about. You need to patch things up with her. Tell her god will save you. Go on now. Tell her you know how to get out of this one.*

I said, *But I don't know how to get out of this one.*

"Get out … what?" she asked.

"Just thinking out loud," I said. "Did you try to kill Sylvia?"

Skinny-Dude popped his head around the corner. Ms. Sabel took a shot at him before answering. "She pointed a loaded gun at me. I brushed her back, that's all."

"She doesn't know anything about weapons. Where did she get a gun?"

"I darted the gold-tooth guy. She took it off him." Ms. Sabel sighed. "She let the barrel wander all over. I'd switched to bullets—so I couldn't just kill her."

"WHAT?" My voice hit a high-pitched shriek. "You could shoot me but not her?"

"She made a deal with Roche. I want her to testify against him."

Skinny-Dude's minions had worked their way through the narrow gap and were now poking their heads out to get the layout. We were one pit bull and thirty seconds away from dying in a crossfire.

"Do you have any real bullets?" I asked. "All I've got is six darts. My gear is in the limo."

"Same here." She squeezed off another dart. "Damn. He crouched, and I accidentally darted the dog."

"Sylvia won't testify for you." I fired two more darts at the minions. "She doesn't know anything. Cyril made a deal with Roche and forced her to go along."

Mercury pointed to my left, where someone's grandmother stood at a window with an arm curled around a five-year-old, shaking her head. No doubt pissed off that the white folks didn't keep their gunfight in their own damn neighborhood.

"Jacob." Ms. Sabel shook her head. "Cyril works for Sylvia. She's not who you think she is."

"That's impossible." My stomach fell out of my body. "She was taken the same time they took me."

The minions took another chance. I fired two more darts to keep them at bay.

"That was for show. When I rescued you, Cyril was beating you with a stick. He only looks like he's running the show because she wants it that way. Sylvia was walking around the house with a gun in her hand. She was not tied up. She was not beaten. Jacob. Sylvia is in charge."

My soul followed my fleeing stomach. My gut was empty.

Things started falling into place. She lusted for each other like mad, but she didn't take me back to her crib, she took me to some random actress's condo. She slapped a guy on a boat before going to Corsica. She was not tied up when I rescued her. As a matter of fact, she was ticked off that I saved her. Then she led me, just like Mercury said, into a trap. I said, "Holy Minerva, you're right."

Hold up a second now, homie. Mercury stood behind her looking stunned. *Are you telling me you finally figured out Sylvia's evil—because a white woman told you? And a mere mortal at that? All this time, you didn't believe me? Is that how you are? Oh. I am hurt, my brutha. I am SO hurt. I can't even.* He walked away. *Don't forget Miguel. You left your squad here for a reason.*

Ms. Sabel was looking at me funny. "Holy—what did you say?"

"It's an expression."

"Amicu," Skinny-Dude called from his vantage point. "Put down guns, Pia and Jacob. Hugo want only talking to you. Make deal. No problem here, yes?"

"There was a CIA guy following her." I chewed my fingernail and waited for them to play their end game.

"Following Sylvia?" Ms. Sabel pressed her back to mine again and aimed at Skinny-dude's hiding place. "I need to talk to that guy."

"When I get us out of this, I'll introduce you."

"You can get us out of this?"

With two darts left, I risked switching over to the comm link we used for situations like this. Ms. Sabel clicked in a second later.

"About time you remembered me." Miguel's voice was like a warm blanket in an ice storm. "We're on the street side, about to make our move. Try not to shoot us."

"You had boots on the ground in Tremé and didn't tell me?" Ms. Sabel sounded ticked off.

"I kinda forgot." I thought up an excuse. "I was busy processing who shot me."

A few seconds later, Skinny-Dude's body rose in the air, suspended between heaven and Earth by an unseen force. Miguel stepped out of the gap holding the man by the scruff of his neck. Dhanpal and Tania herded the other two into the arena.

Mercury popped up in front of me. *Cops are on their way, dawg. You have two options. You can run off with someone who has legions of lawyers and a jet. Or you can stay and pretend the prosecutor won't hang all this carnage on you because you're an easy target.*

He had a point. Besides, Ms. Sabel was heading back to France. If I tagged along, I might get to ask Sylvia a couple questions that had been bothering me since Madame Huppert threw a lamp at me.

We tied up the Corsicans, carried them out, and tossed them in the limo's trunk. Sirens approached. We left as the cops streamed past us.

Ms. Sabel and I didn't speak for several minutes.

"I need you with me in Paris." She held up her phone with a text from Virginia Goillot. It said Hunter had gone to Paris for a state funeral. "I need you on my team, Jacob. I apologized. So ... are we good?"

"Who the hell is Virginia Goillot?" I asked.

Mercury opened the divider between the front and back and leaned in from the passenger seat. *I checked, homie. It's still OK for rich people to shoot poor people. Nothing's changed on that score in the last ten thousand years except the choice of weapons. So, answer the woman. Hell, yes, you'd love to go to Paris with her.*

CHAPTER 44

PIA PUT A FINGER TO her lips, shushing the wait staff of the exclusive Paris restaurant, Le Gabriel. She opened the door to the private dining room and walked in. Her agents followed her, frog-marching the thugs from New Orleans ahead of them.

To keep her edge and not give in to anger or paranoia, Pia replayed everything Willy-Mac had said to her. His soft baritone bubbled like a mountain stream in the background. She faced the targets of her surprise visit.

"Don't get up," Pia said. "Put your hands on the table."

Her hostages did as they were told.

"Hugo is comfortably sleeping off the effects of a Sabel Dart in the next room." Pia glared at Mikhail Yeschenko. "When he wakes up, he can have his boys back."

Jacob and Miguel dropped their three bound captives on the floor.

Pia faced the Vice President-nominee, Veronica Hunter. "Your people are bound and gagged. We thought it would be inappropriate to tranquilize American Secret Service agents. However, Dan and Catherine took the opportunity to register their extreme displeasure at being forced to share security arrangements with Mikhail's hit men. Making any formal complaint against me about this would bring up an investigation into your unsavory associates."

Hunter lowered her eyes. Pia had expected anger. Hunter's odd behavior toward her intrigued her.

"You're making a big mistake," Yeschenko said.

"Not telling you to fuck yourself at our last meeting was a big mistake." Pia bent down to meet his gaze. "This man is Jacob Stearne, my most trusted agent. But you knew that already, didn't you?"

Yeschenko shrugged.

"Did you really think I would live in fear of a hundred gangsters when I have thirty thousand seasoned agents on my payroll? As we speak, five hundred of them are rehearsing for a drop on Corvo. Let's check our calendars and find a mutually-satisfactory date for my invasion."

"Pia, may I speak to you alone?" Hunter rose and touched Pia's arm.

"Not yet." She brushed Hunter's hand away. "Although, I accept your apology."

Hunter turned away. Pia watched the former president's oddly deferential manner for a moment. Once again, a different Veronica Lodge Hunter.

Pia faced Yeschenko.

"What do you want?" Yeschenko asked.

"Your confession was quite well done." Pia dropped an SD card on the table. "My people examined it. You mentioned everything on DeLano's checklist as Roche required of you. But they don't exactly line up with the invoices between your companies and Santalum. It was clever and nuanced, but my attorneys caught on right away. You managed to give Roche what he wanted without giving him anything at all. I need you to correct the record."

"Why would I help you?"

"I have the real invoices. The ones that would interest Russian prosecutors. Not to mention the ones that would raise the ire of your RULE members."

Yeschenko chewed the inside of his cheek.

Pia tossed some paper copies on his plate. He glanced through them and exhaled. Her first confirmation they were the real invoices.

"Fine." Yeschenko smiled broadly and tossed up his hands. "Tell me which invoices you need explained. I'd be happy to incriminate the owners and Roche."

Pia looked him over. Too easy wasn't the word for it. She reeled in all the facts as best she could recall them from the complex web of international banking transactions. She stepped back to think it through while Jacob stepped forward.

"These are the accounts," Jacob pointed to printed spreadsheets he placed on the table, "invoices, and companies we think are yours. How accurate is this?"

"I do not keep numbered accounts in my head. However, some of these transactions stand out." Yeschenko kept his gaze fixed on Pia. "Tell me something first, Jacob. Does it bother you that your benefactor shot you?"

"Are these the accounts?" Jacob jabbed a finger into Yeschenko's neck, stopping the flow of the Russian's jugular vein. He then turned his finger to the sheets. Yeschenko got the message. The two of them went over the transactions and dates.

"Pia," Hunter slid next to her. "It means a lot to me that you forgive—"

"Why did you take the VP spot?"

"Mikhail can be an adversary or a friend. Alan always saw him as—"

"This murdering gangster is your friend?" Pia asked, keeping her eyes on Jacob and Yeschenko.

"Like Alan, I see potential alliances as goal-oriented rather than an opportunity to feel smug and superior." Hunter touched her shoulder again. "I could help you. Advise you."

"Then advise me now." Pia faced her. "Why is Mikhail so helpful?"

Hunter backed up half a step. Her lips began to form words, then she blinked and looked away. "I don't know."

"Accepting your apology is one thing," Pia said. "Earning my trust is a different matter. Let me know when you want to get real."

Pia formed a theory about Yeschenko. He'd hinted at something back on Corvo. *Your father was quite helpful at times.* She tapped Jacob on the shoulder. He stepped away. To Yeschenko, she said, "You don't think my evidence will ever see the light of day. Why?"

"Because you don't want my counterpunch." Yeschenko rose and matched her gaze. "Sabel Industries enjoyed explosive growth in the early days. Huge investments went into the satellite business long before it became profitable."

Pia backed up. When she'd taken the reins after Dad's funeral, an accountant had raised questions regarding the company's historical cash flow. The woman said she couldn't account for how Alan had funded the launch of so many advanced satellites in the first two years of the business. The other accountants told her it was water under the bridge, ten to fifteen years ago. Now the accountant's concern began to make sense. As Yeschenko spoke, Pia knew what he would say.

"Your dearly departed father—" Yeschenko picked his champagne flute off the table and tilted it at Pia "—may his soul rest in peace, helped me move a lot of money from the Russian oil business into the international shipping business via Sabel Industries. He was so helpful that I referred him to several friends. He did all RULE's laundry for years."

"You're expecting a truce?" Pia asked.

"If you leave Jacob behind."

"The Secret Service has a prearranged call," Hunter said. "If Dan and Catherine don't check in, they send in the cavalry."

"We know." Miguel held up a timer on his phone. "Four minutes left before they arrive."

Hunter looked surprised.

Miguel shrugged. "They're slower than usual because you're outside the zone they told you to stay in."

Pia studied the former president. Hunter nodded at Miguel as if she admired the thoroughness of his planning. Another out-of-character reaction for her. Why would Hunter warn Pia of the limited time remaining?

Pia returned to Yeschenko. "I'm determined to bring down Roche."

"And I'm willing to help in exchange for Jacob."

"Jacob is off the table. I'm aware of Dad's accounting gaps and have lawyers and publicists ready to shred anything you might say." She pointed at the gangsters face down on the floor. Miguel picked up one of the sleeping Corsicans, shook him, and dropped him nose-first on the floor. "Other than that, you're all out of threats."

Yeschenko's face flushed with anger before he relaxed and blew out a breath.

"You win. But I'll refer only to three accounts."

Some negotiations are better settled than dragged out. Especially when the Secret Service would arrive in three minutes. She took the deal with a nod.

Yeschenko sat down, straightened his tie and jacket, and looked into Jacob's phone camera. He made a clear and concise statement naming the three numbered accounts and shell companies relating to the invoices in Pia's possession. He explained the specific transactions in which he paid Santalum huge sums for nothing of real value.

Even with his statement, she wanted to know why. He had to have a reason to pick those three accounts that didn't apply to the others. Then it came to her. "Ownership of the three accounts was transferred to someone else?"

He made a face, *maybe*.

"I can work with that—it still incriminates Roche." Pia nodded. "Who owns them now?"

"Yuri Belenov." He smiled. "He stole them from me."

The recognition colored Pia's face. A man she hated almost as much as Roche. She glanced at Hunter. "How's the wine?"

"Excellent." Hunter looked confused.

Pia reached across the VP and took Hunter's wine glass and handed it to Tania. Her agent bagged it in a sealed plastic bag. Her people cleared the exit in front of her. Yeschenko looked wounded. Hunter wore an odd expression of both pain and pride. Pia hesitated a moment to gloat, then gave them a little salute and left.

CHAPTER 45

CHUCK ROCHE SAT IN THE presidential limo, staring at the magazine cover that named him, "the healthiest president who ever lived." He liked that. He made a mental note to order hundreds of copies to place around the White House. He even considered granting them an interview.

The Secret Service agent holding the door coughed again. He stepped out into the cold air of Pittsburgh holding his magazine. "Looks like Aleppo in the dark. Even kind of spooky on a foggy, moonless night."

"Yes, sir," his Secret Service agent said. "Sorry about the magazine, sir. It won't happen again."

Roche looked a question at him.

"Uh." The agent squirmed. "I believe *The Onion* is satire, sir."

"Burn it." He slapped the publication to the agent's chest. "Now."

Roche planted his silver-handled cane and strode toward the glass auditorium. He liked it when senators begged for his benediction in tight campaigns. It was an opportunity for the ungrateful whiners to understand his importance. The groveling senator of the day waited by the door.

Roche stopped ten feet away and waited.

The senator looked uneasy for an awkward moment before finally understanding the minimum requirement. He ran to Roche and dropped to one knee. He kissed the fingers of Roche's right hand. "You are the greatest president of all time, sir. There is no higher honor among men than to be your servant. Please consider me yours."

The man looked up with pleading eyes.

Roche patted his head. "Rise, my friend. I'll send instructions on how I want you—"

The auditorium doors flew open. A phalanx of FBI moved in a circle around a suspect. The man in the middle wore handcuffs, ankle cuffs, and a belly chain.

The man saw Roche and screamed. "You did this! I know it was you! I'll get you—"

An FBI agent Tased the suspect. He screamed and convulsed.

The senator looked up at Roche. "Wasn't that General Bates, your chief of staff?"

"Terrible thing," Roche said. "Turns out he had a Chink girlfriend. Sent her classified documents on our naval deployments in the South China Sea. Can't trust anyone these days."

The senator said, "You should consider my daughter to replace him. Top of her class at Stanford Law."

"I have high standards for women in my administration. Is she hot?" Roche looked the man over. "Never mind. Couldn't be."

Roche followed his agents inside. Someone introduced him to the crowds. He strode up to the stage, swinging his cane and doing a jig or two. He soaked up their adoration on stage left. Then soaked up their adoration on stage right. People in the crowd cheered louder every minute. Some of them took a knee and prayed.

When he reached the podium, fifty giant screen TVs lit up in the ceiling and beamed his smiling face to everyone in the building, those outside, and the poor, unfortunate souls left at home. It was a wondrous rally. The kind he deserved in spades. He owed the people more chances for them to adore him. He resolved to do more rallies while their applause shook the building.

He slapped the lectern and waved his arms, trying to quiet the crowd, but their enthusiasm for him knew no bounds. It kept coming and coming like endless waves on a beach. Finally, they calmed themselves enough for him to speak.

"You're going to be hearing things in the coming days that are all lies. Foreign gangsters like Mikhail Yeschenko are teaming up with American scum like Pia Sabel to create lies about my money. Don't you believe them for a minute.

"How do I know this? Because I finally got our intelligence service to work on protecting the United States of America from real criminals. Oh yes. I've whipped them into shape. They used to cry and whine about Russians bringing down Flight 1028, but they never found any real proof. Now they've been ordered by me—because I'm the only president who keeps them focused—to search for people plotting against this great country. And they're doing it. They reported an incident just hours ago in which Pia Sabel attempted to kidnap your new Vice President. Can you believe it?"

The crowd fired up his favorite chant, *SABEL SUCKS! SABEL SUCKS! SABEL SUCKS!*

Roche let them enjoy themselves for a few minutes before continuing. "Aren't you sick of the scientists telling us how our cars are wrecking the weather? I mean, seriously? What do they know? Nothing. They're idiots. And how about those doctors and lawyers and economists and professors who look down on us and tell us we're the stupid ones. News flash—WE'RE NOT THE MORONS. Those fancy, over-educated, born-rich elites, THEY'RE THE MORONS."

The crowd shouted his refrain, *THEY'RE THE MORONS! THEY'RE THE MORONS! THEY'RE THE MORONS!*

The crowd went wild, as well they should. How long would they let educated people tell them what the truth is?

"How about that special prosecutor? He's been after me for years, and all he has to show for it is fifty phony indictments and a bunch of guilty pleas from liars and whiners and innocent people caught in their witch hunt. Some of the Russians don't even have their own lawyers. He's just bullying them. He should stop right now before he finds anything more."

Half the crowd cheered, and the other half looked confused. Roche made a mental note to leave off the last five words next time.

"I've been protecting you. But the media never tells you about it. Just hours ago, I discovered that my own chief of staff had fallen in love with a beautiful woman. Yes, he is married. But. Could happen to anybody. You know? He fell in love with a girl and gave her some secret documents that he shouldn't have. Turns out, she was a Chinese spy. So, he's gone. Watch how the press makes that my fault tomorrow. You know why they're going to blame me? Because they're the ones trying to destroy this country. They're the ones tearing us apart. They try to make you mad at me every day. Me! Your freely-elected president. What's wrong with those people?"

The crowd cheered that one. Then they took up the phrase that had fast become the loudest chant at all Roche rallies, *WRECK THE REPORTERS! WRECK THE REPORTERS! WRECK THE REPORTERS!*

No one liked the press anymore because they failed to appreciate how hard Chuck Roche worked to protect the common man from terrorists and spies and billionaires. If anything bad happened to them, it would be their own fault.

"We need to get organized." Roche waved forward a group standing backstage. "We need to take matters into our own hands. We need to protect the news cycles to make sure they print what's really going on in this country."

Ten men in bright red suits came on stage and stood behind Roche. They wore blue shirts with white ties and white shoes. They looked over the crowd with a steely, determined, confident gaze. Anyone with a brain knew these were leaders in the fight to protect President Roche from his enemies.

"We've been working in secret for months on a little project. Tonight, you get to be the first people to see our new organization of protectors. These men are the commanders of a new group pledged to guard our nation against phony news. They will organize and give orders via Twitter. All their contact information will be made available right after this rally. But only to true patriots. We don't want any reporters infiltrating this group."

Thunderous applause met the ten men in red suits. They stepped forward and waved to the crowd.

"I need ten thousand men of strong character to volunteer for a special nation-guarding assignment." Roche gestured at the men. "Under the command of these red-blooded loyalists, the Redjackets, they will protest in front of every TV station and newspaper until the press finally writes about the great things that are going on in this country. Who will join the fight?"

Throughout the crowd, young men raised their hands. Some raised their Roche Replica canes, made of authentic Chinese plastic with a silver-like handle—only $99.99 each, and available online at the Re-elect Roche website.

"I am the one who lowered your taxes," Roche shouted so all could hear the glory of his mighty deeds. "I am the one who stopped the hordes of drug-dealing children from streaming into this country. I am the one who defunded your healthcare. I am the one who levied tariffs on those filthy Canadians.

"You have given generously in the past, my friends." Roche held his hands up. "I'm calling on you to give again. I can't afford to fight this battle alone. Look around you, find one of my helpers carrying a basket. Give them everything you have. Don't hold back. I need your money."

With that, he stepped back and let the waffling little senator come to the podium. The man raised his hands, then brought them to his chest in prayer. "Ladies and gentlemen let us pray for the greatest president of all time. After all, he came down from his fine penthouse in Manhattan to help us, the little people."

Roche noticed how some people in the crowd already knew the words. These people were impressive. Their love for him almost drove him to tears. But they could do more.

"He has endured a crucifixion in the press." The senator's voice picked up steam. "He has suffered indignities that no other president has ever suffered. Not Lincoln, not Kennedy, none of them have suffered as he has suffered. And yet, no matter how many times they try to knock him down, he has risen again and again to sit in the Oval Office. We have given him, and only him, the power to judge the citizens and the terrorists. May his administration HAVE NO END!"

The crowd roared their newest chant, pronouncing the president's name the way every red-blooded American did, Row-SHAY: *ROCHE EVERY DAY! ROCHE EVERY DAY! ROCHE EVERY DAY!*

When they exhausted the chant, they cheered the senator's name and stomped their feet.

Which could only mean one thing. The son of a bitch was hogging all the limelight.

Roche pushed him aside. "Make sure you know whose side you're on tomorrow. Make sure your friends and relatives are on the right side. Then ask yourself, who are you going to believe—the man you elected president or the liars and terrorists who are trying to tear apart my nation?"

They cheered wildly. *ROCHE EVERY DAY! ROCHE EVERY DAY! ROCHE EVERY DAY!*

"Join the Roche Redjackets," he shouted. "Protesting is the American way. Exercise your right to free speech. Go to the buildings where the liars hide and write their little lies. Make them write the truth! Let nothing stand in your way!"

And the crowd started a new patriotic chant, *WRITE THE TRUTH! WRITE THE TRUTH! WRITE THE TRUTH!*

CHAPTER 46

When we got off the jet in Nice, Ms. Sabel had arranged a separate car for me. She said, "You still can't believe Sylvia betrayed you. I can see it in the way you're dragging around. Go to Monaco, talk to her. If you believe her, stay with her. If you want to give it all up and go home, I'll understand. I'm hoping to save democracy, Jacob. If you can forgive me, I want you on my team. Which means you need to figure out your future."

She and my squad got in a pair of limos and left.

I hopped in the Uber with Mercury who was still wearing his formal toga. He always wears his formal toga in Ms. Sabel's presence. It had red trim with gold threads and covered more of his chiseled body than his porn-toga. He fiddled with his seat belt like someone who'd never used one before.

After getting tangled up, he evaporated through it and then reconstituted himself on top. He tugged his toga straight. *Is she right, homes? You haven't committed to Pia-Caesar-Sabel yet? You still have a hole in your heart for that traitorous little ... Get it together, dawg. Sylvia's nothing, Pia-Caesar-Sabel is something. One of them has never done you wrong, and the other had you beaten within an inch of your life.*

I jumped on him, pounding him with my fists. *Never done me wrong? She shot me!*

The driver said something in French. He sounded surprised and a little frightened.

My fists were striking the door while Mercury flew on the other side of the window. My used god smiled and waved.

"Sorry. Sorry." I straightened up and wiped my face. "Just another American with issues."

Mercury reappeared next to me. *We talked about that. She shot you because you were asking for it. Get over it. Whoo-doggie, I see why she sent you on this mission now, man. You have problems letting go of the little things.*

The Uber dropped me on the square in front of the Casino. I hopped out as a Lamborghini drove down the sidewalk and came within an inch of my toes. The driver honked and swore at me in Arabic.

After scanning the square for more potential threats, I called the Major. I asked, "Why did Ms. Sabel leave the National Team?"

"I thought she told you."

"She's given me reason to doubt her stories."

The Major hesitated. Then she took a long, deep breath. "I'm not a psychologist, I don't know the correct term, but she had a breakdown. With all the traumatic events in her life, you can understand—"

"What happened?"

"They were playing a friendly in Kazakhstan. She'd internalized everything for years. Her PTSD built up like a volcano. She started lashing out—"

"What happened?"

"She beat the crap out of a coach." The Major exhaled slow and long. "She'd become paranoid and delusional. She thought everyone was involved in a conspiracy to kill her."

"Turned out she was right. Two presidents have gone after her." I thought about what she'd dealt with in her life and found a little sympathy. "Did you know she shot me in Tremé?"

After a long silence, the Major said, "Yes."

When I clicked off, Mercury stood in front of me. *See, bro? No big deal. Everybody knows, and they don't have a problem with it. Can we move on now?*

I said, *Being used as a paper target might not be a big deal to you, but it bothers me. I'm making a big decision between life and death here.*

Mercury said, *That's not what you're doing, young blood. You're choosing between what's good, honorable, and true—and Greeks.*

Why do the gods always make things complicated? I looked him over. If there were any other god in the world who would answer my prayers, I'd go with them. A Mayan frog-god would do.

"You're going to leave me hanging?" Peter Hammond stood behind Mercury with his hand outstretched.

"Sorry, odd phone call." I shook hands. "Why is a CIA agent watching a Corsican gangster?"

"I can't tell you that." He looked disappointed. "And a guy with your resume should know better than to ask."

"The Berlin station has zero authority to operate in Monaco. A Berlin agent has zero reasons to be following a gangster on this end of the continent. You're operating outside your mandate, outside your authority. I'm willing to bet your boss has no idea. You're so rogue, I'll bet the *New York Times* would put it on the front page."

I lifted my phone and pretended to dial.

He crossed his arms. "What do you want?"

"An exchange. I tell you what I know, and you tell me what you're doing here." I watched for a sliver of agreement.

"My boss does know." We strolled around the fountain. "But you're right, it is a rogue mission. Someone in our agency traced some odd calls from the White House to Cyril. Call us deep state, call us patriots, whatever, but we found that disturbing. A couple weeks ago, the calls stopped. Our little cabal of intelligence agents wanted to know what happened. I volunteered to find out. My boss is covering for me. You don't want to know more than that."

"Is there a Virginia Goillot in your patriot-gang?"

Hammond looked at me funny. "How do you know her?"

I showed him my stream of odd texts.

"Virginia Hall Goillot, first woman in the CIA to receive a Distinguished Service Cross. She was number one on the Gestapo's hit list, but they never got her. Volunteered to work the entire war inside occupied France. Helluva lady. But that—" he pointed at my phone "—is a codename for one of our rogue operators in the Secret Service. Someone mistook you for smart."

"Says the guy I played." I gave him a fist to bump. He left me hanging. "Who runs the operation here, Sylvia or Cyril?"

"Interesting question." He frowned and stared off into space as if it had never occurred to him. "I'd always assumed the gang was run by the gangster. They do defer to her, but that could be out of respect for Cyril. Why?"

"Someone told me she's running the show after making a deal with Chuck Roche in the hallways at Sabel Gardens."

He stopped walking, touched my arm, and looked me dead in the eye. "I need to speak to that someone."

"And she wants to talk to you." I looked at his hand. Then gave him my soldier stare. He let go.

"I need to talk to Sylvia," I said. "Where is she now?"

"I lost them after your boss trashed their safe house. Haven't seen her since."

I pulled my phone and dialed my certified gambling advisor. "Pierre, where can I find Sylvia Lallouette?"

"The jet you rode in on, Monsieur," he replied. "It is not your own?"

"No." I sighed at the thought of losing my personal gambling advisor. "But the lady who owns it will host her next board meeting at your place if you tell me where to find Sylvia."

I could hear the calculator in Pierre's head working the numbers. Who would deliver more revenue long term: the lady who was laundering a bit of graft off fake art, or Pia Sabel of Sabel Industries? He said, "You will discover her in *Salle des Amériques*, monsieur. Shall I tell her to expect you?"

"Let's make it a surprise."

Hammond chose to wait by the fountain on his own accord rather than be darted first. He wasn't fond of his last nap.

I popped up the steps and into the *Salle des Amériques*. On the way in, a TV displayed President Roche delivering a speech in Pittsburgh. He was surrounded by men in red suits with blue shirts and red ties. The scroll at the bottom indicated he was raising a private army. Exactly like my dream. I pointed at the screen and looked at Mercury, unable to form a question.

Mercury said, *Dude, you get messages from god—and you think it's just a nightmare? So, are you going to respond the same way you did in the dream?*

He loomed over me to intimidate me. World problems were one thing, but I had personal issues to deal with. I didn't know if I could trust my boss. And the evidence against my girlfriend was piling up faster than a snowdrift in Buffalo.

I said, *Not my problem.*

At a tall electronic gaming machine, Sylvia held a glass of wine in her hand. Cyril looked over her shoulder.

They watched a screen intently and didn't notice my approach until I'd landed my fist just above Cyril's belly button. He had little to say as I drove that fist upward, compressing his diaphragm into his lungs. All the air in him flew out over my shoulder. I lowered him gently into an invisible chair. Then I stabbed him with a handheld Sabel Dart.

His bodyguard came at me with a baton that fell to the floor when I stabbed a dart in his thigh.

Seven seconds. Getting slow in my old age.

Sylvia watched me with fear in her eyes.

A guy stood next to her with a stunned look on his pale face. Ms. Sabel had described him to me. I caught his gaze and asked, "You DeLano?"

"Uh, yeah." His voice cracked. "Maybe."

"Ms. Sabel's disappointed you haven't called yet. Did you do what she asked?"

Sylvia snapped a killer-glare at DeLano when she processed my words.

"Kinda." He glanced at her, then me, then choked. "Complications. I … I can explain—if you promise not to kill me."

"Wait outside by the fountain."

He handed his drink to Sylvia and fled like German soldier catching the last train out of Normandy on D-Day.

She stood and shouted after him. "You're a dead man, DeLano. You hear me?"

"It's true, then?" I asked.

Mercury leered over her shoulder. *What've I been telling you all*

*along? Greek-sympathizers are evil. Zeus runs one seriously wrong
religion, dawg. Yours is the one—*

I said, *Shut up.*

Sylvia said, "I haven't said anything yet."

"You ran a lucrative operation for Roche. Why do the art scam?"

"Roche didn't get rich by paying his people." She looked around at
the gambling salon before squeezing her eyes shut in shame. "And I
developed a problem that burns cash."

"I thought we had something real."

"We did." She started to give me the big eyes and moved forward, her
hips leading the way. When I didn't melt, she realized it was a losing
battle. "Why can't I be rich like Pia? I just wanted a big score—just
one—that would set me up for life."

"Life in prison." I huffed. "What happened to the woman who gave
me Desmond Tutu's *The Book of Forgiving* and asked me to hang up my
guns for good?"

"Forgiving isn't profitable." Sylvia sighed. "Chuck Roche rode into
the White House on a wave of hate, not love."

We stared at each other. All my dreams of her success on the Iowa
dinner-theater circuit flashed through my imagination. The dream died
deader than an ISIS fighter in front of my smoking muzzle. Similar
fantasies were crashing and burning in her mind as well. In unison, we
tightened our mouths and faced off like fighters.

"Ms. Sabel wants to know if you'll testify." I waited a beat. "I already
told her you'd never admit your crime to yourself, much less anyone
else. But here's your last chance. Will you testify against Chuck Roche
to save your country?"

"I'm French."

"Only when you want to be." With deep regret, I closed the Sylvia
chapter in my head. "Have a nice life."

CHAPTER 47

PIA ASKED FOR GUENIÈVRE AT the front desk of the *Centre Hospitalier d'Antibes Juan-les-Pins.* The young swimmer met her in the visitors' lounge. In wretched French, Pia said, "Thank you for letting me know he's alive. Have there been any updates?"

"Madame is angry that I told you anything." The girl twisted her knees and fidgeted. "She is most upset that you came. You must leave."

"Is he awake?"

"For a moment, then asleep, then awake for one moment more. The pain is most horrific."

"I'd like to speak to Vivian. Will you show me the way, please?"

"Non." The girl held up a hand. "I will ask again. But you should not impose."

Guenièvre ran around the corner.

The Major called. Pia weighed her available time and took the call.

The Major said, "We thought Yeschenko and Roche had a falling out, but it seems Yeschenko gave the president information about your dad laundering money. Roche tweeted about it a few minutes ago."

"Is it true?"

"Honestly, I don't know." The Major breathed. "I quizzed the accountant you mentioned. She said there are large cash deposits that lack the proper paperwork. It was years ago. The statute of limitations is seven years. The most recent questionable transactions are over twelve years old. You were in high school, I was in the Army."

"*Before my time* is not the moral high ground."

"With Roche, there is no moral high ground. Our customers have stuck with us through some scary headlines over the years. When Roche attacked us the first time, they stayed but with less enthusiasm. Money laundering might be too much. There is only one way to move forward. We have to consider it, Pia. It's time to genuflect before Roche. It's the right thing to do. You can save tens of thousands of jobs."

"Is that what you would do if you were me?"

"No." The Major scoffed. "But your dad picked me out of the ashes of my military career. I still had plenty of matches and gasoline and more bridges to burn. He taught me to make—"

"—no enemies," Pia said. "I know. I've heard that speech."

Pia clicked off with a promise to think about it.

A second later, Vivian powered around the corner.

"The only reason you're here is to seek absolution." She stuck her finger in Pia's face. "Well, you aren't getting any. I told you he was all I had left. I told you not to get him involved in anything. Now he's on life support."

Guenièvre watched from the corner.

Pia said, "I came to offer help—any way I can."

"You can't buy your way out of this." Vivian fisted her hips and leaned into Pia's personal space. "Not this time. You can't hire someone to pick up after you. He's in intensive care. They pulled three bullets out of him. We still don't know if he's going to make it."

Teared welled in Pia's eyes. She willed them back down. Tears would send Vivian into a deeper rage. Pia knew because she'd been in Vivian's place more than once.

"I deserve that," Pia said. "I just came to pay my respects, offer my prayers, and thank you both for—"

"Get out." Vivian pointed at the exit and held her posture like a statue.

Pia waited for a moment, hoping for a crack in Vivian's angry façade that never came. She nodded and turned and tried to make her leaden feet move. She shuffled her way down the hall, heading for the parking lot.

Behind her, a flurry of French swirled between a nurse, Guenièvre and Vivian. Their voices rose in argument, then ebbed and settled.

"Wait," Vivian called out. "That old fool wants to see you."

Pia returned and stood like a student waiting for a critique. "It's up to you, Vivian. You can tell him I already left."

"I'd rather no one had told him you were here in the first place." Vivian gave Guenièvre a withering glance. "But I didn't build my marriage on lies. Get in there. Don't say anything to upset him. You get sixty seconds. Nothing more."

Pia nodded and followed the nurse around the corner and down the hall.

Willy-Mac looked terrible. His proud, strong face was gray, his forehead clammy. A tube was taped in his mouth. His eyes were closed.

She took his hand.

His voice came small and quiet. "Did we win?"

"Not yet."

"Find it? The …" he took a labored breath, "… evidence?"

"Not yet."

"Ready to…" he paused for two breaths, "… give up?"

The lump in Pia's throat clogged her larynx. She kneaded his hand as tears rolled down her cheeks. Giving up was undecided, yet in her heart, she knew the Major was right. How long could she play the righteous avenger before she looked like a mad woman on a Quixotic mission?

Two of his fingers squeezed hers. He said, "The fight always rages. Dr. King wasn't the first, nor the last. Never give…"

He took such a long, labored breath she considered calling the nurse. When she looked up, the nurse was already on her way in. She spoke in upbeat French, indicating Pia's time with Willy-Mac was up.

She stroked the old man's hand one more time and let go.

"Better to die…" Willy-Mac opened one eye just a sliver, "… fighting the tyrant."

He slipped out of consciousness.

Pia found her way back to the visitor's area. Tania was talking to Vivian. Pia kept walking on a path that would take her past them and out the exit.

Vivian stared her down. "Your people tell me you're going to quit."

Pia faced her. "That's the least bad of several bad options."

"You put him in that damn ward." Vivian stepped up to Pia with fire in her eyes. "You better not let his agony be in vain."

CHAPTER 48

CHUCK ROCHE LET HANK GRUBER, Secretary of the Treasury, kiss his fingers while only bowing from the waist. The man claimed bad knees. Gruber's attitude stuck in his mind as the rest of his people took a knee and kissed the presidential fingers before filing into the Cabinet Room. It seemed as if Gruber didn't think the ritual was dignified.

When they were all seated, Roche said, "The national security problem I've called you here to discuss is of utmost importance. We have new information from a source code-named Cyril. He reports that Pia Sabel has come into possession of six video confessions from international businessmen. These videos make appalling claims about you people. The last time we met, I tasked everyone with creating accusations against Sabel."

He let that sink in while the lazy bastards looked at each other.

"Only one of you has bothered to do anything about the problem." He gave each one of them a long hard stare. "What's the matter with the rest of you? Is something wrong? Is something bothering you? Don't you like it here?"

They looked at each other like schoolboys caught throwing eggs at old man Patterson's car. Especially Gruber. That guy was the worst of them all. Always thought he was so smart because he had a PhD in economics.

"Something bothering you, Hank?" Roche asked. "Speak up. I grant you blanket immunity to speak your mind."

"Well. Now that you mention it," Gruber said, "I think I speak for everyone here when I object to the medieval abasement you now require. We are learned men, all of us." Several heads nodded agreement. "We have matriculated at the most prestigious universities and enjoyed distinguished careers. We are highly regarded by our peers and have held significant positions in the commercial sector. We never agreed to take part in a kakistocracy. Our academic—"

"Anyone else agree with Hank?" Roche glared around the room.

"Not me." CIA Director Nora Ratched waved her hand.

"You know what I hate about you, Hank?" Roche sneered at the man. "I can't understand a damn thing you say. The basement was here when I moved in. And, I heard you've been saying some nasty things about my Redjackets. Not only did you fail to create any useful evidence against Sabel, you undermined my authority. You know what that means?"

Hank pursed his lips and shook his head.

"YOU'RE FIRED!" As soon as Roche's voice stopped echoing off the walls, two guards appeared by Hank Gruber's side and yanked him out of the chair.

Gruber railed treasonous slogans as they dragged him from the room. Proof that the man was unfit to work in the greatest administration of all time.

Roche went to Gruber's empty chair, picked up the folders and notebooks, and dropped them in the nearest trash can. Then he looked at the rest of them. His cabinet officers looked at their fingers. He made a note of the three who looked at him and smiled. O'Brien, Ratched, and Danvers understood the important part they played in the grand plan.

Hunter kept her eyes fixed on him with no hint on her face of whether she agreed.

He said, "Maybe now we can put tariffs on anything we want, huh? Won't that be a nice change?"

No one answered.

"Anyone else have a gripe? No? Good." Roche took his seat. "As I was saying, we have intelligence that Pia Sabel has doctored up confessions by criminals that will harm your reputations. One among you has contributed ideas to save your miserable hides. You will recall that I promised the person who helped the most would become Secretary of State. Well, let me introduce you to your next peer, Nora Ratched."

The CIA Director, now Secretary of State nominee, rose and smiled and bowed to the president the way good cabinet secretaries do.

Veronica Hunter stared at the younger, firmer blonde—and not in a nice way.

"I know," Roche continued, "I said Hunter would be the last woman I'd put in an important position, but Nora did some terrific things for me over the last few days. She's good at quite a number of positions, ahem, in the administration. One of those things was having the initiative to work with our informant, Cyril."

He explained how Pia would return to the states at any minute and conspire with several traitorous senators to get her evidence in front of Congress. When that happened, the special prosecutor could see them. And the press would post them all over the web. That would be a disaster.

"Excuse me, sir." Sinclair, National Security Advisor, raised his hand. "Who is this Cyril?"

Nora Ratched scowled at the man. "You of all people should know these things. President Roche had the foresight to groom this contact personally."

Sinclair winced. "I meant, who cleared him? Who did the background check? Who is this guy?"

"Asked and answered," Ratched said.

Roche said, "This is a grave matter, people. Pia Sabel must be stopped. Now, the next item on the agenda regards going to war against Saudi Arabia."

The room erupted in shouts of astonishment because too many of his people did not have absolute faith in the president's infallible wisdom. Someday, he would get rid of these slackers and replace them with true patriots who understood how and when to get with the program.

"SHUT UP." He slammed his cane down on the table. "What the hell is wrong with you? When I say we're going to war, you don't start arguing. You fall in line. Now, listen to Secretary of Defense O'Brien's report."

"First, I must say it is a blessing to be in your cabinet. Thank you, sir." O'Brien stood and delivered. "Over the last forty years, Saudi Arabia has poured over $100 billion into spreading Wahhabism around the world. These extremist Muslim views inspired Al-Qaeda, the Taliban, and hundreds of radical imams. They've exported terrorism and revolution from Afghanistan to Yemen. They don't allow a free press or freedom of speech. They murder dissidents, editors, and reporters. Under Ms. Ratched's patriotic leadership, the CIA revised their guidance and now calls them an active threat against the United States of America."

"Wait," said the Secretary of Commerce, "they're our allies."

"If they're so bad, why weren't they included on your Muslim ban?" another disloyal secretary asked.

"Goddamn it, listen to him." Roche slammed his cane on the table again. "They're going to be our next enemy. This is a talking point. Whenever someone asks you about one of my tweets, or what the special prosecutor is up to, Saudi Arabia is your new answer. Start preparing your departments for a war against them in case we need one."

"You can't go to war like that. You need—"

"Do you guys know what happened to Bates?" Roche shouted so hard his face turned red. "I happened to Bates." He jabbed his finger at his own chest. "Wanna know what happened to Ripley? I happened to Ripley. And Kurtz, and all the others, too. When someone thinks he can take me down, I take him down first. Don't think for a moment that I won't ruin you too, motherfuckers." He slammed his cane on the table. "Now quit arguing and start doing what I tell you—or you'll be the next one to get Kurtzed."

CHAPTER 49

I grabbed DeLano by the scruff of the neck. "Ms. Sabel told me you got all salty and threatened her in Antibes."

"Cyril made me do it." He glanced back at the Casino.

"Any idea how close you came to needing facial reconstruction surgery?" I started dragging him around the fountain to where Peter Hammond, international rogue spy, waited.

"I'm a schoolteacher, man." DeLano shifted his eyes left and right and over his shoulder.

"You're a schoolteacher who owes Ms. Sabel a bucket full of SD cards. Where are they?"

Hammond looked us over. "Most people butter up the schoolteacher with an apple, Stearne."

"I don't have any patience left."

"You didn't have any last time I saw you." Hammond stepped back as if he'd said something funny. "What's on the SD cards?"

"I don't care." I looked around for a cab. "I'm going for a career change in about five minutes. First, I owe you and Ms. Sabel a bit of closure. Then, I'm going to open a café."

"You won't be alive in five minutes," DeLano said in a whisper last used by the French Resistance. "Cyril's got juice. We gotta get out of town."

"What's this 'we' shit?" I asked. "I just put Cyril down for his afternoon nap."

DeLano did his shifty-eyed look again. "I heard him talking to POTUS this morning. Cyril told Roche that Pia has six SD cards. The president went ballistic. Did you hear me? Dude. The president. Cyril's that deep. I'll bet he's got CIA watching him. We gotta get off the streets right now."

Hammond and I shared an ironic glance. Then Hammond leaned in to sniff DeLano's collar, checking for the reek of alcohol.

Mercury appeared behind him. *Ain't this the best, homie? Can you really turn your back on this life of international intrigue?*

I said, *She shot me.*

Mercury said, *Are you as sick of saying that as I am of hearing it? Was I right about Sylvia?*

I said, *Yes.*

Mercury said, *And I'm right about Pia-Caesar-Sabel. She's trying to do what you built your career doing: saving your country. Why would you turn your back on that?*

I said, *I can't trust her.*

You were asking for ... I mean, you were being a dick. He shook his head. *Think about your options, dawg. You're never going to sell your mini-asparagus and Japanese mushrooms back in Iowa. Best you can do there is meatloaf.*

I said, *It's all about rutabagas now.*

As much as I hated to admit it, meatloaf was the edgiest dish I could serve between Omaha and Dubuque. But my days of taking bullets for—or from—beautiful women were coming to an end.

Hammond and DeLano were looking at me funny. I wondered if my pious meditations were spilling into my daily life again. Hammond pointed at DeLano. "If Cyril's really talking to POTUS, I need that phone. You gotta go back and—"

I reached in my pocket, pulled Cyril's burner and slapped it in his hand.

Hammond stared at me as if I were the messenger of the gods. "Have you ever considered joining the Company?"

"Good idea," I said. "But tell me the truth, does the lobotomy hurt?"

Mercury said, *Why are we wasting time with this loser, dude? You need to find the SD cards and get them to Pia-Caesar-Sabel.*

I said, *Maybe the CIA would be a good fit.*

Sure, with little hard work, you could be the assistant manager in the cafeteria at Langley in ten, fifteen years. C'mon, my man, you're burning daylight.

"Guy like you, wouldn't feel a thing." Hammond pointed up the street. "Do you need him?"

DeLano was half a block away, sprinting like an amateur in a suit. I took off after him. Hammond followed with less enthusiasm.

I collared DeLano three blocks away, in front of the shoe store I'd visited earlier. The shoe-guy with the pompadour was adjusting the window display when I tackled DeLano. Pompadour put his fingers over his mouth to contain his surprise at my violence. When he recognized me, he shook his head. His words replayed in my head: *American, you know. Beats her. I've heard.*

I shrugged at the guy and dragged DeLano to his feet. "Where are the SD cards?"

"Can you get me into the witness protection program?" he asked.

Hammond pulled up breathing hard. "What's on these SD cards?"

"If she trusts you," I said, "Ms. Sabel will tell you."

I hailed a cab. While we watched it pull up the block, I filled Hammond in on where to find Ms. Sabel in Nice. "Tell her what you're doing, and she'll help."

I texted Miguel to expect Hammond, then stuck the spook in the cab and waved goodbye.

I put my arm around DeLano and started walking back to the Casino. "Does Cyril have the SD cards?"

"No. Cyril thinks Pia took them, but I hid them." He looked up as we neared the end of the fountain. "I could only find six."

"Where are they?"

"Near here. I want a guarantee first."

"I guarantee you'll have two broken ribs and a crooked nose if Ms. Sabel doesn't have them in an hour."

"I mean, immunity. Can you do that?" He realized we were about to cross the street and enter the Casino. "Hey, where are we going?"

"To see Sylvia." I gave his shoulder a squeeze. "Look, buddy, I don't care. I've quit my job several times in the last week. Nobody takes me seriously. But this time, it's going to stick. Now, you seem like a sober fellow, so here's a bit of advice. Find the SD cards, take them to Ms. Sabel, or go in the Casino and throw yourself at the mercy of Sylvia Lalloutte."

"You mean my options are suicide or suicide?" He grabbed my shirt. "You gotta help me."

Mercury laughed. *You're not going to sacrifice the schoolteacher, are you, homie?*

I said, *Not my problem. I'll take my chances in the Midwestern culinary scene. At least, next time I fall in love, it won't be with an actress-turned-gangster, and I can raise a family.*

Mercury said, *To thine own self be true, And it must follow, as the night the day, Thou canst not then be false to any man—I helped Shakespeare write that smack, fat lotta good it did me. Now it's time to be true to you and me both homie. Who do you want to be, lead chef at Denny's or Jacob Stearne, awesome servant of the Roman pantheon?*

I said, *Does Denny's have health care?*

Mercury said, *Don't be like that, brutha. I'm serious here. Pia-Caesar-Sabel has a little problem with anger management. But she's trying to save your stinking country. You used to care about that. You went to war and killed a boatload of terrorists and a few unfortunate bystanders so that decent Americans can play Fortnight, cheat on their husbands, and eat Flaming Hot Cheetos whenever they want. That's the American way. You gotta help her, bro.*

I said, *Don't call my country "stinking."*

Mercury said, *As long as the predominant religion is based on that sandal-shod poser, I'm gonna call it what it is. You gotta help Pia-Caesar-Sabel so she can tell everyone about the one true pantheon. Besides, have you seen what Chuck Roche has done to the NFL? He still harbors a grudge because they wouldn't let him buy the Buffalo Bills. That's how vindictive and petty he is. You should drag him outta office just for messing up sports.*

The one point that always stuck in my head when considering a career change was the fact that cutting a head of lettuce in half doesn't give me the same satisfaction as shooting a bad guy between the eyes. And nothing a chef can do measures up to the job satisfaction I get when saving the United States of America from her enemies. Especially when they're powerful people. But, could I trust Ms. Sabel?

I said, *Give me one good reason why I should work for the woman who shot me.*

Mercury pointed at the row of exotic cars. *Do you get to shoot an Arab prince and steal his Lamborghini in Iowa?*

At the end of the row, the drunk Arab who nearly ran over my toes chatted up a supermodel while leaning against his Lambo.

For the record, I said, *I never shot a bystander. I'm pretty sure.*

And then there's the fact that there aren't any Lambos in Iowa.

I brushed DeLano's hands off me and grabbed his collar. "I'll give you a one-time offer that expires in three seconds. Think carefully before answering. Will you lead me to the SD cards?"

DeLano swallowed. "What about immunity?"

"No problem."

I let go of him and strolled over to the Arab. In his language, I said, "Drunk? And without your thobe? What will your father say?" I turned on my sergeant's voice and shouted in his face. "Straighten up. Look at me when I'm talking to you. Suck in that gut. You call that a salute?"

While he looked confused, I slammed my last handheld dart in his leg and caught him when he slumped. A mean glare sent the young lady away. I parked the Arab on a nearby Maserati and swiped his key.

I texted Ms. Sabel not to leave Nice without us. I shoved DeLano in the passenger seat and pressed the starter. "We're stealing a car in a city that has more cops than streetlights. I can disappear in an instant and leave you to answer for my crimes. If you want to stay out of jail, DeLano, start pointing the way to the SD cards."

CHAPTER 50

PIA MET JACOB AT THE top of the airstair just after midnight. She pointed at the Lamborghini on the tarmac. "Where did you get that?"

"A friend lent it to me." He grinned.

One step below him, DeLano shook his head. Without looking, Jacob kicked DeLano. DeLano switched to nodding with enthusiasm and mouthed, *Yeah, legit.*

"We don't steal cars." She fisted her hips. "The police came asking about it."

"But—you stole my Porsche," DeLano said.

"Not exactly." She thumbed at the hangar. "It's over there."

"I texted the owner." Jacob held up his closed hand between them. "Told him where to find it. We're good."

She held out her palm. Jacob dropped six SD cards into it.

She thanked them both and ushered them inside and told the pilots to take off. The chairs had been turned down into beds. Miguel, Tania, and Dhanpal were already asleep. Jacob and DeLano joined them. Pia went to her room and closed the door and plopped down in the chair. The jet rumbled down the runway, nosed up, and took off.

Her lifelong insomnia gave her little hope for sleep. She plugged them in her laptop, confirmed the SD cards held what she thought, then uploaded them to Bianca for analysis. She started to text Senator Jeff Smith, a family friend, about appearing before his committee.

Her finger hesitated over the send button.

These cards cost her several weeks of effort. This was the evidence she needed to bring down Roche. To get them, she had burned nearly everyone she knew. Yet, everything involving Roche went sideways.

She'd paid a high price to get here. Now it was time to determine the cost of moving forward.

The engines roared outside while her agents slept. A layer of moonlit clouds below blocked her view of southern France.

The business decision was simple. The Major laid it out, and there was no arguing with it. Roche won. Businesses everywhere either loved or hated him but all kept quiet. Among big company executives, she alone had challenged his immoral behavior. And for that, her employees were about to pay the price. It wasn't fair to them. They didn't ask to be laid off. They didn't ask her to challenge his power. Some had even voted for Roche. Right or wrong, misguided or inspired, the people of a democracy had spoken. The sensible thing to do was to capitulate.

So why had Vivian changed Pia's mind? *You put him in that damn ward. You better not let his agony be in vain.*

Guilt accounted for a small fraction of her motivation. She wanted to save the country from the most incompetent and dishonest president in history.

Alan taught her to consider the pros and cons of big decisions. She started to make a list in her head.

What were the pros? They were easy to articulate: Expose Roche; force his resignation; get the economy off the debt-cliff; clean up the rampant corruption; restore healthcare; repair relations with allies. But those were details best left to the politicians. Since Hunter would soon be VP, the country might go back to relative sanity.

Pia almost laughed. She used to loathe Hunter's administration. Now it sounded like the good old days. She moved to the bed, stretching out on top of the covers.

What were the cons?

Roche always lies. That's huge. Defending yourself against a liar is hard. And Roche would attack with a tsunami of lies. How would he respond to the videos themselves? He'd claim they were Hollywood productions, digitally altered. Everyone knows how post-production works.

Then he would attack her character. Would he accuse her of leading a pedophile ring? Yes. It was only a matter of time. Would he drag her sex life into the public eye? Yes. And Stefan would help. Stefan wouldn't need to lie, just telling the truth about her explosive anger would be damning enough.

The thought of public humiliation scared her. Roche counted on that fear with all his adversaries. He had no sense of shame which made it his preferred battlefield. Her pride was a silly vanity in contrast to saving the country, but a very real fear nonetheless.

The public clamored for stories of the great and powerful falling from grace. The paparazzi was an industry created to watch the crash and burn of those who reached a pinnacle. From Princess Diana's dating habits, to Britney Spears' youthful nights on the town, to Kendall Jenner's ill-advised advertisements, anyone in the public eye was ripe for humiliation for the tiniest infraction. And she was about to infract the president big time.

Was it worth it? A sudden rush of empathy for celebrity suicides flowed through her. They had taken a path they hoped to be quiet and peaceful. Perhaps suicide would be a better path than raucous exposés and character assassination tweets. But would that end be truly peaceful? Or would it be an eternity filled with regret? Monsters worse than Roche might wait in that bleak darkness for all anyone alive truly knows. And yet, death presents an inviting alternative to defamation on national platforms from *Twitter* and *Facebook* to *CNN* and the *New York Times*. Everything Roche said was reported because he said it, not because it has any basis in fact.

Who wants to be boiled alive in that hellish cauldron?

The cowardice of vanity was the foundation of Roche's success. No one would call him out for fear of falling into his pit of despair.

It wasn't just faith in herself she needed. While her cause may be true, and her movement may gain traction, the unresolved question came down to one consideration: when presented with the facts, would Congress choose to preserve their nation—or their party's leader?

What did Willy-Mac say? *The fight always rages. Better to die fighting the tyrant.*

Easy to say. Harder to do. Yet Willy-Mac had gone bravely into that warehouse knowing the danger. She could only hope to equal his courage.

Another thought scared her even more. Would Roche turn his Redjackets against her? She checked her phone for news about his version of Brownshirts. Three thousand "volunteers" had stormed the *Miami Herald* and vandalized the building. Another group had shut down the *Chicago Tribune* for three days by barricading the streets. Several other protests had closed *CNN* offices across the country. Reporters were beaten, their cars destroyed, their cameras and microphones crushed or stolen.

Sabel Security's agents were better trained, better organized than the Roche Redjackets. But how could her agents defend freedom of the press? Could they handle a flash mob organized via Twitter? There weren't enough darts to go around. Her agents would be effectively neutralized if she sent them out to stop the Redjackets. Did Roche know that? Was it part of his plan? No way. He wasn't smart enough. Yet, when he felt threatened, he fought with Herculean intensity. With his back to the wall, his survival instinct magnified his intellect. Planned or not, he would discover this advantage eventually.

Those were the cons she could think of. How many more had she not yet considered?

She pushed the pillow under her head.

Dad sat in the chair across the aisle. "Every individual will eventually rise up. Some will rise up too late. Some will rise too soon. When will you rise, Pia? When will you say, 'no more?' This is your time. Even if it seems impossible, you must resist."

She examined his face. He was at rest, naturally relaxed. She asked, "Did you launder money for Yeschenko?"

"Don't let that be your excuse to back down." He met her gaze with a cold glare.

She sat up in the dark. "Chuck Roche? Fuck Roche."

She texted Senator Smith. "I have videos that expose Chuck Roche's corruption. I want to testify. When can I get in front of your committee?"

CHAPTER 51

CHUCK ROCHE LOOKED UP FROM the head of the table in the White House Situation Room. US Marshals pushed Yuri Belenov toward him. Roche waived a hand at the Russian. "Leave the handcuffs on him, take the rest of that off."

Nora Ratched and a few other executives from intelligence and defense agencies sat at the table.

One of the CIA guys said, "You can't bring this man in here. He's a Russian national tied to Mikhail Yeschenko."

"This is why no one trusts you." Roche spun to face him. "You're wrong. This man is a double agent who's been doing valuable work for the administration."

"Impossible." The CIA officer frowned. "I'm in charge of double agents."

"Not anymore." Roche rose and slammed his cane on the table. "YOU'RE FIRED!"

The man picked up his things and shook his head. "Inevitable in this admin—"

"Leave that." Roche pointed at the man's notebooks. "Your security clearance is revoked."

Secret Service agents seized the man's arms and led him out.

"Sir, with all due respect," another deep state official spoke up. "I must object to sharing intel with unvetted sources. We have very sensitive—"

"You don't need to be here," Nora Ratched said.

The man figured out her message quickly: *get out before you get fired.* He snatched his laptop and fled.

A marshal shoved Belenov into the chair next to Roche. Hate bled from the captive's eyes like a caged animal.

"You were pretty smug last time I saw you." Roche patted Belenov's hand. "You've learned an important lesson today. My guys can track down any miscreant, Yuri."

Roche waved his hand at Ratched. She fiddled with her laptop. The screen at the end of the room showed an intelligence seal warning all kinds of pain to unauthorized users. She clicked a few more times until the screen filled with a nighttime image of an office building in downtown Santos, Brazil.

"Recognize your office, Yuri?" Roche grinned.

Ratched zoomed the camera in closer. She flipped the image from full-color night vision to infra-red sensors. Human heat signatures nearly as clear as daylight photography shocked the Russian into a gasp.

"Is that your associate, Petr?" Roche asked.

Belenov glared back at him. "You gave us pardons."

"So what?" Roche grinned. "What about that other guy? Isn't his name Igor?"

"What is this?" Belenov's words were venomous.

"This is SHaRC headquarters." Roche leaned closer. "Those are your hardworking lieutenants standing guard on the night shift. Loyal guys. Making millions for you."

"Why are you showing me this?"

Belenov was trying to hide his fear behind his rage. It wasn't working. The clammy skin and the trembling lips of a coward under pressure were obvious. Roche found himself excited at the prospect of making the arrogant young man scared. It was more fun than calling someone fat and ugly on Twitter. It was more fun than calling war heroes losers. Hell, it was more fun than having the wife and children of a terrorist killed.

"That drone has two missiles onboard, Yuri."

Belenov took another look at the screen. "Why does the picture say 'Sabel Technologies' at the bottom?"

Roche squinted, unable to read the subdued grey lettering in the lower right.

"They make the only silent operational UAVs," Ratched said. "Sorry, sir. The Air Force is working on alternative drones."

Roche drummed his fingers on the table and stared at her until she hung her head in shame.

Then he turned back to Belenov. "I can drone them while you watch. Just to make sure you understand the seriousness of what we're doing here. I'm rich, I can shoot whoever I want. And I'm President of the United States of America, so I don't even need a gun."

They stared at each other long enough to make everyone uncomfortable. Roche was used to long silences. The quiet worked because he was so smart it took several minutes for most people to catch up to his brilliance.

"Oh, I know what you're thinking," Roche said. "You can run to the press and ruin me with whatever. Well, newsflash, Yuri. Nothing ruins me. NOTHING! If you can find a news outlet that hasn't been shut down by my Redjackets, they'll think you're a whacko conspiracy nut."

Belenov looked at his handcuffs. The rage inside him was evident. His head quivered, and his face was red.

"One missile can wipe out your entire night crew," Roche said. "Or we can wait until morning and wipe out the day crew. Either way, you're email-reading, insider-trading operation is over."

Belenov tightened up while staring at the screen. His anger could slice through cold steel, yet Roche knew he had the lowlife scum by the balls. Belenov built his little group of SHaRCs by hand. It was his baby. To lose it would mean losing everything he had in his miserable life. He would break. Everyone who challenged the great Chuck Roche broke eventually.

Belenov slowly turned to face Roche. "What do you want?"

Roche smiled and held up a hand as if saying, *hold that thought*. His gaze swept the rest of the officials in the room. "Everyone out."

Nora Ratched closed the screen, rose and led them out.

When the last man had shut the door, Roche faced Belenov. "First thing I want is a guarantee you'll never act like a smartass again. No guarantee, the nightshift dies. Second thing I want is an apology followed by you kissing my fingers."

Belenov had looked agreeable until Roche mentioned the fingers thing. It was like anal sex—no one liked it the first time. But just like butt-stuff, there's no better time to get started. Roche reached for the big red button Ratched had left on the table. He pulled it close and let his left hand hover over it. Then he held his right hand out and put his fingers within Belenov's kissing range.

Belenov looked at the now-blank screen, then the dangling fingers. "I will never again act like the smartass in front of you. I apologize for my rudeness and lack of manners."

He took a deep breath and kissed the fingers.

"That wasn't so hard, was it?" The president liked it when people understood their place in the world. The keepers were the ones who knew enough to take a knee without being told. Belenov might learn eventually. At least for now, Roche had his own version of the Red Army hackers. He didn't need Hunter. And both of those were good things.

He pushed his Top-Secret phone in front of Belenov. "These texts show the checking accounts that come up in six stolen videos. Your mission is to make a few adjustments."

"If I refuse, you blow up my offices?"

"That's not all." Roche roared with child-like glee. "If you tell anyone or move your offices or do anything I don't like—everyone dies."

HUNTER LOOKED OUT AT THE magnificent moonlight glittering on the Atlantic off the coast of Corvo. "What a marvelous view."

Yeschenko awoke and shook his head and pushed one of the blonde girls off his chest. "What was that?"

"I remarked on the view."

"To wake me?"

"Yes." She rolled a finger around at the three women and one man who lay naked and strewn about the room as if by a tornado.

He took the hint and clapped his hands. "Thank you for coming in. Your services are no longer needed. Tatyana will show you to the servant dorm."

The four got up, picked up their gossamer clothing, and followed Tatyana.

"We have a problem," Hunter said. "Pia is walking into a trap."

"I've never had someone MC an orgy before." Yeschenko stood behind her and wrapped his arms around her. "Your friends, if that is what you want to call them, are truly gifted."

"At a certain age, I realized people are too timid to demand what they want out of sex. They want someone to take charge." She curled her hands around his. "I'm serious about Pia."

"She is a problem," he said. "She will turn on you."

"I have spies in the White House. Roche is up to something that might delay our plan."

"You're not the only one with spies." He let go and wandered until he found a robe. "Did you wonder how she found us in Paris? She followed you. She has a spy in your operation."

Hunter wheeled on him. She started to speak, then caught herself. Fury colored her face. She stormed out of the room and down the hall. She looked in several rooms before she found her Secret Service agents.

"Dan, Catherine, good news," she said. "You've been promoted. You're going back to White House duty immediately."

CHAPTER 52

Ms. Sabel was thoughtful enough to have Anoshni delivered from the farm when we landed. My dog had taken to rolling in Joyce's compost barn before running through the cow pens. Which meant the pup was spending my day off at the groomer's. When they trotted him out, he smelled like lilacs, had a bow in his hair—and he was ready to bite me. He was a reservation dog, rescued by Miguel on a visit home. Miguel had given me the pup as a "sorry-about-that" gift after running off with my girlfriend. I got the better end of the deal. My dog worships the ground I walk on while the girlfriend walked out on Miguel a week later.

I waited until we were in the car before ripping the bow out and roughing Anoshni's fur. An act of kindness he appreciated. I fired up the Ferrari Ms. Sabel had given me to replace the one that had been blown up by her enemies, which itself was a replacement for an older car that had been blown up. I forget how far back the chain of destruction goes.

With the convertible's top down, the dog stood on the armrest and stuck his head into the wind. He knew we were heading for the dog park. The cool spring air flowed through his nose and over his face.

I needed a break from the tension at Sabel Gardens. Consultants and lawyers were swarming Ms. Sabel with advice and practice sessions and corrections and notes. Nobody needed shooting, so my expertise was not in demand. She looked anxious when I left. Not in the romantic sense; more in the guilt sense.

She wasn't sure if I'd forgiven her yet. I wasn't either.

Joyce called, offering a welcome distraction from such heavy philosophical problems. She said, "Do you like Louis Kirby?"

"He didn't clap me in irons when I killed four men in the front yard. He seems reasonable enough."

"I mean—" she hemmed before she hawed "—do you think he'd be a good fit in the family?"

"Wait, I never heard what happened with Dan Sweeney. I thought you two—"

"You always do that!" She yelled so loud, I pulled the phone away from my ear. "You've always got to bring up whatever you can just to … Oohh. That's so childish, Jacob. Just sibling rivalry, that's all."

"Uh. OK." My turn to hem and haw. "Didn't Louis used to run Kirby Farms before he became sheriff?"

"Those rumors aren't true." She yelled with less volume this time. "He didn't go bust. His brother wanted a share, but there wasn't enough money in it for two of them, little place like that. So he went into the rounding-up-drunks-and-vandals business. That's the real story, and don't you believe otherwise, no matter who you hear it from."

It took me a few seconds to figure out what the call was about, but I replayed her original question in my head, and it came to me. "He'd fit in fine, Joyce. You have my blessing."

"I don't need your blessing. I'm a grown woman—and accomplished too. Why, as a matter of fact, I—"

Family.

I held the phone up to Anoshni's ear so he could share my pain. He gave me a sad look. When I brought it back, she was still going. "—and at seven times the yield of any cock-based-farmer in the state. You try that sometime."

I noticed a rental car in my mirror. Behind the wheel—the quiet guy. Ms. Sabel had called him Hugo. Cyril wanted information about him. I put the phone on the car's Bluetooth and pulled my Glock out of the holster in the car's central tunnel. I took a turn onto Democracy Boulevard, crossed I-270 and drove by Montgomery Mall. It's a wide street that made Hugo easy to keep an eye on. Joyce kept bragging about organic farming in the twenty-first century while I made a left onto Seven Locks Road. She was running out of air when I made another left onto Bradley Boulevard, a mile shy of completing a full circle from where I first spotted Hugo.

There were no aggressive moves. No sudden acceleration. No burning rubber on tight corners. No assassins who might lean out the passenger window and take a shot. All of which meant Hugo wanted to talk, not fight.

"But that's not why I called." She rested for a second. "Crazy as it sounds, we talked and, well … we want you back."

Hugo waved and pointed to the side of the road. I stuck my hand in the air and indicated a U-turn. If he was planning to kill me, at least we could have it out at the Cabin John Dog Park. I owed that much to Anoshni. I turned around in the Bethesda Country Club driveway and headed back.

"Did you hear me?" Joyce asked.

"I'm flattered." More like shocked they wanted another brush with danger but saw no reason to bring that up. "I'm not sure farming is my—"

"It's not about you and farming, ya dipshit." She gave me her signature huff. "Mom just can't take it with you being gone, getting shot, killing people, and all that. You need to be back where it's safe to raise a family, where you don't have to lock your doors, and the sheriff gives you a lift home instead of the thirty days. We crunched some numbers and came up with a plan."

Hugo made the turn and followed at a respectful distance. Too respectful. I watched his hands and face to see if he was talking to someone on a comm link. With the dog's muzzle visible from all sides, even a Corsican could work out where we were going.

"Are you listening to me?" she asked. "Do you want to know what the plan is?"

"Yes, ma'am," I said.

Hugo's jaws didn't move, his hands stayed on the wheel, his eyes on the road.

"We're going to invest in your new restaurant. We're thinking someplace like Fort Madison, but we're willing to go as far as Davenport or Des Moines if you force the issue. Whatdayasay?"

Mercury held the dog in his lap and petted his clean coat. *Yeah. What do you say, bro? Hugo came 4,500 miles from Ajaccio just to blow your brains out. Think an extra 700 will stop him?*

I said, *Can you guarantee me Ms. Sabel won't blow my brains out if I erase Hugo?*

Are you still hung up on that? Dude, she will never, ever shoot you again. Until next time. Now blow off your sister and deal with the Corsican. He carries a Ruger SR9 under his shirt and is hoping to use it.

I said, *Hoping?*

Mercury said, *He's on a mission from Yeschenko, with orders only to shoot in self-defense.*

"We found a little place next to Lost Duck Brewing on the waterfront." Joyce spun out her dream for my future. "Perfect for you. Nice people who might like to experiment with crazy—"

"I'll think about it and get back to you." I clicked off and pulled into the park. Unless something had changed since 1885, Fort Madison's "waterfront" was a railroad track and a reconstruction of the original fort that was abandoned in 1813. I'd be lucky if the locals went for cuisine as radical as chives in the mashed potatoes.

It was a question of comfort and security. Did I want to be comfortable and safe with my only care in the world being the flooding of the Mississippi? Or did I want to live on the edge, fighting for the truths we hold to be self-evident? Which life would make me feel good about my days on Earth?

I ruffled Anoshni's fur and clipped on the leash.

Yeah, killing bad guys is the life for me. Corpses don't complain if the béarnaise sauce is runny.

Mercury backed against the car and crossed his arms, a smile stretching across his face. *Now you're talking, my man. The greater the difficulty, the more glory in surmounting it, as Epictetus liked to say.*

I said, *OK.*

I got out and stretched with my back to the Corsican, the warrior's body language that says, *You are no kind of threat.* Which was bluster because his pistol was right where Mercury said it would be. But he wouldn't kill me until after he delivered his boss's message.

A frisson of excitement rippled through my muscles at the prospect of a life-and-death struggle against a seasoned gangster. Who needs farm life?

I faced the man. "What's up, Hugo?"

CHAPTER 53

PIA ASKED HER ATTORNEYS TO take a separate limo. She climbed in hers with Jacob next to her. Hugo's message should be kept between the smallest number possible. They faced front, their eyes on the divider between them and the chauffeur.

"Hugo doesn't speak English much," Jacob said. "Hell, he doesn't talk much either."

"He didn't pull a gun or anything, did he?" She realized it was a bad question for her to ask.

Jacob glanced her way then faced forward again. "He was shaky, a slight tremor in his skin. It was either fear or hate, most likely a combination."

"What did he want?"

"Yeschenko wants you to contact him." Jacob watched the trees go by on River Road. "Through Hugo, no less. Yeschenko says you're still a member of RULE. And that RULE can help you. He wants you to get in touch with Belenov. He is willing to arrange that."

"What did you tell him?"

"N-F-W."

"No way is right. Eventually, we'll need to expose or destroy RULE, but today, we focus on Roche. We're an hour away from delivering the coup de grâce to his administration. The last thing I need to do is connect with murderous gangsters."

Jacob nodded his approval.

"Y'know, I hadn't realized it before now—but that is what we're doing." She smiled at Jacob until he met her gaze. "We're ending Roche madness. After today, he's finished. Isn't that great?"

Jacob stared for a long time. "You were right about Sylvia. I'm sorry I didn't trust you right off. I wish there had been a different ending to that moment in Tremé, but I'm glad we've arrived here together. You've done the right thing. I'm proud to be on your team."

It felt as if he had forgiven her. Almost. She hoped that's what he meant, but she couldn't take it for granted. She knew how betrayal worked, it ate at you until you moved on. But on this day, she took his words as a big step forward. Her mood lightened, and she began to feel the imminent victory like a drug in her veins.

"Was that all Hugo wanted?" she asked.

"He also had a message from Hunter." Jacob twisted his face. "I'm not sure why, or what it means, but she plans to boost your public image against Roche."

"She's trying to help. I'm good with that." She thought about it. "But we don't need either of them. As long as DeLano corroborates the videos, we're golden."

"You don't find it odd, Hunter and Yeschenko hooking up?" he asked.

"Strange bedfellows, as they say. But they both hate Roche."

"I think they're more than friends."

They both curled their noses at the thought.

Before long they pulled into the secure entrance for the Dirksen Senate Office Building. She left Jacob in the marble lobby and joined her attorneys.

Under the guidance of Senate ushers, they marched into the Senate Judiciary Committee hearing room and took their seats. Pia sat at the small table in front of the expansive dais where senators whispered to flocks of aides. Around her, photographers swarmed in for close-ups. Behind her, a wall of reporters texted out updates on their phones. To her left and right, video cameras live-streamed.

After the legal authority of the committee had been established, Pia's requirement to testify truthfully under penalty of federal law was confirmed. The basic questions of name and residency followed. Then came the friendly opening statement by the Chairman, Senator Jeff Smith. He cited their life-long friendship and vouched for her honesty and patriotism.

Then came the ranking member, Senator Frederick Krueger, whose opening statement was gently hostile. Which was understandable considering his unswerving support of President Roche.

Then Pia made her an opening statement. She said, "In the videos forwarded to you earlier, you watched six international businessmen detail how they laundered money at the direction of Chuck Roche. They explained how they circumvented American sanctions and broke international laws. All six of them explain exactly how they paid bribes and extortion from accounts filled with ill-gotten gains to shell corporations. In exhibits PS-00230 through PS-00235, you will find the owners of these shell corporations.

"Separately, we have supplied to you the invoices, exhibits PS-00237 through PS-00372, showing the fraudulent transactions that paid those bribes netting $348 million in profit for Santalum Corporation. In exhibits PS-00373 through PS-00508, you will find the invoices and transfers of cash from Santalum for the exact amounts to the US company called Roche Enterprises, owned by Chuck Roche, President of the United States of America."

Half of the reporters ran to the hallway to file their reports. A couple TV reporters stood and started reporting in place, breaking all the hearing rules in a mad dash to scoop their competitors. Senator Smith banged his gavel for some time before the noise abated.

"To back all that up," Pia continued, "we will make Michael Todd DeLano available to confirm the authenticity of these recordings."

For the first time in months, she exhaled.

She felt good.

Justice would be served.

Senator Smith followed with a windy thank-you for her efforts. He recognized the great sacrifices she'd made to deliver her evidence. He lauded her courage to testify in a hostile environment, knowing the slings and arrows a bitter and rancorous president would hurl at her. He asked her if it were scarier than facing down Brazil in the Women's World Cup. The room had a little laugh.

Then it was Senator Krueger's turn. He said, "Ms. Sabel, this is indeed impressive work. How long have you been prosecuting financial crimes?"

"I'm not a prosecutor, sir."

"Where did you get all this wonderful expertise in the nuances of complex international accounting?" Senator Krueger smiled when he spoke.

"Since my father's death, I've been involved in Sabel Industries financial affairs. We are an international—"

"As the sole owner of Sabel Industries, you take your fiduciary responsibilities seriously, don't you?"

"Yes, sir. I think it's important—"

"In the execution of that responsibility," he looked over the top of his reading glasses, "are you aware of the major transactions of your holding company as well as all your subsidiaries?"

"I do my best. It is a sprawling—"

"You are a remarkable young lady." Krueger smiled and nodded at her. "Not many can take on such multifaceted bookkeeping problems without going mad. Are you involved in the day-to-day operations of international finance at Sabel Industries?"

"To a certain extent, but not daily—"

"If Sabel Industries were to launder money, you would be aware of that, correct?"

"We would not launder money. I would never allow that to happen on my watch."

Senator Krueger smiled and leaned back. He tapped his pen on a stack of papers in front of him while he stared down Pia.

After an awkward silence, he bent forward. "I would expect no less from you in sworn testimony. As your friend, Senator Smith said, you are an upstanding citizen who would never lie, cheat, or steal. You do not allow money laundering because you keep everything under personal control, is that right?"

Pia's stomach began to twist in a knot. "Well, the company is my responsibility—"

"You suggested that Chuck Roche, President of the United States of America, is the beneficiary of these transactions, correct?"

"I did not suggest." Pia's anger rose. "I stated the facts."

"Then help an old man understand your *facts*." His voice was silky smooth. Too smooth. "Where is the connection?"

"An example would be that money flows from Co A, owned by Mikhail Yeschenko, to Santalum Corporation. Then Santalum turns around and transfers the exact same amount to Co B, owned by Chuck Roche."

Krueger's voice rose in volume. "To be specific, I will refer to exhibit PS-00373. Using your example, Co B is actually Gumb and Smythe, LLC, is that right?"

"Yes."

"And yet Gumb and Smythe, LLC is not in fact owned by the president or Roche Enterprises, is it?"

"Check the record, Senator Krueger, you will find it is."

"Well, young lady," Krueger shouted angrily, "I did check the record. Gumb and Smythe, LLC is a wholly owned subsidiary of Sabel Industries. In fact, all the companies referred to in these invoices are wholly owned by Sabel Industries—are they not?"

CHAPTER 54

PRESIDENT ROCHE SAT ON HIS couch in the Oval Office watching TV. A stack of intelligence reports about threats and stuff sat on the coffee table. They were single-spaced and full of big, boring words. Someone in the CIA should learn a thing or two about how to make reports interesting. He'd listen if they made a video with some drones strikes and fireballs. Those were fun to watch.

Then Veronica Hunter walked in.

She fisted her hips. "What did you do to Pia?"

"Who the hell let you in?"

"Answer the question," she said, "or I come clean about everything on national television."

"I don't know what you're talking about."

"Pia would never have come forward with that paper trail if she owned the companies. How did you turn that around on her?"

"She testified against me in Congress." He wondered why Hunter didn't understand how Pia had committed a treasonous act and deserved the death penalty. "She can send you to jail. I couldn't sit there and let that happen."

"You lied."

"So?" He stood and faced her as the heat of anger pushed into his head. "I don't need truths and facts. When I say stuff, they put it on TV. If I say Pia Sabel's a traitor—SHE'S A TRAITOR. Anyone who says different is fake news. You lost because you don't get that."

"You're falsifying records just to cover your ass? Don't you care about getting caught?"

"I always have," he hissed, "and always will, destroy anyone who gets in my way. Remorse is a waste of time. Apologies are for the weak. Losers like you blow hours pondering morality. You can debate ethics all day. While you vacillate, I act. And my actions are what make me successful. No one has ever stopped me. And nothing can stop me now. I'm President of the United States. As soon as I figure out how to get rid of you—without making me look bad—you're gone."

"You'll never get away with this." Hunter paced the room. "Pia's smart. She'll figure out what you did."

"What did I do, Veronica?" Roche crossed the room and got in her face. "What are you saying?"

"I haven't figured it out yet, but Pia will. Why don't you tell me about it?"

"If you're trying to record this conversation, I've learned my lesson. I've had this room fitted with devices that electronically wreck digital recorders." He grabbed an old-fashioned micro-cassette recorder off his desk and held it between them. "Now tell us about your new boyfriend, Mikhail Yeschenko."

Hunter shook with rage, gritted her teeth.

"You swore you'd get rid of the special prosecutor," Roche said. "Don't come back here until you make good on that promise."

Hunter started to speak but could find no words. She stormed out.

Roche yelled for his chief of staff. When the man came in, he said, "Never, under any circumstances, let that woman onto the White House grounds again."

"But she's going to be your vice president tomorrow."

"Did you just argue with me?" Roche formed a half circle between his thumb and fingers and held next to his waist. "Choke yourself."

His chief of staff got on his knees and pressed his neck into Roche's hand. He pressed himself harder until he could no longer breathe.

Roche's harsh but necessary penalties had saved many a career over the years. It was a shame he wasn't allowed to beat people with a cane. It brought a much more primal satisfaction.

The man struggled to keep his neck pressed hard enough against Roche's hand to fully cut off his air supply. The will to survive is strong in some, weak in others. This man was weak and lacked the courage to take his sentence like a man. Roche decided to be merciful. "Rise."

The man stayed on his knees. He struggled for air and swallowed. "There is one other thing, sir. Check the news."

"Are you all right?" Roche asked. "You better not throw up on my rug."

"I apologize for my mistake, sir. Thank you for your leniency." He gasped and choked again. "The news, sir."

With that, his chief of staff ran out of the office.

He took a seat in front of the big screen and turned up the volume. Five senators stood at a podium, the scroll beneath them read, *Senate leadership demands the disbanding of Roche Redjackets.* The next segment showed a bipartisan group of representatives saying the same thing. The ungrateful fools were caving to the press. Right when he had the little mole rats in the media cornered, the elitist politicians were letting them off the hook. That was exactly what was wrong with Washington: they always caved when they should turn up the heat.

The next segment was worse. Bianca Dominguez stood before a large screen at a press conference. She was a young woman who was so hot she could've been a stripper. Instead, she blew her talents on being the CEO of Sabel Technologies. And she was a lesbian—what a waste. Worst of all, she was a Mexican, or Columbian, or something bad. Why had those stupid judges, and the NSA guys, and the Joint Chiefs forced him to keep the contracts with Sabel Tech?

Conspiracy, plain and simple.

Dominguez pointed to charts that showed the original owner of the companies that he'd had Belenov transfer to Sabel Industries. Her charts were impressive. So was her data. She had dates and claimed to have sworn testimony from Panamanian bankers who testified they were coerced into making the transfers. The press was lapping it up. She hadn't traced the last step, though. Yeschenko's name had not been mentioned.

If they traced things back to that crazy Russian, he would take a five-year stretch in the big house just to ruin the unbelievably fantastic Roche legacy.

How the hell could he smear Pia Sabel and make it stick? And once he did, how could he keep Hunter from blowing up his plan? He broke it down into three problems. He needed a plan for Pia Sabel, another for Mikhail Yeschenko, and a long-term just-in-case plan. He would tackle the low-hanging fruit first.

The long-term plan required a little manipulation. Roche walked over to his desk and pawed through the pardon applications until he found one. He called the admiral who had filed it, Admiral Annie Wilkes.

When the woman answered, Roche jumped right in. "Shame about your daughter being locked up for shooting her commanding officer. He sexually assaulted her. She should get a medal."

"I'm glad to hear you feel that way," Admiral Wilkes said.

"I'm thinking about her pardon." Roche let the last word hang in the air for a second. "I'm wondering if you would be loyal to me if I did that."

"Yes, sir." Wilkes sounded excited. "I would be eternally loyal to you."

"You recall the *USS Maine*?"

She paused a second. "You mean the cruiser that mysteriously blew up in Havana and sparked the Spanish-American War?"

"That one, yes." Roche liked this admiral. "There was a good deal of speculation at the time that the explosion was not perpetrated by the Spanish, but by a few sailors paid off by William Randolph Hearst."

"I've heard the speculation, sir. I'm not sure that's ever been—"

"You are in charge of the ships in the Persian Gulf, right?"

After a long pause, Wilkes said, "Yes."

"I'm going to keep this pardon application on my desk. At some point in the future, should things get tense in Washington—maybe someone starts using the word *impeachment* too much—I'd like to hear that the Saudis attacked our fleet. If I hear about an explosion, maybe a ship sinking, I'd sign that pardon right away."

"I would never… that's too much to ask… Not even for…" Wilkes was still sputtering when Roche clicked off. You can never tell until it happens, but Chuck Roche had a deep optimism about human nature. People always went for the incentive.

Yeschenko was an easy enough problem to solve. He picked up the phone and dialed Nora Ratched. "Remember that drone strike on Corvo we discussed when you were still running the CIA?"

"Hiya, Chuck." She purred like a kitten. "I haven't been invited over in a long time."

"I need you to fire that missile."

"Um." There was a pause on the line. "You need to sign an order. Then it goes to the Senate Intelligence Committee for their sign-off. But, don't worry, I'll make sure it's written just right so they'll expedite approval."

"Do it."

"Shall I bring the paperwork over?" She was purring again. "Say, in time for dinner?"

"I'm not going to marry you." He liked to ensure relationships had boundaries before anyone could say *paternity suit*. Then he remembered it had been a couple days since his last *briefing*. "Yeah. Come over after dinner."

She might've been trying to say something when he clicked off. Nora Ratched was just as bad as Hunter with all her wheedling to get into his bed. But then, they were both women, so it was understandable.

He paused and looked at his reflection in the window. Why was Hunter so interested in Pia? Why did Hunter make that ridiculous apology for the way he demonized the witch? What was going on between them? And how could he stop them from digging farther into the shell companies? If they did, they might discover where he'd stashed Belenov. They could wreck everything—unless he wrecked them first.

And he knew just how to do that.

The great President Roche strode into the press briefing room where his press secretary held her daily time-waster. He shooed her away from the podium.

"What's wrong with the press in this country?" He came out shouting. "I'm in the middle of authorizing a drone strike on a financier of terrorism—and someone interrupts me because a whole bunch of senators can't stomach the Roche Redjackets. What a bunch of losers.

"Did you hear them today?" He looked at each camera, right in the lens, the way they'd taught him on the *World's Meanest Boss* show.

"They were whining about the 'rule of law.' I mean, what is that? Why even have rules if you already have laws? The people of this country elected me to break the rules and make the laws."

The room was dead silent. A second later, it sounded as if everyone were inhaling at the same time. The reporters were finally starting to understand his real genius.

"Look, folks," he said, "this country is getting worse and worse all the time. More drug dealers are sneaking into the country to get your children hooked on Vicodin. Terrorists are applying for refugee status every day. Busloads of people are trying to vote. Pia Sabel is forging papers to cover up the companies she owns. Lesbian orgies are going on at Sabel Tech headquarters every day. Teachers are trying to ban your machine guns from schools. Where will it all end?

"The FBI won't do anything. They keep throwing around bureaucratic nonsense like evidence and probable cause. Sergeant Anton Tarasov will testify this week about how Pia Sabel murdered a Russian diplomat. How much more evidence do they need? And Congress? Don't get me started on those bums."

He looked at all the cameras again. "People need to stand up and rid this country of the animals trying to destroy it. That's what the patriot-volunteers in the Redjackets are trying to do—save the country from our enemies. This is the time to stand and be counted." He pounded his fist on the podium. "This is the time for every red-blooded American to JOIN the Roche Redjackets. They're the people doing something about vermin like Pia Sabel. Who else is going to rid our great nation of this ugly Chihuahua who claims to be an athlete?"

CHAPTER 55

I JOINED MIGUEL ON 2-BY-8 planks suspended between the rungs of two ladders a couple yards apart. It gave us the elevation we needed to see over the wall separating Sabel Gardens from the rabble outside. Roughly two hundred armed Roche supporters meandered in the cul-de-sac beyond the gates. About a third of them had red jackets in one style or another. Only two of them had the whole red suit, blue shirt, and white tie thing going. They'd given up on the white shoes. Too much mud.

Mercury whispered in my ear. *Dream or message from the gods? You decide, homie. But these Redjackets look awfully familiar, don't they?*

I said, *They don't look organized. They look and act like a flash mob. Brought together by Twitter and Snapchat. They're dangerous for their unpredictability but easily routed.*

Don't get cocky, dawg. Mercury gave me his serious stare. *Roche's been working on these Redjackets for a long time. Some of these guys are digging tunnels, caching arms, building up stores. Others are just partying. This bunch doesn't look like the A-Team. Meaning, the A-Team is using these guys to buy time.*

The crowd had swelled a good deal in the last hour. Several signs rose above their heads. One read, *Make Pia Pay!* Another said, *Surrender Sabel.* Every now and then, someone would shout at us, *What happened to Popov?* A guy with a bullhorn rallied them with periodic chants of, *Lock up Sabel!* A couple people rolled out a banner that read, *Roche: Love him or leave!*

Sabel Garden's grounds were fenced in by an eight-foot view-fence on the other three sides. It was meant to be neighborly. Without the infamy that comes with ridiculous wealth, the other homeowners had gone fenceless. That allowed some Redjackets to moon us from the woods behind the grounds. They were chased off by homeowners, but it was only a matter of time before the Redjackets overwhelmed the locals.

Miguel scanned the left. He said, "Want me to handle Tarasov when he comes to town?"

I scanned the right. "I got him covered."

Montgomery County Detective Czajkowski, CJ, had been dispatched because he'd investigated the shoot-outs that had, from time to time, happened at my house. He tried to disperse the crowd but was badly outnumbered. CJ waved to us and pointed to the gate. I used the comm link to authorize his entry. In a few seconds, he joined us on the platform.

"People don't like you, Stearne." Detective CJ crossed his arms and grinned. "They've clogged River Road all the way down to Falls. The town is shut down. After sundown, they're bringing out the torches and pitchforks."

"Nice. Is that your official reaction to heavily armed, drunken clodhoppers making threats?"

"Ever hear of a sheriff named Louis Kirby?" He paused for an answer I didn't give him. "Kirby claims you gunned down four people in your parents' driveway. You're the threat. You're a serial killer, Jacob. How many people have you killed?"

"In this country?"

"Hey." Miguel poked CJ's chest. "Who's your sheriff's biggest campaign contributor?"

"Uh." He looked at the ground.

Ms. Sabel had kept up her father's habit of giving politicians plenty of money. There were benefits.

"Where's the SERT?" Miguel referred to the Special Event Response Team, otherwise known as the riot squad.

"My boss didn't want to escalate things right off. Getting twenty cops involved in a shootout with a thousand civilians is bad press. He wants you to defuse the situation."

"How?" I asked.

"You're problem, not mine." CJ shrugged. "There are more Sabel

Security agents than Montgomery County cops, so, deal with it."

He jumped off the platform and scurried back to the main gate. We watched him twist his way through the crowd back to his car.

Mercury leaned around Miguel's large frame. *Why are you standing here, my brutha? Go out there and shoot a couple of those guys. That'll scare them off.*

I said, *They're all carrying weapons. I'd be dead in a minute.*

Gnaeus Julius Agricola would do it.

Who? I regretted asking the minute my words came out.

Homie, he rolled his eyes, *you really gotta grab the books. Agricola conquered Britain, Scotland, and Wales when he was your age. And you can't even clear a street?*

Miguel scanned the crowd with binoculars. "Remember Corporal Sumter? He's out there."

"Was he the guy who took one in the battle of Marjah?" I raised my binoculars and scanned the Redjackets. They were mostly redneck males under thirty. The realization that there were decent people who'd been misled by Roche depressed me.

Miguel nodded.

Mercury said, *You gotta do something. Did you notice what happened to Bianca's press conference? Did her exposé on the shell companies get noticed by anybody? No. Roche started this mess, and all the reporters came here. They didn't even stop at Hunter's press conference.*

I said, *Who cares about a VP's press conference?*

Bad attitude, dude, Mercury said. *Hunter backed Pia-Caesar-Sabel, but her story is buried so deep, not even Google can find it. The reporters would rather see blood in the streets.*

My forgotten god was right. Reporters and cameramen wove through the crowd, interviewing everyone before the shooting started. Many of the Redjackets smiled with missing teeth. Now that they were the story, their collective attitude toward the press had swapped ends like a teenager driving an icy road.

A pistol fired.

The crack sent the crowd huddling against each other for safety. Their eyes rose to where our heads stuck up above the wall. A telltale puff of smoke wafted above a man near the front gate. I pointed at him. The crowd followed my finger. The guy waved at his comrades as if he'd won a prize.

"Fricking idiots with firearms," Miguel said. "Gun permits should have a minimum IQ requirement. One more accidental discharge like that and this powder keg blows."

One of the Redjackets in a suit made his way to the moron and took the gun away. He checked the weapon, then handed it back to the owner. Brilliant.

Miguel said, "He should deputize them all as Barney Fifes. Put one bullet in their shirt pocket, take the rest away." He turned to me and looked me over. "So, what's the plan?"

A bus pulled up at the back of the crowd and dropped another fifty Redjackets. They chanted, *Give us Sabel.*

Someone lobbed a rock. It sailed toward us, off by a foot. Neither of us flinched. Still, I felt like a medieval knight watching the Golden Horde from Mongolia mass outside my thirteenth-century city walls. Brave as I tried to be, the growing numbers made for an inevitable showdown that would not go well.

Yeah, bro, what's the plan? Mercury gave me a Cheshire Cat grin. *Haven't got one, have ya? Want to know what your favorite god would do?*

I said, *As long as it doesn't involve grenades or machine guns, I'm all ears.*

Aw, dang it, brutha. Mercury looked away. *This coulda been bigger than the Battle of the Catalaunian Plains if you'd come out on full-auto.*

There were times when Mercury brought messages that sounded more like Mars, god of war, than Minerva, goddess of wisdom. I needed wisdom to lower the tension a few levels. Ms. Sabel would be returning well after dark. An explosive hour in the world of paramilitary death squads. As I thought about it, lowering the tension level wasn't all that difficult. It just took more courage than I had.

"The plan is—" I jumped off the platform "—body armor and our scariest looking automatic weapons."

Miguel followed with a skeptical look, but he wouldn't ask. We'd been through too many battles to question each other. We put on armor and donned helmets with Sabel visors. We chose the Heckler and Koch M110A1 variant of the HK417 bristling with mounts, rails, scopes, guards, and extra-large magazines. We marched out to the entrance.

Miguel stood behind the massive wrought-iron gates with his rifle across his chest, his hand on the grip. I stepped through a small opening. The guards closed it behind me. A feed from our camera gave me a bird's-eye view of the crowd in the corner of my visor. The air was still but filled with tension that rippled like electricity before a lightning strike. I carried my rifle ready for action without being immediately threatening.

The few soldiers in the crowd were easily identified by their relaxed posture. Combat veterans know a man's intent by the look in his eye. The rest were skittish at the sight of me decked out in full combat gear. The modern soldier looks like an alien about to lay waste to your city. Which we have been known to do.

I walked into the group, looking for the red suits. The rank-and-file backed away, leaving me in a circle twenty feet around. Someone pushed a fat man in a suit forward to the edge. He had a red nose, his eyes were bloodshot, he reeked of alcohol. He reminded me of the guy who stands behind the bully repeating his leader's words with a snicker.

I adjusted my rifle. The civilians flinched. The veterans backed deeper into the crowd. The smarter tactical move. If you don't have armor, put a couple bodies between you and the guy with the gun.

I faced the suit. "Nice shirt."

He trembled. His afternoon was getting real, and his bully wasn't there to protect him.

"You in charge?" I waited. He continued to tremble. "Got a name?"

Someone pushed his shoulder and gestured to me as if urging the leader to speak. Beads of sweat broke out on his forehead and ran down his cheek.

"Listen up." I raised my volume to full Master Sergeant. "Maryland is not, I repeat, not, a stand-your-ground state. The state of Maryland has a 'duty to retreat' law. That means that if you are being attacked, you cannot resort to deadly force or self-defense if it is possible to safely avoid harm."

The suit adjusted his tie and swallowed. I gave him time to speak. Nothing.

A couple rows deep in the crowd, a young guy raised a pistol. Corporal Sumter stood next to him. Sumter smacked the gunman in the chin with an elbow, relieved the young guy of his weapon, and tucked it in his belt. Sumter and I exchanged a respectful nod.

"As you can see, I am surrounded by your gang on all sides. Even though I knowingly put myself in harm's way—in the hope of reasoning with you—I have no option to retreat. I have no way to avoid harm should someone in your group decide to threaten my life. That means I have every right to open fire if I feel threatened."

Murmurs sounding like *holy shit* circled the group in a second.

Things were getting scary for the weekend warriors.

"This is a variant of the HK417. It can fire a 7.62×51mm NATO round at a rate of 600 per minute." I paused for effect and wondered if I should tell them the rifle was fitted with Sabel Darts. Nah. "While you might kill me within a few seconds, at least sixty of you will feel one of these rounds pierce your organs before I'm neutralized. But I am not here to threaten you. I am here to offer you a way out of a bloodbath."

They all exhaled at once. They hadn't breathed since I started talking.

"If you all go home," I said, "and think about the Golden Rule, then come back tomorrow, we can have a friendly chat."

"Good idea." The guy in the red suit nodded double-time.

He turned and swam through his surprised men. They looked me over and weighed my reasonable request against my confidence and my significant arsenal. Slowly, they began to disperse. First the row closest to me, then the weaker guys behind them. Soon, it turned into a hasty retreat.

As the crowd parted around him, Hugo remained rooted in place, cleaning his fingernails with a hunting knife. When we were alone, he approached. "Roche drone Corvo hour ago. Missed Yeschenko with inches. My boss talk to Sabel, tonight."

CHAPTER 56

THROUGH THE WINDSHIELD, PIA WATCHED the limo's headlights illuminate the mobs lining both sides of the road. Jacob reported that the early throng had been replaced. The new group was better organized with more professional leadership. Gone were the random chants and handmade signs. In place were evenly spaced men with bullhorns who led coordinated chants.

Blackout windows concealed her identity as the limo's occupant until the gates opened. The chants picked up their pace, *Surrender Sabel! Surrender Sabel!* Eggs pelted the car as it pulled through. Something hard hit the glass.

Clouds of smoke erupted behind them as they cleared the gates.

"Those are our smoke bombs, ma'am," the driver said. "Jacob thought it best to obscure the driveway."

He dropped her off at the side entrance, not visible from the front. When she made the ten-yard walk, shouts came from the southern end of the property. Spotters with binoculars. She would need to play cat-and-mouse to go anywhere.

Inside was safer. And marginally quieter. She met her personal detail in her home office.

"The county can't handle the crowd," Jacob said. "They think there are five hundred now with buses pulling up every few minutes. They blocked the streets farther down River Road, but a Redjacket general showed up with a court order a few minutes later."

"General?" she asked.

"My term, ma'am." Miguel pointed out the window. "For every fifty men, there is one guy in a plain red jacket. For every four plain jackets, there is a red suit. We see the regulars deferring to them. That's a paramilitary hierarchy."

"We need to get you out of here," Jacob said. "It's not safe."

"These men are after me, not you. They'll harass me anywhere I go."

"You have a condo in New York. That city has the resources to protect you. You have a ranch in Wyoming that's too remote for them to send numbers."

"Move my problem to NYC or the Tetons?" She waved him off. "Imprison myself to avoid their tactics? No thanks. I'll think of something else."

"We have thirty rubber bullets, sixty-two darts, and three thousand conventional rounds. We could—"

"Under no circumstances is anyone to carry lead bullets on these grounds. The last thing we want is to hurt one of them."

A bright flash outside was followed by a loud explosion that shook the windows. They rushed to get a look. A fireball engulfed the guardhouse near the gates.

Jacob and Miguel ran for the exit.

"Wait!" she stopped them. "No bullets."

They nodded and sprinted down the hall.

Hunter called.

"I received a welcome home from your administration," Pia said. "The first Molotov cocktail just landed at my gate."

Hunter inhaled sharply. "Get out of there. These people are out of control. I've been trying to reason with Chuck for the last hour. He claims he has no control over them."

"You could talk to them on his behalf. After this afternoon's confirmation, you're officially part of the administration. Will you stand by and do nothing—again?"

"I'll do what I can," Hunter said. "The reason I called was to warn you about Tarasov—"

"Until the Redjackets disperse, your warnings mean nothing." Pia clicked off.

She headed out the kitchen loading dock to make her way to the guardhouse.

"No injuries." Tania stopped her. "Miguel had the guards keep clear of buildings in case they tried something like this. But you're their target. You need to get back inside."

Another Molotov cocktail came over the front wall and landed on the brick drive. While it fell far short, Pia was clearly the target. They looked into the dark skies above.

Tania, wearing a night vision visor, lifted her rifle and fired three rounds. A drone fell thirty yards away. She sprinted for it.

Pia ducked back inside and dialed former FBI Director Shikowitz.

He answered right away. "Pia, are you back inside?"

"Yes," she said. "How did you know—"

"The Redjackets are live streaming from their drone."

"How is any social media platform allowing that?"

"That's a problem without an immediate answer." He drew a breath to deliver the bad news. "I don't have any official capacity, but some people still take my calls. I've spoken to the FBI Terrorism head and the county sheriff. The state cops are stalling, presumably, because the governor is a Roche supporter. The FBI has orders from the attorney general not to act against Redjackets. They're appealing that, but it will take days. The sheriff is mustering his team. His SERT arrived at the intersection of River View Lane and River Road. They've met stiff resistance and can't move forward. You need to leave the building."

"What do they want?"

"They're repeating a demand that you surrender to them. They feel the FBI is compromised by deep state operatives—otherwise known as people who follow the rule of law. People we used to call patriots."

She thanked him and clicked off.

Before she could think, it rang again. The caller ID read Yuri Belenov. Which made her curious since he had always called her on an IP phone that had been routed through ten different hacked computers.

She texted Bianca to record and trace the call, then put her on a parallel speaker phone to listen in. Jacob walked in to report on the mob. She held a finger up to silence him and pointed to the phones. She answered Belenov's call on speaker.

"Yuri Belenov," Pia said, "what an unpleasant surprise. I promised to track you down and turn you in for your part in killing 365 Americans in the Flight 1028 attack."

Belenov responded in a rushed voice. "I'm calling to warn you that Sergeant Anton Tarasov will testify before Congress tomorrow that you killed Viktor Popov."

Jacob scribbled a note and pushed it to Pia, *I have Tarasov handled.*

She put her faith in Jacob's promise. "How considerate and dramatic of you to 'warn' me, Yuri. Sergeant Tarasov's testimony is already on record and concurs with the testimony of four decorated American veterans who were there. No warnings required."

"Pia," Mikhail Yeschenko's rattled voice came on the line, "you joined as a lifetime member of RULE—"

"You tried to force me to join." She talked over him.

"—and the membership has voted. The result was unanimous. You must eliminate Chuck Roche."

Why Yeschenko was on a call with Belenov, who had recently robbed him, made her wonder. A second later, it came to her.

"I heard you barely escaped a drone strike just hours ago. Now you advocate violence against the United States of America? And you want me to do it for you? You and your friends in RULE illegally aided Roche's campaign because you thought you could control him. Why is that my problem?"

Belenov spoke up. "Confession is good for the soul, Pia. Tell me about—"

Bianca texted her, *West Wing.*

A wave of fear chilled Pia's body. Of all the twisted, illegal things Chuck Roche might do, this one indicated he'd reached a new, dangerous level in his quest for an autocracy.

"If confession is so healthy, Yuri," Pia said, "confess to the world how you executed the plan between candidate Chuck Roche and Russian spymaster Viktor Popov to crash two American airliners—just to aid his campaign. As for you, Mikhail, do you know why Mr. Belenov set up this call for you? Do you know his call is coming from the West Wing, where Roche is holding him? Have your lawyers file a motion for habeas corpus. That will expose Roche for you."

Both men were uncharacteristically silent for a moment.

Pia continued. "Do you know Roche is recording this call to make the public think he's a hero and to legitimize your murder?" Something about the connection sounded off. "Are you there, gentlemen?"

Silence.

Jacob looked curious.

"Roche tried to get something incriminating on me." She sighed. "He must have Mikhail scared for his life after the attack on Corvo. And he's kidnapped Belenov."

"Bold," Jacob said. "And illegal. He's above the law now?"

"He is the law. He's just figuring out how to use it to his advantage. Imagine what he'll be like in six months if we don't stop him."

Jacob's brow crinkled. "How?"

Pia dropped into her executive chair and thought. A thousand alternatives to launching a war between the Secret Service and Sabel Security ran through her mind. Her congressional testimony had been undermined. Roche's followers cared little for the truth as long as Roche gave them a plausible narrative to follow. They would never have to face the fact that they were complicit in one of the most treasonous periods in American history since the Civil War.

Her choices were the same as when she started her ill-fated adventure, take a knee before the king or die fighting him. What options did she have? Dad had asked her, *When will you rise, Pia?* Well, she tried that. The angry mob was outside, endangering her employees while waiting to tear her apart. She considered what Willy-Mac had told her, *Better to die fighting the tyrant.* But long before that, he'd said, *To topple an autocrat, you need to expose his moral compass.*

"There's only one way." Pia patted Jacob's arm. She left the office.

She went to her room and changed from her business suit into her athletic wear. She marched downstairs and out of the front door. She crossed the turning circle and the long driveway to the front gates. She slipped through the small door within the larger gate. She continued through the stunned crowd straight to the man in the red suit, blue shirt, and white tie.

"I surrender."

CHAPTER 57

CHUCK ROCHE LISTENED TO HIS nephew prattle on about the problems his administration faced. He didn't need some snot-nosed punk to tell him things were tough. DeLano was set to testify in the morning. So was Bianca Dominguez, who had traced the six accounts from Belenov back to Yeschenko. The press would claim that proved Roche had an extortion game going on. They would make it sound like Pia Sabel and Michael DeLano were right about his scheme. Sabel looked good on television; people would believe her lies.

He couldn't let her get back on TV.

Tarasov's testimony would follow in the afternoon. He would accuse Sabel of murder. It might be enough to destroy her. It might not. Then there were the Four Marches planned for the weekend. The Free-Press March, the Women's March, the March for Our Lives, and the Invest in Education March, coming from four different directions, would all trek through Lafayette Square in front of the White House.

With his nephew going on about all the problems, he couldn't think straight.

He needed someone with the right attitude to attack his adversaries. That's how President Roche always won—attack first. Attack hard and keep attacking until every one of the seditious fools who stood in his way were dead or emasculated.

He was staring out of the Oval Office window at the Rose Garden when he stopped listening to his nephew because he saw someone who shouldn't be there. He ripped open the outside door. "Hey, isn't your name Dan?"

"Yes." The gray-haired Secret Service agent faced him from across the lawn.

"I had you and your girlfriend assigned to Hunter."

"She had us reassigned back. We put in for a transfer to counterfeiting."

Roche went back inside. He never had the impression Dan or Catherine would take a bullet for him. And that was their job, the only thing they were good for. He texted the head of the Secret Service to expedite the transfers.

When he looked up, his nephew was staring at the TV screen on the wall. On it, newly minted Vice President Hunter was making a statement. She was encouraging the Redjackets to go home. What a loser. When the going gets tough, you don't back down, you double down. Attack, attack, attack. He sent out a tweet: *Redjackets are patriots doing this country a favor when the FBI and Justice were too timid. Redjackets should be revered and encouraged. Join the Redjackets! Get Sabel! (Obviously, we'll need to get rid of another VP.)*

As he pressed send, the Fuchs News host interrupted with breaking news. Pia Sabel had just surrendered to his people.

Victory was inches away. President Roche pumped his fist in a well-deserved celebration.

Then his chief of staff walked in with some legal documents that he handed to Roche. "An attorney claiming to represent Yuri Belenov has filed a motion of habeas corpus."

"So?"

"That means we have to hand him over."

"Well, he's not here." Roche waved his arms around the Oval Office. "Besides, if we turned him over, he'd testify against me. That would wreck our chances in the next election, so—obviously—he's not here."

"Sir, if the special prosecutor were to ask me if we held—"

Roche stepped nose-to-nose with his chief of staff. "Tell this attorney Redjackets are roaming the streets looking for Muslim-lovers and terrorist-supporters. He should keep an eye on his offices before someone breaks all the glass in his windows."

The chief of staff lowered his nose and left without another word.

Roche's phone rang with a call from Deng Zhipeng. "Mr. Deng, are you ready to testify against Pia Sabel?"

"You have Yeschenko wok fo you. You have Belenov wok fo you. I not wok fo you. I not testify—"

"Wok?" Roche asked. "Oh. You mean work. Learn to speak English, damn it. Either you testify that money went to Sabel, or I'll drone you too."

"I live Beijing. You shoot missile here?" Deng waited in silence like a smart ass. "I testify fo DeLano and Sabel. I be there next week—"

"Fuck you." Roche clicked off.

Who needs disloyal losers?

He started to text Nora Ratched about droning the Chinaman next time he left home. Then he stopped before sending and erased it. Someone had warned him that his texts were transcribed and kept for the public record. The press would get hold of that text and make a big deal out of it.

"WHO THE HELL CAN I TRUST ANYMORE?" He yelled so loud the windows rattled.

"Uh, you can trust me, Uncle Chuck." His nephew sprawled across one of the couches, watching TV with an empty bag of Cheetos next to him.

"You're the only one left." He waved at the empty bag. "Can I trust you to get more Cheetos?"

The young man looked around the room for staff. There weren't any. "OK."

He got up and trotted out.

Roche checked his Twitter feed. Senators were lining up to denounce the Redjackets for kidnapping Sabel.

"I'm saving the country," Roche said when his nephew returned. "I'm saving us from the immigrants and the coloreds and the weaklings with preexisting conditions. I'm saving us from NATO and South Korea. I even saved us from Canada for Christ's sake! I'm working hard to make allies out of great nations like Russia and North Korea. I work day and night to make sure everyone has a job, and everyone is making money. And what do I get in return? Judgments. They all judge me immoral, unfit, unhinged. Well, fuck them."

"Who is that, Uncle Chuck?"

He stared into the darkened Rose Garden. It was time to double down on all of them. Time to attack—and attack big-league. The plans had been drawn up by General Kurtz, the mad warrior. They were ready for just such an occasion. It was time to go for it.

He marched to the press office and woke up a cameraman. "Want an exclusive?"

"I'm a pool reporter," the man said.

"You're going to love this." He went behind the podium and waited for the guy to give him the signal. When the light came on, Roche cleared his throat.

"Ladies and gentlemen tonight, I am asking Congress for a Declaration of War against the sad shithole of a country called Saudi Arabia. They make too much money selling us oil. Fifteen of the nineteen hijackers on 9-11 were Saudis. I don't know why my people left them off the Muslim-ban, but we're going to fix that. They wear dresses, and they speak Arabic. It's time we put an end to this mad religion. Shortly after this goes live, I expect terrorists to begin attacking our nation. For that reason, I'm demanding Congress declare martial law."

CHAPTER 58

I GAWKED AT THE TEN-FOOT-DEEP ditch and wondered how the Redjackets had managed to dig it so deep and wide overnight. They'd built a classic Roman palisade with a twelve-foot spiked wall around a central courtyard of more than two acres. Surrounding that was a stake wall, long sharpened spikes buried in the dirt at a forty-five-degree angle. The outer ring was a moat, dug at the specific angle to trap tanks. They hadn't had time to fill it with crocodiles yet. Anyone who charged the compound would end up stuck in the ditch, impaled on the stake wall, or shot while attempting to scale the final defensive wall.

They called it Fort Roche.

Four of us stood on top of a rise at the Cabin John Park off MacArthur Boulevard. From right to left, the county sheriff; an FBI agent who didn't bother to introduce himself; Miguel, and me.

Make that five.

Mercury leaned around the FBI agent. *Homie, it's time for a death-charge. You won't live long, but you'll look brave trying to save the damsel in distress.*

I said, *There must be a better way. You're a god, think of something.*

Mercury said, *I discussed fourteen million six hundred and five alternate futures with the Dii Consentes and all of them wind up with you dead. So why not go out in a blaze of glory? Think of all the romance novels that'll be written about you, dawg. The tragic hero who dashes in to save the woman he loves.*

Won't work, I said. *Romances end with happily-ever-after. What else you got?*

"I got nothing." The FBI agent looked at me funny. "She wasn't

"

kidnapped. Period, the end. 'I surrender' doesn't qualify. You're on your own, kid."

"They laid siege to her home," I said. "What was she supposed to do, let it escalate until someone got killed?"

Miguel nudged my shoulder, his reminder not to punch a federal officer for being a jerk.

"We're about to go to war," the Feeb said. "Terrorists are sneaking in from Mexico as we speak. And you want me to worry about your little princess?" He smirked and nodded at the Montgomery County Sheriff.

"We did what we could," the sheriff said. "There were too many."

"I'm going in there." I turned back to survey the opposition. I saw several heads looking over the ramparts with binoculars.

"I'll arrest you before—" The sheriff started.

"The Bureau would look on that as a terrorist threat against American patriots." The FBI man crossed his arms and leaned back.

"Patriots?" I screeched. "What happened to you guys? When Shikowitz was Director, the Bureau cared about investigating crimes and taking down bad guys. Here's a fortress, built overnight in the Cabin John Park by renegade vigilantes who've kidnapped a local philanthropist—and you laugh it off?"

"Wanna know what happened to us?" He shoved me. "Shikowitz got fired, that's what. Several other agents got fired too. Those who weren't fired had their careers destroyed by Presidential tweet. Think I can afford to talk shit about the president? Think we're all going to quit and work for some kinda soccer star? Hell no. We got with the program. Chuck Roche is the greatest president who ever held the office. He says those Redjackets are patriots—therefore they are. Not vigilantes, patriots."

The sheriff and I watched the agent stalk away.

"So. That happened." The sheriff glanced at me sideways. "I'll have to round up some aid from the neighboring counties, maybe lean on the governor for some National Guard support."

"Pull your men back from the perimeter at 2 AM, and I'll take care of this."

"No can do." He held up his binoculars and took another look. "Drones show more than five hundred armed civilians in there, Jacob.

Another five hundred have been seen milling about the neighborhood. First thing they'll do when you attack is kill your boss. Let me handle this my way. I just need to get some help. We need more teargas. I'll have to call the governor."

"The governor is a huge Roche supporter. You won't get shit."

"I know." He toed the dirt.

My phone rang with a video call. I clicked in. Ms. Sabel's face filled the screen. Her shoulders were pulled back, her hands tied tight behind her. Her eyes glowed with intense anger—the kind I'd only seen in the final second of a life and death struggle.

"Remember me, Sergeant Stearne?" A voice behind the camera sounded familiar. "I'm Corporal Sumter."

"Couldn't forget you. Took a bullet through the lung in Marjah. You launched two more grenades before collapsing. I was proud of you, corporal—back then."

"Well, yeah, you'll be proud this time too because…" Someone in the background smacked him and told him to get on with it. He shouted off the phone, "I got this. Lemme alone."

Ms. Sabel looked straight into the camera. The intensity of her glare felt like a slap.

The sheriff looked over my right shoulder. Miguel looked over my left.

"Look, they have some demands." Sumter traded terse, off-screen whispers with someone. "We. We have demands."

"Let me guess," I said. "When this is over, you want me to sew your head back on so your mom can have an open casket?"

A fist slammed into Ms. Sabel's chin. She went flying off camera.

"Fuck you, Stearne." The screen jerked around until an ugly face filled the frame, the collar of his red jacket barely visible. "You work for this slime bucket, you're going down with her."

In the background, Sumter complained about treating their captive according to the UCMJ, Uniform Code of Military Justice.

The Redjacket told Sumter to shut up.

Mercury tapped my shoulder. *Dawg, that's Roche's first campaign manager, Gordon Lisko. The boxer-lobbyist who propped up dictators from Minsk to Tbilisi and all stops in between.*

"We demand that she confess her crimes," Lisko said, the camera angle showing his blue shirt and white tie. "She's refusing. Talk some sense into her."

He grabbed her hair and yanked her in front of the camera. Her left cheek was red and swelling fast. She shook free of the man's grip. "Don't worry about me, Jacob. Get DeLano to the hearing."

Lisko smacked her a second time.

He glared into the camera, then clicked off.

Mercury said, *Now do you believe me? You need to go in there with two rifles on full auto. One in each hand. Kill as many as you can, and maybe Pia-Caesar-Sabel can escape while you're distracting them by dying.*

Miguel held his watch up where I could see it. I knew what he meant. Tarasov would testify soon. I had to deal with that before rescuing Ms. Sabel. Otherwise, they would have her on murder charges.

"I'm going in." I turned to the sheriff. "I'm not asking permission."

"I won't let you do that." The sheriff planted his feet and gave me his toughest glare. "I can't believe the Feds walked away from this either, but we can't go rogue. Law enforcement is what separates us from turning into Libya or Venezuela. Which is where we're headed if President Roche keeps bad-mouthing everyone who investigates his party. Doesn't matter. I'm the law around here. We do this my way."

"You're outnumbered by civilians, a hundred to one." I pointed to the palisade. "You can't do what needs to be done."

"We have a professional hostage negotiator talking to them now." He followed my gesture and grimaced with the pain of a public servant caught between two factions of constituents. "I know they won't negotiate while they have the president's backing." He exhaled. "Give me twenty-four hours to settle this legally."

I couldn't get the look in her eye out of my mind. "What do you think they're going to do to her in those twenty-four?"

He pursed his lips and stared at the ground.

"Zero two hundred." I shouldered past him. "You don't have her out by then, you're dead to me."

CHAPTER 59

PIA CURSED HERSELF. OF ALL the victims in the world, she was the least likely to freeze when she needed to act. Yet that's exactly what happened. Four times now.

She sat with her back against twelve-foot pine logs sharpened to spikes on top that formed her cell. Eight feet by eight feet. No roof. No heat. No bed. Dirt floor. Three men hung around all night and into the morning. Mike, Jeff, and Sumter. Others had come and gone from guarding her, but those three took her incarceration personally. She sat where she could watch the door. A hastily cut hole only five feet high covered by a piece of plywood hinged on straps served as the entryway. Her handcuffs chafed. At least her ankles were free.

Her mind raced through what happened. Why did she freeze?

She once volunteered at a homeless shelter where a woman in therapy had berated herself for freezing when she had been raped. Her trauma led to a loss of coping skills and eventually the homelessness that landed her in the shelter. For years the woman had blamed herself for not resisting. The session ended in sobs of empathy from every woman present.

At the time, Pia thought that would never happen to her. She was an international soccer star, an elite athlete who'd once considered a career in boxing. She'd taken self-defense courses like Krav Maga and Model Mugging among others as part of her athletic training. At an early age, she'd trained with former Secret Service agents when extortionists threatened her life. She'd trained extensively with weapons both manufactured and improvised. Few women in the world had her skill set.

She was tall. She was strong. She was brave. She was capable.

Yet. She froze.

Four times in one night.

Each time, the man they called Sumter had intervened before anyone touched her. But his guardianship was dissolving. With little command structure in place, rapists had volunteered to guard her, and now they were taking over. Good guys like Sumter were outnumbered.

Mike's words stung her memory. He was the big guy who'd brought water and a bucket for waste. "Lookin' pretty tight in those leggings, bitch. You tight in all the right places? Guess it don't matter none. You soccer cunts are all lesbians anyway. Probably never had no dick. You'd feel different about it if you had some prime beef like mine, baby."

Tonic Immobility. The clinical term for paralysis under stress. Deer in the headlights. That had been her reaction. No witty response like, *Bitch-cunt-baby, the trifecta of what women love to hear.* Nothing like, *Did your mother teach you the art of seduction?* No punch to his gut either. Something she could've delivered, handcuffs and all. Instead, she'd stood still. Like a statue.

There was some consolation in the fact that hundreds of Mikes and Jeffs loitered outside, eager for an excuse to pounce on her. But the odds of survival never stopped her before.

Surrendering had been the only way to save her employees from the escalating violence. She had no regrets about that decision.

She took a deep breath and rethought her options—again.

Psychologist Dr. Walter Cannon had identified the male flight-or-fight response back in 1915. All Pia's self-defense classes were based on the male reaction to an aggressive threat. It took more than eighty years before UCLA Professor Shelley E. Taylor revealed that females have a different response to stress. Taylor called it the *tend and befriend* response. The response that calmed and soothed wounded hunters, tired gatherers, scared children, damaged warriors, and conquering invaders for millennia. And in so doing, women preserved the tribe, the families, and the future. Tending and befriending have been key instincts in the successful evolution of humans.

Taylor found that compared to men, women produce much lower levels of adrenaline and testosterone when encountering threats. Women don't respond with immediate fear. They respond with a caregiving approach, tending and befriending. Her work showed that the tending process begins at birth and molds the child with genes that express themselves through caregiving.

The instinct helped women survive indignities and humiliations.

Jeff was skinny and average sized, a little shorter than Pia. He'd brought her fast food just after dawn. She batted it away and stared defiantly. He leered and sniffed her neck. She froze. With one hand, he pushed her down. He grinned and tore her legging at the calf. Then Sumter came in.

Could she use *tend and befriend* to prevent what she feared would happen? Would anything work on these mouth-breathers?

She'd thrown herself into the situation hoping the publicity would advance her Roche-corruption narrative. She wanted people to look at the evidence. If the Redjackets ended up raping her, would people finally look at all the clues? Or would they see her as weak? Would they ask, *Why didn't she fight?* If it did make them look at the mountain of evidence, would it be out of pity?

Why did rape always fall back on the victim?

Pia had no intention of surviving that form of humiliation. She had an agenda: put Roche's corruption in his supporters' faces so they could no longer deny it. That called for an aggressive response. She needed to fight. And fight hard. She refused to emerge as a victim. She would come out as a victor.

And yet. Tonic Immobility.

A voice whispered in French at the door. A clandestine whisper asking for her attention. The regulars couldn't pronounce buffet, much less speak French. She crawled closer. It was DeLano, the last person she expected. She answered in French.

"Cyril sent me several recordings," he said in English after he proved his identity. "He has more. He wants you to get him immunity through Hunter in exchange. Can you do that?"

"Why would he think I can get Hunter to help?"

"Oh. Right." He moved to where she could see him in a crack by the wall. "You haven't seen the news. She's been on all the talk shows. Every time, she ends by telling them that you're the last honest person in public life. She thinks the world of you."

"I still don't trust her." Pia thought for a moment. "I can't promise Cyril anything."

"I know why Roche—"

"HEY!" Mike's aggressive voice stormed toward her door. "You're that damn clown done testified at Congress."

The narrow view provided a glimpse of DeLano, wearing a red jacket, rising to meet his accuser. Mike pounded him with a right cross that sent him sprawling backward. "Who the hell let you in here?"

Several men gathered around DeLano. They kicked him while he was down. Each man getting in a lick. DeLano curled into a ball. They kicked his back.

"Stop it, you animals!" Pia screamed through the thick wood. "You're hurting him."

Strike after strike landed on DeLano with a sickening thud. He didn't respond in any way. He stopped moving. The kicks kept coming, six or more men taking several kicks each. Then four of them dragged him away.

Pia shuddered and backed from the entrance.

Mike slammed the door open and ducked in. He glanced in the corner where her breakfast remained in the wrapper, untouched. "You ain't getting lunch. Unless you want some sausage."

She said nothing.

"Look at me when I'm talking to you." He grabbed her hair and pulled her to her feet and looked her over. "Not bad looking for a skinny bitch."

She tried to force herself to slam her cuffed hands into his stomach. She didn't move.

Jeff stepped into the room.

"You think she's got any titties?" Mike said.

Jeff came over and squeezed her left breast. "My brother has bigger boobs."

Mike grabbed the collar of her long sleeve crew and yanked hard. The neckline ripped halfway down, exposing her racerback sports bra.

"Hey, meatheads—" Sumter's voice shouted from outside "—get out of there."

Mike smiled. Jeff sneered.

"Your boyfriend's gonna be relieved of command after Tarasov testifies." Mike ran his finger from her neck, down her chest, and circled her nipple. "Then you're gonna confess."

Sumter barreled into the cell, seized Mike, threw him against the wall. "That's not what we're about. Get outta here."

Jeff punched Sumter in the lower back. Sumter sprawled face-first into the dirt and crushed against the pine wall. Mike reeled back and kicked him in the ribs.

Pia ran through several scenarios that might save Sumter. Mike and Jeff's movements were not professional, not trained to maximize power and position for a fight-ending strike. Her feet were free. She could kick the living daylights out of them both.

She remained rooted where she stood.

"Fuck you, Army boy." Mike kicked Sumter again. "You ain't shit where I come from. We got homeless veterans all over the place back home. Bunch of losers."

Jeff turned to Pia. "You're gonna confess. Got that? You're gonna confess to making up all that shit about Roche. And for killing that Russian. Tarasov is going to put the last nail in your coffin, bitch. After that, we got permission to do whatever."

CHAPTER 60

PRESIDENT ROCHE MET HIS LOYAL senators in the Cabinet Room. They were all fine men who had proven themselves by standing up for him when the going got tough. To celebrate their support of the greatest administration in history, he brought out the champagne. They were supposed to be planning the war against Saudi Arabia, but that would wait.

"Senator Krueger—" Roche raised his glass of apple cider "—your questioning of Bianca Dominguez was brilliant. The look on her face when you accused her of having a love child with James Franco was priceless."

"And the press scrambled out of the room to file their stories!" A random senator slapped Krueger on the back. "How did you get that juicy bit of intel?"

"I took a page from the president's playbook," Krueger said. "I made it up."

A round of laughter went up.

"Remind me," Roche said, "to make you my next VP—which won't be long!"

Another round of laughter rang out.

An aide opened the door to announce someone. Before he could speak, Hunter pushed past him into the room.

"Which is so funny?" Hunter asked. "Planning a war or martial law?"

She really knew how to toss a bucket of ice water on a party. That's why no one liked her.

"Ripley plans to give me a box of your old records." She curled a finger at Roche and pointed to the Oval Office. "A word. Now."

If there was one thing that made Roche mad, it was a demanding woman. Another thing that made him mad was people blackmailing him. He looked at his hand-picked senators. "Update your resume, Krueger. I'll be right back."

He strode through his secretary's office that joined the Cabinet Room with the Oval Office.

Senator Jeff Smith, Pia Sabel's toady of a backstabbing senator, waited inside. Roche stopped his tracks.

"You first," Roche pointed at Smith.

Smith held up a stack of documents from Bianca Dominguez. "You don't have the votes for war. You don't have the votes for martial law. When your charade is over, the public will read the Dominguez report, and you'll be run out of office. I'm offering you a way out—"

"Fake news, Jeff." Roche snatched the report out of his hands and threw it in the trash. "Everyone knows she's a gay Mexican. No one believes her. If you back her alternate facts over my story, you'll be voted out of office."

"You can resign." Senator Smith looked at Veronica Hunter. "If you leave now, she might give you a pardon."

"What for?" Roche pointed to the door. "I didn't do anything wrong. Get out, Jeff. And think about this on your way out: I could stand in the middle of Lafayette Park and shoot somebody, and I wouldn't lose voters."

Senator Smith scowled and headed for the exit like a dog with his tail between his legs. He stopped at the door, "For what it's worth, Dominguez was born in Bethesda, Maryland. Her parents immigrated from Columbia legally. Your mother was an immigrant too. From Scotland, right? Dominguez was a highly regarded analyst at the NSA and is respected by everyone in the intelligence community. They couldn't have made a better pick to run Sabel Tech."

"Intelligence community," Roche said. "Oxymorons, the lot of you."

"He's right you know." Hunter crossed her arms and stared at Roche. "After everyone realizes your war with Saudi Arabia is a distraction, they'll come back to Bianca's report and DeLano's testimony."

"No one went to DeLano's session." Roche pulled out his phone and thumbed out a tweet: "If you are one of the people who helped the Mexican-lesbian Bianca Dominguez forge the documents submitted to Congress this morning, report to the FBI immediately. They will offer immunity in exchange for information."

"There, my legions will take care of her." He looked up at Hunter. "Now—why are you talking to Ripley?"

"He offered me your records." She fisted her hips and stuck out her chin. "The ones with the canceled checks. They prove you paid the hitmen who killed Pia's parents."

"Forgeries." He leaned into her, nose to nose. "How'd your boyfriend like my surprise?"

"He's back in Moscow. And he's demanding to testify about your use of drones."

"So what? A foreigner complains about an explosion on a remote island? I've loaned the Portuguese a few of our disaster experts from FEMA. They've already determined it was a gas leak."

"I plan to testify at your impeachment that you paid the killers. I will testify that you asked me for men to spy on the family. No one said anything about murder. I was shocked and horrified and too scared to come forward until now. All of which is true, and you know it. They won't let me pardon you because I'll be a co-conspirator. We both go to jail."

One woman like Hunter could ruin the best president of all time. In what kind of world is that fair?

With a former president's testimony, his denials and distractions might fall apart. Roche paced the room, thinking. Droning only worked on foreigners. Even Ratched refused to drone Americans. And Ratched was willing to do anything. Anything at all.

"What do you want?" he asked.

"Resign. I'll pardon you."

Everyone was jealous of his popularity. Everyone wanted to be Chuck Roche. That's why they attacked him so much. He should pity them, but they made him mad. Especially Hunter.

"YOU'RE FIRED!" He pointed to the door.

"Doesn't work that way." She smiled. "You need a vote from the

House and then two-thirds of the Senate to get rid of me."

That sneaky traitor probably read the Constitution. Tiny book full of words for nerds. But she knew how these things worked. She had him by the short-and-curlies. She was worse than the Russians. Which meant one thing: attack. Did he have footage of her orgy with Yeschenko? No, she'd stayed out of the window the whole time. Would Yeschenko testify against her? Worth a shot. Maybe if he helped rebuild Corvo Island, Yeschenko would come around. What about Belenov? One of those scenarios would play out.

She said, "I've taken the liberty of writing a resignation letter for you. Too much bickering, too many lies in the press, you're sick of the mess and retiring to spend more time watching TV."

"You can take your resignation letter and shove it up your ass."

He stormed out of the Oval Office and barreled straight into the Roosevelt Room.

"Gentlemen, did you miss me?" He laughed.

"We have a little problem," Krueger said. "We don't have the votes for war."

"Yet." Roche stared at the weak senator. "I've heard about your failure. Keep the faith boys. You'll have a nearly unanimous vote in a day or two."

They glanced at each other. No one asked how. Slowly, they raised their glasses to him.

Senator Krueger excused himself. As co-chairman of the Senate committee, he had to be present for Sergeant Tarasov's testimony.

Roche strode to the whiteboard at the end of the room where Nora Ratched had two bullet points written: *Declaration of War* and *Martial Law*. He added a third.

"We have one more thing to do that will help us get rid of the VP." He wrote, *Endorse and Encourage Redjackets*.

CHAPTER 61

MIGUEL AND TANIA WAITED FOR me in the limo. I ran in, slammed on my dress uniform. It was the blue Class A ASU, carefully cleaned and maintained despite its lack of use. It still had the medals from my last day in the US Army. The Bronze Stars, my Purple Hearts and all the others. After a serious check in the mirror and a couple quick fixes, I was good enough for inspection. I headed back out.

Mercury stopped me at the door. *Dude, you're not going without your Distinguished Service Medal. Two senators would recognize it across the room.*

I looked at my chest and remembered I kept it in a display case. I ran back, pinned it on, and ran back out. When I jumped back in the limo, Miguel and Tania gave me the inspection once-over.

"Your beret has a dog hair on it," Tania said. "The rest of you looks ~ meh."

Tania, the go-to gal for moral support. I brushed the hair off and snugged the beret back on. I put my hands on my knees, stared straight ahead, and wondered if my idiotic plan would work.

Mercury craned around from the passenger seat. *Whatever it is, it damn well better work, dawg. If Pia-Caesar-Sabel goes down for murder, you're gonna be plagued by phthisis.*

I kept looking straight ahead, ignoring him. There was no need to look up phthisis because it had to be something gross and disgusting and Roman.

"I came up with a plan," Miguel announced. "We attack with all the darts available, then switch to rubber bullets. We drop Dhanpal straight into her cell." He handed me a photo of the layout taken from a drone.

"While the three of us attack the gate, he can make a getaway. Might work."

"What's wrong with you?" Tania asked. "There are way too many heavily armed civilians in there. They'll get scared, do a major freak, kill each other and us."

"Sacrifices." He looked out the window.

Mercury said, *Monster Slayer and I are on the same page, bro. Take out as many as you can before you die. What've you got?*

I said, *Nothing yet, but I'm working on it.*

We rode in silence to the Senate building. Each of us thinking up a plan that would free Ms. Sabel with a minimum body count. Which wouldn't matter much if Tarasov told the US Senate what really happened on Attu.

"What's your plan to wreck Tarasov's testimony?" Tania asked when we pulled in to the parking lot.

"Something risky."

I left them in the limo and strode into the hearing room.

Aides were still setting up. I found the chair I wanted, slightly forward and to the left of the table where Tarasov would sit. Someone was sitting in it. I stood in front of him with a serious stare. He looked over my medals and slid over a seat. I sat and waited.

Sergeant Anton Tarasov, looking like Central Casting sent him to play the hero in a Battle of Stalingrad documentary, marched in flanked by a translator. He wore his dress uniform. It looked a lot like mine. Same stack of stripes on the sleeve. His were gold vertical stripes on a red background; mine were gold chevrons on green. He wore a single Cross of Saint George, similar to my Bronze Stars. I stared straight ahead at the wall beyond him.

Tarasov whispered to his translator and put a stack of papers on the table. He did his best to ignore the press. Someone swore him in. He took his seat. The photographers swooped in and snapped a thousand pictures. While the cameras clicked and whirred, Tarasov glanced my way.

My gaze remained fixed on the far wall. Slowly, I moved it to meet his. He gave me a nod that was imperceptible to anyone else in the room. Professional courtesy. We had once been enemies. He had kidnapped

Sylvia. With the help of my derelict god, I saved her and spared his life. Later, we met on another battleground, the island of Attu. I spared his life a second time. At the time, we both knew we were professionals doing what soldiers do. No hard feelings.

He looked straight ahead at the dais full of senators. He moved his hands over the stack of papers in front of him as if he were going to tear them up. He took a second glance at me. I returned his imperceptible nod. He faced the senator who was clearing his throat to begin proceedings. There was a hint of a smile on Tarasov's grizzled face.

It worked.

Maybe.

I left.

In the hallway outside, I streamed the live proceedings on my phone. There was a commotion going on. Senator Krueger said, "That is not the testimony we understood. Could you explain your response?"

Through his translator, Tarasov said, "Emissaries of President Roche contacted me in Moscow. They paid me $130,000 to read this statement to you. It is garbage."

Tarasov tore the stack of papers in half and threw it on the floor. Reporters dove for the scraps.

The translator continued, "Pia Sabel did not kill Viktor Popov as President Roche paid me to say. We met her on the island of Attu. She exposed Popov's crimes against the Russian Federation. When I saw the evidence she presented, I was enraged that Popov would steal from the country I loved. I shot Mr. Popov nine times—with my pistol."

It was the best lie I'd ever heard.

Ms. Sabel shot Popov nine times—with the pistol I'd confiscated from Tarasov—for killing her parents and several other horrific crimes. Tarasov and I watched her in awkward silence. I offered him the chance to be a hero of the Federation. His option was to die in the middle of nowhere. He accepted my offer. He returned home to a hero's welcome, which included the Cross of Saint George. He owed me.

He had just paid in full.

Professional courtesy.

Senator Krueger's voice rose an octave. "Sergeant Tarasov, did you take President Roche's money?"

"Of course."

The room broke into laughter.

"Are you going to return it?" Krueger asked.

"Nyet."

I turned off the phone. What would Roche do, sue him in Russia? My appreciation for the hero of Stalingrad went up a notch.

I rolled out of the Senate building.

Tarasov inspired me. When I beat him, he respected me. In an instant, I appreciated all the things soldiers have done throughout history, some good, some bad, some clever. My mind opened. Creative ideas spilled like water coming over a fall.

That's when it came to me. I knew how to save Ms. Sabel.

Mercury marched alongside me. *Homie, you finally got down with my going-in-with-guns-blazing plan? They'll make movies about you. They'll write songs about you. You're going to be the most famous dead man since Paul McCartney.*

I said, *Nope.*

Mercury said, *Tunnel your way in wearing a suicide vest? Not as heroic, but they'll make a movie about Pia-Caesar-Sabel. Just remember to call out before you die that you owe it all to Mercury, the winged messenger of the gods!*

I said, *Nope.*

Mercury said, *Dawg, if you have an idea and it didn't come from the messenger himself, it just ain't gonna work. Let's talk about this for—*

I said, *That's the beauty of it. It was your idea all along. Remember what you told me about Paris?*

Mercury was shaking his head when I climbed in the limo. I knocked on the driver's glass. "Take us to the nearest liquor wholesaler."

CHAPTER 62

PIA'S AFTERNOON WENT BY SLOWLY. Many voices argued and joked outside her prison. Mike and Jeff were a constant noise. Sumter's voice hadn't risen since they dragged him out of her cell. But they'd left her alone.

Many of the Redjackets watched the hearings on their phones. After a while, an angry shout went up. People were pissed off about something. Tarasov's name came up surrounded by swear words.

Lisko shoved the makeshift door aside and ducked in. "What did you do?"

She held up her handcuffs with a question in her expression.

"How did you get to Tarasov?" He punctuated his question with a punch to her gut.

She brought her hands up fast. The cufflinks shredded the sleeve of Lisko's jacket and tore skin from his forearms. The force of her blow slammed his own fist back into his face. For a split second, both froze. Pia because she was proud of herself. Lisko because he was shocked. He pulled back to punch her face.

Pia twisted left, allowing Lisko's fist to skim her ear instead of landing. When she twisted back, her doubled hands slammed into his midsection. His breath left him. He staggered a couple steps.

She ran for the doorway.

Mike stepped in and wrapped her up. With her hands bound, there was little she could do. She kicked and missed. He pushed her backward. Lisko slammed a fist into the small of her back. She stifled a scream.

Lisko pushed her to the wall and pinned her arms. Both panted from the exertion.

"Get her hands cuffed behind her," Lisko bellowed. "The hell is wrong with you?"

Mike pushed in from the side. He uncuffed her. Lisko pulled her forward while Mike yanked her hands behind her. She struggled with all her might, but two big men proved too much to overcome.

All three were panting when Lisko spoke again. "How did you get to Tarasov?"

"I've never spoken to Tarasov." She tried to catch her breath. "No one who works for me has spoken to him since we left Attu."

Lisko looked at Mike. The junior man shrugged.

Lisko turned his back and pulled out a phone. "She says her people haven't talked to him, sir." He paused. "Yes, sir. One way or another, she'll read the confession."

He clicked off, put the phone in his pocket, turned and faced her. His hands went to his hips. Silhouetted against the doorway, he formed a menacing hulk.

Mike pushed her a step forward, got behind her, wrapped his arms around her torso and held her tight against his body.

Lisko stepped up and slammed a right hook into her cheek.

Pia's world darkened, spun, and flickered. She blew out a breath and spat. "Your mother must be proud, Lisko."

"Tarasov didn't live up to his contract. He stuck to the story you cooked up last year. How did you get that kind of loyalty out of him? How much did you pay him?"

"There's a difference between right and wrong. You don't have to pay people to do the right thing."

Mike fondled her breasts. She twisted and fought in his grasp.

"In twenty minutes, you're going to read a confession on Facebook Live. You don't, and I'm letting Mike and Jeff loose."

Lisko punched her gut before leaving.

Mike grabbed between her legs and mumbled in her ear. "President says this is OK."

She bent at the waist, curling her shoulder as she moved, throwing him to the ground. She tried to kick him.

He rolled out of reach and jumped to his feet. A tremble shook his knees. "Watch it, bitch."

A second later, Pia was alone with her thoughts. She sat on the floor and wriggled her butt and feet through her cuffed hands. Getting them around front offered a small comfort.

The door opened six inches. A few paper-clipped pages landed in the dirt in front of her. The door closed. The bolt on the other side slapped in the lock.

"Boss says you commit that shit to memory," Mike shouted through the wood. "So's you don't sound like you're reading it."

Read a confession live. Or get raped. Great choice. She doubted Lisko would hold back the rapists either way. She scooted to the papers and picked them up.

It was only days ago when she had enjoyed the tranquility of Willy-Mac's backyard. Vivian and Elise came home. They chatted as if the battle was far away. Now she was a prisoner, and he was in intensive care. *Better to die fighting the tyrant.*

She wondered what Elise thought of her now. Would the girl be ashamed of Pia for giving in and reading the confession? Would she find out Pia was raped afterward? Should she stand defiant and determined, taking their blows live on camera?

They could kill her. The Redjackets were immune.

Unlessshe could think up something clever that would change the game.

She looked skyward at the gathering clouds.

There was something. Maybe they would rape her no matter what—but she could be clever, and that would be their undoing.

Pia read the pages. She committed them to memory. She rehearsed them until she knew them inside and out. Until she could say it in her sleep. Until she could think of something else while saying the words. It would be difficult, and her vocabulary would be restricted, but she could do it if she concentrated.

What little daylight remained was fading when Lisko returned with a tripod and a chair. Mike and Jeff followed her in. Mike held a baton. Jeff held a rifle.

They pushed her into the chair, took off her cuffs, and turned on a super-bright light.

Lisko stood next to her, the camera phone in a cradle on the tripod. Mike trained on him. Mike mouthed, *live*. Lisko said, "Thank you for tuning into the Redjacket Facebook Group. President Roche, the greatest president of all time, who is making this country safe for white, uh—all—people, told you Pia Sabel killed a Russian diplomat. Many of you didn't believe him. Well, now it's time you learned the truth. Those who doubt President Roche will learn the error of their ways. Pia Sabel is now going to confess her crime."

The camera swung to her.

"My name is Pia Sabel." She blinked slowly, then followed it with two short blinks. "Tonight, I confess to murdering—" she blinked twice followed by a longer blink "—Viktor Popov on Attu Island on November…"

CHAPTER 63

IN SOME BACKWOODS STATE FAR from New York, Chuck Roche followed his security people toward the elevators in the basement parking garage. The fundraiser for Senator Bobby Moore would be critical to keeping the majority. Why a man would wait to kiss his fingers until after five women accused him of sexual harassment while they were underage was a mystery. But Bobby Moore had finally come begging for help and gladly kissed Roche's fingers.

Roche read the email from his press secretary. She told him to stop using his favorite line, *A child molester in the Senate is better than a Democrat any day.* She'd said it would backfire. Maybe she was right, but he figured people never care about morality when the economy is up.

He heard someone running toward him and looked up. Fuchs News' hottest reporter stuck a microphone in his face while her cameraman shouldered his camera and flipped on the light. He thought about asking her to join him on Air Force One after the dinner.

"Mr. President," she asked, "how do you respond to Deng Zhipeng's statement?"

"Say, you're nice and trim." He looked her over slowly, the way women liked. "You look good."

She pursed her lips and frowned. "But Mr. Deng said—"

"I have no idea what you're talking about."

She turned to her cameraman and gave the cut signal, a hand drawn across her throat. The bright light went off. The camera drooped.

"Where is your press secretary?" the reporter asked.

"Stayed home. Something about a sick child." He tapped his cane on the cement. "Don't know why she can't leave the kid with a nanny. I guess some people think kids are more important than their president."

The reporter's mouth hung open for a second before she shook her blonde locks and composed a sentence. It had to be his charm that made her speechless. Happened all the time.

"Deng Zhipeng made a statement in Beijing today," she said. "He said you extorted money from him just like you did Yeschenko. He had invoices just like the ones Ms. Sabel and Ms. Dominguez gave to Congress. Senator Smith and he have been arranging a time when he can testify before the committee."

They stared at each other for a long time.

"Who cares about what a Chinaman has to say?"

She squinted. "Maybe you should talk to your deputy press secretary before we go on the record. I'm looking for a reaction we can put on the air. We're trying to help you, sir."

He didn't see the problem and continued to the elevator. His deputy press secretary ran up and squeezed in just before the doors closed.

"Sir, Mikhail Yeschenko has just confirmed Bianca Dominguez's trace on the account ownership."

"Well?" he asked. "How do we counter? He was financing terrorists. Yeah. That'll play well. And I was forcing him to give me the money instead."

"Uh." The deputy shook his head.

"OK, then, I was tracing the money." He tapped his cane on the elevator's floor for emphasis. "Ratched will back me up."

"Sir, Ms. Ratched is the Secretary of State now. You put Mr. Duke in charge of the CIA. He won't play along."

"Sure, he will." Roche looked around at the Secret Service agents. The two troublemakers weren't there. He had to be careful talking in front of Dan or Catherine. "Before I appointed him, I asked him if he is loyal to me. He said he is."

"He didn't mean that way."

Roche didn't like the way the deputy had emphasized *that*. He looked the man over. "Are you loyal, Rudy?"

"Yes, sir. Um, it's George, by the way."

"Got a better idea?"

"No, sir." The man swallowed hard.

"Then call Duke, tell him I want the proof sent to me in an hour or he's fired. If he doesn't get it, get Ratched on the phone. And have the press release ready by the time I'm done with my speech."

The doors opened. The deputy press secretary darted away. What a useless coward. He was living proof that some people are born to be cannon fodder.

Roche stopped in his tracks. He listened. In the distance, he heard shouts of, *Stop the madness. Redjackets are Brownshirts.*

He turned to one of the good Secret Service agents. "What's that noise?"

"Protestors, sir."

"What are they protesting?"

The agent backed away three feet, out of cane-reach. "The Redjackets seem to disturb them."

"What's wrong with Redjackets? They've done some great work."

"Kidnapping a citizen was hard for a lot of people to…" He noticed the president's glare. "I believe the local TV station was shut down for a couple days. There was some backlash from that."

"Get the governor to call out the National Guard." Roche resumed his way to the banquet. "I'll show those whiners some backlash."

His phone buzzed with a text from his real press secretary. "The French have indicted Sylvia Lallouette and Cyril Cahuzac for art fraud. Neither has been apprehended yet. Cahuzac's lawyer claims he was doing clandestine work for you. He's shopping a plea. How do you want to handle?"

"Deny it. Cahuzac's a fraud."

She texted back. "He claims there is a phone with logged calls and texts from you."

Roche stopped in his tracks. The bastard kept the phone? He was supposed to burn it and take a cyanide capsule. Wasn't there anyone he could trust anymore? Cyril could unravel everything if Sabel got hold of him. For the first time in his life, Roche felt a noose around his neck. He couldn't breathe. His heart pounded. Outside, the crowd was growing louder. *Lock him up. Lock him up!*

His phone rang with an incoming call from Hunter. He knew what she wanted. He considered it. Resign, walk away from the mess with a pardon? She might threaten to testify against him, but she never would. She was an egomaniac. He could call her bluff any day. But the other problems were mounting. He bounced the phone in his hand, resisting the urge to hurl it against the wall. Then he sent her call to voicemail.

When you're in deep, go deeper and harder and stronger. Life is no place for wimps. Chuck Roche was the kind of guy that, had he been a gangster, would've died in a hail of gunfire rather than surrender. Times looked tough, but things always went his way when he gave the world the finger. He could get out of any jam. He was invincible. After all, he was Chuck Roche!

He arrived at the side door to the fundraiser.

"Golly, it's an honor to meet such a great man," an aide standing by the door said. He stuck out a hand to shake. "We're just about to announce you, Mr. President."

Roche stared at the man's hand. Why did random lowlifes think they could shake his hand? Whatever happened to manners, decorum, knowing your place?

Other thoughts weighed on his mind. Would this be his last night as president? Was this the end? Should he take Hunter's deal? He could walk away now and spend the rest of his life blaming the media and spinning conspiracy theories.

Another text came in. This time from Gordon Lisko. He was live streaming Pia Sabel's confession.

Yes! Everything was working. Proof that God loved him more than anyone else in the world.

He smacked the aide with his cane. "Stop grinning like some carnival clown and get in there, goddamn it. Have them start playing *Hail to the Chief*."

CHAPTER 64

WE ARRIVED AT THE LIQUOR distributor's warehouse and found the proprietor. He wasn't keen on my idea until I flashed my American Express Centurion card. He snatched it and gave me a tour of his operation.

We picked out a tractor-trailer covered with the Budweiser logo from bumper to bumper. The owner gave us space to work and left. The engineering crew from Sabel Security's operations center met me and—after calling me crazy—went to work on the rig.

"Why won't you tell me what this is all about?" Tania waived her arm at the mechanics and welders.

"Because you'd laugh at me."

She turned to Miguel. "Do you know what his plan is?" When Miguel shook his head, she got in his face. "Then why the hell are you going along with it?"

"He gets messages."

"I know all about his damn *messages*. If you ask me, they come straight from Looney Tunes."

Miguel cocked his head. "Got a better idea?"

Tania stormed off to an open loading bay and watched the gathering clouds.

Mercury stood next to me, watching a man cutting steel with a carbide circular saw. *Y'know, if Scipio Aemilianus had those things, the siege of Carthage would've been over in a day, not three years.*

I said, *Is this going to work?*

Mercury said, *I don't know what you're talking about, homie. This is all you and your wild imagination.*

Which was not the encouragement I was hoping for from my imaginary god. It was a tough decision. If my plan worked, hundreds of lives would be saved. If it failed, which was more than likely, it might cost my friends dearly and explode into a loss of life unseen since the Cimbric wars.

Mercury said, *Dude, you've been reading up on Roman history. I am impressed for a change. Indeed, the mighty consul Marius defeated thousands of Cimbric Celts on the Raudine Plain.*

I said, *I was thinking of the earlier Battle of Arausio. Proconsul Caepio lost nearly a hundred thousand Romans.*

Hey now, Mercury said. *We don't talk about that one.*

Corporal Sumter called me. Which saved me from another history lesson.

He said, "They fired me."

There was a silence. Instead of explaining, Sumter sighed.

I asked, "Is that a good thing?"

"They're going to make Pia confess in a couple hours." He sighed again. "They're planning to beat her up before, then rape her afterward."

My fist clenched. I wanted to reach through the phone and beat the crap out of him for aiding them. But I wouldn't learn anything that way. I cooled myself down. "Thanks for the heads-up, corporal. I'm hoping to spoil their party. Why the call?"

"I want to switch sides."

In covert operations, there are a thousand protocols to go through before trusting someone to switch sides. Sumter might be a false flag, a double agent, a cut-out, or any number of things we didn't want. But I needed intel on Fort Roche.

"Why?" I asked.

"This Redjacket deal ain't straight, sir. I thought we were going to show the liberals how they were wrong about President Roche. But these guys aren't conservatives. They aren't Christian. They aren't anything but degenerates serving themselves and their false prophet."

Time had faded my memory of his evangelical streak. His language brought it back into focus. He'd thumped his Bible more than anyone I'd known before or since. But he'd been a damn good soldier.

"Why did you join that particular operation?" I asked.

"They said Pia Sabel was making up all that stuff about the president. They said she was trying to tear him down because he was going to bring prayer back to the schools and end the war on Christmas." He took a deep breath. "I realized they were wrong. After seeing how she stood up to them, silent and unafraid—I knew she wasn't the one doing the lying. She turned the other cheek, Jacob. In real life. She stood like a statue when they said bad things and touched her and threatened her. Not many can do that."

"She's brave." My stomach turned at the thought of what she was going through.

"To me, that meant Roche is the one lying. She says he's extorting millions and laundering money. All he has to do is release his taxes, and he'd prove her wrong. But he never did. And he won't, that much is clear. I realized he must be hiding something. Ain't no reason for an honest man to hide his taxes."

"Meet me in person," I said. "Tell me what you know about Fort Roche."

"I know where the tunnel is. The one they're using to bring in food and water."

Mercury said, *Whoa dawg, you ARE planning on going out in a blaze of glory. Whatever bomb you're planting in the beer truck won't stop the reinforcements in the tunnel. You won't get them all, but you'll go down on full auto. Eminem's gonna rap about your tragic heroism. Don't forget to call out my name out while you're dying. Oh, this is gonna be epic, my brutha! Epic!*

I said, *You and the Roman pantheon are always fighting against the Greek pantheon for believers, right?*

Mercury said, *Yeah, always. Ever since the Christians took over and spun the narrative that we're all mythological, it's been tough.* He waved his arms around at the workers who couldn't see him. *See what I mean?*

I said, *If you get Bacchus and Venus to descend on Fort Roche, will Dionysus and Aphrodite swoop in to take over?*

So now you're feeling the struggle, homie. Mercury gave me an approving look. *I am feeling a frisson of excitement. Hell yeah, those posers would muscle in.*

Can you tell your guys to let Aphrodite win that battle?

Mercury said, *Hold up there, dawg. Just what the hell are you smokin?*

I said, *You won't want the Redjackets on your side when I'm done with them.*

Mercury thought about it for a minute. *OK, but this time, you have to tell Pia-Caesar-Sabel exactly who saved her ass. And she's gotta finish that temple. I mean, it's only a stack of marble right now. It's been a freaking year!*

After I made more promises than a gigolo in a confessional waiting for his STD test results, Mercury took off on his bronze wings to sell my idea to the Dii Consentes.

The engineering team finished up and asked me to inspect the truck. Just as I gave my approval, the proprietor returned.

"Sixty kegs of beer spiked as requested…" He stopped talking when he saw his truck. "What the hell did you do?"

"I'll pay for it."

"Like hell. You're gonna buy it."

"OK."

He did a double take. "That truck's worth a hundred grand."

"OK."

My boss was worth a lot more. Besides, who wouldn't want to have their own beer truck for company parties? We could paint it white and write *Sabel Industries* across the side in royal blue. I held up my Amex.

"I meant," the proprietor said, "a hundred and forty grand."

"It's used."

"Fine." He took my card and went back to ring up the balance.

Not too much later, we had the kegs loaded on the truck and drove it out to Cabin John Park. We pulled up behind the sheriff's entourage. He had special response teams and armored cars and communications vans and ambulances. I found him in the communications van with their crisis negotiator. No progress at all.

That's when Ms. Sabel's confession aired.

She was bruised and beaten. Her eyes were black and blue. She held her head up and spoke clearly. Everyone watched it on their phones. To people who disliked Roche, it was horrific. To people who supported Roche, it was proof that she was an evil witch who should be burned at the stake.

It made me sick. Literally sick. I stepped out of the van and puked on the street. I should've stopped her from leaving Sabel Gardens. Dragged her back inside. I could've saved her from the pain. She didn't deserve that. No one did.

The sheriff patted my back. "I agree. We need to get her out of there. But I don't see how. Our drones are counting hundreds of armed civilians. This could wind up ten times worse than Waco."

I spat out the last and took the bottle of water he offered. After a swig, I said, "I've got a plan. The less you know, the better. But—no dead bodies. Guaranteed. Or, a minimum anyway. No telling what a drunk redneck with an assault rifle will do to himself and his friends. I need a mobile bridge and about six hours."

"You gave me until zero-two-hundred. We're not even—"

"My plan involves setup time. We won't move until zero-two-hundred. You work something out before then, we'll stand down."

We argued for a while before he admitted he didn't have any options.

I went up on the berm to survey the fortress. Off to my right, the county had a surplus AVLB—armored vehicle launched bridge—stretching its folded links across the moat near the fort's front gate.

Miguel joined me. "The others are asking me if you're off your rocker. Again."

"Yes and no."

"Mercury?" he asked.

"Sort of. I'm not convinced I have his version of history straight."

"Why not tell me the plan?"

"You'll laugh."

"On my honor as a soldier—" he patted my shoulder like a big brother "—I will not laugh at you."

I looked around. A hundred yards back, the obnoxious FBI agent had returned and was heading for us. Otherwise, we were alone. Miguel had always backed me up. Sometimes at personal cost, but he was always there for me. He was as solid a friend as anyone has ever had. I could trust him with any secret.

So, I told him.

He doubled over, convulsing with laughter. Not just some random chuckle—it was deep and consuming like a horse braying. Snorting when he gasped for breath. He stumbled forward as he hooted, his hands covering his stomach.

I rolled my eyes.

When the FBI guy finally arrived, Miguel was still laughing.

The FBI guy wheezed a few seconds, then asked, "What's so funny, Tonto?"

Miguel snapped out of it, grabbed a fistful of the agent's shirt and shoved the guy to his left, throwing the Feeb's balance off. Miguel's hold kept him from falling on his ass. Miguel suspended him in mid-air at waist-level. The agent's arms windmilled, trying to grab hold of something to pull himself upright.

"When the European aliens illegally entered our continent," Miguel said angrily, "they asked the Chiricahuas what the tribe living north of them were called. The Chiricahuas joked that the Dilzhe'e tribe were the brainless people. Like you might describe Ravens fans. The Spaniards were dumb enough to think that was the tribe's real name and labeled them the Tonto Apache, or foolish ones. Whites have been using that ignorant term for three hundred years. I am not Dilzhe'e. I am not even Apache. I'm Diné, what whites call Navajo. That makes you the *Tonto*."

"Hey, sorry, I, uh…"

"American history is important. Native culture has many…" Miguel looked up at the wall at Fort Roche. He was quiet for a long time.

Then he looked over his shoulder at me. "Smoke signals."

I said, "What?"

He dropped the FBI guy, who flopped down the berm.

"Smoke signals." Miguel pulled out his phone. "Morse code. Look."

He replayed Ms. Sabel's forced confession. I watched. Her blinking was not random. It was specific. A long blink followed by two short ones. Then two short ones followed by a long one. Our clever boss has blinked the Morse code for D and U.

Miguel held the phone and backed up the video while I took notes. She spelled out, DURESS/RAPE/THREAT/GORDON/LISKO.

CHAPTER 65

Pia kept her ear to the plywood door, listening for them.

When they left her after the live-streamed session, they were quite pleased with themselves. For a while, the groups outside sounded as if they were clapping each other on the back and celebrating. One voice said, "We got people to quit talking about those stupid invoices. Nobody cares about that when the lady handing them out just confessed to murder."

He was applauded.

Then the reports came in. First from Emily Dominguez at the Washington Post. They whispered it to each other: Pia had embedded Morse code. She heard them replaying her confession and swearing when they figured it out. Some of the Redjackets complained that it had gone viral on Twitter and Facebook and Instagram.

A voice shouted out, "Those damn senators are lining up to condemn us. What the hell's wrong with them?"

"Give the president time," another voice said. "He'll come through for us like he did after Charlottesville."

Many voices drowned each other out, incredulous they were not hailed as heroes.

Mike stormed toward her cell, arguing with someone. "Get outta my way, damn it. I'm gonna teach that bitch a lesson. I'll show her who's boss."

Through a crack in the plywood, she could see part of the scene outside her cell. Silhouetted by generator-powered work lights, Lisko held a sawed-off shotgun at his side. A handful of men stood behind him. Mike and three or four others faced him.

"She put my name out there," Lisko said. "Nobody's going near her til tomorrow when we see how this thing plays out."

"I don't care about you," Mike shouted. "I get what's coming to me."

"Wait til President Roche speaks out. He'll clear some room for us to operate."

There was some bickering back and forth, but the balance of weapons behind Lisko tipped things in his favor. After a few tense minutes, Mike and his crew left. Lisko posted more reliable types at her door. She felt relatively safe for the moment.

For the first time since giving herself up twenty-four hours earlier, her exhaustion overcame her. The stress and anxiety of being surrounded by hundreds of hostile men had drained her more than she realized. She fell over in a heap at the back of the cell and looked up at the night sky. Before she knew it, she was asleep.

Dad loomed over her. "Didn't mean to wake you."

"It's OK." She rubbed her sleepy eyes with her cuffed hands.

"This is my last visit."

"No." She sat up quickly. "It can't be. I need you."

"These things aren't up to me."

"But I still need help. Who will help me if not you?"

"You're never alone." He kneeled next to her. "At one time they called them spirits. Maybe you prefer instincts, ancestors, voices, angels, the force, whatever you call it—you have what you need right here."

He tapped her forehead.

"How do I stop Roche from starting a war just to cover his ass?" she asked.

"You don't."

"I'm not going to let this go." She reached out to him. "I'll put the evidence out there. There must be a way to make people understand."

"After Helsinki, there is no doubt about his allegiance. What you want to do is force the people to act. But, you can't." And then he was gone.

She pounded her fists on the dirt floor. What did he mean by that? Why couldn't she make people act? Negatives were not his style. He always had a solution to every problem. Yet he'd given her nothing. Why did he leave her feeling so powerless? How could she bring the national nightmare to an end?

CHAPTER 66

PRESIDENT ROCHE WATCHED HIS FAVORITE classic movie, *Hare Trigger*, starring Yosemite Sam on Air Force One. He needed a little entertainment. The fundraiser for Moore lacked energy. People at the dinner were on their phones instead of listening to him. They were quiet as church mice when he finished. He hated when other people in the news distracted his crowd. After all, he was the best speaker of all time.

His communications director knocked on the door and poked her head in a narrow opening. She hadn't been around much since her testimony in front of the congressional committee. Which was a shame—she was easy on the eyes. Maybe he shouldn't have lost his temper and called her a stupid bitch. But then, she did testify that she told white lies on the president's behalf. She's lucky he didn't cane her for that one.

She said, "There are eight senators in a video conference demanding they speak to you, sir."

She used the remote to switch his TV to the video conference, then pulled the door closed as she slipped out.

"You have to send out the US Marshals." Senator Krueger was beet red with anger.

"This Redjacket crap has to stop," another weakling blurted.

"Have you seen the demonstrators outside the White House?" a third voice asked.

"What's wrong with you morons?" Roche asked. "She confessed to murder. They caught a killer. You should be singing their praises."

"Oh, my god," Krueger whined. "You haven't seen the latest."

"She was beaten, bruised, and bloody," the Texan said. "She blinked in Morse code."

"Protestors are filling the streets and Lafayette Square," a feeble voice added. "They have four big marches lined up tomorrow."

Krueger filled him in on Pia's message.

"I will not abide rape," Krueger said. "The women voters won't stand—"

"Why do you let yourselves get pushed around like that?" Roche shouted. "Look at me. Women still voted for me after that audio tape surfaced. Jews still voted for me after David Duke endorsed me. Blacks still voted for me. You guys gotta grow some balls and stand up for what's right. I'm what's right. I'm saving this country. If you don't support me, you'll never see another term in office. Pia Sabel killed a man in cold blood. She deserves whatever she gets."

They all started shouting at once.

Roche rose and slammed his cane on the table. "What the hell do I have to do to get through to you idiots? You don't get ahead by backing down. You only get ahead by intimidating people. And let me tell you, they are easy to intimidate. Yell at those chumps. Scream at those reporters. She murdered a man! If she got beat up, so what? Hell, if I hear another whiny word out of you gutless faggots, I'll have the FBI investigating you in the morning. Now get out in front of the reporters and start backing me up."

They were silent. They looked gray.

Spineless bastards. What he'd give for a few manly men in the Senate.

"Alrighty then," the Texan said, "help me out with one problem I'm gonna have back home. In Texas, you can get away with killing a man if you can prove he needed killing. If there were ever a candidate for the needed-killing part, it would be that commie, Viktor Popov. Y'know one time he—"

"Popov was a friend of mine." Roche slammed his cane again and again. "He helped me out with big loans when the other banks wouldn't touch me."

Their mouths dropped open.

"Oh, come on now, don't tell me you've never financed an oil refinery through Russian banks. Everybody does it." He stared at them.

They stayed silent. "Yeah, and they expect me to scratch their backs now and then. That's how business works. You guys think about this: if I go down, my party goes down with me. Now get with the fucking program. Get out there and bad-mouth Pia Sabel. If you say it over and over, people will believe you. I've done it all my life, it works."

"This isn't going to blow over," the woman from Maine said.

"HEY!" He pounded the table with his fist. "Where is that Declaration of War? Why don't we have martial law?"

Krueger shouted back. "You're not getting martial law when something like this is going on."

"How do you expect to get past 'what's going on'? War and martial law, that's how." He shook with rage. "As soon as you give them something else to worry about, they'll forget all about her and a little rape. Besides, she said it was a threat, right? Probably hasn't even happened yet."

"We haven't even taken up the bill, and the price of gas has already hit $10 a gallon. Every Muslim nation from Senegal to Pakistan has lined up to support the Saudis. We'll get—"

"I've heard enough. Get out there and back me up—tonight. Get my war on track or live under liberal rule the rest of your lives. Get it on the schedule in the morning. If you don't, I'll start defunding your states. I'll withhold any federal funds—education, roads, healthcare, whatever—until I get what I want."

"You can't do that," another wimp said. "We'll sue—and we'll win."

"Sure, about five years after your constituents have you drawn and quartered. You heard my orders. Get to it. Chop, chop."

He disconnected the call and stared at the TV remote. Which buttons did he need to push to get back to Yosemite Sam?

His phone rang with a different video conference request from the attorney general. He clicked on and saw Attorney General Michael Myers's ugly mug on his screen. He almost dropped the phone.

"We've reason to believe Pia Sabel is being held against her will," the jerk said. "We're required by law to investigate. If we find any connection between you and the Redjackets, we will—"

"You too?" Roche slapped his forehead. "Why do you think I had anything to do with it?"

It was beyond belief that everyone blamed him. Was he responsible for every petty crime in the country?

"You made a speech, an ill-advised speech, glorifying the Redjackets because, and I quote, 'They're the people doing something about vermin like Pia Sabel.' End quote."

"I never said that."

"It was broadcast, they have the videos," the treasonous bastard howled. "In that same speech, you said, and again, I quote, 'Who else is going to rid our great nation of this ugly dog.' End quote."

"You should be investigating Hunter. She's been sleeping with Mikhail Yeschenko, a spy for the Russian government—"

"You're not getting off this time." The attorney general's face turned red. "We know you have Yuri Belenov held captive in the West Wing. Several people on your staff have complained to me about it. They don't want to be part—"

"He's an extra rendition. A criminal terrorist."

"You mean extraordinary rendition? Doesn't matter. You can't kidnap a man. Especially after his lawyer served you with—"

"Whose side are you on, Mike?" Roche felt like caning the man. "Aren't you on God's side? You heard the evangelicals. God sent me. The Almighty is protecting me, why aren't you? You're supposed to protect me from Belenov's lawyers. You're supposed to keep investigations from getting out of control and pointing at me. Hell yes, I gave the Redjackets an order to make that slut confess to murder. Hell yes, I ordered our covert ops people to bring in Belenov. How do you think I got all the shell companies reassigned to Sabel Industries? Belenov did that, and he wasn't going to do it willingly. All those things are matters of national security. It's up to you to keep me—"

"Oh, my God," Myers said. "The Justice Department prosecutes criminals. And you've just admitted to three crimes."

"That's covered by attorney-client privilege."

"You idiot, I am not your attorney. I'm the people's attorney." Myers slapped his hand to his forehead. "I have no choice but to resign."

"You do," Roche whispered through his teeth, "and I'll sick Belenov on you."

"Watch me." Myers clicked off.

That worried the great president. He shouldn't have to bother with these petty issues when he wanted a war with the Saudis. He was a busy man who had busy things to attend to. He stared at the remote with fifty buttons on it. Which one changed it back to Yosemite Sam?

And what did Michael Myers mean by "watch me?" What was he planning to do? Open another investigation? Every time Roche turned around people were complaining he was doing something illegal. He had to put a stop to that.

He thought through a few options. Then one came to him. He tweeted: "Will anyone take care of Attorney General Michael Myers for me? He's accusing the patriotic Redjackets of doing something wrong when they caught a murderer!"

Still, "watch me" bothered him. Would that rat go to the press and lie about him being involved in something illegal?

He picked up the remote and clicked until he saw a news channel. They were flashing a banner that said, "Breaking News: Attorney General Michael Myers Resigns." The talking heads were telling everyone to stay tuned, they'd have an interview with Myers right after a few messages.

Those ads went on forever. During that time, Roche began to regret picking Myers. The man had been trouble from the beginning. Could he distance himself? Call Myers a liar? Were the things Roche said all that bad? He admitted to holding Belenov. And to ordering the Redjackets to get a confession. But he never told Myers the rape was his idea. That was just talk. Guys always joked about that kind of thing. Lisko would stay loyal and never tell anyone Roche gave him the idea. Lisko would know a pardon was coming.

The screen flashed to a reporter outside the Justice Department. Myers walked toward her with a piece of paper in his hand and a sour look on his face. The two did a little back and forth, Myers confirming he'd resigned. Myers asked to read a statement. The reporter got out of the way but kept the microphone in front of him.

"Just a few minutes ago, the President of the United States made statements to me that I believe were illeg—"

A shot rang out. A black spot appeared on Myers's forehead. Blood began spurting out of the hole. His eyelids fluttered. He dropped the pages. He fell backward.

A man with a pistol stepped in front of the camera. "Hey, y'all. Looky what I done. I took care of Myers. I did it for you, Mr. President. We're gonna make America—"

One of Myers's bodyguards jumped the gunman and threw him to the ground.

President Chuck Roche looked to the ceiling. In a moment of crystal clarity that comes once in a lifetime, he realized those whacko evangelicals were right. The signs were clear—God had indeed sent him.

CHAPTER 67

Energized by Ms. Sabel's clever use of Morse code, we donned our battle gear. Rifles with two magazines of Sabel Darts, pistols with one mag of darts, and an extra mag with real bullets. Using real bullets could open us up to lawsuits and criminal charges, making them the last resort. If we put down one Redjacket with each dart, we would incapacitate a small number of the enemy. Maybe that would intimidate the rest into surrendering.

We donned our liquid-metal armor and helmets and night vision visors. I prayed to Mercury, Minerva, Juno, and Jupiter that the other half of the plan would work.

Mercury reassured me with a grin and a slap on the back. *Don't worry about a thing, brutha, it might work. Probably not—but at least you'll die like a hero.*

We took our positions. In cramped, hot conditions, we waited for our fate in silence. Each of us wondered the same thing soldiers always wonder about in those last moments before battle. Deep meditations begin in that quiet time after the artillery shells stop flying overhead and before you're given the order to attack. The pre-fight tension grips a soldier's gut tighter than at any other time in life.

We were moments away from facing death. Our thoughts swirled with the questions we would never ask out loud: Will I be brave when I need to be? Will I be smarter and quicker than the other guy? Will we win? Will I live?

The sheriff's negotiator convinced the Redjackets that the beer truck was a gift from a fan who thought a celebration was in order. He said the county was calling a truce until morning. The sheriff drove the big rig across the portable bridge to the main gate, then retreated on foot. After a long time, the main gate opened. A couple scouts came out to inspect the truck.

They found no reason not to drink free beer. And it was the good stuff, not light.

There were arguments shouted from the ramparts. Followed by rebuttals from the scouts which consisted of one repeated four-letter word: *beer*. Eventually, the siren song of brewskies won out over those convinced it was a bomb. They drove it inside and closed the gate.

More arguments followed. They should be careful, someone said. Give it a full inspection, another shouted. Agents of chaos battled those in control. A chant went up, *You gotta fight for your right to party!*

Outnumbered and out-shouted, the generals finally gave in. They knew enough to avoid a mutiny. After the first kegs were pulled from the racks, they gave the order to celebrate responsibly.

Which didn't happen.

Inside Fort Roche, a loud, raucous party exploded into the night. Beer flowed, men laughed, fights broke out, dances started, music played. As the hours went by, they went from happy to stupid, then slurred, followed by angry, and finally, tired.

Overhead, silent Sabel drones circled the fort, peering through a thickening fog with high-tech sensors. HQ relayed their signals to the Major who oversaw a team of strategists. Our visors live-streamed video of the situation.

Many of the Redjackets assigned to guard duty had abandoned their posts and partied with their fellow criminals. While that lack of discipline reduced the number of our adversaries, the remainder were sober men who were growing increasingly suspicious and concerned. Paranoia could lead to the worst of our fears: trigger-happy, untrained civilians with high-powered semi-automatic weapons, mountains of ammunition, facing us across a pile of drunk civilians unable to get out of the crossfire. It was a monumental disaster waiting to happen.

Mercury squeezed in next me. *Homie, I'm impressed. For a mortal, you're not as stupid as we thought. Close—but this is quite an improvement from your last dumb idea. Maybe all my divine guidance is finally paying off.*

Yeah, I said. *Thanks. I think.*

Mercury said, *I gotta tell you bro, Venus and Diana thought we should drop a boulder on your head for suggesting we give these Redjackets up to Aphrodite, but Vesta and Neptune were digging your vibe. And it's working. Listen to these guys throw down!*

I said, *What convinced them?*

When you mentioned Paris of Troy. I reminded them that it was Aphrodite who convinced Paris to open the gates and let in the Trojan Horse. Which—contrary to scholarly interpretations of Virgil's epic poem—was a boat, not a literal horse. I mean, c'mon, how many warrior dudes can you cram into the belly of a horse? Now, carving a horse's head on a boat's prow was all the rage back in Ulysses's day. They called them hippos, *as a nickname. That's Greek for horse. Ulysses and his men hid below a false deck—kinda like what y'all are doing here in the beer truck.* He sniffed. *Although they bathed more often.*

After midnight, things were winding down. A few hearty partiers kept going for another half an hour or so. The sober few kept checking the truck. By one in the morning, the fort was quiet. The occasional voice rang out as one sober guard checked in with another. Eventually, those voices trailed off.

The Major updated us in the comm link. There were eight bodies in motion. One of them figured out the kegs had been spiked because the partiers could usually last longer than closing time at the local pub. They were pissed.

Five against eight gave us decent odds. We were ready to go. The adrenaline was flowing like a drug in our veins. But something didn't smell right.

Out of five hundred guys, there should be more than eight non-drinkers. And given the stakes, even more would be wary of a free beer truck. I had the Major rescan the area. The drones reconfirmed the eight moving bodies. Their sensors detect body heat and normally could tell the state of a person because body temperature drops a couple degrees when sleeping. But there were too many people huddled for warmth in the night chill to be one hundred percent accurate.

I assigned our targets. Dhanpal would open the main gate for the county cops. Sumter would open the secret tunnel and bring in the rest of the cops. Tania, Miguel and I would take out the eight guards. The Major floated the idea of getting Ms. Sabel out as the top priority, but we all agreed that our boss would never leave until her people were safe.

I gave the plan one last thought. Based on our intel, the odds were in our favor. Mercury gave me a shrug. The die was cast. I tugged on the rope that released our trap door. We rolled out from underneath the truck and into the night.

After the president bad-mouthed Sabel Industries, the Army bought all the remaining large drones from Sabel Tech. We were working with smaller, experimental drones that carried little more than a pistol. The Major had one drop a phone and a gun to Ms. Sabel. They updated her on the mission.

We charged into the courtyard and took out two Redjackets before my worst nightmare came true. Wary combat veterans had hidden from our drones among the drunks. More than ten opened fire on Dhanpal before he could open the gates. Miguel dropped two before going down. Tania took out three. I hit a few before giving the order to hide. We snuggled into piles of drugged Redjackets.

Our armor protected our torso, upper arms, and upper legs, but we could still be wounded or killed from a face-shot or other vulnerable spots. Our helmets were the strongest available on the market. They would stop almost any bullet from a handgun, although the impact from the larger calibers, like a .357 Magnum and up, could snap a spinal cord or deliver a grade 3 concussion. Military rifle rounds, on the other hand, could pierce Kevlar. Most of the Redjackets carried smaller caliber pistols, but there were plenty of Smith and Wesson M&P 15s, Daniel Defense DDM4s, and Bravo Company Mid-16s lying around to kill us all.

Dhanpal and Miguel reported in with broken ribs. Sumter made it to the secret passage and lost the comm link in the tunnel. His mission would take the longest to pay off. The only intel we had was that it terminated in a suburban house. No idea which direction it ran or how many Redjackets waited on the other end. We could only hope he made it.

Linking to a speaker we'd mounted on a drone, I made an announcement to the Redjackets. "Surrender now and avoid being responsible for friendly fire injuries. Or deaths."

No one answered.

Mercury tapped me on the shoulder. *Three bodies to your left, homie.*

Where he pointed, I saw wide eyes peering over the backs of knocked out Redjackets in the dark. I had the advantage of a Sabel NightVision visor. He had the advantage of a half-second lead. His bullet bounced off my helmet as I ducked behind three of his buddies. I rolled right and took a shot. He'd scrambled, and I missed.

Tania reported two men heading for Ms. Sabel's cell. She nailed one of them. The other returned fire, killing a Redjacket at her feet.

Dhanpal recovered and made another attempt for the gate. He took fire from three points. I nailed one of them. Miguel took two more bullets in the armor but managed to fell another hostile. Dhanpal's helmet rocked from a direct hit. He dropped out of sight behind a group of sleeping enemies. He made no response to calls on the comm link. Miguel lumbered over to help.

A man landed on top of me. I shook him off and tried to dart him before realizing he was already drugged. That's when the bullets started flying from the three guys who'd tossed him at me. Their fake out landed me on my knees in a vulnerable position. But the heat of battle throws off the untrained shooter's aim. They managed to fire three rounds each, nine shots total. All of them missed.

I didn't.

All three were sprawled on the ground a second later.

Several of the sleeping Redjackets were disturbed by the gunfire. They groaned and rolled over. They were groggy and drunk—and armed—which made them scary as hell. But none of them could manage to stand. The ground looked like a horror movie: acres of sleeping, brain-dead zombies writhing like a pile of worms.

The Major alerted me on the comm link. "We outfitted a couple drones with spotlights."

A few seconds later, she had one lighting up two men trying to crouch behind a food cart. They made the mistake of trying to shoot the light out of the drone. Instead, they made themselves larger targets by taking their eyes off their adversaries. Miguel took out one. I took out the other.

Tania was on her way to Ms. Sabel's cell. It was her idea to be the first one there. If they had raped Ms. Sabel, having a woman open the door might be a more welcoming site. I didn't argue.

Dhanpal hadn't responded, so Miguel and I moved toward his position. We found him shaking cobwebs out of his head. His comm link was the only casualty. We covered him while he made his run to the gate.

Mercury elbowed me. *Don't look now, but you have three admirers aiming assault rifles at your head.*

I dropped and pulled Miguel down with me. When he landed, I pointed at the threat. He crawled off wide right, I went left. We pincered them with me coming in from behind. Miguel is a *yee naaldlooshii,* or skinwalker. A Navajo warrior who can take the form of an animal and sometimes control his enemies through eye contact. It was dark, and I had my eyes focused on the enemy, so I didn't see him become a bear. I heard a grizzly roar, followed by a Redjacket screaming. The other two Redjackets held up their hands and begged the third Redjacket not to kill them when he turned on them for surrendering.

I don't put my faith in mythology. I darted the two, while Miguel darted the third.

Mercury said, *Damn straight, dawg. Skinwalkers are mythological. I am not. I'm real—for all you know. Don't start thinking your friend Monster Slayer there is an alternative.* He nodded at Miguel. *Anyone can do that bear trick.*

I said, *Oh really? Turn me into a bear then. Or a coyote. That's what skinwalkers start with, right?*

I could do that. Mercury pulled his chin up. *But I'm not feeling it right now. You gotta be in the right mood, y'know.*

Dhanpal pulled the large gate open and hailed the county cops. They were across the moat, and nowhere near ready to roll. Apparently, they had had not put any faith in our plan and expected us to have died by now. While they scrambled to grab their gear, I wondered if Ms. Sabel's campaign donations might back a different sheriff in the next election.

Five bullets grazed my ear.

The Major had a spotlight on the perpetrators before I could ask for help. When you work with someone long enough, you operate on a type of telepathy.

Miguel and I fired at the same time and bagged them.

Throughout our ordeal, we could hear Tania muttering to herself in the comm link. "Take that motherfucker." Which was often followed by, "Ha."

Miguel and I ran to offer her assistance.

One man stood by Ms. Sabel's door. He planned to hold our boss at gunpoint as a last resort.

Tania channeled my loudspeaker and addressed the last man. "You have an option, surrender or take one in the face, asshole. You've got three seconds to think it over."

Which was a mean trick because she didn't give him three seconds. While he considered her offer, she rose, drew a bead on him, and put him down—all in half a second.

The last remaining defenders had had enough. One held a white t-shirt over his head as he rose. The others called out and laid down their arms.

A horde of sheriff's deputies streamed in from the main gate. Sumter called in that he had secured the tunnel. The deputies began the long and thankless task of cuffing the drunks with plasticuffs and securing their weapons.

Tania opened Ms. Sabel's cell and stood in front of our battered and bruised boss. She looked weak, in a lot of pain.

Mercury said, *Dude, don't just stand there. You gotta help her. Find out if she's been raped. Get her a doctor. Do something.*

The idea of asking such a question felt way out of line. I hoped Tania would handle the hard parts. At the same time, leaving it to someone else felt like a copout. There are problems in life I'm capable of handling. Others, not.

Standing there humbled and emasculated, I had no idea what to say or do. I wanted to give Ms. Sabel a hug and tell her everything would be all right, but that was wrong. And so I stood there, feeling like an idiot representing a gender that is all too often aggressive and abusive. I was tempted to find the perpetrators of her injuries and put a bullet through their skulls.

Ms. Sabel and Tania whispered while I remained frozen in place. After a minute, Ms. Sabel waved me closer. I stepped up, wincing at the sight of her injuries up close.

She said, "Take me to Lafayette Square."

CHAPTER 68

AFTER PIA'S MORSE CODE CONFESSION and dramatic rescue went viral, invitations to speak at that day's protests poured in. She told the doctor not to dress the abrasions. She skipped makeup as well. When she took the podium to address the marchers, she wanted every injury to show. She even wore her torn and bloodied shirt. Ice and bandages could wait.

Four protests were timed to pass by the White House in succession. The Women's March protesting sexual assault, asked her to speak. As did the March for Our Lives, the children's protest against gun violence; and Invest in Education, which sought to bring American schools back into the top 20 worldwide; and the Free Press March that directly protested the Redjackets. She chose the Women's March for no better reason than she could get there in time.

To make the timing work, the city had assigned each group a different major street on which to assemble and parade past the White House. Two groups would come from the northwest, one on Pennsylvania Avenue and the other on Connecticut. The other two would come from the northeast, on Vermont and New York Avenues. Smaller parks at the beginning of each route were assigned for the warm-up speakers like Pia to address the assembling marchers. The marches would continue down their street, through Lafayette Square, past the White House, and on to the Capitol where the main speakers would address the combined crowds on the National Mall.

Pia arrived at Farragut Square as an actress addressed the crowd about her first fan letter. After debut movie role at the age of twelve, the fan detailed his fantasy of raping the underage actress. The next to address the march was a well-known TV personality who extolled empowerment in a raucous, upbeat, fist-pumping speech.

While the crowd was still cheering wildly, Pia took the podium.

This was her moment to destroy Chuck Roche. Since senators had chosen to ridicule her, this podium allowed her to make a direct appeal to the public. It represented everything she'd worked for over the last several months. Many people had paid the price to bring this story to the people. She had shot Jacob. Willy-Mac sacrificed himself. She had nearly gone mad. She worried if she could follow the motivational speaker with anything.

From the crowd, a voice shouted, "You're safe with us, Pia!"

With every eye on her, the kind words gave her strength. She took a deep breath.

Pia began with the story of Santalum and the details of shell company transfers and buyouts. Drawing a line from France to Corvo to Brazil, she told them about money flowing from one country to another before landing in Roche's pockets.

Marchers began looking at their phones and wandering to the porta potties.

Pia brought her voice up to nearly a shout. She explained how Roche extorted oligarchs and dictators and royalty. She explained how he laundered money to make it harder to trace.

No one seemed to care. The marchers talked to each other.

She stopped. International business accounting is not fun. Which is why despots always get away with corruption. No one wants to hear about one company buying another for excessive multiples of its unleveraged assets and intellectual properties. Even she didn't like it.

One person can make a difference. You are that person. Or so Stefan insisted.

She always thought he meant she alone could fix the country. She wanted to bring the country together while Chuck Roche sought to divide it into pieces. For weeks, she had been operating under the assumption that, if she only tried hard enough, she could force her will to triumph over Roche. It wasn't working. Thinking one person can save the nation was the rallying cry of fascists and autocrats. Dad was right, she couldn't force people to act. They would only succeed against tyranny if they acted together.

Willy-Mac had pointed out the individuals making up the crowd behind Martin Luther King. Her soccer career had only been successful because of teamwork. From Aesop to the New Testament to Patrick Henry, the only way the people succeeded was summed up in one powerful phrase, "United we stand."

The crowd began looking at her, wondering why she was silent. A woman on the side of the stage asked if she was OK. A couple voices shouted encouragement from the crowd.

How could she explain her revelation?

She tossed her notes, pulled the mic up close to her face, and let indignation power her voice. "A few hours ago, a man in a Redjacket grabbed me between my legs and said, 'President says this is OK.' Is that right? Can we let that go?"

The crowd bellowed a long and drawn out *NOOOO!*

They cared about her. Warmth flowed through her skin.

"Throughout the history of this great nation," she said, "Americans have risen to defend our country from slavers, fascists, and terrorists. Americans always have, and always will risk everything to defend our eternal principles: those truths we hold to be self-evident—life, liberty, and the pursuit of happiness. Today, those principles are threatened."

Faces lifted from their phones. People heading to the porta potties turned around.

She continued. "Outrage-driven TV and clickbait websites stoke our fears without facts. Politicians hurl slurs at citizens like schoolyard bullies. They drive wedges between friends and neighbors. They want to divide us. They want to weaken our resolve. We can blame many causes, but the real blame lies with us. We have not demanded better."

A silence fell over the crowd. Pia wasn't sure if it was good or bad.

She charged ahead. "When the president told his lackeys to attack our free press, did we demand that our elected officials tell him to stop? When the president accused people of crimes without a shred of evidence, did we call his state-run channel to demand proof?"

Several voices answered, *No!*

"When he bragged about sexual assault, did we call his office to demand an apology to all women?"

More voices replied, *No!*

Rage energized her inner-athlete. She pulled the mic off the podium and crossed the small stage, no longer able to stand still. "When Roche's top aides pled guilty to felonies, did we demand he resign for his incompetence?"

A thunderous reply came back, *NO!*

"When he villainized immigrants, political adversaries, and prominent minorities, did we demand he retract his inciting rhetoric?"

People shouted, *NO!*

"Dare we sit still and take this abuse any longer?"

The answer came long and loud and interspersed with shouts and stamping feet. When they quieted down, Pia took a deep breath.

"Humans have two million days of recorded history. Today is just one of those two million. But the course of the next two million will be determined by what you and I do, right here, right now. Today, we can choose to shut down Chuck Roche. You can make the difference. We can bury him with demands for his resignation. United, we can confront his appointees and demand they work for the good of the nation—not to protect their ranting tyrant."

Cheers and applause swamped her. They weren't cheering her, or her words; they were feeling empowered. They'd had enough and were sick of it. She paced while thinking what to say next.

Over their applause, she said, "I will rise up today and make my voice heard. Will you rise up with me? Will you demand this liar leave office? Will you demand our elected leaders stop enabling this criminal? Will you stand united with us?"

The cheers grew in volume and intensity. Pia waited for them to slow down. When they did, she brought her voice down to a softer volume, making them strain to hear her.

"We can challenge Roche ten times, and he might beat us every time. But we must try again and again. We must fight the tyrant until victory is ours. We must never again surrender to humiliation and degradation and division. We must never settle for less than our birthright: life, liberty, and the pursuit of happiness."

She had more to say, but the cheers overwhelmed her words. Filled with their energy, she shook her fist while she strode across the stage. The people shook their fists right back.

In the corner of her vision, she saw herself on the giant screen, her torn shirt exposed a good deal of her bruised shoulder. The camera closed in on her black eye and battered cheek.

She tugged at her shredded top. "Whatever pains we must endure, whatever agony we may face, we have to resist with every fiber of our being. When we take Patrick Henry's words to heart, 'United we stand,' combined with our individual commitment to winning at any cost, we will triumph."

The cheering became sympathetic. Most women in the crowd had either suffered her fate or lived in fear of it.

"We have a choice to make. If we choose to go forward—to challenge Chuck Roche outside his window, in the offices of appointed officials, in the voting booths of our precincts, in the streets of our cities—our path will be hazardous. But ours is a uniquely American path. It is consistent with our national character, the path of peaceful, deliberate, and democratic revolution. Our other choice is to remain passive and submissive, allowing this president to trample on the American values of decency, civility, equality, and honesty. That is a path we have been led down for too long. One we can no longer bear."

Pia stopped there because she'd run out of ideas. The people waited. She closed her eyes and thought of the ten thousand half-time speeches she'd heard. Some were good, others were not. But they always finished with a specific goal. What was hers?

"Our goal," she said, "is not a victory of the people over the small ruling class of billionaires bent on manipulating voters. Our goal is to vindicate our American values of truth, justice, and respect. We must accept our responsibilities and commit ourselves to do more than we expected, to endure more than we imagined, so that a hundred years from now, your grandchildren will say, 'She stepped up that day and changed the course of history.'"

The cheers rose up louder than ever. She wasn't sure if anyone heard her, but she pointed in the direction of the White House and yelled.

"Let's tell them how we feel. Are you with me?"

They responded in unison. "United!"

She crossed the stage as several celebrity speakers swarmed her. They gave her hugs, patted her back, and shook her hand. As she descended a small stair, the crowd surged in and continued the congratulatory hugs. The chant grew louder, "UNITED WE STAND!" They flowed out to the street.

Someone called her name. It was a familiar voice. She looked over the heads of the women around her. To her left, Guenièvre of Antibes waved to her.

The teenager pushed her way through and faced Pia. She rattled off something in French far too fast for Pia to understand. Something about the speech. Given the girl's big grin and the fact that she spoke little English, Pia wondered what the girl had understood.

"The energy is electric," Guenièvre said in French.

Replying in her broken French, Pia asked, "What are you doing here?"

"Vivian sent me to experience what Americans and French have in common: protest marches."

Pia laughed. On nearly every trip to Paris, she had encountered a strike or march.

The crowd began to pivot, heading for Lafayette Square before going on to the Capitol Mall. Pia realized she'd exited the wrong side of the stage. Jacob and Tania were a thousand people away. She texted them and linked arms with Guenièvre. She took a sign from a bin and gave it to her friend. The chants alternated. Pia translated some as best she could. Guenièvre tried to chant along in English.

The crowd slowed in the block between Farragut and Lafayette. People swarmed in from every direction. Confusion among the remnants of the earlier protest doubled the crowd. An unseen force pushed them in different directions.

Without warning, shouts and screams rose up a short distance away.

Pia pushed through people, heading for the desperate cries of strangers. A tight wall of shocked men and women formed a small circle around a fight. Over their heads, Pia saw a man in a red jacket beating another man with a stick. Behind him stood ten more Redjackets.

Pia slipped between the stunned observers and snatched the Redjacket's baton. She made eye contact and pulled back her right fist. He yanked his weapon free, watching her fist. Using his distraction against him, she slammed her left palm into his chin. The man sprawled backward into his crew, knocking them down like bowling pins.

She dove into the mass of men scrambling on the ground, stole a baton, and swung it in front of them. "Beat it."

They turned and jumped the barricades and ran back to the office building from which they'd launched their attack.

The marchers behind her cheered. Guenièvre swung a fist, mimicking Pia's fight with a triumphant beam.

Pia watched the fleeing Redjackets. They'd overwhelmed the DC policemen from office lobbies and service entries and jumped the barricades. A coordinated, pre-planned attack. Pia tightened her muscles. Hers was no victory. The fight was just beginning.

Near the White House fence, more screams and shouts went up. Pia ran toward the problem with Guenièvre on her heels. Texts pinged her phone. Jacob and Tania trying to find her, she guessed. She would catch them later.

At the high black fence that separates the White House from the park, more Redjackets attacked marchers. This time, the Redjackets numbered in the hundreds. They grabbed signs from protestors, clubbed people, and kicked children. Pronouncing the president's name *row-shay*, they chanted, *Love Chuck Roche—or leave the USA.*

Pia paused at the edge of a line of marchers and assessed the scene. In an open space of fifty feet, a Redjacket swung a long, heavy chain around his head inside a circle of men who faced the crowd and chanted. No one had yet attacked the outer ring, much less taken down the man with the chain. He swung his chain and turned in place, intending to attack anyone who dared challenge his circle. His chain intimidated the crowd.

Pia shoved the baton in the back of her athletic shirt and bolted for the nearest man. He readied a fist to meet her. She turned her shoulder as she reached him, sending his fist over her back. Her shoulder hit the man in the chin, spiraling him into the ground. She landed on his back.

The chain-wielding man stepped toward her, accelerating the speed of his weapon. She yanked the baton out and held it in the air over her head as her momentum spun her around on the tackled man. Her club caught the chain mid-length. The chain pivoted on its new fulcrum. The outside half whipped around to smash its wielder in the face.

Two down. Hundreds to go.

Redjackets materialized from commercial buildings, surprising and swamping the police. Others, having hidden among outside observers, donned red t-shirts or jackets. They jumped barricades and overwhelmed the police. Their chant grew louder: *Love Chuck Roche—or leave the USA!*

DC cops blew whistles and blasted air horns. The Redjackets assaulted them as well as the protestors. Flailing and beating anyone in their way, they surged into the crowd with extreme malice.

Thousands of marchers fought back, stripping some of the Redjackets of their chains, knives, and clubs. Many protestors fell. More kept fighting despite terrible injuries.

Pia fought off one man and turned in time to see Guenièvre pound her fist into a man's face. The girl pulled her knuckles back, staring at them in painful disbelief. The first thing a street fighter learns is not to use an unprotected, clenched fist. Knuckles and metacarpals break easily. Pia's French friend took her eyes off her adversary to examine her throbbing hand.

The man charged the girl.

Pia spun on her heel, landing her left elbow on the attacker's chin. He collapsed on the ground.

She took a baseball bat off him and handed it to Guenièvre. The young woman smiled and tested the bat in her hand before swinging it into her assailant's ribs.

They waded into the riot, hauling Redjackets off women and children.

Police moved in with riot gear and military tactics designed to subdue a single, rebellious mob. The effect made things worse. They compacted marchers and Redjackets into an ever-decreasing space against the White House fence.

Concerned for the presidency, the entire Secret Service contingent on duty flooded the north lawn, facing the riot from behind the iron. They had no intention of letting the fight breach the grounds. The agents stood ready with their hands resting on their holstered weapons. They stood twenty feet apart, wary and uncertain. While there had been many peaceful protests over the years, never had such a large march been attacked by outside agitators.

Pia and Guenièvre were pushed against the fence. They subdued two more Redjackets and were holding off four more when police pushed through to them. Many of the Redjackets melted away.

Children and their parents from the March for Our Lives group flooded into the vacated space. Some were bloody and beaten, others wary, and all were scared. They recognized Pia and Guenièvre as allies, not Redjackets.

For a split second, Pia thought they had turned the tide. The police were handcuffing the remaining troublemakers at a rapid pace. All four marches continued flowing into the park, squeezing out empty space and pressing crowds toward the White House.

Behind her, Chuck Roche stormed toward the fence, yelling at his Secret Service. "Don't just stand there, shoot them. They can't do this. This is an attack on the president. SHOOT THEM!"

Pia recognized one of the agents, Catherine. The woman turned and stared at the Commander-in-Chief. "We're not going to do that, sir."

Roche raised his cane up and brought it down hard on the woman's head. He grabbed the pistol from her holster and shoved her to the ground.

Roche pointed the gun at the protestors.

The crowd went silent. No one moved. The air was still.

More marchers poured into the area, pressing them tighter against the fence.

"Get out of here!" Roche screamed. "All of you! Get off my lawn, or I'll shoot!"

Pia took five steps to her left, moving directly into his line of fire. She stretched her arms out to protect as many people as possible. "Put the gun down, Chuck."

"YOU!" Roche flushed and shook with rage. "I should've known it was you launching an attack on the White House."

"This is a peaceful protest, Mr. President." Pia steeled herself.

Life is a fleeting thing. All too often, she'd seen her loved ones lose theirs. At this point, she had no reason to live and every reason to join her beloved family in the life hereafter. If Chuck Roche wanted to shoot someone, it might as well be her.

Guenièvre moved next to Pia, mimicking her protective stance, trying to help.

Over her shoulder, Pia said in French, "Get behind me."

The girl followed the order as best she could in the crowded space, squeezing half behind Pia.

"Get your goddamn people out of here, you nasty woman!" Roche's voice strained as he shook his pistol. "Get them out of here, or I swear to God I'll kill them all!"

"Don't take it out on them." Pia stared into the muzzle. "You don't want to hurt these people."

"Damn right, it's you I want to kill."

"Lower the weapon, I'll come inside the gate—away from the innocent bystanders—and then you can shoot me."

A slow, collective inhale of disbelief was the only sound in the square. Parents' arms curled around their children, pushing them back, hoping for safety. People too far back to understand the danger pushed forward. The equal forces offset, creating a solid wall of people, all unable to move. Pia recognized their tonic immobility as fear permeated the air.

"I have Cyril Cahuzac's phone." Pia lowered her voice, hoping only she and Roche could hear. "His testimony is meaningless without it. I'll give it to you."

"You're lying." Roche's eyes bulged, his face grew redder. "You'd never give it to me."

"Take my offer, Chuck." Pia stretched farther. "No need to hurt anyone else."

"Fuck that." Roche squeezed his finger around the trigger and closed his eyes. He turned his face as he fired. An amateur move to avoid the loud noise and blinding flash. His actions pulled the barrel to Pia's left as it fired.

Guenièvre groaned and dropped to the ground.

CHAPTER 69

IT WORKED! THE TERRORISTS IN the square began running for the exits, proving once and for all that Chuck Roche always knew the best way to solve a problem. The president considered putting another round in the fallen dog, but that big Sabel woman was giving the extremist first aid.

"We have them on the run!" Roche turned to the agent on his left. "Don't just stand there, shoot them all."

The agent stared at him with cold eyes. It was that traitorous bastard, Agent Dan.

The man just stood there, gaping like a chump. Then he dared to reach for his weapon and aim it at the greatest president who ever lived. But Dan's bluff was easy to call.

Roche faced the treacherous fool. "You swore an oath to protect me with your life."

"I'm afraid that's a myth, sir. There is no such oath." Dan stared down his pistol barrel with deadly seriousness. "I will not hesitate to protect the citizens. Drop your weapon."

For a moment, Roche thought he might die right there, shot to death by his own man. A trickle of wetness flowed down his inseam and into his sock.

He heard footsteps behind him. Running. Son of a bitch. Dan had been distracting him.

Agent Dan was going to get his ass fired, that much was for certain.

Three agents landed on the president's back and drove him to the ground. One of them kicked him in the balls. He heard someone scream like a wounded child before realizing it was him. He doubled over, clutching his jewels and twisted around to see which criminal had kicked him. Catherine. Just like a woman to do something so sneaky.

Handcuffs snapped around his wrists. Rough hands grabbed him and hauled him to his feet.

They dragged him back inside the White House. Catherine followed with a smug look on her face.

"Get her out of here." He shouted, but his personal detail ignored him. "She kicked me in the balls."

"No, I didn't." A smile played across her lips.

"Don't lie."

"Why not?" She shrugged.

The guy in charge, a blockheaded guy, checked the president's cuffs and shoved him in a chair in the foyer. Then he turned away, speaking into his comm link. Roche heard the blockhead use phrases like *arrest* and *attempted murder* and *assault with a deadly weapon.*

If they played it that way, he would ruin them just like everyone else who had ever challenged him.

"Take these cuffs off me." He glared at the rebellious dupes.

The blockhead turned back to him. "She's in critical condition, sir. They don't know if she's going to make it."

"Who?" Roche looked around. Agent Catherine looked fine except for the gash on her forehead and the blood running down her face and neck.

"The girl you shot."

"What's the big deal? Rich people can shoot poor people. All we have to do is say she was breaking into my house and I was standing my ground."

"That's not how that—"

Roche recalibrated.

"She was trying to storm the White House." Roche pushed to his feet. "She had a weapon in her hands. We were under attack. I defended the property of the people. Now take off these goddamn cuffs."

"I can't do that, sir." He took a deep breath and looked at the other four agents. They huddled together, whispering to each other. Every now and then, they'd glance over their shoulders at him.

Roche could see where this was going. They were all deep state people who'd had it in for him from the beginning. He should've fired them all when he took office and brought in his own people from his refineries. He had hired all the best men in the business after John Gotti got locked up. Those boys would've done this job right. They wouldn't have whined about shooting a few terrorists.

But, maybe this time, he'd gone too far. Maybe. If the girl died, the liberals would blame him. And then her parents would sue him.

Blockhead broke the huddle. The agents flanked him. The big guy said, "We're going to arrest you and book you for assault with a deadly weapon."

That would be terrible. The finest administration in the country's history destroyed because some random teenager got in the way of a bullet meant for Alan Sabel's adopted punk? Chuck Roche couldn't let that happen. Even his allies would tell him to resign. Hunter would come running to preside over his final moments.

The stock market was up. Unemployment was down. Why? Because Chuck Roche was the most brilliant businessman to ever hold the office. He wouldn't let a few rogue agents deprive the world of the only man who could save it.

President Roche had learned many things in life. Some of which were: never back down, never apologize, always attack.

"You're not going to arrest me. I got rid of the Civil Service so I could do this..." Roche leaned in and stared down the blockhead. "YOU'RE FIRED!"

He looked at the others. He couldn't promote Catherine. She'd kick him in the balls again. He spat in her face. "You're fired too, toots. Turn in your badge and gun and get the hell out of here."

Catherine and the blockhead stepped back with their mouths open. As if they'd never been fired before. The other three shifted their feet. Slowly, they looked at each other. It took them a minute to realize they couldn't arrest a man who could fire them. Then they understood why the Justice Department couldn't indict him. They were powerless to stop him.

"Get those two degenerates off the property at once," Roche shouted. "I've determined they're a threat to national security."

The three minions didn't move.

"Do it now, or you're fired." Roche stared at the only one who wasn't sweating.

The man looked Roche in the eye. He swallowed hard.

"Yes, sir." He turned his gaze to his former boss and steeled himself. "Sorry, Mike, I must relieve you of your sidearm and credentials."

Roche turned to the next least-likely-to-pee-his-pants. "Get these cuffs off me."

When he yelled in his presidential manner, people responded. It took five minutes to fire all the whiners and get the smart guys to reaffirm their loyalty.

During that process, one agent showed enough initiative to arrest agent Dan for threatening POTUS. Roche put that guy in charge.

He gathered his loyal staff in a meeting room and made them swear an oath to serve him. He was done with non-disclosure agreements. His new oath required suicide for failure or disloyalty. Nora Ratched, Robert O'Brien, and Mr. Danvers helped.

Over the next half hour, he drilled the facts of his brilliant and heroic last stand against the forces of anarchy and terrorism. The marches started out peaceful, but they had been taken over by radical fanatics looking to overthrow the duly elected government. The riot had been full of Muslims and Mexicans, as anyone would see if they watched the videos. People honored Dolly Madison, and all she did was save a painting. He had done much more because he was brave and courageous. He had saved the country by grabbing a pistol at a crucial moment.

He tested each of his staff on the facts. Anyone who didn't get it was fired.

As they filed out to spread the good news, he gave them one last piece of wisdom, "My administration did not undergo a purge. We released many deep state agitators who conspired with Muslims and Mexicans and outsiders. Don't let anyone in an interview say otherwise."

The remaining few braced themselves and left.

"Get me the Attorney General," Roche yelled as he strode to the Oval Office.

"He's already in there waiting—" His chief of staff fled before finishing his sentence.

Standing in the office was a small man. He had a tiny body, a big face, and ears that stuck out on both sides. He wore oversized glasses last seen in the 1970s. Roche made a note to be more careful about putting people in cabinet positions when they looked terrible on TV.

"Who the fuck are you?" Roche asked.

"I'm the acting, uh, Attorney General," the little man said. He clammed up and trembled like a mouse before a panther.

"Good. What's my best defense strategy then?"

"Uhm, sir, I'm not your personal attorney. I represent the interests of the American people."

Roche stepped up close, nose to nose. "Yeah? Can these 'people' fire your ass?"

"Well, uhm, not directly."

"Can they send a tweet and have you shot on live TV?"

The little rat stood there with his mouth opening and closing but no words coming out. His eyes were as wide as bicycle wheels.

"Then what's my defense?" Roche asked.

The mealy man shook his head as if he were a dog drying his fur. "The Justice Department is not defensive. We're the prosecutors. We prosecute people who, uhm, commit criminal acts."

Roche started to think the worm was going to accuse him of something. He looked the guy over, up and down. "Do you think some crime was committed?"

"Well, uh, there are those who might consider shooting a—"

"Terrorist. Is that what you were going to say? Shooting terrorists is some kind of criminal act now?" Roche pushed the man back. "Is that what my *acting* Attorney General thinks?"

"We can't sweep this under... uh. The ambassador has already called—"

"Ambassador? Do citizens have ambassadors now?"

"Oh, no, sir." The little guy swallowed hard. "The girl was not an American."

Roche liked the sound of that sentence. Indeed, God had smiled upon him. All kinds of possibilities opened up like a blossom. He grinned and tapped his cane on the floor. "Tell me she was an illegal alien."

CHAPTER 70

IT WAS AFTER MIDNIGHT WHEN I went home to catch some sleep. Ms. Sabel had gone back to Sabel Gardens after sending Dhanpal to the intensive care ward to keep watch over the French girl. I clicked the button to open the garage door from half a block away. I clicked to close it before I hit the driveway. My timing was perfect. My low-slung Ferrari slipped neatly underneath as it rolled down. I trudged inside, looking forward to a nice soft pillow.

My keys slid across the kitchen counter, my gun and holster landed next to them. But something was off. Anoshni's wagging tail was not there to greet me.

Mercury stood in my kitchen, *Keep frosty, homie. Ain't no rest for the wicked.*

I said, *Who you calling ...*

An odd noise came from another part of the house.

My hand hovered over the lights. I decided against turning them on and reached across the counter for my Glock instead. Moving forward, one careful step at a time, I cleared the kitchen, the dining nook, the living room, and the foyer. That left three bedrooms, one of which I used for a home office. Or, more accurately, my armory.

A faint panting noise came from the master bedroom. With one eye on the dark rooms behind me, I reached in and flipped the switch.

Sylvia Lallouette was scratching Anoshni's ear. She straightened up and faced me in a flash. An emerald green, off-the-shoulder sheath dress set off her auburn hair. Pale blue eyes glowed above her tanned cheeks. An electric smile stretched across alabaster teeth. She was the most beautiful woman in the world.

Mercury stepped out from behind her. *You mean second-most. Don't forget Inbar Lavi.*

I said, *Well, yeah, obviously not counting Ms. Lavi.*

"Miss who?" she asked. "Oh, did you miss me?"

And how.

My love muscle throbbed with ideas about how we could ignore certain aspects of our relationship, like having me beaten within an inch of my life and working for Roche's international conspiracy ring, not to mention endless lies and forgeries. Those are minor infractions when sex is an immediate possibility.

My brain started fighting for control. I stuffed my pistol in my belt behind me.

Mercury said, *That's it brutha, don't give in to Aphrodite.*

"I'm here to thank you for Monte Carlo. You could've turned me in." She slow-danced her way to me, her hips swinging with the mesmerizing cadence of a samba. I smelled roses. She produced a bottle and a pair of glasses from behind her back. "A little toast for old times' sake?"

Whoa, now. Mercury held up his hands. *Don't touch that stuff. It's a love potion from Corsica. It's called mirto rossa. It's a liqueur made with myrtle berries.*

I said, *So what?*

Mercury said, *Dude. Myrtle is one of Aphrodite's symbols. Along with roses and sparrows and swans.*

I said, *I don't see any swans.*

Sylvia looked at me funny. "Do you have swans?"

"As in swan song," I said. "That's what this is, right?"

She draped her arms around my neck, still holding the wine. Her breasts pressed against my chest. "You're referring to the ancient Greek metaphor for one's final performance before death?"

Those big pale blue eyes telegraphed a lusty notion. Sylvia's ruby red lips parted.

"Uhm." I cleared my throat. "Is that what it was?"

"The Greeks believed the swan never sang until she was on her deathbed."

"Or just before sentencing." I pushed her back. "Why are you here?"

"I need help, Big Boy." She set the glasses on the dresser and opened the bottle. She glanced over her shoulder. "I don't know why I'm attracted to you. I just can't help myself."

"Maybe it's because the French have indicted you for several crimes."

"Yeah. And there's that." She poured two glasses. "I barely made it out on my American passport. Will you help me? I'll do anything for you. Anything."

Mercury bent over my shoulder. *Ever wonder why desperation is both pathetic and erotic at the same time? Cause you mortals are just plain sick, that's why.*

"I've never had a threesome." She handed me a glass and raised hers. "Would you teach me?" Her gaze dropped below my belt. "It looks like so much fun in all those pornos I've been watching. You know how it is. I've been lonely without you."

The downside to wearing boxers is their inability to conceal your enthusiasm.

She assessed her feminine power and pressed against me once more.

Mustering more courage than it took to get me through the Second Battle of Fallujah, I stepped away from her. "What kind of help?"

"I can testify against Roche. I need a lawyer who can help me negotiate immunity. Then I could stay here with you and—" she closed the gap and twirled her finger into my belt loop "—we could explore all kinds of ideas you once thought of as 'sick and wrong.'"

"Word up. Cyril beat you to the punch." I set my glass down. "Your best bet is to see if Ms. Sabel gives a shit about what happens to you— because I don't."

"Don't say that. You want me as much as I want you. You want to settle down and have a life and a family."

"I dreamed that once." I looked at Mercury, who stood behind her gloating and feeding me words to say. "Since then, I've come to terms with what I really am: a serial killer in the service of Ms. Sabel."

"Caesar?" She looked shocked. "Did you say you're in the service of your Caesar?"

"I said, Sabel."

"No, you didn't." She backed up. "You said, Ms. Caesar. Holy shit.

Are you … Roman?"

"Doesn't matter." I spread my arms wide. "I'm done with you. You're leaving now. Want me to drop you at Sabel Gardens or Montgomery County Police?"

She crossed her arms. "Pia's place will do."

I grabbed her wrist and pulled her down the hall. Three steps later, I stopped in my tracks.

Someone was in my home office. I pushed Sylvia back, pulled my Glock, and reached around for the lights.

Yuri Belenov, looking pale and thin, spun to face me.

"What the hell is this, Grand Central Station?" I asked.

Belenov's right hand lingered on my gun cabinet lock.

"Facial recognition latch," I said. I waved my barrel at the tiny lens built into the cabinet lock, then holstered my weapon.

Belenov's eyes took in Sylvia in a single sweep. He raised an eyebrow at me, which, in the universal unspoken language of men, meant, *Duuude*. His gaze returned to the latch. He checked it out with a hacker's appreciation.

"A gift from the president of Sabel Tech after I talked her girlfriend into accepting her marriage proposal." I parked my butt against the desk on the opposite wall and crossed my arms.

Belenov looked like he wanted to say something but didn't know where to start.

I started. "You looked a good deal more prosperous last time I saw you. What happened?"

"Your president happened." Belenov had very little accent due to his years studying in the US. "He kidnapped me. Held me hostage in the West Wing. He is an animal."

"You got out early for good behavior?"

"Escaped." Belenov spread his hands. "Roche purged his ranks after something happened at the march. He purged the men guarding me and didn't calculate the result."

"You broke out of the White House?" I asked. "I'm impressed."

Mercury mimed behind him, acting like one of the Marx brothers from the *Duck Soup* mirror scene. *And he came to your place. You don't find that suspicious? If Roche's Stasi had him followed, you're harboring a terrorist.*

I said, *Roche has the Stasi working for him?*

Mercury said, *He's turning the Secret Service into a true SS unit as we speak, bro. When you can't trust anyone, you form your own Praetorian Guard. But aren't you a bit curious? What's this Belenov dude want with you, anyway?*

"No worries," Belenov smiled, "I wore a face mask getting on the subway, then sunglasses getting off. They can't even trace me with facial recognition."

"How do you know where I live?"

"Roche had me hacking for him. And the White House has access to everything, including your Social Security profile. Your boss gave you big bonuses. You must be … uniquely qualified."

"Don't go there," I grabbed his arm as he paced near me, yanked it behind him, and shoved my Glock in his nose. "It's not like that. I saved her life several times. That's it."

"Of course." He hid his pain when I let him go. "I meant no disrespect."

"Why here? Why me?"

"Because Redjackets are still swarming Sabel Gardens. I need you to take me there." He held up his hands to stop my protest. "I know, the only place you want to take me is to jail. Hear me out."

Roche had forced him to forge emails between Saudi officials about bombing the *USS Caine*. Belenov left digital fingerprints in them to prove they came from the West Wing. His story didn't make sense to me because there hadn't been any bombings lately. But he might've had something Ms. Sabel or Bianca could use to stop Roche.

I dialed Miguel.

"I'm sleeping," he said.

"I need to borrow your G63."

"What's wrong with your Ferrari?"

"It only smuggles one fugitive at a time; I have two."

CHAPTER 71

PIA ENTERED HER DARKENED MANSION through the kitchen. When her father was alive, Sabel Gardens sparkled with parties and guests and debates. Her unchecked anger and her questionable mental health stifled the glittering revelries. Now she lived alone, surrounded by paid staff who treated her like a poison—carefully and with arms fully extended. Albeit with perfect politeness. Her childhood nightmare had arrived. She was utterly alone.

Chef offered her dinner. She asked for comfort food, served in the library.

As she walked away, she realized she'd never done as much for her staff as Vivian had for Guenièvre. She could benefit from that woman's wisdom in her life. She'd never had a role model to develop her tending and befriending instincts.

The fireplace crackled for her. She sat and contemplated her day of success and tragedy. She should be celebrating her triumph over Roche. Instead, yet another life hung by a thread after falling into Pia's orbit. If she truly believed in her Episcopal upbringing, she would pray for Guenièvre. But her occasional and mechanical church attendance made any attempt at prayer feel empty. At least she'd accomplished one act of decency. She'd sent a jet to fetch the girl's mother.

Matzo ball soup arrived on a tray, delivered by Chef's new helper whose name Pia couldn't recall. She thanked the girl and soon found herself alone in silence. She thought about getting a dog like Jacob's. Someone who might wag his tail when she came home.

Chef's assistant knocked on the library's open door. "Vice President Hunter to see you, ma'am."

Hunter slid in before her announcement finished. She crossed the long room and stepped softly to the hearth. She watched Pia for a moment before speaking. "I thought you could use some company. You've never liked being alone."

Pia glanced at her. Even an enemy was better than loneliness. She returned to her soup and scooped a chunk of matzo.

"Roche is going down this time." Hunter clasped her hands behind her back and faced the fire. "He'll never dig up a distraction big enough to cover up shooting that poor girl."

Pia slurped a spoonful as loud as she could.

"I'll be president soon." Hunter twisted to see Pia's reaction.

"The country gets out of the devil's clutches only to be snatched up by his girlfriend." Pia finished her soup and set the bowl down.

Hunter crossed her arms. "I came here out of genuine concern. There's no need to be impertinent."

If it were anyone else doing the *tending and befriending*, Pia would be more receptive. As it was, she felt a tinge of guilt. Hunter was reaching out. Pia had a thousand reasons to be cynical about Hunter's motives, but at some point, she would have to control her temper.

"I'm sorry." Pia leaned her elbows on her knees. "It was nice of you to come. Please, have a seat."

Hunter looked at the chair. Her eyes calculated how the wingbacks would isolate their view of each other. "I like the fire. I'm feeling chilly at the moment."

"Will this really be the end of Chuck Roche?" Pia asked.

"There used to be a saying, 'When a rich man shoots a poor man, the poor man comes back for more because he needs the job.'"

Pia thought of Jacob. She closed her eyes. A shiver of guilt passed through her body.

"That's not true anymore," Hunter said. "At least I hope the electorate will demand his resignation."

"Congratulations in advance then, Madame President."

Hunter watched her closely. "Join my administration, Pia. I'll teach you everything you need to know about politics. Together, we can reconcile our country."

An electric shock of anger jolted Pia's bones. "I would never join you."

She lashed her gaze to Hunter's.

"Did you ever ask yourself how Chuck found out about Tarasov?" Hunter asked.

It was a question Pia had asked herself a million times. Tarasov would never have contradicted his own story. And her people would die rather than reveal her secret. She could feel Hunter's gaze reading her body language. "How?"

"I had a drone video your entire encounter on Attu." Hunter's voice turned sharp. "It was one of those Sabel Tech drones the Army uses. There isn't any sound, but the images are remarkably clear in high resolution."

Hunter reached in her purse and pulled out something small. She tossed it into Pia's lap. An SD card.

"Luckily for you," Hunter said, "Chuck has no idea which branch of government holds the original video. He knew it existed, but people loyal to me acted deaf, dumb, and blind when he demanded it. That's why he tried to bribe Sergeant Tarasov."

Pia tossed the card into the fire.

Hunter sat on the edge of the wingback, staring at Pia. "When I take over, I can destroy the original."

Pia felt nothing but revulsion and told Hunter so with her eyes.

The fire crackled and snapped. Neither spoke for a long time.

"You can't escape my reach, Pia." Hunter reached out a hand. "I can elevate you. Make you the American Queen."

"Or destroy me?" Pia turned to the fire.

"You don't understand the power in your future. You have the strongest personality I've ever seen. With the proper guidance, you can expand your appeal and develop your charisma. In time, you will become the most important woman in the world. You can wield that importance to heal our divided nation."

"Power?" Pia asked. "You have more than you can handle. You're like a drunk driving a Maclaren. You'd drive this world straight off a cliff."

Hunter straightened her pantsuit and faced the fire. They sat in silence again. In a new, softer tone, Hunter asked, "Did Alan ever tell you about your birth mother?"

Pia stiffened.

"After he died, you must have gone through his records." Hunter waited, but Pia didn't reply. "Did you find your birth certificate? Were Sandra Velocitane and Lloyd Aston named on it?"

Pia snapped an angry look at Hunter. "You know they're not."

Hunter stared at the fire with a stone face. She slowly turned to Pia.

"Why did you take my wine glass from the restaurant in Paris?" Hunter asked. "DNA test?"

"You let rogue agents kidnap and torture me." Pia leapt to her feet, her fists clenched at her side. "You never cared about me for one minute. You never lifted a finger to help me. How could you abandon—"

Hunter jumped up. "You can destroy Chuck Roche. That's why he's afraid of you."

"—your own child? I've been adopted twice, and still, I have no one."

"You have me now," Hunter shouted.

"After you finally realized how mad Chuck Roche is, you turned to Yeschenko. But he made a tactical retreat to Moscow. He's useless to you now. Then, and only then, you remembered the daughter you pawned off on a young couple years ago. Why? Because you have an insatiable lust for power and you need my money to get it."

"Men want the world to grovel at their feet. We're different. We want to heal and to nurture. You and I can fix this country, Pia. You can make a difference. You can be the one to bring everyone together, befriend the alienated, heal the divided, soothe the wounded."

"If your desperation for power has driven you to this pathetic depth, I can only imagine the humiliations you suffered for Roche and Yeschenko."

Hunter watched the fire. "The things we do for men are simple—not humiliating."

Disgust twisted Pia's face. "Why did you give me up?"

"I had a career." Hunter looked away. "I was going places. I was destined to be president. I would never have had the time to raise a child."

"I was inconvenient?" Pia asked. "Did you pay them, Aston and Velocitane?"

"She was an athlete with lots of talent and no money. Aston was a trust-fund kid who'd been cut off by his parents. He was an engineering genius, but they were forcing him into med school. He ran out of cash."

"You had her killed—in front of me."

"That wasn't the plan." Hunter dropped into the chair. Tears streamed from her eyes. "No one told me that was the endgame. They were just going to break in and steal his data. They never said anything about killing anyone. That was between Roche and Popov."

"Then why did Alan adopt me? Where were you?"

"I couldn't get near that horrific scene. I couldn't be tied to it in any way." Hunter drew a deep breath. "I made Alan a deal. If he took you in, I'd land him big contracts for the CIA and NSA. He had a little company—"

"You paid him?" Pia regretted the screech in her voice. "How dare you mock his memory."

Hunter's eyes wandered the paneled room. "It worked out well for you."

Pia remembered Vivian's lesson. "Money doesn't solve problems. It's no substitute for …"

Neither woman spoke. The fire popped and flickered.

After a long time, Pia said, "Get out."

Hunter rose. "Think about my offer. I've done a lot of regrettable things in the past, but together, we can get this country back under control—"

Pia extended her finger toward the door. "GET OUT NOW."

"Whoa," Jacob's voice came from the entryway. "Should I come back later?"

Sylvia Lallouette and Yuri Belenov stopped behind him.

"Veronica was just leaving." Pia kept her finger pointed.

"We might need her help," Jacob said. "These whackos claim to have incriminating evidence about Roche."

"After today," Hunter said, "Roche is finished."

Jacob shook his head. "That guy will never be finished until a thousand vultures tear the last morsels from his bones."

Hunter looked at Pia for a reprieve. When Pia shook her head, Hunter tightened up, straightened her posture, and began the long walk toward the exit beyond Jacob.

Chef's assistant ran in, brushing past the others. She stopped halfway in between. "The Saudi's have blown up Admiral Wilkes's flagship." She looked to her left and right at everyone. "We're at war."

THANK YOU!

Thank you for choosing my book. I hope you enjoyed reading it as much as I enjoyed writing it. As an independent writer, I am dependent on word-of-mouth referrals and book reviews. If you liked this book, please tell everyone, and leave reviews all over the place. I will be eternally grateful.

When you do write a review, send me a link to it and I'll put you in the next drawing for an autographed book. I run at least three or four drawings a year.

If you can't get enough of Pia, Tania, Miguel and Jacob*, checkout the series at SeeleyJames.com/books. While you're there, join my newsletter to get discounts, drawings, fun, news, outtakes, and more about the Sabel Agents club on Facebook! Every week (or so, sometimes I'm lazy), I'll let you know about the book in progress, personal triumphs & tragedies, what I'm reading and other fun stuff. I even had one person write to me to say, "I don't like your books, but I love your newsletters." To which I replied, "Thanks, Mom." Yeah … whatcha gonna do?

I'd love to hear from you. Please write, message me on Facebook, let me know what you think.

*I like you already.

NOW THAT YOU'VE READ THIS BOOK, WHICH ONE SHOULD YOU READ NEXT?
HTTPS://SEELEYJAMES.COM/BOOKS

ACKNOWLEDGMENTS

My heartfelt thanks to the beta readers and supporters who made this book the best book possible. Alphabetically: Miguel Rodriguez, Pam Safinuk, and Gloria Shirley.

- Extraordinary Editor and Idea man: Lance Charnes, author of the highly acclaimed *Doha 12, SOUTH, THE COLLLECTION, and STEALING GHOSTS.* http://wombatgroup.com
- Medical Advisor and Character Diviner: Louis Kirby, famed neurologist and author of *Shadow of Eden.* http://louiskirby.com
- Amazing Editor: Mary Maddox, horror and dark fantasy novelist, and author of the Daemon World Series and the fantastic thriller, DARK ROOM. http://marymaddox.com

A special thanks to my wife whose support, despite being reluctant to say the least, has been above and beyond the call of duty. Last but not least, my children, Nicole, Amelia, and Christopher, ranging from age nineteen to forty-five, who have kept my imagination fresh and full of ideas.

ABOUT THE AUTHOR

His near-death experiences range from talking a jealous husband into putting the gun down to spinning out on an icy freeway in heavy traffic without touching anything. His resume ranges from washing dishes to global technology management. His personal life stretches from homeless at 17, adopting a 3-year-old at 19, getting married at 37, fathering his last child at 43, hiking the Grand Canyon Rim-to-Rim several times a year, and taking the occasional nap.

His writing career ranges from humble beginnings with short stories in The Battered Suitcase, to being awarded a Medallion from the Book Readers Appreciation Group. Seeley is best known for his Sabel Security series of thrillers featuring athlete and heiress Pia Sabel and her bodyguard, unhinged veteran Jacob Stearne. One of them kicks ass and the other talks to the wrong god.

His love of creativity began at an early age, growing up at Frank Lloyd Wright's School of Architecture in Arizona and Wisconsin. He carried his imagination first into a successful career in sales and marketing, and then to his real love: fiction.

For more books featuring Pia Sabel and Jacob Stearne, visit: SeeleyJames.com.

facebook.com/seeleyjamesauthor

instagram.com/seeleyjamesauth

bookbub.com/authors/seeley-james